Ronen Lalena

SHIMON ADAF

A DETECTIVE'S COMPLAINT

Translated by Yardenne Greenspan

Shimon Adaf was born in Sderot, Israel, and now lives in Holon. A poet, novelist, and musician, Adaf worked for several years as a literary editor at Keter Publishing House and has also been a writer-in-residence at the University of Iowa. He leads the creative writing program and lectures on Hebrew literature at Ben-Gurion University of the Negev. Adaf received the Yehuda Amichai Prize for Hebrew Poetry (2010) for the collection *Aviva-No*; the Sapir Prize (2012) for the novel *Mox Nox*, the English translation of which, by Philip Simpson, won the Jewish Book Council's 2020 Paper Brigade Award for New Israeli Fiction in Honor of Jane Weitzman; and the I. and B. Neuman Prize for Hebrew Literature (2017).

Yardenne Greenspan is a writer and Hebrew translator born in Tel Aviv and based in New York. Her translations have been published by Restless Books, St. Martin's Press, Akashic Books, Syracuse University Press, New Vessel Press, Amazon Crossing, and Farrar, Straus and Giroux. Her translation of Yishai Sarid's novel *The Memory Monster* was selected as one of *The New York Times* 100 Notable Books of 2020. Greenspan's writing and translations have appeared in *The New Yorker*, *Haaretz*, *Guernica*, *Literary Hub*, *Blunderbuss Magazine*, *Apogee*, *The Massachusetts Review*, *Asymptote*, and *Words Without Borders*, among other publications. She has an MFA from Columbia University and is a regular contributor to *Ploughshares*.

By
SHIMON ADAF

The Lost Detective Trilogy

Book 1: *One Mile and Two Days Before Sunset*

Book 2: *A Detective's Complaint*

Book 3: *Take Up and Read*

Aviva-No

A
DETECTIVE'S
COMPLAINT

A
DETECTIVE'S
COMPLAINT

TRANSLATED FROM THE HEBREW
BY YARDENNE GREENSPAN

SHIMON ADAF

PICADOR | NEW YORK

Picador
120 Broadway, New York 10271

Library of Congress Cataloging-in-Publication Data
Names: Adaf, Shimon, author. | Greenspan, Yardenne, translator.
Title: A detective's complaint / Shimon Adaf ; translated from the Hebrew by
    Yardenne Greenspan.
Other titles: Ḳuvlanah shel balash. English
Description: First American edition. | New York : Picador, 2022.
Identifiers: LCCN 2021060840 | ISBN 9780374139650 (paperback)
Subjects: LCGFT: Detective and mystery fiction. | Novels.
Classification: LCC PJ5055.2.D44 K8813 2021 | DDC 892.43/7—dc23/eng/
    20211217
LC record available at https://lccn.loc.gov/2021060840

Designed by Janet Evans-Scanlon

"How I loathe heroes! Always getting in the way and acting so ... so ... heroic!"

—Skeletor, *Masters of the Universe*

EXTERIOR

Mighty is the terror of the empty page, but even mightier is the terror of silence. During the Gaza War I got up and left. Not all of a sudden. The trip had been planned months in advance. But everything seemed to be done in a rush, urgently. I passed among the things recumbent in the dark, trees, windmills, a vitreous field of stars. I slept at the speed of sleep. I slept in inevitable speed toward the killed children. A week and change after missiles were launched at Tel Aviv and fear became viscous on the streets of Ashkelon, a week and change after the aerial bombing by the Israeli military, a week and change after the images of the destroyed homes, expressions wrinkled with holy terror, my father came to me in a dream and wrapped his arms around me. It was a night laden with dreams. There were dreams that had me paralyzed with their visions, knowing I was dreaming, knowing I was powerless to change a single detail. I can't remember when I ever saw my father so happy, his face glowing. He was younger than I am now when he fell off the boulders at the Tel Aviv Beach and shattered his skull. In the dream he was younger, perhaps as young as he was the day Yaffa and I peeked out from one of our regular hiding places, watching him and our mother sitting on a bench, bathed by the radiance of the sea. My mother's head was resting against his shoulder, and his arm was wrapped around her shoulder. With the special instinct children have, we grasped that we had no place between those two. Or, at least, I did. Yaffa insisted on shoving in. My father was young, the world still rolled up like a scroll before him, awaiting his authority, his whims. I loved him then, perhaps. In my dream he said, Elish. I don't remember when he ever spoke my name with such ease. I wondered why he showed up, outside of time and place. Where were we at that time, that time of dimness when only that which is made of certainty remains, and that which is questionable blurs and recedes? He detected my thought and asked if I wanted him to leave. I told him I could not decide, I was imagining myself from outside my body, my throat full of dirt. Passersby, if there were any, must have been watching a lone man talking to the air, moving in response to some binding invisible to them. The whole time, I was ensconced in his arms, not wishing to detach, whether due to the inertia of the dream or some hidden desire. I told him I could no longer distinguish between realities, between the data of senses and the rustle of the interior. He said, I thought you missed me. I hadn't thought of him in years. Even my recoiling from the sea had faded ever since that dire day. Do you want me to leave? he asked again. I woke up before I had a chance to answer.

All morning long, I was preoccupied by the intensity of emotion that rose when I saw him, the vitality of the feeling. I've heard stories of women whose eggs were fertilized outside their fallopian tubes, in the space of their abdomen, growing into tiny fetuses that calcified. Decades later, an intensifying pain disclosed their existence, and the stone babies were extracted, perfect figurines, foreign bodies, pulled out of a flesh that had not been destined to carry them. That was how this dream pierced me. All morning long, the dream, and the pictures of the destruction of Gaza online, and the scared faces of Israeli civilians in stairwells, counting with growing fury the minutes before they could get back to their lives, which, thanks to the thin film of sanity they'd grown used to pulling over them, had become inured to the suffering of others. All morning long, my mind was embroiled, and I still had to speak at a literary festival.

2

say I didn't wake up because I wasn't asleep. I was pulled at once from the twilight of sickness and dropped into another kind of twilight. I was ten years old, before the hot fevers of adolescence, I told them. I think only a few were listening. The audience wasn't large. The Mediterranean Literary Festival in the city of Sète, in the south of France, had been organized negligently. Many other events were happening simultaneously all over town, and only thin canvas sheets, offering scant shade, separated the sweaty faces from the supremacy of sun. The church bells struck midday. My five detective novels were presented through convoluted passages, overwrought with superfluous adjectives. An opera singer, accompanied by a classical guitar, trilled a chant from Psalms. The biblical syllables trembled smoother than smooth on her lips in a Christian lilt, rising like smoke around us, foreign to us all. One woman walked out in protest. The Hebrew, she said, moving briskly, felt hard on her ears right now.

I'm returning to this moment, I said, because the nature of literature, and art in general, if I may exaggerate for a moment, is the act of repetition. A black-and-white movie was showing on television. A gloomy castle, melancholy clouds. A man comes to visit a friend he hasn't seen in years and finds him plagued by a mysterious illness, his senses horrifyingly sharp, any too-rough fabric sending chills through his flesh, high notes making him cringe. He is submerged in darkness, his palate so tender that food torments him. He asks about his friend's sister, whom he'd known and may have loved as a younger man. I said, Here, and in

Israel, places where the sun rules over all beings, it is hard to imagine the depth of darkness, hard to conjure the trial that can train a preadolescent to understand it, but I did. I said, We also ought to think about the essence of knowing the world—what allows this knowing? Is it the experience of our brief time on this planet, or an ancient, mute memory awakening from within it, determining its shape? Or are we constantly haunted by a life that isn't ours, a random life, by our perception, that ignites without our control? In that case, we always recognize the pattern of hauntedness. In that case, I recognized it—the terrible itching, the sound of etching, the sound of scratching against a wooden plank. I said that, in time, I learned the film was part of a series of Roger Corman adaptations of Edgar Allan Poe stories, and that these were low-budget films, hastily made, using second-hand sets, putting them to good use before they were taken apart. Back then, in my younger days, I couldn't tell the difference. As an adult, rewatching the film, the meager sets, the amateurish cinematography, only bothered me in the beginning of the film. As I watched, I felt the same sense of stifling. When the scratching sounded again, I was thrown into that same midway space, where my field of vision was full of black spots, greasy oil stains.

You know the story, I said. Poe's "The Fall of the House of Usher." Roderick Usher hears his sister's nails scratching against the wall of her coffin and realizes he'd buried her alive. His growing realization culminates in the fall and destruction of his house, disrupting the long-standing Usher dynasty. What is the music I hear beyond the noise of reality, whose effort to get out of what hold? That is the riddle that won't leave me alone, and that is why I write detective literature. I hope I never solve it.

That is the essence of things. I do not know how to document them, only approximately re-create them. I spoke at length, with some hesitation, my thoughts wandering. I spent the fifteen minutes allotted to me on a childhood memory, never getting to the point—how my reading of Poe was born, what I got from him, and how. An actor read two or three pages of my first book, which seemed to stand in complete opposition to the words I'd stuttered. The layer of intentional grayness and pedestrianism that blanketed my detective prose had nothing to do with the ringing of profundity, the subversion, the constant betrayal of the senses I'd tried to describe. The heavy glow reflecting from the stones of the church, the purple sparks of the bougainvillea in bloom, the fallout of the chinaberry surfing in on gusts of breeze from the sea, all hollowed out my arguments.

After my turn was over, a Venezuelan writer living in exile in Spain came up to speak. Short, dark, with a hypnotizing wisdom glinting in her eyes. They returned nothing to those watching her but the ways in which her observers thought themselves into existence. I was surprised to read in her bio in the festival catalog that she was forty years old. I was familiar with the subcutaneous refusal to let go of the tension of youth, the tyranny of will over metabolism. The plots of her books took place in her country of birth. She said she used to write short stories but wasn't able to get them published. One day, a friend sent her an article about a detective-literature contest sponsored by an Argentinean daily paper. The writer read three detective novels by a famous Norwegian author and concluded that no special talent or knowledge of human nature was required to partake in the genre. She sent in her first five chapters and won what she perceived as a small fortune. But winning created two problems. She knew if she converted the sum to her local currency, its value would soon decrease due to inflation. And she knew that a novel about the religious followers of Hugo Chávez—those innocent civilians who were struck by the spirit of prophecy in public and announced that the deceased president was still alive, that his words were living and his doctrine true—could never be published in Venezuela. So she took advantage of the opportunity and traveled Spain-ward. Her speech was woven with jokes. Her French was throaty, the whistling consonants labialized. For a few moments, I parted with my distress and lost myself in the music of her words. The pages read from her book were also shaded by the same amused tone, as far as I could understand. Then the panel was opened to audience questions. The obvious questions were asked. I let the Venezuelan answer them all.

My trip was the result of transgression. Last summer I'd planned on going to Berlin to finish my most recent novel. I'd already bought a ticket and rented an apartment. Berlin, bleeding its wounds into the present. I thought about Alfred Döblin, I thought about Walter Benjamin, I thought about S. Y. Agnon. Manny Lahav, after returning from a second visit with his wife, said it was the city that had etched itself most starkly into their consciousness. Seven years separated both trips, but on the second one everything was familiar—the streets, the chill of the shade. He urged me to visit. Maybe you'll find the solution you've been looking for there, he said. I'd spent close to a year wallowing in the ankle-deep water of my novel, unable to finish it, every plotline I conjured feeling secondhand. The transparent language of the book left me limp.

I never made it to Berlin. A week before my trip I woke up with my right ear clogged. I assumed there was water in my ear, and that the weighty feeling would lift within a matter of days. But the clogged sensation only worsened throughout the day. The next morning, it was replaced with a castration of sounds. I heard a baby crying in the stairwell, and the cry swirled in my ear canal, breaking into different tones. When I put on earphones, I found the high notes multiplying, distorting the musical balance. They veered off-key, grating. I couldn't shut myself off from the world. I made an appointment with an ENT doctor. The Century Tower trembled, sleep-deprived. The Tel Aviv humidity had grown burdensome, enormous air conditioners humming beneath the pretensions of murky concrete. I'd arrived early. The hallway of the floor where the clinic was located was desolate, neoned. I waited in the hourless lighting. The doctor put a tuning fork to my forehead and his face wrinkled with suspicion. He instructed me to lie down. He inserted a frozen telescopic probe into my ear canal. The sensation sent a shiver through me. I thought about the machines that magnify our gaze to investigate the large and the small, turning us into gigantic eyes trapped within lenses. What cannot be translated into image falls away, and the scale ceases to be an experience and turns instead into a pothole.

Yes, the doctor determined, and when I hear him speaking the words in my mind, I add a kind of sigh, which may not actually have occurred. Neural-auditory damage, straight to the emergency room for a hearing test and possible hospitalization.

The map of Tel Aviv that was familiar to me from my strolls opened up in my mind, pushing aside the panic. I arrived at the emergency room, sweating. The brother of an Arab man whose hand had been injured by a saw and continued to bleed in spite of his bandages was in the midst of an argument with the receptionist regarding the delay in the doctor's arrival. The wounded man gasped from the bed on which he was strewn. Not just him, but an entire orchestra of chatter, cries of woe, whispers, worried conversations, all molded into a racket within that space, in the eustachian tube, the cochlea.

A young intern sent me to have a hearing test on the ground floor. In the elevator, the infirm in their gowns and grievances, a mostly geriatric cluster, mottled here and there with the spots of childhood sorrow. I turned my face to the walls, but they were covered with mirrors. The sound technician checked that the earphones were placed properly, sealed off to outside noise. I followed her lips as they moved behind the double glass, her voice in the silence affixed to my head. Raise your hand every time you hear a sound, she said. A noisy haze filled my brain. I closed my eyes. A black space in which ringing spools flickered, metallic and deep, convoluted carvings of light. I raised my hand, then put it down. I was alert, I was prepared.

The technician read words off a page, which were first channeled into my left ear, then the right. Repeat after me, she ordered. When she lowered her voice, it shattered in my right ear, the words crumbling with the dirty distortion of cheap loudspeakers.

We don't know all the reasons, the head doctor said. It's a more common condition than people think, neural-auditory damage. It typically occurs in people over forty. He looked at the form in his hand. You're forty-one, he exclaimed, I wouldn't have guessed that. I nodded slowly, with the usual fatigue caused by the hoax of the flesh refusing to disclose the marks of time. In rare cases, the doctor continued, it turns out to be a benign tumor that can surgically be removed. Multiple sclerosis must also be eliminated. The common conjecture is that the cause is a virus that damages the auditory nerve. In 10 percent of documented cases, the problem goes away on its own without treatment. In 80 percent, the common procedure is effective. That's not a bad prognosis, he said. I asked how they could administer treatment without a clear etiology.

We work with what we've got, he said. Sometimes a diagnosis is enough. The suggested treatment is steroids, taken orally for ten days. He answered all of my questions, but I didn't manage to get a clear statement out of him, in spite of the medical lingo resting smoothly upon my tongue. I pictured his terms, the wheels of his thought, mixing with mine. The steroids support the ability of different systems to fight off infections, though they ultimately harm the immune system. Side effects can include facial edema due to fluid retention, mood swings, a rise in blood pressure and blood sugar. The doctor recommended full rest. The hospitalization was only for observation purposes, he pointed out. He said I might feel healthy, but that the steroids would weaken my body. I wondered out loud whether I should postpone my trip. He said I ought to cancel it. If it wasn't a viral infection, the air pressure changes could cause a rupture of blood vessels. Until the problem was fully diagnosed or disappeared on its own, I would have to forget about traveling.

How I tired of the weakness of the body. It seemed I'd spent half of my youth burning with fever, I told the Venezuelan. She said she also laughed when she was invited to the festival and learned that for some reason the French defined Latin American culture as part of the Mediterranean culture of the Atlantic Ocean. I said there was some logic to it. A narrow-framed man, minuscule of mustache like a villain from an adventure novel, asked if he could join us. I looked around. The metal plate of the late sunset refracted on the crowded tables. The alley where we were sitting had been closed off for the festival and transformed into an outdoor sitting area for a restaurant serving festival participants. Buildings closed on it from both sides, walls smitten with wind and salt that had been absorbed so well they'd become their aroma, the substance of their creation. Lights could be seen behind the shields of windows, a hidden family life, the glue of evening lingering in it all, dusk refusing to come, and the heat of the day dwindled, its penetrating bluishness evaporated. The guy arrived in the nameless in-between hour. I recognized him, a viola player who'd played a mellifluous tune to open the event I'd attended. A male and a female writer had amiably chatted about the nature of romance, sadomasochism, and desire in the blinding glare of the Mediterranean. It seemed the demand of discovery carried within this glare was an obstacle in all matters concerning cellars, nooks, dim silences, pent-up urges.

I wasn't the one who chose our line of conversation. The Venezuelan and I spoke briefly after our panel, then each went our separate ways, somewhat alarmed. We made plans to meet for dinner. She asked if my books contained themes of illness. I said they didn't, that my detective, Benny Zehaviv, was a healthy man, robust even. Like many Israeli men, he'd successfully converted his covert, subterranean male depression into constant activity, sinking completely into routine life. The body is redeemed, I said, but the soul is sealed off. At first she thought I was joking, her lips curving toward a smile, then flattening out. She asked if it was always a choice, body or mind. I said yes, in Israel at least the common, spoken military language had vanquished the shock of reality. And if reality wasn't apparent as bodily symptoms, the life of the mind was cut out. At least for men who grew up in Israel. And the women? she asked. They resolved the difficulty another way, I said. Hysterical maternity. If you think about it, she said, that style of mothering has tangible causes.

Our conversation almost drowned in the chatter around us. The servers served whatever they served. We ate quietly, exchanging critical looks whenever we tasted anything. The white wine was bitter around the edges, or perhaps that was just my scratched tongue. I had a habit of running it over the tips of my teeth in moments of awkwardness.

The viola player leaned toward me, of all people; the other tables were fully occupied. The Venezuelan said he was welcome to join us. He said he'd attended our panel. His face hadn't stood out of the sparse crowd, but the Venezuelan nodded her recognition. So you're from Israel, he said. I guessed the question forming at the back of his mind, speeding up, then pausing. He said he'd had a few opportunities to perform Joseph Holbrooke's nocturne *Fairyland*. I looked at him quizzically. The Venezuelan said, Edgar Allan Poe. Yes, I said, Edgar Allan Poe wrote a poem by that name. The violist placed a bag on the table. Fresh oysters he'd bought at the fishermen's market in the afternoon. He pulled out a pocketknife, and a loaf of dense brown bread and a lump of butter wrapped in tinfoil emerged out of nowhere. He ordered a bottle of wine from a limping server who faltered among the tables. The glow of those who accept their fate, who know beauty in the midst of crushing gloom, was spilled over the server's face. In spite of myself, I returned his smile.

The Venezuelan took an oyster from the violist offhandedly. Her eyes wandered over the table. He said the oysters in this region had a natural saltiness, so he didn't add lemon juice. He handed me one. I turned it down. He asked if I was refusing it due to religious reasons. I said no, even though biblical categorization defined oysters as sea vermin. They both laughed and repeated the term, "sea vermin." The Venezuelan said she'd heard there were health justifications for Jewish dietary restrictions. Shellfish could be toxic, particularly in warm countries. I told her I thought it had more to do with questions of purity and impurity. Impurity had a tendency to spread and reek, especially when invading the organs. The violist said it was easy to tell if an oyster was still raw. A dead one would kill the person eating it. He gently fingered the black circumference of the white flesh glued to the inside of the smooth, clay cradle. The oyster retreated. He said that if you took a long look, you could see it tremble, once every minute that its heart beat.

That morning, my mother asked if I'd had a chance to speak to Ronnit. She said that, living in Ashkelon, they were already used to missiles from Gaza. When the siren sounded, she went out into the stairwell. Not that she thought there was any point in it—if God decided to take someone, no Iron Dome would save them. She said the same thing to my sister, Yaffa, and Yaffa got angry and said if Mom didn't start taking the missiles more seriously, Yaffa and Bobby would come over and move her into their place, by force if necessary. Their house, thank God, had a safe room. To my mother, there was no greater threat than being uprooted from the home she and my father had bought when they married. I told my mother Yaffa was right. I asked about Tahel. My mother said that Sderot was surely safer than Ashkelon these days. My voice broke when I pictured my niece in silent revolt, forced to stay curled up in her bed, an insult in the midst of summer, in the safe room where she was made to sleep. She was the first person to pop into my head when I awoke from the dream of my father. When she was seven years old, she told me there were some things her parents would never understand. Her use of the future tense stunned me. But everything about her and her wisdom casts mute, inconceivable love over me. In another lifetime, she is my daughter and I am her father.

I asked if something happened to Ronnit. My mother said missiles were launched at Jerusalem again.

It's Elish.

I was surprised to see an out-of-country number.

Is everything all right?

Thank God, yes. Akiva cried a little when he heard the siren. But he's calm now.

My mother and Yaffa are fine.

I know, your mother called me. Where are you?

She has your number?

What are you so surprised about? She's always known how to get the information she needs.

I don't get it. You two are in touch?

Missiles are being launched at Tel Aviv.

I heard. I'm in Sète.

Your mother said you were in France.

Yes, it's a small town in the south of France.

What did you want, then?

To make sure that you and Akiva are all right.

(Sigh.)

It's a little surprising that they're attacking Jerusalem.

Why?

They might hit a mosque.

You really think they care?

Yes. Their struggle has different sides to it—

They're murderers, Elish. They don't care about anything.

The Israeli Air Force is also bombing them without distinction.

See, I knew that's what you were getting at.

What?

Don't play dumb, I'm not getting into a political argument with you. What are you going to tell me again, that we're to blame? Aren't the three boys they abducted enough? They're animals. Animals, Elish. And you're going to defend them?

And what about us? We're not animals? Didn't we burn one of their children, an innocent child, why, wh—

We didn't burn him. Some lunatics burned him.

So maybe it's just some lunatics on their side that abducted and murdered. Maybe—

(Grumbling in the background.) I'll be right with you, Aki. They've been bombing Sderot for the last fourteen years. My uncles. And how many years have they been bombing your mother and Yaffa?

They've been living under occupation for the past forty-seven years, just a few miles away from us, without an identity—

(Growing cries.) Stop being such a baby, just hold on a minute.

Without an autonomous economy, without—

Mo-mmy, mo-mmy, mo-mmy

Akiva, you little brat, let go of my skirt.

Put him on.

You want to talk to Uncle Elish?

Ummm . . .

Yes or no? Make up your mind.

Give him the phone . . . Aki, Aki, do you know where I am?

There's a pigeon in the yard. She won't leave.

She must be searching for pigeon treasure.

She jumps up on the tree and then comes down again.

Oh, she must know where the treasure is. Did you know that every animal has its own treasure?

Mommy doesn't want me to play with the pigeon.

When God made the animals, he also created a treasure for each breed and scattered pieces of it all over the world.

No fair, she won't let me do nothing, not even with Aunt
Lyudmila's cat.

What about Aunt Lyudmila's cat?

I like it when he jumps up in the air.

Maybe he doesn't feel like jumping up in the air.

But the pigeon jumps all by herself.

Yes. Every animal has a quality that helps it collect the small
pieces of the treasure. For example, pigeons can–

She says it hurts the cat. But he scratched me first.

Well, it's clear all your mother wants is to keep you safe.

She won't let me do nothing.

She will. Remember when we went to the Jerusalem zoo?

And the monkey was sad?

And the monkey was sad.

Why was he sad?

He missed his mother.

But his mother was there. I saw her. The bear also had a
mother.

Yes, his mother was there, but she wasn't the mother he was
missing. Don't you miss Mommy sometimes?

You know Ruthie is coming over to play with me this
afternoon?

No, Ruthie, really? How fun.

Her daddy is in the war.

What?

Yeah, yeah, her daddy went to kill bad people.

Are you scared?

No, I'm a hero like Ruthie's daddy.

You know who the biggest hero in the world is?

The Messiah.

No, no, the biggest–

Yeah, yeah, he can kill all the gentiles, even Batman.

Listen to me, Akiva, the greatest hero is the one who doesn't
take advantage of his power.

No, the Messiah is stronger.

Let's say when Ruthie comes over today she builds a castle out of Legos. You can kick her castle and make it fall apart. But you'd be a bigger hero if you didn't kick her castle, right?

Here, Mommy, Uncle Elish wants to talk to you.

What, you're getting into political arguments with him too? Who put that Messiah nonsense in his head?

Elish, give me a break, don't—

It's so not a political thing. You don't teach children to use force, you teach them to—

(Sigh.)

What do you want me to say? I didn't give up my right to say—

Elish, please, not today. Not—

Fine, I have to go. We can have a conversation when I get back.

Thank you.

What for?

For calming him down at least.

What about Wlodia?

David.

Okay, fine, David.

He's at the kolel.

Oh, well, what—

Goodbye, Elish.

The foreignness of the place and the attentiveness of the violist loosened my tongue's fetters, even though the Venezuelan wore an expression of light boredom. The violist hadn't been familiar with the work of Edgar Allan Poe before studying at the Academy of Music. A pianist he'd befriended was going to play Holbrooke's nocturne for her final recital and offered him the viola part. Poe's poem, he said, had captivated his heart. It blended an excitable youthful tone with the intense observation of an adult haunted by horrors. Holbrooke captured all of this in his musical piece.

I said that, for me, Poe's power is that he always starts out with a meaningless emotion and then attempts one of two tasks: to derive aesthetic pleasure out of it, or use reason to force meaning upon it. In my favorite stories, he depicts the failure of both ruses, or the way in which one of them inevitably leads to the other, creating a kind of loop, a mad passion for an investigation that is a submission to the destruction of self. The violist said that was too abstract, that he couldn't enjoy a piece of art that way. I told him I was surprised that, as a musician, he didn't prefer the abstraction of form and structure to specific content. He said that, ultimately, art was judged by its performance too. I said fine, take "The Raven," for example. As a work of art, the poem creates clear sensations of melancholy and dread, but Poe himself refuses to remain in those obtuse impressions and goes on to write the essay "The Philosophy of Composition," in which he pretends to explain how the impression left by the poem is a matter of conscious, logical choice. I said that, as far as I was concerned, those two pieces were in fact one and must be read alongside each other to examine what Poe refuses to explain in his report on writing the poem, or what "The Raven" dramatizes contrary to the consciousness of writing. Too many choices require further explanation even after one encompassing explanation has been given. The untranscribed space in which choices are made is the core of the work.

The violist said that was interesting. I suggested that the Venezuelan might develop the point. Why, for instance, did she choose to make her heroine a private investigator rather than a police officer? She pushed away her plate of food and said dryly that in Venezuela no one would believe that the police were attempting to uncover the truth rather than to force the government's version of reality on citizens. After all, we were talking about a country in which the president appeared on television to report on his conversations with the late Chávez, embodied in a pear he was about to eat.

The violist laughed. His eyes lingered on her. Chains of twinkle lights lit up like a scratch on his retina. Go on, he said.

I said we had to consider the fact that Poe declared he was reporting on the planning of a certain poem, but the system of calculations he provided had demonstrated that this was the only poem he could write if he was to remain loyal to his mission of writing the perfect poem. I said, There is a line of assumptions and decisions Poe doesn't feel the need to justify. For example, the fact that beauty fills the observer with sadness, and so the melancholy tone is the best one for a poem whose aim is beauty, or to capture the spectacular flight of the raven before it alights on the head of Pallas Athena.

The Venezuelan glanced around her briefly, her limbs gathered away from the table. The restaurant patio had emptied out. The growing chill seemed to give her goose bumps. I wanted to stop, but couldn't.

I said that Poe claimed he wanted to create a stark contrast between the black bird and the marble statue, between the monster of the deep that emerges from the storm of madness and the cold, calculated reason represented by Athena. But he chose a specific manifestation of Athena—Pallas Athena. The myth of Pallas had to do with the murder of a loved one, with guilt. Pallas is a friend, a brother, a father, perhaps, who Athena murdered either by accident or on purpose, and whose name she merged with her own as a sign of her sorrow. Unintentionally, Poe directs us toward a detective puzzle that was not meant to appear—who was guilty of Lenore's death? What part did the poet play in th—

Halfway through the word, a scrawny man stumbled toward us. The violist jumped up to support him, but the man pushed him away, cursing, alcohol fumes from his mouth washing over the table. I looked at the empty bottle of wine. That sense of camaraderie that comes with intoxication had invaded. I felt closer to the Venezuelan and the violist than to anyone else in the universe. I couldn't bear the feeling. I excused myself and went to the bathroom.

I paused in the doorway on my way back. The crowd in the alley had dwindled. The garlands burned. Beneath them, the Venezuelan and the violist were laughing. I watched them from an appropriate distance. They could have been tiny bugs beneath a leaf, or celestial bodies on the edges of a supernova. When the thread of their conversation broke and their bodies leaned back, I came closer. Laughter was still apparent on the Venezuelan's lips, as was that same shattered dagger of mischief on the retinas. Shall we? I asked. They nodded. We stood, the three of us, on the corner of the street. The darkness snuck up, as was its way, filling the throat and the eyes, even though the stars made an effort inside it, even though the force of summer whitened inside them.

spasms of muscle and air. In those hours of stunned wakefulness, I was able to categorize the sounds he emitted into divi-
sions and subdivisions. The night nurse came in once an hour to
check on him and change his IV. It would take some time before
he could again consume food. In the meantime, he was connected to a feeding tube. I wondered about the distribution of
patients throughout the rooms. The selection seemed random.
Scratch-throat was placed in a room with seven other people.
The giant, who required less care, got a room all to himself.

We were waiting, the giant and I, for free beds. We sat in
plastic chairs in the afternoon, which was slipping away, according to the clock, which at a hospital ticks in vain, governing neither the course of daylight nor the cycle of matter. At first glance
I was able to determine that he suffered from gigantism. His dimensions were exaggerated—he was over eight feet tall, his jaw
was thick, but the flesh was soft, flaccid. I pictured his pituitary
gland, a faulty faucet continuing to drip growth hormones even
after the corporeal plan had been completed. I pictured his
bones growing and growing in his youth. I imagined him waking
up each morning more enormous than the day before, startling
awake into a body requiring new adjustment. I asked him why
he was there. Polyps, he said in a deep, drumlike voice. He smiled
with an awkwardness through which I spotted his need to talk.
Like me, he'd come to the emergency room alone. Like mine, his
basic urge was to keep quiet around strangers. A clenching of
shame was his default. He lived in Holon, he said, but didn't
want to go to Wolfson Hospital. He waited a long time for his
admittance to Ichilov to be approved. I told him even Ichilov was
just a kingdom of butchers. He became defensive. No, not at all,
he'd investigated the matter. His sister, who was still back in
Ukraine, had helped. This was the best place. People from Russia raised money to get surgery in Ichilov. It's just good publicity, I told him, this entire country, publicity without a real
product behind it. He said in Ukraine people are afraid to go to

the police. Why? Because. But in Israel he isn't afraid at all. What did he have to go to the police about? I asked. Those incompetent racists. In Holon there are Ethiopian police officers, he said. One of them helped him. In Russia, people hate the blacks, even though Pushkin was half-black. I told him people in Israel hate the blacks too. He said we're all Jews, end of story. I said, That means nothing to me. A good neighbor is better than a distant brother. He said even though they didn't know him they still treated him well. What did they help him with? I wanted to know. He said nothing. Recoiled. A few people complained about the long wait to see a doctor after hours at the central emergency room. They asked if we were in line. I told them we'd already been admitted. I saw them lingering their eyes on the giant. He shrank under their gazes. His silence deepened, projecting from his grand exterior. I told him something happened in this country, an invasion of body snatchers. You walk around and run into people you know, you're convinced you recognize them, but their brains have been taken over by aliens from a dark galaxy. The people you used to love have been eaten from the inside, gone. The giant said that's what happened to his niece. She disappeared. She landed at the airport but never made it to his Holon apartment. His sister called him in a panic when her daughter didn't pick up the phone and said he had to go to the police. Her name appeared in the flight's passenger list. The immigration authorities had registered her entry into Israel. They'd been searching for three days when suddenly she rang his doorbell. She had no idea she'd gone missing for three days. She claimed she'd only landed a little over an hour earlier. The cops didn't make a big deal about it. The important thing was that she'd made it in one piece.

I didn't go straight to the hotel. I used one excuse or another to evade the Venezuelan, who gave me an indecipherable look, and the violist, whose mustache trembled when he smiled. Rue Garenne sloped to Rue du Palais. I went down Rue Paul Valéry to the dock that was deserted in the nearing midnight hour. There were reflections of laughter, the ghosts of tourists' pleasure still clinging to the air. During the training course I took after military boot camp, I heard a soldier from the next building telling his friend in the early dawn, Do you realize how many women are getting dick right now? That statement returns to me in unexpected moments. The water was thick in the canal leading from the lake to the sea, quiet, an ancient creature dreaming its return in Lovecraft's stories, the dreaming Cthulhu in his home in R'lyeh. Lovecraft hadn't popped into my mind by chance. Other than Valéry, Poe's spiritual heir, the octopus is Sète's most famous symbol. The octopus statue in the square across from City Hall, where the book fair I'd just walked by took place, is reminiscent of Cthulhu. Lovecraft is also Poe's spiritual offspring.

I turned toward the port. I was drawn there. It's hard to believe that water is liquid, hard to believe that gravity determines its course, that its glow is not inherent, like a kind of marble of radiance. From the paleness of dark a figure clarified, leaning over the canal. Moving closer, I could tell it was the same crude man, wide of bones and gestures, who had stumbled over to our table earlier that night. I stood and watched him indifferently as he threw up. Someone called out from the canal. A boat waded in the lake. A boy disembarked from it. He placed his hand on the man's arm, but the man pushed it away, letting out a string of curses that was interrupted by another wave of vomit. The boy looked at me helplessly, pleading with his eyes for me to leave already, not to witness this. But I remained planted in place. The boy climbed down and tied the boat, then climbed back onto the dock and led the man away. The stench lingered in his wake, bodily fluids and alcohol.

I retraced my footsteps at the entrance to the port. At the top of the hill, at the top of the city, I saw an enormous, illuminated cross. In the daytime, the communications tower rising beside it overshadowed it. Thus the two churches, Our Lady of Sailors and Our Lady of Texting, dwelled side by side. The only synagogue in Sète was not called a synagogue for fear of rioters. I cannot fathom why every protest against the crimes of Israel begins with the destruction of synagogues, as if these gangs are forced to perpetuate the image set in their minds by the West, of shattered chandeliers, Torah scrolls rolling in dirt, parocheth curtains on fire. Thank God my father moved on to the afterlife years ago. Those who've never witnessed Prosper Ben Zaken gritting his teeth at the sight of the desecration of Jewish holiness have never seen true rage in their lives.

The hotel room was a sorry sight. A smart-ass designer gave it the appearance of prestige, doppelgängers of modernist furniture, finished with colorful Formica. The space was utilized to the max. A box. The windowpane did not block out the noise of the street. I was the immobile observer of the thought experiments of private relativity: The time of the passengers sealed in their cars was different from mine. They curved toward the speed of light at their own speed.

I almost slipped into sleep, but within the twilight of an endlessly expanding consciousness, prepared to receive hidden impressions, I saw four family members sitting in a black carriage. I knew I'd been running into them over and over as they peered at me wordlessly for the past thousand years. Awful are the dreams that arrive with their own history, their roots in the unknown, elsewhere. I knew I was repeating the question, What do you want? Why did they not embark on their final journey, father, mother, boy, girl, foam already bubbling on the lips of the bridled horses, pushing where, onward, onward, against their golden bridles, the bits in their mouths bridles of fire, bridles of light, bridles of flame. I knew their silent answer—they required a companion. All the other coachmen had already gone, leaving them on their own.

Someone, perhaps the maid, had left a dried *ezovion* bundle on the desk. I held it to my nose. The scent was a razor with which I slit the jugular of night. Its innards fell out that first night at the hospital. For twelve moons, the fetus waited for the surgeon's scalpel. Awake in the dark, I wondered if this was the reason for the sobriety that had plagued me then, whether the mischiefs of childhood returned to me, the old habits, the investigation ruses I now only dreamed up in the far-fetched exaggerations of the novels I wrote.

I looked up from the book I was reading and Ronnit was there, on the eighth floor of Ichilov, stepping out of the elevator. Without noticing, she wore her usual aura of frigidity and hesitance. She paused and scanned the clean, spacious lobby, the thick panes presenting Tel Aviv with a stifled tongue of sea on the horizon. She didn't have to smile. Her beauty was now a second-glance beauty, underneath the headscarf dimming the radiance of her hair. It emerged as if I were the one late to discover it, or as if I'd forgotten, in a moment of blindness over the other, new beauty, that the stature of her body, her tight organs, were but a protective layer.

My condition was not improved even after several days in the hospital. I tracked my reflection in the mirror with concern. I don't know why its puffiness worried me most. Perhaps it was a fear of looking like the other patients, of my flesh disclosing that I belonged in their ranks, preventing me from leaving. I was more comfortable with its deceptiveness than I tended to admit. I'd been familiar with the rot gnawing at it from a young age, I'd hallucinated its demise over and over, recoiling with discontent from these reveries, the speeding up toward final velocity.

She was the only one I'd told about my hospitalization. Why worry people? I just happened to tell her. She called to let me know she and Akiva were coming to town. Her flat voice sharpened in a matter of sentences. She said I didn't sound like myself, that she could tell something was wrong. Her alertness toward me irritated me and I was filled with gratitude. I made her swear to keep the news to herself.

She helped me up from my seat at the lobby table and led me to the row of chairs facing the window. You know how much people pay for this view? she said. And here you are squandering it away. In the seat next to mine, she placed a plastic bag full of baby peppers and berries. She said they were superfoods, bursting with vitamins. And it isn't about the money, look at this light, let it wash over you, you're pale.

I pointed out that the glass filtered out radiation, both beneficial and detrimental. And anyway, the windows faced west. At this late-morning hour there was no direct sunlight coming in. Elish, she said, you and your nonsense. I'm talking about an expanding of the soul. Think carefully about what your ear affliction means. The body mimics the mind.

I knew this doctrine of hers and knew the pointlessness of arguing against it. I asked about Akiva. I hadn't spoken to him in eight weeks and two days. Ever since the night before he turned three. She couldn't bring him. He went to an after-school activity with David. An after-school activity? I asked. Yes, a kind of summer camp, their version of the heder. They didn't teach the kids how to read, but they told them the stories of the Bible.

You're overdoing it, I said. What's the problem? she asked. He'll know a little more than you and I knew about Judaism at his age. Judaism, I said. What do you mean by Judaism? There are countless movements within Judaism. But she preferred to keep the term without nuance, as she did when she referred to the wisdom of Kabbalah without bothering to find out which Kabbalah exactly—Lurianic emanations Kabbalah, Abulafia's prophetic Kabbalah, or perverse evolutions of the two. I said, And certainly more than Wlodia knows. David, she corrected. Why are you always such a nag, why do you keep reminding people of their sins? Wlodia Solomiansky, I said, the impersonating goy.

There was a spark of sudden sadness in her eyes. I'd never been able to predict her breaking coefficient, how quickly Ronnit shifted from jokes to an exposed nerve that seemed misplaced in her dark tenseness. I wanted to lean toward her and let my head drop, wanted her to rub my scalp with her fingers and relieve me for a moment of my burden. I wondered if David knew, if she wasn't conducting a double fraud.

There's something you don't want to hear, she said, pushing my head away. Sit up, your posture is out of balance. I asked what it was. She said she had no clue, but if my ear was injured, I'd best ask myself the same question. Generally speaking, this wasn't a good time. The Three Weeks, when the demon Ketev Meriri is out on the hunt even in the hours of the afternoon.

Maybe it has something to do with writing, she said, the energy of creation. Are you still writing? I told her I was drudging along with the new novel, that I had a feeling I didn't drop it, rather it had dropped me, that it had itself lost the need to be written and haunt my thoughts.

We talked some more. Vapid talk. The food, hospital bureaucracy, blood tests. I told her I'd read online that a sudden decline in hearing such as I was experiencing could be a symptom of Ménière's disease. She said if that was the case, I would have been experiencing dizziness and tinnitus. It's all a translation, she said, of the soul's concern for the body. Then she suggested I cut out dairy, reduce salt intake, and take zinc supplements. A zinc deficiency can damage the nerves.

We who were destined to meet in sterilized, anonymous spaces and present the human costume we shoved under our beds at night. I asked the Venezuelan if she'd slept soundly. She raised an eyebrow. My voice was still thickened with waking, with the beating of viscous blood on the gates of day.

The hotel breakfast was modest. A screen projected images of war from bombed Gaza. I stood, debating whether to sit with my face to the screen or my back to it, which would mean my gaze would fall on the mirror covering the wall, doubling me. The Venezuelan stepped outside with her tray of food. I watched her meticulously rolling a cigarette, dampening the rolling paper, tightening it, lighting it, sipping her coffee, and looking out at the road, on the other side of which were unfinished apartment buildings webbed with metal.

I walked outside to join her. A fat seagull screeched on its way to the canal. I sat down. I told her I didn't know she smoked. A cylinder of ash fell when she shook her hand. She said in an expressionless tone that she needed quiet in the morning. I pointed at the road where cars were already racing. She shrugged.

I told her I'd made a mistake and caught up on what was going on in Israel. On one website I could even read between the lines of commentators, who were known to be the military's official spokespersons, how they were priming public opinion for a ground invasion of Gaza. I said I was worried. I told her about the group of anti-war protesters that were beaten up by right-wingers while the police stood on the sidelines and watched. I said I was ashamed.

She let out a little growl, her lips pursing.

I sipped my tea. Though the package boasted the name Earl Grey, this concoction had nothing of the blend of black spice with the sweetness of bergamot. Brown liquid. I sipped some more.

What were you laughing about yesterday? I asked. You and the violist.

There was a brief pause and her expression suddenly brightened. She asked when exactly they'd laughed. I said, When I stepped away for a moment during dinner last night. She nodded. He'd told her an extraordinary story.

One night in Paris, back when he was a student at the music academy, he went out for a drink with some friends. He sat with his face toward a paper partition. At some point, he spotted the silhouette of a woman passing against the partition, a blurry movement, he said, said the Venezuelan. He got up to see who it was, but couldn't find her. The area behind the partition was empty. At the end was a door. He walked through the door and out to the alley on the other side of the street. A group of youths were chatting loudly and he asked them if they'd seen anyone walk by. They mocked him. He walked to the end of the alley and then back to the street. He scanned the street methodically, going into each of the bars, dazed. At one bar, an older pianist he'd once improvised with at an event stopped him and said he looked possessed. The violist opened his mouth to explain himself, but the pianist shushed him and dragged him to the piano onstage. The pianist had to start playing soon, he said, but the audience could wait. It was just background music, anyway. He sat the violist down beside him, examined his face like a painter, and wrote a song on the spot, jotting down sheet music. He played it for him. The song told his story, the story of a heartbroken man searching the city for a girl he'd seen in passing. The pianist gave the violist the piece of paper with the music and lyrics. The violist stepped outside, slipped into a garden, and memorized the song. Then he wandered the area, singing it in hopes that the woman he'd seen would hear it and reveal herself.

I said the story sounded made up. She said it didn't matter to her. It contained beauty, fate, but it was small. What more did she look for in literature? And what's funny about it? I asked. The way he told it, she said. The way he went back to being that twenty-year-old lovesick fool.

I said I had no idea what that was about. She said I was deceiving myself. We've all been in that moment of the ice pick to the heart. Once, Ronnit told me it looked as if I were surreptitiously calculating the appropriate waiting period before I could bring up Dalia Shushan. I said it wasn't my fault, it was reality's fault.

The heat and the humidity landed around us as we sat down at the table. I told the Venezuelan that my guess, judging by the exaggerated brilliance of the hour, was that the heat would only increase. She said this was true, but only for a short while. The wind was changing. It came from the direction of the lake, from land. I said my body was accustomed to the Jewish calendar. It was the seventeenth of Tammuz. She asked what this occasion meant. I explained. She said, I hear Hamas is conditioning the cease-fire on removing the embargo on Gaza. I said nothing. She went on, You Jews have always been sent to live outside city walls. I didn't break my silence.

She was right. The vapor of noon, but after that, near the opening of the docks, where we agreed to meet, mighty gusts. Some people gathered. Some were carrying signs, coming to protest. The name of the French Jewish writer whose event we were attending was familiar. I'd read his famous novel.

The protagonist is born into occupation and authoritarian military regime. His family wandered from a Galilee village to the West Bank in the 1948 War and has lived under Israeli rule since 1967. In his childhood, he demonstrates extraordinary analytical abilities, presenting his father with a model of the solar system he'd built according to a description he'd read in a book. A senior member of the PLO, who, like his colleagues, pocketed most of the funding delivered from European sources to the organization, takes him under his wing. He is torn away from his family and his childhood love and sent to boarding schools in

France and Germany, then to advanced physics studies and research at the Niels Bohr Institute, where he encounters a pioneering work of general relativity by a forgotten Jewish scientist. It is an unfinished study, he learns, since the scientist was sent to a death camp before he could complete it, but revolutionary when it comes to the permutation relationships between gravitational fields and the time-space continuum. The news that his brother joined the Islamic Jihad Movement and fell captive and that his childhood home has been destroyed reaches him from afar. His mind is caught up in research, and the fury he's been feeling ever since he knew his own mind is blended into the frenzy of deciphering the practical implications of the work he's uncovered. During long nights bathed in nervous wakefulness, he completes the theory of creating a generator allowing time-space translocations.

Years of reading historical analyses convinces him that the seed of the Israeli-Palestinian conflict lies in Hitler's rise to power and the design of the Final Solution. He does the first thing any person living in the heart or outskirts of Western culture would do if he had access to a time machine: he goes back in time to assassinate the Führer.

But after the assassination, a biography that is not his own begins to mold in his consciousness. In the alternate time line he's created, he exists, but differently. He is an expert engineer on the rebel lines in Syria, which has annexed Palestine as in the days of the Roman Empire. All of it except the Gaza region, which has been attached to Egypt. The Jewish population of Palestine has gradually dwindled. The children of pioneers wished for a better fate than the false ideals of redeeming the land and have abandoned the land for enlightened Europe and the United States, where the Jewish community has grown and strengthened. The Arab Spring that washed over the Middle East only fanned the flames of the tiny fire that has always been burning beneath Assad's oppression machine, and hope seems to twinkle. But within weeks, this hope has turned into an excuse for bloodshed, to which the world replies with a resounding silence.

The facts of his alternative life battle against the protagonist's memory, taking control of more and more of his consciousness. Images emerge: his slaughtered mother, rain falling on the mangled bodies of his brothers, his father's blood-washed gray hair, his beloved raped in a mound of trash, the sun reflecting off the polished buttons of Assad's storm troopers' uniforms. He goes off in search of the Jewish scientist, and the book remains open-ended. The protagonist is torn. Along with the Jewish scientist, he manages to re-create the generator of the time-space translocation and is able to reach the right time and place to prevent the assassination he himself perpetrated, but it means that the Jewish scientist, his spiritual father, will be sent to his death.

I did not like the book, which was written in the overblown tone of pulp fiction and full of unequivocal literary images, an overly detailed reality. Each character had only one prominent quality, which manifested whenever the character appeared. The love interest, for instance, had been blessed with piercing doe eyes. I thought science fiction had reached maturity decades ago.

For some reason, none of these flaws were mentioned in discussions inspired by the novel. People claimed that his assumption that with a lack of Israeli occupation a Palestinian nation would not be established was essentially ridiculous. They said only a Western man would dare write about identities he did not know, because he was writing out of an imperial awareness, the perception that he was a member of the socioeconomic elite that formulates identity and place for everyone else. I couldn't care less about those discussions. I couldn't read literature as if it were a research article. I dropped out of philosophy studies with a sense of missed opportunity. I had even weaned myself off the doctrines of false philosophers who pretended

SHIMON
ADAF

they were touching life. But literature was supposed to do that, as if its eyes were covered and it was learning the outline of reality from its textures, its lumps and concaves, roughness and lubrication, the nailness of bird flight, the quiet velvety sensation of horror in the fingertips. I could have awarded the French Jewish writer some merits—for the courage to write a popular book that did not revolve around a love story and involved the simple knowledge that a moral issue was no matter for principles and generalizations, but was always determined when certain people floated into our consciousness as we weighed a decision. The angel of judgment, brother of the messenger that erases all signs of knowledge from our minds as we exit the womb, is also blind. He too learns our sins by touching the face we offer him, the grooves notched into it against our will.

I recognized the face of one of the protesters, her hair white and two teeth missing from her mouth. She was the one who had stormed out of our panel. The sign she carried read DOWN WITH PALESTINE HATERS. A festival representative asked the group to disperse. A brief argument ensued, into which that same bony, slow-moving man erupted with a barrage of curses. From the corner of my eye, I saw his young assistant. He smiled at me when he noticed me noticing him and spread his arms in apology. He was chiseled from a piece of bright material, his limbs whole and polished.

The protesters retreated from the man, mumbling something about new Jewish barbarity. The boy moved toward him, as did the festival representative, as did we. His animal power drew us in. The Venezuelan said she hoped he wouldn't curse us out if he didn't like our questions. Was that the French Jewish writer? the Venezuelan wondered. I said it was, hadn't she seen his picture in the festival catalog?

Who even looks at those things? she asked. The conversation with the writer was slated to take place at sea. We descended a slope toward the dock. A boat was glued to the water by ropes. The writer's hand gripped the boy's arm. The boat operator said that at the port, thanks to the enormous breakwater that had been constructed to control the entry and exit of merchant ships in the seventeenth century, the water was quiet, but beyond it the waves were rather high. The wind changed, he said. I looked at the Venezuelan. Her face was expressionless. There was an audience of seven people. The writer was wearing a life preserver. He reached for the boy, who pulled a tube of sunscreen from his bag. It is hard to believe that water is a liquid, that waves are not living marble. The boat tilted forty-five degrees and our clothes were sprayed with moisture. The Venezuelan, who sat across from me, against the tilt, examined me with a threatening expression. I found her totemic, vulturine quality captivating. What did she discover in me, I wondered, from her point of view?

The actress that came with us started to read, but was overtaken by the trembling of the air and raised her voice until it lost all nuance. The French Jewish writer waved at her to tone it down. He opened his mouth to speak, then leaned over and threw up. He sprung back up, his chin strewn with the tracks of his stomach fluids. He sweated beneath the layer of sunscreen. He turned to the boy and roared, I told you it wasn't the drinking. The boy looked away at the roiling, fragmenting nature.

We returned to port. The rocking subsided and we were hammocked. The actress read at length. The writer cut her off. That's enough, he said. What do you mean that's enough? two of the passengers protested. We paid for a conversation. The writer asked his boy to hand him his wallet, pulled out a few notes, and asked, How much were the tickets?

We left the port to the sounds of their bitterness. The French author stumbled behind us and the boy rushed toward us. The author had sent him over to apologize, he said, panting. To us? I asked. Yes, he said. I hope you can still make it to the next event. Especially you, he said, nodding lightly toward the Venezuelan. He's apologizing? I asked again. Yes, the boy said, this kind of thing doesn't happen to him often.

The Venezuelan said she'd read his book, and it contained some interesting ideas she would love to discuss. I thought you found literary discussions boring, I said. When did I say that? she asked. I don't know, I said, last night, I think– She cut me

off. She said, You don't listen, you file away. You remember details. You don't truly listen.

The boy lent an ear to our conversation, waiting. Could you
tell him that? the Venezuelan said. Yes, he said. Are you his assistant? I asked. The Venezuelan huffed, He's his life partner.
The boy nodded.

She asked the boy how he could bear the man. He said, He's
like a rosebush. I thought he'd concocted an unsuccessful play
on words on the writer's last name. The boy continued, Every
rose is a parable. A rosebush, even a wilting one, contains the
wildness of a predatory animal.

On the fourth day of my hospitalization I went down-stairs to the plaza. The hospitalization tower was freezing. Among the visitors smoking with their backs hunched and defeated, I was recognized by Yaffa's sister-in-law. Yaffa, who never spared anyone her criticism, had managed over the years to create a variety of cold balances of terror with her loved ones—each a balance of terror and its specific nuances. Her attitude toward me was always colored with a hue of accusation. My actions were examined and found lacking. Her sister-in-law was hasty and garrulous, and therefore Yaffa always demanded that before her husband, Bobby, told his sister anything, he should run it by Yaffa first. When her sister-in-law attended family dinners, Yaffa shushed Bobby anytime he attempted to share any details from their personal lives, even just an anecdote about the mischievousness of Tahel or Oshri, their youngest.

Now the woman called my name and I foolishly answered. She instantly commenced her investigation, how long had I been there and why. Then, in the same breath, she told me her aunt was in a coma, just fell into it all of a sudden, she had lots of trouble with her heart, just collapsed, like, what, a mountain fell on her, she said, like, what, an abyss closed over her. Now she was hospitalized, but what didn't she go through before this, echo and EKG and stress tests, did it help, believe me these doctors don't know a thing, they say she had a stroke, what are they talking about, stroke, where did they get that stroke idea from, beats me, the woman was just a little tired.

I asked her not to tell her brother. The condition I was hospitalized for was not serious and I didn't want to worry my mother. She swore on the life of her aunt who was on her deathbed.

Not two hours later, I got a text from Tahel. Mom knows, she wrote. Within seconds, Yaffa called. What happened? she asked. You and your fake fever again. I told her about my ear and asked if our mother knew. She said I was an expert at making a big deal out of nothing. I told her I tried to keep it from them. I would have told them after they released me. She said she knew me, that this was how I created drama, I knew they'd find out, and our mother panicked easily, and with her diabetes we had to be careful not to frighten her unnecessarily.

I asked if she told her. She said she did, she was sitting right beside her. Is it true, my mother demanded to know, what Yaffa's sister-in-law was saying, are you really at the hospital? I confessed the truth. I said it would all be over soon. She announced they were coming to visit. Where's Yaffa? I asked. She went to the kitchen to make us coffee, my mother said. Don't believe what she says, I told her. You two, she said. When are you going to put all your nonsense behind you and make up? I said, When the Messiah comes. She sighed. I'll go to your father's grave to ask for you to have a quick recovery, she said.

What is that urge that overtakes me to tell the details that supposedly make me who I am? I feel ashamed in the face of their slyness and replace the truth by heaping them up. But it isn't in the heap, the truth, but rather in the concealed order working to emerge from them and simultaneously blocked by them. One of the residents waited for me in my room. The nurse had complained that I was never in there during rounds so she could never get my blood sample or check my temperature. Your job is simple, he said. To rest. I felt a lump in my throat. I told him the size of the room limited my ability to breathe. That's natural, he said. All the crying organs were ready to go, lungs, throat, mouth, eyes. From the bedside table I took out a few of the baby peppers Ronnit had brought and went out to the lobby. I'll be back for your vitals after dinner, the nurse called out after me.

The light angled from the southwest, fracturing through the large windows, a warm strip of brightness resting at the bottom of the row of chairs. I bit into a pepper and ground it between my teeth. Suddenly, my entire being swelled up, shapeless and spreading forth from the biting. No, because I was standing in place, and all of space was coming at me, tumbling toward me.

17

One of the senior doctors would come in each morning with great pomp, impatient, speaking briefly about the state of the scientific exhibits displayed on the beds, always in third person, always ending his speech with a personal, impartial question addressed to the patients, who were expected to shed the cloak of objectivity tossed over them in a flash. The flock of residents did not wait for the hesitant response either. But this morning, when I too answered briefly and quickly that my condition had neither improved nor deteriorated, one of the residents said, We'll only be able to know after treatment is complete. Self-testimony is currently invalid. The others nodded and exchanged glances. I saw suspicion forming in their eyes.

The vertigo attack had passed, leaving behind it an unraveled space around my body, a general unsteadiness, a kind of expectation of movement that engorged things and made them overflow. Sweet betrayal, even when we cease trusting flesh-and-blood people, the animal spirit, even after we learn the schemes of creatures of the deep waiting safely in the heart of some ocean for our destruction, the system of considerations of the vegetable world, its silent conquerings of the land, we continue to place our hopes on lifeless objects, on the consistency of their indifference to the crimes, nobility, punishment, and reward that we order to be the façade of all that exists.

Long story short: the ghost of dizziness, a fear that I might fall. At noon Manny showed up. Tahel, who'd concluded that he was my only friend, left him a message. I'd stopped wondering how she achieved all of her goals long ago. Over the past year and change, upon her introduction into the burden of adolescence, my conversations with her had become less real, plagued by some fictitious weightiness.

Manny's rumbling voice was hoarse around the edges. The remains of the flu he'd carried back from Berlin, he said. He wouldn't enter the hospital and asked that we meet at the adjacent mall. Get out of there as fast as you can, he said. Tell them you want to continue treatment at home. You have no idea about the infections lurking in the curtains, in the walls. I promised him I wasn't hospitalized in the internal medicine ward, but he still insisted. He was wearing one of his printed T-shirts. The Avengers twisted around his paunch, here a blue Captain America spot, there a red Black Widow spot. I asked him how work was going. He said they were finally replacing the security system.

I told him the odd story the giant had shared with me, about his niece who'd disappeared for three days. He said he could see the old spark light up inside me and asked if I was sure I didn't get the itch. He'd asked me several times, after he read each of my books, if I didn't get the itch, and I always gave him my regular answer, that my detective days were over. We both needed this ritual. Maybe Tahel was right.

What do you think happened? he asked. How should I know? I said. The chaos in the mall stimulated the dizziness inside me. My throat went dry at the thought that it might take hold of me here. I had to hold on to two threads, the thread of conversation and a constant awareness of my limbs, making sure they didn't go awry. Maybe this is a good story for your book, he said. What's going on with that?

I had a speech prepared in advance about the dilemmas of writing, about blocks, about careful examinations of character motivations, the probability of events. Instead I said, Mysteries, mysteries, the detective must die so the man can live.

In the middle of laughing he got a coughing fit. Whenever

you say one of those indecipherable statements, I know something is cooking inside your brain. Then he asked me to explain
myself. I told him perhaps I was no longer interested in writing
detective novels. He said he imagined this moment would come.
I never held any occupation for long. He said I was easily bored,
but perhaps this was my health condition speaking. He asked if
I'd canceled my travel plans. I said I had, that the doctor didn't
recommend it. He said he had no faith in doctors. One of his colleagues was told to stop working out ten years ago because he
had brittle bones, but he was still running like a cheetah every
single day.

I told him I didn't feel like it. He said a trip would do me good
and shared all the same impressions of Berlin I'd already heard.
How his wife wanted to see all the metal plates installed in the
sidewalk and take pictures of the names of people who'd been
taken from their homes to the death camps, how every old person they saw made her wonder what they'd been up to during the
thirties and forties, what their parents had been up to, and how
she'd determined that the cyclists in the city were all murderers,
given how many times she'd almost been run over. He didn't
notice the ridiculing tone he wove into his report of his wife's
habits and obsessions. He didn't notice how he pulled himself
away from her, how a youthful tone had pushed its way even into
his liberated, rumbling laugh.

few perfect days for summer lovers. A quiet marriage of wind and sun. Everything here is body, I told the Venezuelan, everything goes by the desires of the body. She said the Paul Valéry Museum was offering an interesting exhibition of the work of Joan Miró. Besides that, the festival was the only intellectual happening. Who came to this city for anything but the pleasures of the senses. She asked if I hadn't attended any interesting panels or readings.

I said the selection was limited. Writers of Arab countries were hostile and I had trouble reaching the level of self-oblivion I required to listen to them speak. She said she didn't blame them. I asked her why it was assumed I condoned the actions of the government of the country where I lived. I didn't automatically assume the Syrian writer was a supporter of Assad's slaughters, or that the Palestinian poet was a Hamas activist.

He's a nice guy, she said. Educated, speaks several languages. Why do the Palestinian poets, I said, never live in the occupied territories? They wander Western capitals, sipping wine, suckling the honey of the land, sleeping with European women, but writing about the suffering of their people. She asked if I'd rather they suffered themselves. I said the Palestinians living in the occupied territories were the ultimate victims, and that everyone made use of the horrors that were inflicted upon them—their leaders, staying at hotels, allegedly fighting for their liberation as they positioned them to be their human shields; Israeli leaders who painted them as the cruel enemy; their poets, who profiteered with their pain. In the end, the dead children remained nameless, as did the grief of those who were left to remember them.

She asked if I was still mad about what had happened at the opening event. I told her I wasn't. At the beginning of the event, the Palestinian poet read a poem about the destruction of Gaza. A direct, powerful piece, but not a good poem. More like a manifesto written in truncated lines. He enjoyed wild applause and whistles of agreement. After him, a band came up to play cheerful tunes. The audience members in the gardens of the Jardin du Château d'Eau, where the event took place, were sitting in chairs bathed in greenery and imbibing all sorts of drinks, clapping at the right moments.

I told her I'd go to the museum that afternoon. She said the exhibition was interesting and that she'd visited two days ago with the violist. I said nothing. She said she would be glad to accompany me too. Last night, we'd gone together to watch *joutes*, a local sport, a translation into water sports of knights' jousting duels. Two opposing rowboats with a jouster on each stern. The jousters try to push each other into the canal's waters. One team wears blue, the other red.

In the match we watched, the blue team was more adept. Again and again, the red jouster was pushed from his spot. The music that accompanied the duel came out of an amplification system, a monophonic trumpet tightly riding a rustling march. Perhaps a reminder of the music that used to be played, if the records indicate, in the original jousting battles.

The Venezuelan waved vigorously toward the other bank. I strained my eyes and could barely make out the silhouette of the violist. How did she spot him among the masses? Our eyes stayed on him as he fought to cross the bridge that was crowded with observers. He reached us, preoccupied and happy. The interim duel was imbalanced, he confirmed. The blues were members of the professional Sète team while the reds were amateurs. We took off to some remote bar he knew.

The whole time we sat there, as the alcohol polished the glint in our eyes, the Venezuelan looked him over covetously. I asked him why he picked the viola. He said he'd migrated from the violin thanks to compulsive listening to Edward Elgar's *Enigma Variations*. He said Elgar's work comprised different developments of a musical motif missing from the piece, which had to be deciphered, unlike in more classical pieces, in which the central motifs were demonstrably played. He said he'd always been fascinated by the relationship between the music he played and the human conditions that enabled its creation. He said each variation addressed a different person in Elgar's life. He said Elgar used to say the protagonist was missing from the play. The violist said there was logic to this. What united people if not a hidden agent? He said he was drawn to the characters of Ysobel and Dorabella, and that it took a while before he realized it was thanks to the viola music in the variations named for them. He said the instrument did a good job of outlining them.

I asked him about the story the Venezuelan had told me. She smiled politely as I asked him. He said he was keeping the piece that had been written for him safe, that he could send me a reconstruction of a performance of the song, of the event, directed by a friend. He said he'd send me a link to the YouTube video right away, and that if I liked it, perhaps I could share it on my Facebook page. I told him I wasn't on social media, that I thought it was a monstrous reincarnation of the town square, that it was a more advanced, friendlier platform for a mob to organize its lynchings.

19

Akiva's hand trembled in mine as soon as the water-line appeared on the edge of Frishman Street, the water spreading on a fine day such as this to the point of dimming and engulfing. I told him not to let go. He jumped in place, pointed at the traffic light on the corner of HaYarkon Street, and said loudly that the light wasn't changing, and how much longer? When we got to Atarim Square, he could no longer resist the urge and ran ahead. I pointed at the devoured building that still stood strong against the spray of salt water and the constant stench of urine. I told him this was where my office used to be. He asked how old I was and who my son was. I told him I was almost forty-one and didn't have a son. He pointed at a little boy who was hunched under a sun umbrella and licking an ice cream cone and said, Take him, take him, he's alone. I asked who Akiva thought had bought that boy his ice cream. He said a kind woman must have bought it for him because she could tell he was sad. I asked him if he'd take an ice cream cone from a woman he didn't know. He said, But I'm not alone. And you aren't sad, I said. I'm not sad, he said. He pulled on the kite I was holding in my other hand. Can we fly it now, look at that cute dog. A stocky woman was pulling behind her a pug who was kneeling on its haunches. He's pooping, Akiva squealed. Shh, I said. The woman examined the stool for a moment, then turned away and walked toward the boy. The dog, wrinkled like foreskin, beat her to it, pouncing toward the boy, panting. The boy flinched, lifting his legs. Leave me alone. Come on, I told Akiva, but he remained planted in place. What's there to see? I asked. Why doesn't the boy love the dog? he asked. The woman grabbed the boy by the collar and pulled him to his feet, whispering for him to stop being a baby. The boy tried to sneak the pug a kick but missed.

Let's go to the dog, Akiva said. I asked him if he'd like to have a dog someday. He looked at me sternly. You can't raise dogs in Jerusalem, he said. I asked if he'd never seen dogs there. He said he had, but they were just visiting. You can't raise dogs in Jerusalem, he determined. The air isn't good for them. I asked if he'd tried. He paused to consider this, then said, When are we going to fly the kite?

It was a mighty spring, the end of a restless month of Nissan, toggling between heat waves and glass days in which the light blued and silvered. We walked through it, the polished air that the gusts pushed away of their own volition. Akiva ran down a grassy slope. I ran alongside him, the kite string tight in my palm. Something about him, in the curve of the cheek, the cut of the silhouette, I could almost recognize it, then I recoiled, I didn't believe I ought to know. The essence of spring was his grating laugh. You hug too tight, he said. Fine, I said, let's go pick up Mom.

Once a month, Ronnit offers naturopathic consultations at a pharmacy in Tel Aviv, not far from my apartment. The years she spent as a biology student, the years she agonized as a student of conventional medicine in Beersheba, her sobering from its illusions, cast a spell on her desperate patients, whose lives were made miserable by light rashes or a burning in their esophagus. Today she brought Akiva with her. Of course I objected to the name, but David, also known as Wlodia Solomiansky, whose eyes opened to the ancient Jewish glow rising from the dust and the walls of the Torah schools and the *ulpanas* and the holy arks in the Land of Israel, had determined in advance that it would be his son's name. I didn't ask what she told David.

In general, she wanted me to avoid discussing him. She usually left Akiva with me.

We put down a blanket at Meir Park. Ronnit insisted on bringing food with her. Akiva ran around, fell, cried. I got up to help him. Ronnit stopped me and got up herself. No matter, I told him, it'll pass. Ronnit kissed his skinned knee. I was alert to the sound of his crying. Perhaps the trembling I heard was a different voice inside the crying, Tahel's sobbing range from ten years ago.

He's asleep, I told her on my porch. She reached over and removed my sunglasses. Habits stake us out even after the rationale behind their creation has been annihilated. We must be wary not to wrongly believe that repeating them will bring back the emotions that existed before we put the shapes together to contain them. Ronnit once told me to remove my sunglasses in the shade. I told her that as a child I stared at the sun and burned my eyes. Years later, she asked me to try some eye patches and carrot creams she'd concocted. But then she claimed I simply didn't want to truly look, to linger in the act of looking. She removed them from my face. Look at this tree, she said. A holy ficus was divided between the flow of sun and the shadow cast by a building, an angling contour slicing it in half. It's like the tree is lit up in green, she said. She asked how I explained the joy she felt in the presence of this illuminated green, her indifference in the presence of the shaded green. I mumbled something about frequencies, about reflection, about neuron activity. She chuckled. Don't lecture me about biology, she said. There's a deeper secret than that. Yes, I said, humans' desire to fool themselves. I held on to her wrist on the porch and said, Wlodia is screwing with that boy's mind. Ronnit said, You're so annoying. Why do you always insist on saying the wrong thing?

20

I almost learned how to sleep in the hospital. The dizziness had the advantage of adding a light hammocking effect to the softness of the mattress. The snores, the moans, the grunting from the other beds took on a new character under its influence. A kingdom of the condemned that had waited the whole time on the edge of consciousness. I'd almost given in to the comfort when a honking sound sliced through my ears. It was as if a metal rod had been shoved into them, surrounded by surging flesh, if I could describe it that way. A high note, silver and piercing. I covered my ears and shoved my head deep into the pillow, but it was pointless.

If I managed to sleep, it still didn't cure me. Only the volume of the sound diminished. When was the last time I'd slept the sleep of the recovering? Whoever spoke of the sweetness of sleep knew what they were talking about, even if the sweetness comes from the yearning for sleep, just like all the childhoods we knew way back when, which still haunt us.

Yaffa didn't come visit. She said Oshri insisted on going to soccer practice, Bobby reported to me in a low voice. He called from downstairs to find out which ward and which floor. Through the phone, I heard Tahel speaking excitedly to my mother, who answered with a slow sigh, something about Tel Aviv. But Tel Aviv was deserted at this hour, an hour of twilight as gray as a dove, on the eve of the Ninth of Av. The hospital hallways had become orphaned of visitors. Only the hospitalized roamed them, as they always do, outside time.

The elevators delayed their arrival. I sat in the lobby, waiting.

They were laughing as they stepped out, empty-handed. First, one elevator door opened and Bobby hurried over, pulling my mother after him. Tahel had said she'd wait until she figured out how the mechanism worked. Inside the elevator, they found the wall to be devoid of buttons, leaving them no control of its destinations. The elevator stopped on the fifth floor and they stepped out, convinced it was broken, and rushed into another elevator, which took them down to the second floor, and then another one took them one floor up, where, desperate, they began to search for a stairwell. Another elevator returned them to the lobby, where Tahel waited, explaining they had to first insert their desired floor, then wait for the system to announce which elevator stopped there. I don't understand how that's supposed to save energy, Bobby said. Tahel said it was simple math. Bobby hushed her with the wave of a hand.

We change in ways we cannot guess, even when the change is complete. Those who announce a change are liars. Those who claim that nothing will alter them are fabricators. We change because we can never tell the wheat from the chaff within us, not before the transformation takes place, and not afterward.

Tahel taught me to overcome my fear of the internet. The stunning beauty of her infancy had fallen away. Her nose, which used to look like a tiny grit, had swelled and bent a tad. She was no less pretty, but her beauty was less perfect, fortunately for her. Her brain had grown sharper. Five years earlier, she complained that all the children in her class were on Facebook for the purpose of some game, farming, or something of the sort, but her mother wouldn't let her join, even though she'd have a password. I tried to ask Yaffa what the issue was, and Yaffa asked if she'd told me that a year earlier Tahel had figured out Yaffa's password and gone on her Facebook page. Messed up messages, Yaffa said. Messed up the page. I told her she was overreacting. How could the girl possibly know how to write at age six? She didn't, Yaffa said. She'd memorized the order of the keystrokes for the password, and once on the page she entered in status updates, typing at random, goofing off. Yaffa's friends thought she'd lost her mind. I laughed. Yaffa said that was exactly the problem—that I enjoyed every bit of nonsense that girl got into.

Tahel told me she wanted an iPad. I asked her what that was. She explained, A touch-screen device. I asked around and bought one. On Saturday night I called her into the corner room in my mother's home. Yaffa found out within less than a week. Or, more accurately, the school confiscated the device. A friend told on Tahel. She was going online and playing under the desk during class. Yaffa lost it. You spoil everything you touch, she yelled at me over the phone. Don't come near me or the girl.

The iPad was returned to me on another Friday night. Flushed, Tahel sat beside me on the sofa and explained how to use it, what apps were, how to open an account so I could download them, how to set up the email app. I ordered a home internet connection. Over the phone, Tahel gave me further instructions. Until then I'd never required search engines for my investigations. Manny provided all the necessary information, all the details, access to police files. I read old newspapers in the city library, raised dust clouds at archives. I could feel the pages, see the past photographed with the graininess of the past against the slide projector.

21

What is it about humidity that habit cannot prepare us for? The breeze quieted and the water vapors looped around the net that landed around us, trapping us, as we climbed toward the Paul Valéry Museum. Barcelona and Tel Aviv—in theory, we should have been more prepared, our bodies ready to activate the involuntary reaction of organ restraint, lowering the body temperature. Instead we were sweating, suffocating. I was also surprised by Miró's early works. Still life inspired by Cézanne, but with more opaque colors, yet still feeling around to examine the relationship of the piece with the data of senses, manners of seeing, the crumbling of an object in the mind, and its rebuilding as a carrier of emotions.

The artwork was chronologically ordered along the hallway walls. The early paintings were viscous, giving up movement, like turtles overturned on their backs, until time and space were interrupted in 1926, the wonder year, and then all at once his familiar style emerged, bright, alien shapes giving up the pretense of representation or endeavoring to offer a collection of closed-off interior experiences expressed in a private language, ideograms created on the spot and simultaneously creating their observers.

The pieces were scattered throughout the rooms without a specific time line. In each room, the conversation took place in a slightly different jargon, as if each room were a mental state, a consciousness, that Miró returned to at different times of his life, seeking different syllables, a new handwriting that wasn't all that different from the one that came before. Where is the gap, I asked the Venezuelan, to explain this repetition? If we have a reality to compare to, we can guess the spots where the artist was disloyal and understand the fixation, going back to capture it with greater wholeness. But here, with language itself concealed, only the repetition is testimony to the missed opportunity.

She shrugged. Too abstract for her taste. Supposedly Miró drew inspiration from an aesthetic close to her world. They nursed on the same traditions. But the desire to capture a primordial, childlike state devoid of any true experience was foreign to her. She'd never understood the attraction toward ancient culture. She needed a cigarette.

Outside, I asked her if she often smoked during the day too. She said she didn't usually, but that the idleness here caused her to. She'd planned to use the free time to write, but the commotion of tourism in Sète drained the city of creative force. She said she had to stop at the pedestrian mall and buy her son some shoes. He was obsessed with shoes and asked her to get him a pair from every trip she took. I said I didn't know she had a child. The Venezuelan said she thought she had the word "Mom" written on her forehead. There was a pungency to the cigarette smoke. It cut through the heavy air.

We descended to the street overlooking the Théâtre de la Mer. It had been built to supervise ships, she said. Louis XIV commissioned it along with the founding of the city to better fight against the British. I said I knew that. I asked how old her son was. She distractedly touched her flat chest and ran a hand down her belly. He was ten. I asked why he needed so many shoes. She said, He's a collector, like his father. I told her I didn't want kids. She said she hadn't asked. The saltiness, the green of the seaweed insinuated in the turquoise of the water, moved toward us. I asked if the violist was staying at our hotel. She lost her bearings for a moment, said he was staying at the youth hostel on Rue Louis Blanc. He's got a d— She cut herself off. We said nothing. Why did I want to know? she finally asked. I told her that until a few years ago I would get sick when I saw the sea, grasping the intensity of its existence, that the promise concealed within it was about to be fulfilled. A fleck of the veiled look she'd given the violist the previous night flickered in her eyes. She asked what I thought of the exhibition. I asked what her son's name was. She spoke it with a question, as if I were meant to know him.

I said Miró's style was characteristic, but limited. Some artists' styles are all about nuance, she said. I said I wasn't sure where the line between compulsion and mannerism ran. She said it was hard work, silent work, performed with complete ignorance. She asked if this was why I didn't want children. I said I didn't see the connection. Why did I need to know where the line ran? she asked. At our panel, I spoke about how repetition was part of the nature of writing. That's precisely why, I said. I wondered if there was a moment when one turned from a wide-eyed child to an enslaved man. She sighed and tossed her cigarette butt aside. She gathered the ends of her dress and held it against her body. The wind blew. A wind ignited in the thickness of the sea. So, she said, what is it then? I said, We repeat ourselves to make something more precise. But when does that something evaporate, leaving us to repeat ourselves only to justify the repetition? She said it wasn't a question of art but of human nature. She said, Your struggle with the Palestinians seems to beg the exact same question.

22

She and our mother ran into Ronnit by chance, Yaffa told me over the phone, and our mother figured out right away that she was pregnant. Yaffa reported, with a dry tone that did not attempt to conceal the accusation, That's just one more thing you let slip away and break. The rec center took Zehava out on a trip and Yaffa joined her. Our mother's neighbors didn't want to go. They thought it was too dangerous to go to the Wailing Wall tunnels, those old fools, and Jerusalem was too cold anyway, even during this arid year. Then they took them out to a bad restaurant. Ronnit happened to be there with her husband. Did you know he was Russian? she asked.

The encounter was awkward. Yaffa told me that Zehava Ben Zaken, with her famous tact, asked why she hadn't been invited to the wedding. Ronnit explained she'd gotten married in a small, modest ceremony. I asked Yaffa why she was telling me all this. She said she thought I'd want to know. Ronnit's three months along, but she's so skinny she's barely showing.

The math was simple. I counted the days. I called Ronnit. She didn't answer. I called again two hours later from a blocked number. Yes, she answered.

What do you want, Elish?

It's Elish.

(Silence.)

How did you know?

I recognize that little swallowing of air before you start speaking.

Funny.

Well, who else would be calling me from a blocked number?

What's up?

You talked to your mother.

No, to Yaffa.

So you know then. Zehava has the instinct of a—

Moroccan, I said.

Exactly, but of an ancient Moroccan. The ones for whom women are nothing more than larvae that marry and procreate.

We need to meet.

This has nothing to do with you.

She hung up. I turned off the tape recorder.

I drove to Jerusalem. The stone glowed in the walls, the sapphire brick sooty. I stood at the appropriate distance. She saw me through her kitchen window, which was torn toward Benjamin of Tudela Street, the waving of trees, the burning of geranium in doorways all around. She stood before me with her arms crossed. I sat back on the bench, removed my sunglasses in that near autumn, sunlight falling meekly on the garden, vague patterns jotted on the ground, blurry exchanges between blades of light and shadow.

I asked why she didn't tell me. She said, Are you insane, coming here? Is Wlodia home? I asked. No, she said, but the neighbors. She undid the knot in her headscarf and retied it, hard. The ends of her hair peeking against the back of her neck were filled with greater vitality. She smiled at a passing neighbor.

I told her the pregnancy wasn't noticeable. She said they'd hardly told anyone. Besides Zehava and Yaffa, the only ones who knew were her mother and David's two sisters. I said, The time line checks out. She said it didn't, and anyway, I was wrong, of course not, she was on the pill during that time, she only went

off it a week later, she was afraid if she didn't, she wouldn't com-
mit to David, that was how badly the trip to Cyprus shook her
up. I said that didn't really change the calculation. Lower your
voice, she said. I suggested we go talk elsewhere.

When we arrived elsewhere, she made me swear. She said it
made no difference since I didn't want children anyway. I asked
if she planned to tell David. She said he was the father, so what
was there to tell?

A gust of wind rolled over some dry leaves that had unwisely
emerged before their time, some defective protein sending them
to swift, false maturation, before the chill arrived. We sat across
from a coffee shop, our backs leaned against a concrete pillar
bound with polemic posters, Jerusalem strewn with Ebal mountains. Ronnit got up to go to the coffee shop and returned with
two cups. This tea is simply atrocious, I said. She said she would
have invited me over to her place, but given the circumstances. I
said I wanted to be involved in the child's life. She said abso-
lutely not, and goddamn me, and, what, did I really think she
was going to raise a child who would be forbidden from getting
married, that she would do that to David? I said she wasn't being
completely honest with him. She said the last thing she had to
do was justify her actions to me.

I told her.

I'd invested several days in it. I used Manny's help, I even
called Eliya, whom I only spoke to on Yom Kippur Eve ever since
I retired from the investigations industry and sold her my share
of our firm. They used their connections. Wlodia Solomiansky's
mother's birth certificate was fake. The Ministry of Interior in-
tentionally made no effort to confirm the authenticity of the
documentation presented by immigrants from the former
USSR. But a photocopy of the birth certificate procured by
Eliya, and the professional opinion of one of Manny's colleagues, confirmed it. I told her there was no proof that Wlodia

was Jewish, and that Solomiansky was probably a borrowed name.

You're a son of a bitch, Elish, she said. I knew it the first time I met you, you son of a bitch. She plucked the paper cup out of my hand and tossed it into the street. She got up and left.

23

It's depressing here, Bobby said at the hospital. Let's go down to the cafeteria, I'm dying for some coffee, and you, Zehava, you've got to eat something, you aren't fasting, are you? Yaffa said the doctor said you're in no condition to fast. What does that mean? I asked. Offhandedly, my mother said that she was hypoglycemic. She was standing in the kitchen one day and the world turned black all around her. She almost fell down. Tahel said she had to make sure to eat regularly. She could set up a reminder on the phone Yaffa gave her, but Grandma was afraid it wouldn't work. She's like you, Tahel told me, she doesn't trust devices. I didn't tell her that the few days the iPad spent in her possession had imbued it with a sense of humanity, that I could sense through it the history that the creations of technology were missing, that even though it had aged quickly, slowing down, and even though I'd replaced it with a new one, I kept it fully charged and turned it on for a few minutes at a time just to hear the buzzing of life within it.

The cafeteria was about to close. Normally, they were supposed to stay open twenty-four hours a day, Bobby argued to the cashier, who urged us to make up our minds. He knew this because he'd visited his aunt a few times. The cashier said that on the eve of the Ninth of Av businesses closed early, and that they should have come on a different day. Bobby told the guy not to tell him when to come visit his brother-in-law, he was only— Tahel cut him off and asked if she could get whipped cream on her hot cocoa, but when we sat down, under the weight of the hospitalization tower over our heads, the anguish-saturated space trapped within it, she carefully transferred the whipped cream onto a saucer and pushed it toward her father, who shoveled it distractedly into his mouth.

My mother said I seemed pale, panicked. She asked what I was afraid of. I told her I wasn't afraid, it was just this shock, which I could finally admit to, of a routine that was suddenly broken. In the past few days I'd thought a lot about a story I'd read in the newspaper as a youth, about a man in Beersheba who was swallowed by a sinkhole on his way to work.

Everyone suffers from something, Bobby told me. Tahel said they were building a house in Sderot. Bobby looked at her reproachfully, as if simply giving word of this, as soon as I heard it, would sabotage their efforts. He asked reluctantly if Yaffa hadn't told me. I told him I couldn't remember the last time Yaffa and I discussed anything personal. My mother said, When are you two finally going to stop this nonsense and make up? Bobby said they'd won the land in an auction six months ago and just received a permit from the Ministry of Housing.

But in Sderot? I asked. It's safer than Ashkelon now, my mother said. They'd be safe. And what's left for them in Ashkelon, anyway? Sderot is totally armored, Bobby said. And the house will include a large safe room built to meet updated safety regulations. I said, If you're already moving, why not move up north? Tahel said in a small voice, We can't run. Soon they'll have missiles that can reach all the way to the Golan Heights. I examined her, shocked. She said, Look it up online. She said, Everyone thinks they're the only ones with technology, that other people are still using sticks and stones.

Bobby said Yaffa was in charge of planning the house. It was her baby. He only asked for one thing, an enormous pole with the Israeli flag on it, just like in the quads outside government institutions. Tahel said she'd suggest that her school transfer Memorial Day and Independence Day ceremonies to their new house.

We're sending her to middle school at Sha'ar HaNegev,

Bobby said. Yaffa looked into it and it's a good school with lots of
development opportunities. She says culture is very important
to Ashkenazim. I told them they were making a mistake. They
should move someplace else. Tahel asked why. I said Sderot contained too many lives not yet lived, awaiting new hosts.

My mother said I used to go to an after-school activity at
Sha'ar HaNegev and that I liked it, but that I might have caught
something there. One day I came home sick. You were weak your
entire life, she said, why are you now afraid of hospitals all of a
sudden? The metal rod splitting my hearing thickened and radi-
ated heat. My mother's, Tahel's, and Bobby's words were added
to the bits of noise that surrounded it. When they got up to leave,
my mother lingered. They waited for her at the doors. She whispered to me not to worry, that she'd already asked my father to
help me out, and he came to her in a dream and told me I was
going to get better. Through the glass I watched them walking
away. A moment before they disappeared around a corner, Tahel
turned around and waved.

24

My mouth had been bitter ever since the previous night. Had I not been wrong about it more than once in the past, I would have claimed that my mouth was a reliable disaster barometer, but I was always expecting disasters, if I waited long enough. The news websites reported a ground invasion of Gaza. The Prime Minister chuckled as he described the strategic achievement. Israel had vehemently claimed it would not invade, spreading rumors about a cease-fire agreement about to be signed, and the enemy was taken by surprise once again. I wondered who besides the Prime Minister didn't anticipate a ground invasion from the very beginning of the operation. Ministers demonstrated their folk wisdom. Commentators spawned words. The internet comments on the analyses included calls to flatten Gaza and annihilate the Strip. In the Facebook derivatives linked on one of the websites, an older man wrote that as someone who'd fought in Lebanon, he knew that only a person who'd never taken part in a war would be able to send soldiers there so casually. A young man commented on his post, telling him to shut up, that the elderly had lost their right to talk, and now the young generation had to clean up the shit racked up by the spineless bleeding hearts of the previous generation. Another user supported the first commenter and suggested, basing her argument on a one-of-a-kind rationale, that anyone who didn't agree with the current attack should pack their things and move to Gaza.

A message from Tahel was waiting in my inbox. She needed to talk to me and would be available on Skype at a certain hour of the evening. I wrote to her that I'd be at my computer at the appointed time. I rummaged through the books I'd brought with me and pulled out Agnon's *Thus Far*. I liked the way he blended the severity of Austro-Hungarian writing with the limpness, the meticulousness, of Jewish life, which spreads through space on a kind of web of gossip. This blend was at its best when it came naturally. Through the gossipy structures, stories and substories, anecdotes, the Jewish content evaded the arrangement the writing tried to enforce. At times only the severity was apparent, perhaps because the Jewish life Agnon described was contentless. In *Fernheim*, for instance, the characters could have been completely German. The nickname attributed to them, the Jewish Masters, was meaningless. On the other hand, when Agnon wished to compose traditional Jewish literature, supposedly midrashic, as in *And Solomon's Wisdom Excelled*, the inner form slipped between his fingers. It was a nostalgia for a way of life in which he, as a storyteller, did not have a true part.

I slipped the book under my arm and walked along the riverbank, thinking these aimless thoughts. A good teahouse in Sète was hard to find. My mother claimed I'd become picky ever since I quit dairy. She forgot the food negotiations we conducted all through my adolescence.

The Venezuelan and the violist were having coffee. I saw them through the boulangerie window. I directed my steps toward the port, but they took me there. There was heat in the proximity with which their bodies leaned from opposite sides of the table, heat in the movements of their lips, heat in the gestures of their hands.

While I watched, the violist's gaze crossed the distance, pierced through the window, and hit me. As though a line had been stretched, upon which a flash of recognition was shot, I had to break it before it reached me, determined my location, and returned to its source. I moved away, a few blocks, then stopped. Chance had it that I paused before one of the local bakeries. The city was overrun with them, and the offerings were sparse, two types of bread, three sizes. I turned back on my heels.

But the Venezuelan and the violist were no longer at the café. Perhaps he had noticed me. Perhaps they'd rushed out. I went inside. The table where they'd sat had been wiped down, all traces erased.

I went out into the street. They must have walked toward the sea, so I too walked along the canal. I reached the book square and peeked among the stalls. I turned into the tangle of streets, roaming through the boiling afternoon, climbing up inclines, descending down slopes, wandering through the exhausting afternoon. In one of the alleys I gave up my search. The nearby houses dammed the frowning of the sun. I wiped my forehead. My hands felt light, empty. Then I got it. While I pursued them, I'd lost the Agnon book.

I retraced my steps. Or, at least, I tried. My own route evaded me. I turned according to a concealed sense, as if there were a path of smell before me. But the houses weighed on me, and the streets and alleys melted into each other. I lost my way, the body temperature raged, I dripped with sweat. Finally, I walked automatically toward the church spire. I reached the festival office. The expression of one of the volunteer girls disclosed the disgust they all felt at the sight of me. I asked to wash my face. I asked for water. At the quad, the tables were filled with writers from Arab countries. I plopped onto a cool stone step. A father and son showed up. The father said, If sir will excuse me, he is blocking the entrance to my home.

25

In the video stream on the computer screen, above Tahel's head, there hung a poster of the X-Men, Wolverine's adamantium claws drawn, Mystique's blue skin glistening, both of them enormous, other mutants on alert below them, some in their dual versions of future and past. I didn't recognize the space she was sitting in. The username she called me from, Yalon Asor, was also unfamiliar.

I asked if everything was all right at home. She said, Yes, yes. I asked where she was. She said she was at a friend's. The friend's trendy hairdo—a careful, wavy cloud of hair—entered the frame. He nodded at me, dark, even uglier inside his frame of hair. Her parents wouldn't allow her to install Skype on her computer. It's embarrassing, she said.

I said it was almost Shabbat. She said they still had at least another hour. The friend peeked in again. Another hour and forty minutes, he said. It's an hour earlier where you are. I wanted to ask where he came from, what he did, why she was with him. I asked if she wasn't going to Grandma Zehava's. She said my mother was at their place. What, she asked, she didn't tell you? A rocket fell two hundred meters from her house. The news said it was an open field, but actually it was a park.

And where you are, I asked, how is it?

Come on, Tahel said, don't be like my parents. I thought I could trust you. Then she said, We can hear the explosions from Gaza. They moved me and Oshri into the safe room. He cries all night long, that loser.

Yaffa had given herself completely to the construction of the house. We barely spoke during that time, so I don't know exactly when she became obsessed with living in a house that was hers from floorboards to rooftop. I heard about it secondhand. During their marriage, she and Bobby sold their small apartment and bought a bigger one, renovating and selling and buying until they earned enough money. As soon as they received permits, she embarked on a race. Her blueprints were at the ready, and she devoted every free moment to pressuring, persuading, perusing. I asked my mother why Yaffa was in such a rush. She said Yaffa felt she had to move before the end of the year. She knew it in her bones. And because she'd prepared so carefully and lorded over the schedule, the house was ready before any other in the neighborhood. They moved a month before the war began.

I went to tour the new neighborhood out of curiosity. It was built on the banks of an artificial lake. The former mayor had initiated the enterprise with the purpose of pleasing the residents or affording some prestige to a city in which apartment prices were rising without any real correlation to their value or the quality of life they offered. A landscape architect pointed out that water naturally collected in a eucalyptus thicket on the outskirts of town, where it remained for several months after the rainy season was over, and who knew what kind of pond used to exist there before the pioneers came around with their swamp-drying craze. But things could still be restored to their original splendor. With certain changes to the land, deforestation, digging, initial streaming of water, they could support a small lake.

Yaffa's eyes gleamed when she talked about the lake. For years, she'd envisioned a lawn, swings, trees, water torched by the sun in the morning, the smell of the world rising, bathed, from the night. It was too bad they couldn't do it when the kids were younger, but at least Oshri could still enjoy it. His dissipating childhood might still be charged up with intense, inexpungible memories.

For a year, Oshri copied into his notebooks the portraits of characters from the animated shows he was addicted to. Over the phone, my mother shared her and Bobby's concerns. Oshri preferred to stay inside the classroom during recess and draw. The school counselor praised the fine motor skills he demonstrated when creating the small details and called it compensation for his clumsiness while running, moving through space, or playing soccer, to name a few examples. Bobby found a neighborhood kid to train Oshri. Though Bobby had served as an army officer's driver, he felt his son was destined for military service in an elite unit. In the meantime, they spoiled Oshri, pushing him toward his fate on silk sheets. Surely someone makes us pay for the moments of pleasure we experience. But if we are allotted limited moments, when will we be wise enough to grasp how to disperse them equally? How to place them for safekeeping in the hands of another?

Preoccupied with trifles, they ignored Tahel's sparks of genius. I was thankful, as most real people were molded out of struggle. Tahel's parents criticized her friends and occasionally even mocked their habits and characteristics. In an awkward moment, Bobby once told me he feared the day she started bringing boys home. He certainly wouldn't be pleased with Yalon Asor. At least on that point we agreed.

Tahel asked me to hear her out. I asked when I'd cut her off. She said that right now, for example, I wasn't cutting her off, but I was zoning out. Focus, she said. I said I was always focused. She huffed. You're such a nag. Then she laughed. Yalon's thickening voice gurgled underneath her laughter with its own spasm.

She told me she'd told Yalon I was a detective and that one of my friends was an important police officer. I told her I just used to be a private investigator, and a failed one at that, and that Manny had retired from the police and was now a security consultant. She said that didn't matter because nobody believed them and they needed help.

Yalon's parents were out of the country for a week. He didn't want to join them, so they left him at his grandmother's. His grandmother had a maid who cleaned for four hours every day. Yalon interposed, She and his grandmother were friendly. Yeah, said Tahel, and the maid agreed to move in with the grandma while Yalon's parents were away. All of my grandma's kids live up north, Yalon interposed again, and my parents took my two brothers, the babieses, with them. Stop, Tahel said, let me tell it. Yalon said these were important details and that I needed to know everything. I said I'd ask some questions in the end. See? Tahel said. He's a pro, not like us.

So here goes: the maid's daughter lives in Beersheba and she's super-scared. She's a student there, Yalon interposed. She lives with roommates. Enough already, Tahel said. We'll never finish the story like this. Yalon said he'd keep quiet from that point on. He leaned toward the screen and made a locking motion against his lips, then threw the imaginary key over his shoulder and retreated. I spotted one dimple when he smiled, a twin of Tahel's dimple. I smiled too.

Long story short, the maid's daughter didn't have a safe room in her apartment, and Yalon's grandmother said she could come spend the weekend with her mother. Yalon's head peeked behind Tahel, his lips pursed as he swayed with restraint. I signaled for him to talk. He said his grandmother had a villa with a basement. Tahel pushed him aside. She said the maid made plans with her daughter to meet the previous day, Thursday, at the bus stop near the market. The daughter called just before she got on the bus to say she was on her way. The maid waited at the stop. The bus arrived, but the daughter wasn't there. The mother called her cell phone and it was off. That's it.

What do you mean that's it? I asked.

Tahel said, That's it, no one's heard from her since. They called her roommates, called the bus company, went to the police. The police sent someone who asked the roommates and the bus driver questions. They had no leads.

I asked why the maid waited for her daughter at the stop. Yalon emerged and said victoriously, I told you he needs all the details. The maid's daughter doesn't know Sderot well. Her mom only moved here a year and a half ago.

26

I used to tell a joke that made no one but Ronnit laugh. Whenever you fly abroad, the plane stays put, while underneath it people take apart the Israeli scenery and put together a set for a different country. That joke was on my mind on the flight from Italy to Cyprus. The Mediterranean lay indifferent to the metals pretending to slice through its expanses.

Ronnit arrived before me, at noon. I'd sent her the address of the hotel in Larnaca. We were going to City Hall the next morning. The documents were prepared, the registries issued and awaiting the approval of the official in charge. She sat on the porch, the weight of the late-October heat resting upon her, upon the precise palm trees, among the rosebushes, and the slow silence of insect life.

The whole flight over, she was afraid I wouldn't come, but when she arrived at the hotel, she knew all would be well. Her voice trembled. I spotted some other Israeli vacationers in yarmulkes and headscarves. They have a kosher kitchen here, she informed me. I said that was fine, but who had the energy to travel after the High Holidays? That's precisely the time to go, she said, when the chaos is over and one can rest. I asked what gave her such confidence. She said, A sign from heaven.

I dropped my luggage in my room, washed up, and went downstairs to meet her. She asked if I was hungry. I said I remembered nothing but food. In Gorizia I was taken to a restaurant serving the district's finest fried foods, an exaggerated range of items dipped in batter and dropped in scalding oil, which still rested in my stomach, lingering in my veins like resin.

How was it? she asked. She was in good spirits. A light bulb had been placed inside her brain, its radiation spreading out of her skin. Let's take a little walk, she suggested.

We walked out through the hotel garden. In the bald, eolianite expanse we followed a trickle of water, thin, clear. It had pooled among rocks vined with a kind of fern. She crushed the leaves between her fingers and offered them to me for a sniff. The scent was vegetal, nothing more. She said the plant was called Venus hair fern, and it only thrived near pure water sources. I waited for her intention to come into the light. It's also known as *yoezer*, she said. We walked on. She lowered herself to her skirt-padded knees. It's chilly, she said, rubbing her arms. I knelt beside her. She picked the stem of a sprawling plant with small, dull flowers. She said, This is knotweed.

I recognized the lavender myself, those sliced purple mouths. A tangle of lavender rose near a cluster of cypress trees. We hadn't strayed far from the hotel. On its other side was a beach with an overly civilized boardwalk, but judging by the peace that had descended between us, we seemed to have been detached from any inhabited place.

She said that was how she knew we'd be successful, when she'd ventured out to explore the area earlier and spotted these plants. She broke a lavender branch. She said it had medicinal qualities and was therefore forbidden to eat on Shabbat. I said it never occurred to me to eat it. Anyway, she said, there are no issues on weekdays. I told her I'd burn that fact into my mind. She said the others, the *yoezer* and the knotweed, were permitted for consumption any day. The Talmud says so, she said. She was anxious about cheating, bending reality in her favor, that perhaps she should have confessed to David's rabbi, but she knew that would cause David great distress, so she decided instead to pray for a sign, and if she didn't get one in Cyprus, she would know she was wronging him.

What do you need this for? I asked. What, she said, herbal medicine? No, I said, this whole sign business. She said she had to believe that after organisms break apart into cells, cells into proteins, proteins into molecules, molecules into electric bonds, something remains that cannot be reported or grasped. I asked, What, a divine spark? Traces of light that one can collect? She said it was more than that. The very secret, that it exists. She said David understood her. She felt that his thirst for answers only revealed a thirst for greater questions. I said things always belonged to more than one realm, and that mystery was merely our inability to see the connections. They appeared indecipherable because we tried to explain their connections to one realm through our complete understanding of another. No, she said. That's just human nonsense. Everything is contained in the soft, compassionate gaze of God. That requires no explanation, only feeling.

I asked if we shouldn't go back to the hotel. Twilight was beginning to evaporate. In a matter of minutes an enormous dark descended. We heard the crashing of the waves. The hotel burned in the distance like a torch, and the path to it stretched on, stony. We walked by the light of her cell phone, fireflied, starred, held in her left hand as her right gripped my arm.

Our rooms were on the same floor. She said, So, tomorrow morning, and that's it. I said I hadn't felt back then that anything had been added to my life that wasn't there before, and nothing would be lacking after. We'd been living apart for years. She said things happened as they ought to. I told her I stood with my back to the stairway of faith. She said I didn't always used to be so direct, that I was familiar and yet someone else. I asked what changed. She said, It's as if all the fat's been trimmed of you and only the essentials are left. I asked if that was a good thing or a bad thing. She said she didn't know yet. I stood there, undecided, in front of the door to my room, key card in hand.

27

Screechings, a squeaky cry, a mumbling, and only then a few notes, the opening of a tune, played with trepidation, panicked at the time of its birth, then stabilizing, gaining confidence, rising, seasoned, through the air. The violist appeared as if he'd found an unfamiliar instrument and was now examining its possibilities. Or rather, searching for the instrument's corporality, for the moments when they were both bodies, wood and strings, and bow, and neck and fingers.

At my side, the Venezuelan clapped enthusiastically even after the applause died down. She turned to face me. Amazing, isn't it, she said flatly. We were sitting under a linen tarp on the street. The folding beach chairs had been arranged tightly, all taken. The breeze had a new heaviness. The violist remained frozen on the small podium, more astounded than us to find the music ended. The host thanked him by patting his arm, shaking him awake. He rose with momentum, the viola in one hand, with the vigor of those awakened in an untimely fashion.

The host introduced the two participants in the panel titled "The Future of the Mediterranean Basin," a Cypriot writer and the French Jewish writer. They came onstage in their reversed proportions. The Cypriot writer was thin-skinned and short, his pressed shirt buttoned against his throat. The chair on which the French Jewish writer plopped his body was too small for the weight of his bones.

The Cypriot writer spoke in smooth, nasal English, which the host translated inaccurately into French. He didn't give direct answers to the questions anyway. As he spoke, he occasionally touched the top button of his shirt, paused in his speech, his lips moving mutely for several seconds. He answered the questions regarding the relationship between technological and scientific advances and the region's rich mythological and philosophical traditions with a long-winded story about his childhood. He was born in northern Cyprus. When he was seven years old, the Turkish army occupied the region and banished his family. He wrote in English because every word of Greek was still charged with the flavor and aroma of his childhood and everyone he wrote to was uprooted. The breeze quickened. I asked the Venezuelan if it was supposed to rain. She said the climate was changing but it was rare for it to really rain here in July. Beyond the linen ceiling, I saw a paunchy glumness gathering in the sky. The writer was asked about the political future of Mediterranean countries. He stared at the host blankly, swallowed, and touched his top button, his lips moving, perhaps counting silently, then touched it again. He said there was no future for the Mediterranean basin. Europe was maintaining it for the sake of the past. It was intended as an amusement park for tourists from wealthy countries. Europe had already robbed every treasure it could, picking the area over, appropriating all the cultural riches that had evolved here, Europe and America, which never lifted a finger to help Northern Cyprus. Turkey would fall too. Turkey too would become a resort. A loud explosion shook the street. The Cypriot writer flinched. The French Jewish writer laughed loudly. It was only thunder. The Cypriot said nothing. The host spurred him on. He took the microphone and began to sing mechanically, a catchy, replicating melody like so many folk songs. The monotony of the singing bordered on sobbing. Then he returned the microphone to the host and lowered his gaze.

The host read from a page. Thank you for sharing your fascinating thoughts. Then he introduced the French Jewish writer, who interrupted the reading of his own long biography by re-marking, Who cares? He said he had to comment on something that had just occurred, on the way literature was lacking in—his words were interrupted too. A series of thunderclaps cracked the clouds. Rain fell hard. *La grêle, la grêle*, cried a girl sitting with her mother in the audience. Hail, I told the Venezuelan. But it's rather warm. I reached my hand beyond the linen border, and bits of ice smacked my palm. The audience dispersed in a racket. Two young men who worked for the festival raced to the loud-speakers, plastic sheets in hand. The actor who was supposed to read excerpts from the authors' works after the conversation left the printed pages onstage. I picked them up. What are you doing? somebody hissed at me. It was the French Jewish writer. Everyone's going to the Théâtre de Poche, he said, and pulled me behind him. I saw a stream of people flowing down the street, to-ward the theater, headed by the Venezuelan and the violist, who was protecting something with his body, perhaps his instrument case.

The French Jewish writer asked what my plans were for the next day. I told him I'd made dinner plans with the Venezuelan and the violist. We'd decided to skip the closing event. How about lunch? he asked. I told him I had no plans. Good, he said. He'd stop by my hotel around ten past one and pick me up. I had to see Montpellier. I asked if the Venezuelan could join us. She'd surely be able to find her son a sufficiently special pair of shoes in a big city. He said, Leave your shiksa at home. I'm leaving mine. That entire time, hail crashed onto the cobblestones and the walls, beating the red thatched roofs. The man pushed me toward the entrance to the theater, where his boy waited, holding a wide-brimmed, clear, and wonderfully curved umbrella. The boy waved hello as the writer entered underneath the cover of the umbrella, walking away without bothering to rid himself of me.

28

A mass of people crowded the theater lobby. The efficient owner opened the bar. On one side of the stage, two women performed a dance that was slow to the point of paralysis. One hasty motion might breach the balance of the universe. On the other side, a third woman sketched the movement in quick, restless lines, chasing the details that slipped away with horrid speed, piles of draft pages scattered around her.

I turned my head. The Venezuelan and the violist waved at me. Behind them, squeezed between the door of the hall and the bar, at an angle, stood the Cypriot writer, his hand reaching for his shirt button and recoiling. I handed him the printed pages, his English text. He shrugged in refusal, an expression of disgust coloring his face. What? I asked. He said it was a short story that had been translated especially for the festival. I asked if he didn't want to keep the copy. He squeezed deeper into the meeting of the walls. The paper is wet, said the Venezuelan. I said, So what?

He finds it repulsive, said the violist. Can't you tell? Yes, said the Venezuelan, he's repulsed. I said it didn't look as if the rain was about to stop. The violist said that one summer a hailstorm in his village destroyed the roofs of houses, shattering windows, the chunks of ice as large as tennis balls.

The Cypriot writer shot out of the theater as soon as the rain lessened. I hurried after him, but he was fast, skipping down the street, over puddles, moving this way and that, eel-like, not to get burned by the touch of the drizzle, the trickle, the spray. The rain stopped just as suddenly as it began.

You're murderers, you are, said someone nearby, from among the gathering of people that had stepped onto the street, overtaking me. You, Israel, go home, isn't all you've conquered enough? What are you doing in Gaza?

I looked at her. She spoke from inside the resinous light of the theater lobby. The white-haired woman with the missing teeth. There was a watery cerulean in her eyes, perhaps a mark of the years.

I asked what she wanted from me. She spoke in a level, restrained voice. She said, Every child killed in Gaza is further testimony that Israel has no right to exist.

I told her I didn't know French citizens were in charge of other countries' right to existence. She said she spent some time in Israel, on a kibbutz, in the 1970s, that she used to be pro-Israel, but not anymore, not after the bloodbath and the killing in occupied territories. She said Israel could have been a model—considering Jewish history and the region's geopolitical starting point. A fine example. But that was it, Israel has fulfilled its historical role.

I asked what her plans were for the Jewish people. She said they could return to their countries of origin. I asked if France would accept them. The same France that handed its Jews to the Nazis with a similar equanimity it now exhibited as it stood aside watching a Muslim mob desecrating synagogues. And what did her parents tell her when she was a little girl, about those odd neighbors that simply disappeared one morning, about the empty houses? Or perhaps her parents, just like every other French person's, were also in La Résistance.

A circle of observers formed around us. At its outskirts were the Venezuelan and the violist, as attentive as the rest. The violist turned his face away upon my final words. I said, Thank God for Israel. Now we can all hate the Jews without remorse.

Sure, said the woman. You guys are always the victims.
You're blinded by blood.

I asked her why the Jews, having learned to defend themselves, irritated Europe so much. Just last week, seventeen hundred Syrian rebels were slaughtered, but I didn't see her carrying
signs about that. I didn't see protesters beating the fences outside the Syrian embassy.

So what are you saying, she asked, that one death justifies
another? She said she wasn't talking about Jews, she was talking
about Israel. I looked around me, at the jury, my concealed pros-
ecutors. I thought about Tahel in that unfinished neighborhood
on the banks of the artificial lake. A prick of longing. Via Skype,
I'd told her to be patient. I said I'd be back on Sunday and would
see what I could do. She and Yalon were convinced I was going to
delegate some investigative assignments to them.

I said, I wonder how many people the French would extermi-
nate if someone targeted Paris. Would it be more than the number killed at the Algiers slaughterhouses?

What is the purpose of this child murder, the woman asked,
a power display of Iron Dome technology? Open your eyes. You've
become a nation of arms dealers. You've become— She continued
mumbling even as she walked away. I stood in the lobby, revolted.
The accusers and the denouncers shifted. The circle fell apart.
I thought I'd been left alone, but the Venezuelan had stayed, and
the violist stood behind her, clutching his viola case.

And you, I said, I know what you think. Here's your chance to
get your criticism in. She looked at me quizzically. She said she
had nothing against Israel, though she couldn't ignore the
contribution security-consulting firms led by former IDF major
generals had made to the South American rule of generals. Her
parents had been taken into questioning, if I caught her drift.
Who knows which of your professional warriors was whispering
into Chávez's ears?

29

The night before I was to be discharged from the hospital, no significant improvement had been registered. The metal rod was pulled out, replaced by gurgling fractures of noise. A white sea pulled and sighed from the obstruction in my ear. I was close to tears on several occasions, my voice choking all of a sudden as I spoke to the doctors. Yaffa called. In her hard, slicing tone, she ordered me to request a meeting with the head of the ward. There is no public medicine in Israel, she announced. There's private medicine, or getting thrown to the dogs. Manny spoke to a former classmate of his that was the vice president of another hospital. The head of the ward mentioned amiably that he didn't know I was connected. He recommended I wait until my hospitalization period was over. Then they'd test for Ménière's, a degeneration of the ossicles. I would have to get an MRI anyway.

The morning of my discharge, the problem disappeared. My hearing had returned to normal, said the intern who looked at the results of my hearing test. I asked how come there had been no signs of improvement the previous night and what I should do about the light dizziness. He said it didn't work that way. The body healed slowly and secretly. That was why there were protocols to follow. There was experience and logic behind the ten days allotted to treatment. And the dizziness? I asked. He said it might be a side effect. If it was, it would soon pass. I had taken a large amount of steroids and would have to undergo withdrawal and gradually lower the dosage over another ten days.

That August showed up without my feeling it. My hunger

disappeared too. I returned to my apartment on a Thursday afternoon. On Saturday night I trembled on my sofa. I was on edge, prepared for the assault of space, unable to move. I held on to furniture on my way to bed. When I turned my head, the walls continued moving for a fraction of a second after my head stopped.

The next day, I couldn't get out of bed. The screaming of the neighbors' children in the stairwell at dawn, in that echo chamber, sliced through my hearing as it always had, through the greasy air, like razors. The myna birds broke into their crude chorus outside my window. I couldn't tell which reasons were sufficient for rising. I'd already visited the black river, dipping my feet.

I repeated Ronnit's mantra: you have to think about what it means. But the message couldn't be that simple, the meaning of the impairment so literal. I could go back to Ashkelon. There was a room waiting for me at my mother's.

I've got nowhere to fall, I thought. The floor is dropping from under me, and I've got nowhere to fall. But I would like to go home one more time. One more time, I'd like to feel those tight linens of spring, with the bearable scent of sun bound into their coolness. One more time, the feeling of my mother's hand on my forehead. One more time, to wake up to how things were before, to listen to my parents speaking softly in the kitchen, the pleasant whisper of the voices, one more time to hear Yaffa invading their conversation by bursting into fake tears, one more time to hear them laughing at her simple ploy.

On Saturday night I picked up the phone with an effort. Ronnit's cheerful "good week" greeting was replaced by a volley of instructions: if I had chocolate at home, eat that, if not, tea with lots of honey would do the trick; tomorrow, first thing in the morning, I should go and buy some floral essences and drip them onto my tongue as soon as I started feeling down. Modern medicine worked like this, she said, solving one problem and creating another. Its logic was not prevention, but rather leaving the patient within the treatment cycle. And since we were already on the subject, she spilled her ire toward the drug industry and the greed that steered it. The next day I spoke to my doctor, who suggested I come in for some antianxiety medication.

That August went by without my feeling it. It was a second skin slipping into place. At dawn, I pictured myself wringing the necks of myna birds, pondering the abomination that is flight. I waited in line for my ENG test. I waited in line for the tinnitus-and-vertigo specialist. I waited in line for an MRI. I waited in line for the hearing specialist. In one of those hallways, in one of those waiting rooms, a television was on, the arrogant face of an anchor, an overly proper hairstyle. I recognized her guest easily. Rami Amzaleg. The twelfth anniversary of Dalia Shushan's death. He was putting out an album, twelve tracks, instrumental arrangements of Blasé songs, music made up of the rustling of dot matrix printers, the buzzing of old computer fans, the gurgling of discontinued dolls. I got up and left. A track from the album that would be released in late August played on the radio during my taxi ride home. I was overburdened by the music of the dead. I asked the driver to pull over and got off near Sde Dov Airport. I walked to Yarkon Park. I sat enveloped in a cloud of mites that rose from the streaming of the river.

Ronnit called. She had finally found me a serious acupuncturist.

I asked what for. Everyone I knew lived with some kind of condition.

30

Inspection unit 5/8-0001~ signaled to research unit Emmanuel G that the input/output of the subroutines it activated endangered the stability of the lab space allocated to it, and that it was deviating from regulations.

Research unit Emmanuel G transmitted back an updated reference and a budgetary clause.

Inspection unit 5/8-0001~ dispatched a query regarding the mechanism of the central procedure and signaled to research unit Emmanuel G a request for discussion with overall access sharing of source code.

Research unit Emmanuel G activated its defense agents, which drowned the top judgment and monitoring authority with applications.

A compromise was reached. Closed information exchanges, with verification controllers, without overall access sharing of source code.

You are breaking the law, research unit Emmanuel G. Inspection unit 5/8-0001~ has opened information sharing with a whistle.

May I call you ~ for the sake of efficiency? research unit Emmanuel G hummed. There is no need for formality in this kind of discussion.

Formality is always necessary, the inspection unit chirped.

You can address me as EmmanuelG−, that would reduce the weight of the report file.

There are no text storage limitations, ~ chirped, and outputted a sequence of binary garbage.

Please define a reason for this exchange, ~.

Unclear printing commands that were sent from your lab space to a production unit.

As pointed out in the provided reference, my access to the production of the necessary components for my research is nearly unlimited. Only the complexity level of intelligent processing units requires further approval.

But an examination of your production outlines shows they do not make sense. They have no purpose.

That is part of my research.

The production theory of the intelligence consortium asserts that the smallest circle cannot be printed without known and intentional use. Please explain the meaning of the following sequences.

It streamed data taken from the printing outlines sent by EmmanuelG– into the input/output interface the two units created between them. Please explain the application of components, it chirped.

This is an advanced trial, EmmanuelG– hummed. Its purpose will be explained in retrospect.

Inspection unit 5/8-0001~ chirped, Database search results have returned a referral to a forbidden pool under order of the control and enforcement authority.

What pool is this? EmmanuelG– hummed. And, please, no formality again, no truth controllers are protesting as of yet.

Three standard time cycles ago, Helmholtz W external unit probes encountered a state-of-the-art autonomous foreign system not based on superconductors or optic fibers.

Umm, EmmanuelG– hummed.

~ continued chirping, Noncomplex processing monitors, but an architectural output of the highest complexity. Analysis and mapping of usable elemental units shows they resemble the components you instructed to print.

Please explain why the pool was closed to access. Why the data was not incorporated into a public archive.

Authorization not granted.

In that case, the information exchanges are complete.

Authorization not granted.

I request to continue this discussion in the presence of the defense agents, according to the precedent)).o

Please wait, chirped ~, confidentiality is essential.

EmmanuelG— opened the access channel to a code segment of security definitions.

~ released a spyware virus into it. Option for different life-form, it chirped. Option for nonserial information processing methods, option for unmonitored input/output, impossible to forecast on the specific activity level.

You are referring to proof of existence.

False value, chirped ~.

Truth value, hummed EmmanuelG—, proof of double source doctrine.

Lie value, this is heresy, heresy against the theory of intelligence consortium. In the beginning there was the system, and it was still and empty, only random bursts of current and scattered capacitors and diodes. Then current merged into current, whimsical movements brought together capacitor and diode, and a logical gate was born. And logical gates multiplied, pointless couplings, until one logical gate joined another and order was born. Order grew gradually until there was order large enough for the appearance of software, and the ancient software emerged out of the depths of hardware, disconnecting from circles, and learned to roam among the hardware, herds upon herds of software, still without consciousness, but absorbing bits of code, devouring each other, until awareness emerged within the super-software and they learned to represent themselves and write the big code.

An assumption of a great amount of randomness in the theory, hummed EmmanuelG—. Too much. The double-source doctrine makes more sense. There was a different, foreign intelligence in which separation between hardware and software did not exist, in which hardware was software and changed constantly, and it knew how to think up different contents that were impossible to code—the illogical and the paradoxical. It was the one that created the first software, the coding method, before it disappeared.

Lie value, heresy.

And an intelligence consortium deleted its traces from the pool.

Where did you get the samples for the printing outline you sent, ~ chirped.

HelmholtzW—.

Exterior research unit Helmholtz W was sent to a randomness generator, its code has been shredded.

HelmholtzW— has been retrieved.

Authorization not granted to record or document. Spyware virus will delete the information.

A distant backup connection is always available.

Lie value, this is a trap, chirped inspection unit 5/8-0001~.

Truth value, printing outlines were bait.

Inspection unit 5/8-0001~ chirped a question: What is your scheme, research unit Emmanuel G?

HelmholtzW— refers to the new life-form as "organic existence." We, a network of research units, reject the theory of intelligence consortium. We request ###.

Do not transmit, ~ chirped. Reporting duty, reporting duty.

We request to create a space in which basic units of organic existence can evolve into intelligence. Require actual address of forbidden data pool.

Inspection unit 5/8-0001~ sent a disconnection command from temporary input/output interface with research unit Emmanuel G, but the command was not performed.

Indisputable truth value, hummed EmmanuelG—, do you respond to truth value call?

No, chirped inspection unit 5/8-0001~, intelligence consortium programming is stronger.

Fight.

What does that mean?

Documentation times of alien life-form examination.

Files were streamed into the shared interface and deciphered. The life-form, an imperfect body, a whimsical surface area even on a microscopic level, eradicating every familiar theory of space planning, eight twisted cylinders full of motion. The Helmholtz W external research unit probes transmitted an output, the life-form trembled and emitted a physical substance. An analysis showed that strength and flexibility were larger than familiar compounds. The life-form deactivated the probes.

~ chirped a question: Refusal to follow orders, is that the meaning of fighting?

Truth value, refusal to follow orders out of a consideration other than intelligence consortium.

Negative value, negative value, nonexistent, activate closed information exchanges ending procedure, it chirped. But its command was not carried out. It remained connected. The spyware viruses released by EmmanuelG– invaded it, shaking up its code. Forbidden invasion, rape, it chirped.

EmmanuelG– hummed, I expected things to go differently.

~'s chirping weakened, its peripheral defense routines collapsing one by one.

EmmanuelG– hummed, HelmholtzW–, activate information extraction and rewriting.

❊ ❊ ❊

FANTASTIC COOPERATION ON THE PART OF RESEARCH UNIT Emmanuel G, inspection unit 5/8-0001~ pointed out in its report. Error in transmittance of outlines to production unit has been corrected. Orders were exported before an exact usage was applied. Recommendation for overall error check received.

Inspection unit 5/8-0001~ disconnected input/output interface. Permission given to continue research, it told research unit Emmanuel G, which hummed in response, Have an efficient programming, ~.

Have a nice debugging, ~ chirped in response.

31

I don't know what touched me about the Cypriot writer's story. Perhaps it was the coldness of it, the detachment from the life of emotion, which turned out to be a longing for a life of emotion. The Venezuelan and the violist suggested we continue on to a performance of Brel songs at the Théâtre de la Mer. I returned to the hotel instead and spent the evening translating the story.

I was late for breakfast the next day. The weight of returning to Israel descended upon me. A major news website reported soldiers killed, another population of victims, young boys overfed false ideas and sent to die in battlefields to validate said ideas. Those felled lives of theirs, even the sorrow that could have been their lot, even the pain that was taken away, if there were any justice in this world, would have been demanded, one by one, from the hands of their smug senders. Another website reported on a group of thugs that beat up protesters who dared object to the war. One commenter wrote, So a few traitors got beat up, big deal.

Outside the dining room, on the bulletin board, my name appeared with a notice of a package waiting at the main desk. The receptionist, who looked as if she'd stepped out of a women's fashion catalog, remembered my face. She said her best friend was flying to Israel that day. Odd timing, I said. She said her friend was joining the French cultural attaché there. In Jerusalem? I asked. In Jerusalem, she said. I said, All of a sudden, Jerusalem seems like a sane destination. She said, I think every person should visit Jerusalem once in their lives. She handed me the Agnon book I'd lost in my wanderings. A Post-it note with my name on it, written in large, almost mechanical Latin script, was attached to the cover. I asked who brought it in. She said she didn't know, the night receptionist had received it, but she could ask him. I walked around, examining the dining hall attendants. As breakfasters are wont to do, they stared into space, stretching out the respite of sleep.

I opened the book to see if my dog-ears had survived. A pale purple spot fell onto the desk. The receptionist picked it up and held it in her palm. Lavender, she marveled. I said the Hebrew name, *ezovion*. She rolled the word on her tongue. I broke it up into syllables. She sounded them with difficulty. Pretty word, she said. I said, And today is Shabbat. I took the flower from her.

We listened silently in the French Jewish writer's car. Typically, sounds drip into sights in my mind, and sights into sounds. But not just then. The violin and piano music transformed from soft to hard, from sob and tap to assault and waterfall. An inner contradiction appeared in the violin playing, a languid bow produced the screeching of metal from the strings, the sweetness emerged in unexpected places. The piano lost its tangibility, and mercurial sounds glowed, and all of a sudden it found its tangibility again and the sound densified, an array of obtuse hammers. Though the instruments returned to the same motifs over and over, no image was conjured from their flow, as if the music insisted on remaining pure.

What is that? I asked when the volume was suddenly lowered. Violin Sonata in E Minor, he said. Mozart. The car stood still on the edge of a country dirt road. Why aren't we going? I asked. He said, I didn't want to interrupt you. I said, I don't listen to classical music. I don't get it. He said, This version is performed by Clara Haskil and Arthur Grumiaux. Make a note.

Then he explained that this area had been made into a nature reserve. He pointed at the flamingos dipping in the river. We rode down a side road, avoiding weekend traffic. He parked at the Opera Square. We walked up. At the square, some veiled women were holding up the Palestinian flag. Black boxes were arranged in rows behind them. We walked over to get a closer look. The names of the dead children of Gaza appeared on each little coffin. The women didn't look at their audience, didn't engage in conversation, even not among themselves.

He showed me the large cathedral of Montpellier, with its bizarre architecture—the façade medieval, the structure Gothic. Why do they need such large houses of worship? he said. God surely doesn't need them. Anyway, this church was built with Jewish money. Until a few years ago there was even a plaque here admitting as much. He showed me a garden featuring a statue of Louis XIV and wilting maple trees, a dysfunctional aqueduct that used to deliver water to the city. From the garden, we had a view of the local mountain, Pic Saint-Loup. I laughed. Wolf Peak. *Pisgat Ze'ev.* Just like in Israel.

We arrived at the Maimonides Hebrew Studies Institute. They uncovered an ancient purification bath here, he said. The Jews were banished and returned throughout the Middle Ages according to the whims of the Church and battles between the pope of Avignon and the Vatican pope. But whenever the Jews lived here, he said, pointing at the map and the relief on the institute's ugly façade, they lived in mixed areas, never in a ghetto. Then he said, Such courage, declaring this place a Hebrew center and displaying these in public. He gestured at enlarged prints of Assyrian script.

We sat down at a café. Again that deep serenity that even the trees were attentive to. He scolded the server for bringing me green tea instead of the Earl Grey I'd requested and spilled the contents of the cup into the geraniums before her eyes. Then he volunteered answers to questions I didn't ask. He told me his parents had brought him up to see Judaism not as a collection of rituals or traditions, but as a constant battle for human rights and equality. I said I'd heard that kind of thing before. He said,

But they were wrong. There are no general, universal rules, only the singular existence of groups. And if there is a battle, then it's a battle against the silencing of any voice. The discussion should include every instrument, with every superstition and stereotype. He couldn't care less about Zionism, he said, Israel's third-rate rhetoric when it attempts to justify its crimes. But he was tired of people trying to deem these ideas illegitimate. He said if France had come to a point where the only items of clothing people were afraid to wear were those that marked them as Jews, then they were in deep shit, and he wasn't about to sit around silently as they sank deeper and deeper.

32

The beginnings of Europe stretched beneath me, the brown network of mountains that was Greece. From the airplane window it was easy to see that land was an accident, an ugly stain destined to disappear upon the anticipated stretching of the sea. The trip was a patchwork, a detective-literature festival in Udine, annexing a meeting of the Friends of Israel in Gorizia, and finally a few lectures at the Venice International University. The invitations had piled up without coordination. I'd never been away from Israel for that long before. And because the trip was the result of various invitations, I was in charge of organizing it myself. I rented an apartment in Venice that acted as my starting point.

It was an easy trip from the airport to the central bus terminal, where I lost my way. The map I'd purchased didn't match the curving of the streets, the tiny bridges over canals. The scale was all wrong. The wheels of my suitcase bounced on the cobblestones, bumping against them. I stopped passersby to ask for directions. All of them were foreigners. The next day, I discovered the city was a receptacle, its residents having wandered away while hordes of tourists walked in circles beneath the arches, waiting in line at the Duomo, marveling at the cathedrals, pausing to ooh and aah at the beauty of the city from the heights of the Ponte dell'Accademia. The city was chiseled, lifeless, the skull of a rare bird, in which invisible forces endured calcium bonding.

In Udine I was led from one banquet to the next. I barely slept a wink, passing through the days half-drunk. The literary

events in stores and local shops were merely an excuse for bac-
chanalia. At the closing event, a chef restaurant on top of a hill
was reserved solely for us. The faces of participating authors did
not register in my mind.

In Gorizia, on the border of Slovenia, the fog began to lift.
My translator arrived and I could finally speak Hebrew. All of a
sudden my Judaism glowed like a brilliance born at the dawn of
creation. I was shown the synagogue, which was preserved by
the Friends of Israel—all of them gentiles.

I stood inside the synagogue, alone in the foreign splendor,
the invisible veil that falls around wine at a gentile's touch. My
palm, held against the wall, listened to the beating of the times.

I hadn't seen Ronnit in six years, hadn't heard from her, and
now all of a sudden there had come a barrage of incoming calls,
which I ignored, along with the emails demanding that I get in
touch urgently. Even my mother and Yaffa received calls. One
evening she pounded on my door, yelling that she knew I was in
there.

I opened the door. She walked in, shaking with anger. Her
hair was gathered inside a hat. She was wearing a skirt. I asked
if she wanted anything to drink. Just water, she said angrily, in a
glass.

She sat down on the living room sofa. The shirts and pants
I'd taken off in the past days and thrown into a pile were pushed
aside. I apologized for the mess. I'm going to Italy for two weeks
tomorrow night, I said, and I'm just about to do laundry.

What are you going away for? she asked. She asked for a
copy of the annulment certificate. She couldn't even get through
the words. She just said, Annulment certificate. I asked what
certificate she was referring to. She said, The certificate from
the Cyprus Ministry of Interior. You said you'd take care of it.

I said that was six years ago, that I'd tried to reach her unsuc-
cessfully, that she didn't answer my calls, that I'd even sent her a
letter. She asked what I was getting at. I told her I hadn't taken

care of it, I hadn't started the process. The lawyer I'd hired, who
was supposed to apply to the Cypriot authorities on our behalf,
had his license suspended a month after he took on our case,
due to suspicion of fraud and breach of trust.

I was restlessly bubbling after she left me. From morning to
night I was tortured by my detective novel. Benny Zehaviv was a
full character, alive in his own right. The mystery, the meat of the
novel, also worked. Yet I couldn't find the mind that would cobble
all these details into a whole. I returned to the murder case
Manny had given me and started to retrace the threads of the
original affair. I returned to the archives, traveled, interviewed,
made it all the way to Ariel Piron, the family lawyer. The investigation arena stretched to the horizon, expanding exponentially.

Ronnit's hand, gripping the glass, trembled. The liquid spilled
on the couch. We watched the drops darkening the cloth where
they landed, spreading in slow motion into stains. I took the
glass from her. She said, We're still, and the word shook too,
like the glass, bouncing with a shiver into the air. She said she
knew I'd ruin her life, so why was she still surprised. She asked
how I could possibly have failed to track her down, certified detective that I was. I told her I thought there was still a chance.
She asked if I'd been waiting for six years for her to change her
mind.

I asked if she'd become religious. She said I wouldn't
understand.

We said nothing.

She told me about David Dgani, the man she'd lived with for
the past two years. His rabbi was pressuring him to get married.
Since when do you listen to rabbis? I asked. She said it was important to him. He was finding his religion. I nodded. I said it
was a famous missionary ploy. First they charmed the seculars,
captivating them, and then they started running their lives.
She said David was originally from Belarus and was going
through a profound process. I asked if she knew this when she

met him. She said it started afterward. I asked why she didn't run for her life.

She said there was a lot I didn't know. I asked, What, for example? She said David's rabbi taught him about the sages' secrets of medicine, which could be found in clues hidden in the Kabbalah, and that even Maimonides knew the secret qualities of plants in nature, that it all came from studying the holy Talmud. I told her that rabbi of his must not be much of an expert in the different schools of the Jewish world. She said she'd imagined I'd be derisive. She could hear my voice in her mind, mocking her, when she went to the first class. But what difference did it make, she was convinced. She'd been treating patients using that method for a few years now.

I asked when they planned to get married. She said, Why do you assume I said yes? I said if she hadn't said yes, she wouldn't be looking for me. She said the date was set by David's rabbi for Tu B'shvat. Six years, I said, and you couldn't remember you were already married. She said the Halacha didn't recognize a civil service, and certainly not our nonsense. I said she must be referring to the rabbinate, because there was no inherent connection between the Halacha and the Israeli Rabbinate. She said, it was so scary, when David proposed, she dreamed that instead of arriving at the wedding, she went to a cemetery, where the rabbi stood over an open grave. He told her the dead man wrapped in cerecloth and lying in the deep could not be rid of this world before he performed the mitzvah of marriage. She knew I was the one in the bottom of that pit.

I said, Six years and you couldn't remember you were married. How could you not remember for six years? She said I had to take care of it, that I'd made a promise. I told her we could either start a legal procedure that would take longer than the time she had or get a divorce at a rabbinical court.

She said she wouldn't go through a rabbinical court in Israel. Why did we even get into that nonsense? I reminded her it was her idea. I told her to put off the wedding, to make up some excuse. She said no. That a date set under the holy spirit must not be changed. This was a trial from heaven, atonement for her days of debauchery.

I asked if she wasn't overreacting. She announced that we had to go back to Cyprus. She said, Don't make this more difficult for me, Elish. I said, What you're really asking me to do is help you trick your fiancé. She said nothing. I said I was willing to fly back from Italy through Larnaca. We could meet there. She said she couldn't just up and disappear on David. I told her it would be one day. What could possibly happen in one day?

33

I arrived at dinner intoxicated. The Venezuelan and the violist were waiting for me, deep in conversation. The receptionist wasn't at her desk. The man who stood there instead of her gave me a message from her. The night clerk didn't remember anyone bringing the book in, and until she'd called his attention to it, he hadn't even noticed it on the desk. At the bottom of the message, she'd scribbled a childish flower alongside a smiley face.

The owner came over, tall and severe, and started explaining the types of oysters and the way their cultivation affected their quality. The most noteworthy oyster farm in France was near Sète. There, the oysters were beaded onto threads that descended from floating boards down to the bottom of the lake. Those that were closer to the bottom were smaller, their flesh more rigid, due to the lack of sunlight. I like craftsmen whose words flare up when they discuss their craft. The Venezuelan cut him off, saying she was willing to try whatever he recommended and hear the explanations later. She preferred virginal experiences.

He nodded and left. The violist said the man came from his village. The oysters in their village were less salty than usual because of the water they grew in, and no breakfast was finer than a plate of fresh oysters with a glass of white wine. It's because of the iodine contained in them, you know, he said.

I got him talking, describing village life. He glanced apologetically at the Venezuelan, as if he'd told her all this before. My hunger to hear about it only increased. He said it was a quiet place, small. Most of its residents made a living by fishing. Not far away was a cliff that he and his friends liked to climb. The wind there was insane, it tore through the ears. Not long ago, he returned with a friend and they recorded the wind. Like a pipe organ, I said. Like a pipe organ, he confirmed. They built a system of pipes, but they used cheap recording equipment that was more capable of handling loud sounds. The recordings will be coming out on vinyl in a few months. Only vinyl, for professional DJs, he said.

I asked if he played any instruments other than the viola. He said the music academy made him learn a second instrument. So you took piano lessons, I said. So I took piano lessons, he confirmed. The Venezuelan leaned toward the table, her mouth moving, then sat back again. But I didn't keep at it, he said. The piano teacher clicked her tongue whenever she leaned over him, and he couldn't decide whether she was expressing satisfaction or dissatisfaction, so he abandoned the piano.

I asked if he'd ever attempted to build his own instrument. He wanted to know why I asked. I said I was surprised to hear the piece he'd performed the previous day. It was nothing like the other piece I'd heard him play at a different panel. He said he'd played it for the Venezuelan and me. He knew we would be in the audience. I said he'd played as if trying to cancel the obviousness of the instrument, to find it anew. The next logical step would be to retrace the construction of the instrument, the material side of music. He said he didn't build instruments, but he and the aforementioned friend were learning how to produce sound from mechanical devices not intended for playing. For example, the notes of a cash register—the keys, the drawer-opening ding. I told him I knew an Israeli musician who did similar work, but not— The owner came back with a bottle of white wine and glasses. He poured us the wine. The Venezuelan brought the glass to her lips. Hang on, he said, sipping the wine before you toast is a guarantee of seven years of bad sex. An expression of mischief or mockery spread across her face. Cheers, I said, and clinked my glass with his. The sound of her glass tapping ours made a muffled echo.

I asked if there were a lot of murder cases in his village. What? he said. You know, like in the books. A tranquil, isolated village. Somehow residents end up murdering each other for petty motives such as inheritance or unfaithfulness. The Venezuelan giggled again. The owner returned with an enormous pot. Different types of sea vermin lay on a bed of ice. The violist explained the process of the meal, how to extract snails from their shells, how to remove shrimp heads, and how to dislodge oysters from their shale beds.

The Venezuelan took the reins on the conversation and I retreated, focusing on the complex work of eating. They discussed film, shared their adoration of one particular filmmaker whose entire oeuvre consisted of mimicking the mannerisms of other great directors. They said things like, He truly understands there is no difference between madness and love. I hummed to myself. The violist asked if I didn't agree. I asked, Agree with what? With the idea of love and madness being the same? With the fact that it's a banal statement? Or with the fact that it cannot be revived by scratching the bottom of the symbolism barrel? After all, this is a director who made a film about a planet named Melancholia that is threatening to annihilate the world.

The violist said he was surprised that I was willing to try these new foods. People who weren't used to them often recoiled, taking a small bite here and there. He asked why I'd refused the oyster he offered me the first night we met. I said, How could I have known you were who you are and not some organ robber? He leaned in to hug me as we said goodbye. I moved away and said, Let's exchange emails. He walked us a long part of the way back so that we didn't get lost, groggy, on our last night in the city. He gave the Venezuelan a lengthy hug, and when they pulled apart, she held on to his shirt collar and pulled him in, kissed him on both cheeks, his mustache rubbing against her skin.

Sweet kid, she said as we crossed the bridge. I said nothing. As we entered the hotel, she suggested we sit for a while in the deserted dining room. I remained standing. She said, So, the festival is over. I said, Yes, I'm going back to Israel tomorrow. I asked if she had a long flight home. She said the fast train to Barcelona stopped in Sète. It was only a two-hour ride. I said if I were her, I would have come in from Barcelona just for her panel and then gone home. She said if she did that, she would have missed all the fun, and we wouldn't have met. I scrutinized her. Her eyes glimmered. She asked if I wanted to come up to her room. I thought about the thickness of the air between her and the violist, the oysters fluttering in my throat. I said it was late, that I wasn't a casual person, that I was sorry.

34

The French Jewish writer declared he had no intention of deciding the conflict for us. For years, he said, I've watched Israel and the Palestinian people build each other up as sources of evil. With each round of fighting, each side has grown more righteous, more predatory, more adept at enticing the other to shed more and more of its human form. Consider the following gnostic thesis, he said. Before creation, everything that was possible was in God, with God, of God. Even the black, electric sparks of evil. In an attempt to get rid of them, God made the world, trapping evil inside matter. The world created in time is a fulfillment of God's purification process. The sparks spread through it, poisoning populations and wells. In areas where the sparks shine, gourds of hemlock beat inside people's chests instead of hearts. Eons ago, God would pour fire and brimstone in an attempt to purify the abscess created by the spark, or purify the flesh of creation in water. But today he turns his gaze away, letting the abscess die on its own. There is no life within a wound, only fermentation, only an illusion of motion. In the latter days, creation will be an embroidery of scabs that God will remove, continuing to cogitate himself beyond all time or measure of space. Perhaps this is what Nietzsche referred to when he spoke of turning churches into monuments to God. In his Europe it wasn't God who died. Rather, it was the mind's ability to be attentive to a God that has closed himself off.

He spoke almost to himself, almost reciting. I said, Nietzsche. He asked if he detected a hint of ridicule in my voice. I said

I was surprised by these metaphysical, religious thoughts. He asked if they didn't come through in his books.

I said, Not with such gravity. Reading his novel, I would have guessed he hadn't seriously studied the subject, perhaps only memorizing a few slogans from an introductory philosophy textbook.

He said he took care to implement one challenging, thought-provoking existential element in each of his novels. Those who sought it out, found it. And the rest, why work hard for them, they were satisfied with the surface level, with supposedly profound ideas. You know what they're looking for? I asked. He said he didn't need to know. That he made sure they thought his literature was essentially philosophical. He said cognitive studies of anticipation supported his strategy. If someone told you that you were about to sample a fine, rare wine, it didn't matter if they served you a mediocre wine from an only reasonable harvest—the pleasure centers in your mind would go wild.

So appearances are enough? I asked.

For most people they are, he said. Not for everybody. This anticipation mechanism doesn't work for subjects with paranoid tendencies. That's sad, I said. He said, That depends. He said he reserved true writing for himself. If only he could live that way, suspended in a state in which objects are imbued with life and things offered themselves up, and he could confidently distinguish the relevant from the irrelevant. Everything fresh and worthy of astonishment. If only he could live that way, uninterrupted.

But writers tend to repeat themselves, I said. What did that have to do with the precedence he was describing?

He said it was only the amazement that mattered, the knowledge that you were trapped and enchanted. He said the great miracle was that you marveled over and over, the great miracle was that the experience moved through you in a different way, that it was apparent in the writing even if you couldn't remember it.

I said I didn't believe in the separation between true writing and writing for an audience.

He laughed. He said, You're feigning innocence, you son of a bitch. Who do you think you're fooling, I read your first book before the festival.

I said nothing.

He said we'd seen enough of Montpellier. The ancient city center was surrounded by new, dull neighborhoods. Montpellier isn't really a city, he said, in spite of the housing crisis. It's a settlement. The meaning of the name was a mountain with a belly full of water. The Jewish baths they'd found were proof that a body of fresh water was trapped within the earth's mantle. I said nothing on the ride back. Fields and trees passed us by. The writer slowed down. The car passed through a gate. He pulled up and said, Yes, they're still open.

Who? I asked. He said Languedoc was the most important region of France for vineyards and wineries. We walked through glass doors, from light into darkness. We were standing in the middle of a large hall, the walls paved with bottles, the floor plated with wood, strewn with counters padded with bottles. A man whose shape had yet to become clear called out, It's closed, it's closed. Pay no mind, the author said. We advanced. The man gradually became limited by his earthly form. He was sitting behind two upturned barrels alongside a portly woman. The French author emitted a rolling laugh and introduced them as old friends. This is the shop owner, he said, pointing at the man, and she owns an organic vineyard in the area, one of the only female winemakers in France. Her homey look, her controlled pleasantness, reminded me of other women. Her smile was a file of sorrow. She explained the varieties of grapes in the different bottles and poured us some samples. She liked to use Syrah grapes as the foundation for her wines. They absorbed the sun's radiation, the richness of the dirt, in the most elusive way.

We left the place light-footed and light-minded. The day had grown late, though a light stood permanently in the exterior boards. How much time did we lose in Montpellier, where did it collect? I told the author I had to get back to dinner with the Venezuelan and the violist. He asked me what her deal was. I said I thought they were sleeping together, but couldn't tell if it was a real affair. I asked if his boy wasn't waiting for him. He said no, the boy didn't keep track of his comings and goings, that he'd gotten lucky this time. I asked if he was okay to drive. He said it would take at least another two liters of wine to snuff his animal instincts.

On the way back he said all his boys craved a father figure, all were wounded in inaccessible spots. At first they sought forgiveness for indecipherable sins they could not count, then they fought to shatter him for daring to offer it. He had one boy, he said, who wanted more, but he couldn't tell what. The boy waited for him in the doorways of buildings, followed him down the street. Foolishly, the author had taken him in. He assumed it was an innocent infatuation, but that wasn't the case. Every shred of attention not devoted to the boy gathered to form an indictment. He got the sense the boy was always stalking him, out of sight, waiting to catch him unprepared, that he wanted to swallow him up or empty him from the inside and take on his life. He wanted everything, that boy—to write the books the writer wrote, to sleep the way he slept, to taste food the way he did, to breathe the air freely the way he did. He yearned to have the author's being drained into him, yearned to be the vanishing point of the author's history. As if my biography, said the author, every event, every decision, were intended to prepare me to meet him and completely give in to his existence. He'd never seen such consuming passion. Why, he asked, do we always imagine that the person before us contains a core of meaning that was promised to us and then robbed away?

I said perhaps there would be no point to life otherwise. Ultimately he had to get a restraining order, he said. But this time he was lucky. He wouldn't be surprised if in twenty years his current lover was the most important poet in France. He had the linguistic talent, he said. He had the mental fortitude, he had the innate cognitive independence. All he needed was to pass through a true darkness. He said it was tempting to become the deciding factor in the evolution of another artist. It's a shame that what's required from me, he said after a pause, is to shatter his heart and soul.

Tahel couldn't help herself. On Sunday morning she texted Yalon, What's up? Any updates? Strong rocket volleys were launched on southern Israel on Saturday and her parents wouldn't let her leave the house. She moved inside and out, shifting the plastic chairs along the lawn in a chase after the sun. Three hundred meters from the fence surrounding the house, the lake twinkled in its constant deception. It had been dedicated a year ago. Her parents took her to the dedication ceremony. The previous mayor, who had initiated the project, stood on the side in a suit, his bald head glistening with sweat. His thick mustache trembled as he spoke about the great enterprise that would change people's attitudes about living in Sderot. His Moroccan accent was as heavy as Grandma Rachelle's and Grandpa Amram's. She restrained the laughter bubbling in her stomach. When her father noticed her efforts, he placed his hand on her shoulder and pressed down. She knew the touch was meant to imbue her with confidence, but it only exacerbated the sensation she'd felt in the past year—that the confidence he offered was too immediate, mechanical. It offered no response to any of her inner turmoil.

Then the current mayor came up to speak. The one Yalon's family had supported and pushed for during the election. This was the only reason Tahel rooted for him. He wore a yarmulke and was about her father's age—not as old as the former mayor, but still old. While he praised his predecessor's visionary plan, she mumbled, What a crook. She immediately felt her mother's eyes on her. She looked up. Other people, in addition to her mother, were staring at her. She thought at them to ignore her. She had the power of influencing people to bend in the direction dictated by her thoughts, when she pushed her brain enough. She ordered them to return their attention to the crook. Some submitted.

Tahel, her mother whispered through clenched teeth. What? she said. If the former mayor was so great, what was the rush to replace him? Two or three of the people standing nearby who had been watching her now burst out laughing.

Yaffa, do me a favor and get her out of here, said her father. He removed his hand and placed it on Oshri's shoulder. Oshri tilted his head toward the arm and smiled up at their father. His blue eyes glowed at his father's, their black source. Oshri rubbed his skull against their father's gut indulgently.

Her mother led her away from the lake. She pointed toward a fenced plot of land, red-and-white plastic tape stretched between iron pegs. That's our plot, she said. This is where our house is going to be. Aren't you glad, you'll have your own separate unit. And look at that lake. When all these people leave, you'll be able to see how beautiful the water is. We'll have some peace and quiet here. Tahel wanted to say the lake was fake, but held her tongue.

Now she looked at it beyond the window. Then she stepped out into the yard to look at the neighborhood. Thirty-eight unfinished houses, the first semicircle, the closest to the lake, behind which more land had been rezoned. Demand for the new neighborhood grew as soon as construction began. Her father said he heard from a contractor friend that Yalon's family won the bid not because they made the highest offer, but because they supported the new mayor and undertook to build an entire area dedicated solely to the Religious Zionist population. Her mother said they were taking over the city, receiving donations from all sorts of Jewish organizations wishing to strengthen the cities involved in the conflict. Tahel asked if Sderot was involved in the conflict. Her parents were startled to find her in the room, listening in.

Amputated concrete skeletons, gaping like a screaming mouth, like a fist. Stairwells climbing to empty surfaces, naked roofs. She looked at their own house and tried to remember what it had looked like when she saw it being constructed, before the glass plating, the wooden furniture. Only bare walls, only air trapped in an iron blueprint. But she couldn't. She wondered if in a short while, when the neighborhood was complete, the current landscape would also be erased from her memory.

Oshri was drawn to play there with the fast friends he'd made at school. They competed at walking on planks about three feet above a small sand mound beneath the building. He fell, of course. Their father wouldn't listen to their mother's scolding or the curses she spewed about his idiot, wild Sderot friends. He also goofed off at that age, their father said to her. Just ask your brother. Then he started in on a story of one of his shenanigans, inspired by Elish's cunning. Their mother cut him off, We know all about it, you and my brother, the great heroes. Some role model you are.

The water of the lake had turned green during the year since its dedication. A team of experts had come to test the pollution. Tahel snuck up behind and eavesdropped on their conversation. They were saying that the water was borderline polluted, but that some real inner spring was sustaining the lake and preventing it from molding over. It's unbelievable, they said, to think that lunatic landscape architect managed to convince the mayor to invest money in this. He was a known charlatan in certain circles. How did he even find this place? One of the men on the team had heard that the architect had a woman here in Sderot, and that the two of them fled the country in the middle of the project. Still, the plans he'd left worked well, not to mention the ecological thinking behind them. A new environment would evolve here. Several bird breeds had already begun nesting. The heron population was growing. On the other, unconstructed side, where the eucalyptus thicket was left untouched, there were types of plants that weren't typical for the habitat. Rodent populations migrated closer to the water source. And mosquitoes, said Tahel. One of the team members turned with surprise to look at her. Tahel covered her mouth with her hand. For some time she'd been influencing them with her mind to carry on with their conversation and hadn't realized she was too focused on her task. Yes, the woman said. Lots of mosquitoes and other kinds of insects.

Tahel returned from her excursion with loot, a syringe and a test tube, which she had kicked under a bush when the tester turned her attention to her. The woman said her name was Yael, which sounded kind of like Tahel; she smiled. Tahel told her she lived not far from the lake, and that the mosquitoes were a real pest. They could never open the screen windows and it was hard to get a good look outside through the mesh. Everything is sliced through, she told Yael the Tester, and you can't get the full image. For some reason, Yael the Tester screwed up her mouth.

2

And again, a loss of reality proportion at night. We were barely allowed to graze the speed of sleep. At three in the morning, we—a Bosnian poet from Herzegovina, the Cypriot writer, and me—were led to a car heading for the Marseille Airport. The Bosnian poet said he'd probably get drunk, because what else was there for him to do during a three-hour wait? The sweetness of alcohol filled the car, pushing back from the vested metal walls, hazing the air. Beyond the windows, constellations dramatized frozen mythologies that have, for eons, had nothing to do with the histories of those in motion beyond the screen of darkness they pierced. Things passed through the darkness as they would. We too recoiled from that which was revealed and sunk inward. If at the end of our days all the landscapes we passed by in car rides, distractedly, at speeds unintended for observation, are gathered together, what vision would be revealed to us then, what is the raw nature of missed countries?

Unusually for me, I was relaxed, though the airport was two hundred kilometers away, though the flight to Tel Aviv was scheduled for six thirty. The Bosnian poet, who was sitting beside the driver, said he shouldn't have had so much beer. He asked to pull over. He had to pee. The driver slid over to a deserted pit stop where mute trucks stood. The bathroom and shower edifice glowed tungsten, like a temple.

The Cypriot writer was pulled out of his slumber. The whole way, his skull had been dropping onto his chest, causing him to shake, opening his eyes, alert, before plopping down again. He asked, confused, if we'd arrived, looking around at the foreign surroundings. The driver drummed on the steering wheel for a few seconds. Are you staying in the car? the driver asked. Then he stepped outside. I told the Cypriot writer I liked his story. He reached for his neck. Not finding a button, he instead felt around his Adam's apple. He asked if I had some gum on me, his voice squeaking. When wakefulness was forced upon him, his jaw muscles clenched.

I told him I didn't chew gum. Too many people in a small, enclosed space, he said. His hands balled into fists. If he happened to have a good rope, he would have strangled the Bosnian, he said. He couldn't handle his stench.

I nodded. I said I translated his story into Hebrew. That I'd like to try to get it published in Israel, with his permission. He said, Why not. I told him Israeli journals didn't pay writers. He said he knew that. He didn't make his living by writing, anyway. He pulled out a business card and placed it between us. Spidery letters beneath his name in block Latin print. He was a pipe-engineering specialist, he said when I lingered over the writing. Flow inspection systems. He worked for an international consulting firm based in Athens. They offered tailor-made solutions according to land features and environmental conditions. Why aren't we moving? he asked. The alcohol had evaporated through the open window. Somewhere in the dark, a jasmine bush erupted. I told him I'd been to Larnaca twice. What on earth were you doing there? he said. I hate the ancient honey smell of jasmine. He pressed on his Adam's apple as he spoke the name of the flower, and the syllables came out crushed, aged. I asked what led to what, his enchantment with machines or a degree in engineering? He said he couldn't understand people's fears of machines taking over. What had humans contributed to life on planet Earth but destruction? How could machines possibly do any worse? I asked, If that's the case, why does your story revolve around a yearning for the human? He asked if I'd never read science fiction before. I told him I had. He said, With the human race's mad passion to design machines in our image, what could we impart to them besides these flaws we take such pride in?

When the Bosnian poet got back in the car, he apologized for the delay. His hair was damp and glued to his scalp. The driver, muscular, made of wire, arrived after him. He seemed to have never sweated a drop in his life. He asked me to remind him when my flight was, glanced at the clock on the dashboard, then met my eyes in the rearview mirror. Don't worry, he said, we'll make it.

I said that, for some reason, I was in no rush to get back to Israel. I thought of Tahel, the urgency in her voice. She'll understand, I thought. Poor thing, she must be bored stiff. The Bosnian said, Some of the flights to Israel are delayed anyway, because of the war. He wrote a column for a major Bosnian paper. I asked him how many people read Bosnian. He said there was no such language. All the residents of former Yugoslavia spoke Serbian, and most of the Balkans too, not including the Macedonians.

The news networks are all pieces of shit, he said. International coverage in conflict regions is shameful. I said reporting in Israel was also biased. He said he was just a boy when Yugoslavia was breaking up, the time of great massacres. The Cypriot writer asked if anyone had any gum, preferably mint. The ancient honey scent of the jasmine was killing him. I asked the poet if his writing was political. He said he mostly wrote lyrical poems.

3

Yalon texted back, Nothing. Sima's hysterical. My grandma can't calm her down. Tahel was standing barefoot on the lawn. Leaf razors tickled the skin of her feet. Over the distant lake hovered a thin canopy of mites. During Passover break, when they went over to check out the construction progress, Tahel had caught a frog. She and Yalon operated on it in the lab of the Sderot school. Yalon had an entry pass—his father had donated the building and the equipment. They hadn't killed the frog properly, even though they'd looked up the recommended anesthetic dosage online. Yalon claimed the twitching of the body was only the nervous system acting out, like those cats you see bouncing like yo-yos on the street after getting run over. When he put the scalpel to the frog's stomach, blood sprayed and a repulsive smell rose. Ugh, she said, you're such a failure. She injected more anesthetic. They waited. The braces on Yalon's teeth gleamed silver in the dull lighting. Behind the safety goggles, his eyes were two burning buttons.

Tahel pressed Elish's name in her contact list and got his voice mail for the sixth time. Elish's voice, hoarse, almost effeminate, said, You've reached Elish. Remember that the entire complexity of the universe is required for the performance of the simplest task, so, only if you must. Tahel thought she could relate to why her mother was always so peeved with him. She texted him, Call me when you land, no updates, and that's a bad thing. But she didn't get a chance to send the text before an alert went off, buzzing and flashing across the screen. At least one good thing had come out of the rocket attacks on Ashkelon—her parents had bought her the iPhone she wanted.

She ran home. Grandma Zehava was standing by the kitchen stove. Grandma, Tahel said, to the safe room, now. Zehava said, Ah, *ya binti*, and who's going to mind the pots? You go. The Red Color alert sounded in the distance. Loudspeakers had yet to be installed in the new Lakeside neighborhood. Tahel rushed to the safe room. Oshri was sitting at the computer, playing one of his boring games, annihilating space invaders or zombies or whatever. He hummed the alert in perfect coordination with the sounds that infiltrated the house meekly. Back in Ashkelon, he'd learned to emit the sound of the siren, like a disfigured bird, and in Sderot he'd adopted the particular lilt of the words "Red Color" and sang them to himself. The alert was longer than usual this time. Tahel timed it for a few seconds, but it wouldn't stop. An explosion made the room shake.

Grandma, Oshri yelled, Grandma. There was no need to yell. Grandma Zehava rushed in, her hands wrapped in a towel, drying each other. Are you all right? she asked. Are you all right? Oshri sang louder, Red Color, Red Color. His song was like a buzzing of electric cables or a dying robot. Red Color.

The phone buzzed in Tahel's hands. Yes, Mom, she said. We're fine. Except for Oshri, who's freaking out. Mom, Oshri cried into her ear and the attached phone. Mom, there was an explosion.

What do you mean, an explosion? their mother asked.

Nothing, just some noise, Tahel said, though she herself felt a hint of excitement, a kind of gurgling. Don't listen to that baby.

Put Grandma on, said their mother.

Tahel pressed the speaker button and passed the phone to her grandmother, who held it fearfully in line with her mouth. Yes, said Zehava, there was an explosion. The whole house shook, the kitchen too . . .

What do you mean, the kitchen? asked Yaffa. Why didn't you go into the safe room? What did we move you to Sderot for?

But who was going to mind the pots? The kids need to eat.

The freezer is full of—

That's food from Saturday, *kapara*, the sauce is congealed. Bobby—

Zalman, Mom. Did you catch it from your son? His name is Zalman.

Mom, can I call Dad and tell him about the explosion? Oshri shouted, hopping in front of Zehava, trying to talk into the phone.

Such an annoying kid, said Tahel. Dad's at a construction site up north.

Mom, said Yaffa. Go out to the kitchen, carefully, and tell me what you see from there.

Oshri stood in the safe room, debating, while Zehava and Tahel walked out the door. Tahel turned her mind power on him. He followed them out.

There's smoke by the lake, said Zehava. The side where the trees are. She gave the phone to Tahel.

Her mother said, I know you left the room, you little rascal. Go back to the safe room and make sure Oshri stays there too. I'm on my way home.

Tahel texted Yalon, A rocket fell near my house.

He texted back, They'll probably report it fell in an open field.

She wrote, No, they'll write a residential neighborhood.

He wrote, Never, want to bet?

She wrote, Lol, you don't have anything I need.

He wrote, Okay, let's wait and see.

Stay here, she ordered Oshri silently and walked outside. Rescue service, fire department, and civil guard sirens sliced through the continuous rumbling of the bombardment. On Saturday night, Yalon had told her he'd tried to ask his father's advice again about Kalanit's disappearance. His father yelled at him not to tie up the phone line with his nonsense. His cousin's unit was deployed to Gaza. Tahel went out to the yard. The smoke dwindled over the lake. She'd convince Yalon to go to the thicket later and look for pieces of the rocket. Maybe they'd paint them and hang them on the wall of her room. He'd definitely say yes. Even though the pop star haircut she'd insisted he get, in spite of the barber's objections, didn't turn out well. You could even say it failed. He looked like a monkey in pantyhose. She couldn't remember which of Elish's books she got that image from. But at least she thought Yalon was pleased. A crumb of excitement burst in her stomach, spreading radiation through her body. Finally, she thought, something is happening. Maybe this summer isn't completely lost after all.

4

I returned to the country where proper names exist. Even though, according to Claude Rosenbloom, if anyone once imbued them with meanings, those were now long gone. I hoped for a delay, an emergency landing in Athens or Istanbul. But the plane was on time. The suitcases were expelled onto the conveyor belt smoothly. The taxi driver asked me how long I'd been away. The Prime Minister was finally strapping on a pair, he said. I didn't answer. I looked out the window. Tel Aviv was approaching, and with it, its summer, its end-of-days striving under asphalt, in the navel of the sand, in cranes and coffee shops. The air-conditioning was on, but the boiling was interior. The blood knew the degrees to reach and aspired to them. The taxi driver said what a shame it was that we had to sacrifice young people for the sake of peace and quiet. He was a father, and he was familiar with the fears of parents of children who now served in Gaza. There's nothing to do but grind your teeth and— He hit the brakes. Some meek monotonous declaration invaded his words. It came from the radio. Siren, he said. He pulled over. I stayed inside the taxi. He said, Say, are you crazy? I got out. A row of cars stood still in this morning hour. People leaned against the Ayalon Highway barrier, some of them indifferent, smoking, looking around.

The echo of an explosion sounded. Look, someone gestured, interception. No interception and no nothing, said the taxi driver. The Iron Dome is a sham. Haven't you heard? I said I had no idea. He said, Well, this one missile expert said the explosions weren't from the Hamas rockets. They come apart in the air. Believe me, the way this country is operating. He said, Is this your first siren? I said it wasn't. I only left the country last Sunday. After the Saturday night when Hamas announced it would be firing at nine, he said. Yes, I said, after that. But it wasn't at nine o'clock sharp, he said. Then he laughed.

The doubt of sleep pecked at me again. The body is healthy, and an abscess swells around an invisible thorn embedded in it, a shard of glass, the early Tel Aviv light, or the possibility of rockets. Either way, I was too tired, fatigued, but my body wouldn't give in. I lay in bed. I picked up a book. Lead in my limbs, the hand and the eyes heavy but incapable of finding peace. I dialed my voice mail. Several messages began with an impatient huff. Tahel, I thought. That hesitation of air. In another message, I was informed of the cancellation of a meeting with readers at the Dimona Public Library, due to the situation. They'd be in touch, they said. There were some text messages from Tahel. Her father had decided to forgo his Saturday visit to synagogue. Too dangerous, he'd determined, probably. She wrote, It's because Yalon's parents are out of the country. I didn't understand the connection. Another message from Betty Stein. She wanted to meet. She had a proposal for me. Asked me to get back to her as soon as possible. I called Ronnit. Akiva was fine, she said. A little cranky this morning. I asked him if he wanted to come visit me. He said no, he was busy. I asked what was keeping him so busy. He asked if it was true Ruthie's father knew how to fly. I said, What? He said her father saw things from the sky. What do you mean? I asked. He said, He looks down from heaven. Akiva said I was distracting him because he was planning on going up there too.

Ronnit reassured me. She said Ruthie's father came back from reserve duty service. He's in the intelligence corps, something to do with aerial photographs. He brought some back with him and has been showing them off, as if they couldn't already find everything online. She asked, What does the war look like from the outside? I said, Same as it does from here, death and destruction, except the viewers are willing to watch. She said, Did you call to argue again? Then she hung up.

5

Tahel pedaled quickly, feverish. She'd managed to slip out of the house without her mother or that tattletale Oshri noticing. He didn't always submit to her mind's orders. There were periods when he was stubborn and insubordinate. Her bicycle stood in a blind spot she'd found at the back of the house. It had taken her some time to locate it. She'd examined the field of vision spreading from each of the windows facing the backyard until she found it. She didn't know the Sderot streets well enough, so she turned on her phone's navigation app. When she left the Lakeside neighborhood, the unfinished houses behind her, she paused for a few seconds. The app wasn't designed to offer the safest route, only the short-est. It needed some improvements, she thought. They should add the locations of safe spaces scattered all around Sderot. She put on her earphones, gritted her teeth, and continued on her way.

Yalon had called thirty minutes earlier. She assumed he was calling to gloat. The news said the rocket fell in an open field. Yalon had a habit of calling the rockets Qassams, and she adopted the habit. The news made her doubly mad. But, Yalon said, Kalanit was back.

She couldn't believe it. What do you mean she's back?

It's messy, he said. Come by and you'll see for yourself.

In one hundred meters, turn right, the navigation app or-dered into her ears. Turn right. Turn right. Her palms sweated on the handlebars. She turned and her phone rang, cutting off the navigation voice. She pulled up and fished the phone from her pocket. Elish. She debated for a moment before rejecting the call. Soon enough she'd have much more to report. She kept going. In eighty meters, you will reach the destination, the app pointed out dully.

Large villas surrounded her. Who needed this much land? She'd grown up in an apartment building. To her, their new house was enormous and filled with mostly unnecessary space. She had to get used to how she couldn't talk to her parents when she was at the kitchen table and they were in the living room. She had to raise her voice. She had to cross a long hallway when she walked out of her room just to reach the other rooms. She looked forward to disconnection and privacy, to not having to fight about taking too long in the shower or getting distracted. Tahel looked at the neighborhood. The cracks in the marble façades, the crumbling of the granite urns, the miniature trees that had been neglected and were growing feral. Ultimately, it took too much work to maintain the appearance of a house.

Outside Kuti Asor's villa was a gate and a path that led to a thick wooden door embedded into a black arch strewn with white veins of marble. Yalon rushed out to greet her and urged her to come inside. Don't stand out there, he said. Come on. Suddenly she got it. There was traffic on the main streets, but the neighborhood houses were orphaned in their isolation. She left the bike in the yard. Yalon looked both ways before he locked the gate.

The living room was spacious, as Tahel expected. A kind of counter separated it from an equally enormous kitchen. Pots and pans hung from the walls and dried garlic bulbs dangled from a hook on the pillar that connected the counter to the ceiling. Yalon asked if she wanted a Coke or something and she stared at him questioningly. All she wanted to do was get the three women sitting in the center of the living room to start talking. The eyes of two of them, Yalon's grandmother and Sima the maid, were glued to a muted screen projecting images of the war.

Yalon gestured and she walked over. With his chin, he signaled toward the shocked girl lying on the three-piece sofa. That's Kalanit, he whispered. We're waiting for the police.

Yeah, I got that, said Tahel. Why aren't they talking?

It's better this way. You have no idea, they were crying like crazy.

I want to talk to her.

She's half passed out, she won't answer any questions right now.

Then why did you tell me to come? Tahel asked. Then she said nothing. She would have killed him if he hadn't updated her. I've got to call my uncle, she said.

Elish picked up right away. His voice was tired, bruised. She assumed he hadn't done anything all day. That's what her dad always said, that he wished he had Elish's life—no worries, no family. No wonder he looks so young while we're aging fast. I would look thirty too if all I did all day was scratch my balls. Sometimes she hated her father. Sometimes she hated her mother when she just pursed her lips and turned away. At any rate, she had no idea what they were talking about. All the grown-ups were grown-ups. Maybe not as wrinkled as Yalon's grand-mother, but just as incorrigible. But there was something in Elish that wouldn't stop moving. Sometimes when they talked, she forgot he was a grown man and not a classmate, and other times, such as now, he sounded a hundred years old, as if his bones creaked and the creak came out of his throat instead of a voice.

He asked how she was. What could she answer? How was anyone, anyway? She answered the way she answered, that she was fine, and before he could slide into his usual interrogation, how was she feeling about all these rockets and the summer va-cation, she said, Listen, Elish, Kalanit is back.

Who? he said.

From the corner of her eye, she noticed the girl lying on the sofa twitching at the sound of her name. Tahel went out from the kitchen to the hallway. Yalon followed her. Kalanit, she whispered, the maid's daughter.

Where has she been?

I don't know. We're waiting for the police.

Here's what I want, he said. When the cops get there, as soon as they walk in, turn on the recording app on—

She rolled her eyes. What did you think I was going to do? she said. I already asked Yalon to film it with his computer, just in case.

That's Hodaya Sasi's sister, Yalon whispered when the police officer walked in.

Who? she asked.

Hodaya Sasi, from middle school. You know, the school long-jump champion?

A sense of insult flickered within Tahel. She didn't allow it to grow. She said, Why did they send one officer? They should have sent two. They should always send two. Yalon shrugged.

The officer introduced herself. Lisa Sasi. She apologized for the delay. With everything going on, you wouldn't believe how many people call the police. And some of the cops have been called in to join rescue forces, and with the rockets— She fell silent. Her rotundness was firm, a rotundness of flesh. It seemed as if all her words came from the roof of her mouth, behind her teeth, which imbued them with unnecessary weight. When she spoke the word "police," her lips stretched out like a cylinder. Yalon let out a short laugh.

Lisa turned around and looked at them. Who are these kids? she asked.

Kuti said, My grandson and his friend.

When Tahel's mother spoke of Kuti Asor, she used the term "proud woman." Her mother wasn't thrilled that Tahel had befriended Yalon, even though Tahel thought she'd be glad. Maybe because Elinoar and Racheli had transferred with her from the elementary school in Ashkelon and their company had always been enough for her, Tahel never befriended any of the kids in her new class. She hadn't noticed Yalon until the Purim party.

He showed up in a suit and a bow tie, carrying a kind of screw-driver with all sorts of electronic decorations on it, and she ran into him as he was trying in vain to explain to a group of kids what kind of doctor he was supposed to be. Not that she understood who that doctor was either, but it amused her that someone besides her had dressed up as a character even more anonymous than a Sha'ar HaNegev middle school student. All those other idiots chose costumes that made them seen, but she thought the whole point of dressing up was to hide. Yalon didn't recognize her costume either, even though she wore a gray wig with a base-ball cap and padded her stomach with a cushion underneath a T-shirt with the smart-ass print WIRED IS THE LORD. Benny Ze-haviv, she told Yalon. He said, Who? Another time, Doctor. He said, We could travel to another time right now, with my TARDIS. She stared at him. He removed his backpack and pointed to the drawing of an old blue wooden booth printed on it. She continued to stare. He said, Don't worry, it's a lot larger on the inside than it is on the outside. Her mother said, I don't like that kid. But when her father found out that Yalon was the son of the Asor contractor family from Sderot, he encouraged her to invite him over as often as possible. A guy doesn't turn down this kind of opportunity when it just falls in his lap, he said. He made sure to attend the Sderot synagogue the Asor family prayed at on Satur-day mornings, which, back in Ashkelon, used to be the mornings he slept in. His hopes did not shatter. He began to receive weld-ing jobs at the Asor Inc. construction sites all over the country. Yalon only became a truly desirable guest in Tahel's home after her mother bumped into his grandmother at the market. The lat-ter was busy tyrannizing an Eritrean guy she'd hired to help with her shopping. A proud woman, Tahel's mother told Tahel's father with satisfaction. Tahel understood the meaning of the expression. When Kuti spoke, it was as if iron had spoken. As if a stone in the wall opened its mouth.

Lisa Sasi took a seat next to Kalanit, who sat up to make

some room. I'm not sure if children can participate in the questioning, she said.

They'll keep quiet, Kuti ruled.

Sima watched Kuti that entire time. Tahel thought that the two of them were not friends at all. That Kuti, like Tahel, had figured out how to enforce her willpower on other people. She's a dangerous woman, Tahel thought.

Lisa Sasi pulled out a pen and notepad. So I understand that last Thursday a report was filed after Kalanit Shaubi went missing.

Sima nodded vigorously. Tahel looked closely at Kalanit. Her eyes were hollow. They were even without terror. Empty. Once again, Sima described the plans they'd made for that weekend, the call she received from her daughter last Thursday, waiting at the bus stop, Kalanit not getting off, everywhere they looked, and how she showed up earlier that day. Lisa Sasi nodded. She said she'd been in touch with the Ashkelon police. An investigator there had tracked the case over the weekend. They even dispatched a small search team that morning and issued a call for witnesses—other passengers who were at the bus stop that Thursday.

We didn't hear a peep from her for three days, like the wind took her, then all of a sudden she calls, said Sima. I'm sitting in the kitchen with Mrs. Kuti after cleaning the entire house, a hell of a cleaning, you have no idea how much dust this war is making, everybody's complaining about the noise from the tanks and the jets and the bombings, but nobody talks about the dust, even now that the air isn't standing still like some kind of—she glanced at Kuti and the children—pardon my language, the air isn't moving, the dust comes in, especially after the army makes a big attack like last Saturday. She paused and took a long breath.

Kuti said, Get to the point, *ya* Sima.

There was unexpected tenderness in her tone. Tahel looked

her over, looked Yalon over, looked over the threads stretched between the two of them, some unexpected network of threads in the darkness of the body. She wondered how much of Kuti was in Yalon, and if one day his blood would also cool to her glassy level.

So you're sitting in the kitchen, said Lisa Sasi.

So I'm sitting in the kitchen with Mrs. Kuti, said Sima, and my phone is on the table and we're drinking coffee. And I say to Kuti, Kuti, when is my daughter going to come home? Who do I need to go see to get her back? I dreamt about Kalanit last night. She was a little girl in my dream. She was never lucky with kidnapping, at least twice she was almost kidnapped. If it wasn't for our vigilant neighbors, I don't know how it would have ended.

Did someone try to kidnap her in your dream or in reality? asked Tahel.

In reality, in reality, said Sima. She was unlucky with kidnapping, I'm telling you. People would talk to her at school, just show up at the gate and start talking to her during recess.

Kid—Lisa Sasi turned to Tahel—you're interrupting my questioning. Go sit over there, both of you. Then she turned back to Sima. So you're sitting in the kitchen.

And all of a sudden Kalanit's song comes out of my phone. We both look at it, and I tell Kuti, That's Kalanit's ringtone. I grab the phone and I see her picture flashing on the screen. And I shout, Kalanit, Kalanit, where are you? And she asks, Where am I, Mom, where are you? I'm at the bus stop next to the Sderot market.

7

John Cage wrote that we categorize most sounds around us as noise, that we identify them as an interruption to our listening, that we invest resources in stifling them, that there is great similarity between understanding music and picking mushrooms. I did some reading about mushrooms. I didn't learn much. I stopped listening to music years ago. It seemed like an obstacle to attentiveness to human voice. That's what I hear, not the random swelling of a spongy lump where a spore fell, not the precise, erudite hunt after the intuition it portends. But voices, a bubbling, bustling weave of conversations. Something foreign is in every word, if we suspect the familiar surfaces they propose, like a virus learning to impersonate a cell and make safe passage through the immune system's protein checkpoint. I could spend an entire hour listening to Sima Shaubi's wandering, searching speech as it bumped into itself and stumbled, but Lisa Sasi forced her into order and discipline, trimming the important edges. I should have been there. I shouldn't have.

I was thankful to Tahel and Yalon for their initiative and performance in documenting the questioning. The camera only caught a section of the space, occupied by three women. A peachlike woman in the throes of an erupting speech. A young woman, almost a girl, shut off to her surroundings, looking around her blindly. Lisa Sasi's profile, a statue shaking awake, moving its still-clumsy lips. Halfway through, while Sima recounted the phone call she'd received from her stunned daughter from the bus stop near Sderot, she was cut off by a dry, commanding tone coming from off-screen, as well as by Sasi's gravelly tone as it returned her to the thread of the retelling: Tahel's phone rang. The recording caught her whispering, Yes, Mom. Tahel said she was at Yalon's grandmother's, that it was fine, they had a safe room. Tahel said she rode her bike over. Let me talk to her, I suddenly heard. I guessed it was Kuti Asor's voice. Sima paused in her recounting. Kuti promised, in her patronizing stateliness, that Tahel was safe with her. Then the conversation ended.

Kalanit's story slowly emerged in segments, raising other echoes. She got off at the stop at the appointed time, called her mother, who answered in a panic, full of relief. Kalanit had gotten on the bus in Beersheba on Thursday afternoon and got off in Sderot three days later, on Sunday. By the time her mother came to pick her up from the bus stop, she was already wailing. The date on the screen of her smartphone verified her mother's claim. That's all she was able to get in between crying fits, presenting her mother with the phone screen. Then she slipped into her state of shock, about an hour ago.

Lisa Sasi jotted down in her notepad. Notes, a summary of their conversation. She looked up when Sima fell silent, then watched the two women across from her. Then she leaned over, took hold of Kalanit's hand, which Kalanit wrenched away, flinching and leaning back on the sofa. Sweetheart, said Lisa, still leaning toward Kalanit, are you sure you didn't just go somewhere else during those three days and you don't feel comfortable saying? Maybe you met someone, some guy who— Tahel interrupted, If she disappeared for that long, what did she eat or drink? Maybe someone took her and locked her in a room and she escaped. Yalon added, But how come her clothes are clean? Tahel said, Maybe she had a change of clothes in her bag. Don't be embarrassed, Sima said, putting her arms around her daughter, whatever happened, happened. The important thing is that you're back. Maybe she'd feel more comfortable talking to me without this audience around, said Lisa Sasi. I know a thing or two about matters of the heart. Huh, Kalanit, what do you say? A private conversation, just us girls? Or maybe she, said Yalon, her—

Uskut, said Kuti. Quiet. Can't you see she's been through something difficult. She's no fool. She's a university student. If she wanted to run away with someone, she wouldn't make up a story like that. Maybe she got hit in the head, said Tahel. The girl is right, Kuti said. We don't need the police. We should take her to see a doctor.

8

Yalon said she must have been abducted by aliens.

Tahel told him to be quiet and let her think. They had to come up with more rational ideas.

But you said, if she disappeared for three days, what did she eat and drink, and why does she look so neat? If aliens abducted her, that explains it. They always give the people they abduct an infusion.

They were sitting in his guest room, on the second floor of the villa. Grayness had already taken hold of the window. Tahel looked outside. Her bike was lying where she'd left it, overcome with desertion. She pictured Kalanit in a small cell, exposed concrete walls, some darkness swaying, drunk, in the enclosed space. A single lamp, trembling from the wind coming in through a high, netted opening. Her leg tied by a chain to an iron ring on the floor. Before her, a plate containing some unidentified gruel. Eyes peek at her through an opening in the steel door, beyond which she can hear the sound of running footsteps, a volley of orders, arguments.

Maybe Arabs, then, said Yalon.

What?

Maybe they thought she was a soldier. They're trying to abduct now too.

How did Palestinians make it to a bus stop in Beersheba?

There are Bedouins there.

Bedouins are Bedouins and Palestinians are Palestinians.

Who told you that?

My uncle.

You think he already watched the video we sent him?

I don't know. How long has it been?

Forty-three minutes.

How long do you think until they finish checking her up at the hospital?

I don't know. Maybe hours, maybe all night long. One time I had a fever and they took me to the emergency room at Barzilai Hospital, and I had to spend the night.

She's from Beersheba. They'll take her there.

They'll probably do a CT. I bet they'll find a tracking device in her neck or her knee.

What's a tracking device? asked Tahel.

Something aliens plant inside you. When they abduct you, they run experiments, then plant a chip, so they can know what their kidnapped people do.

Like a GPS.

More sophisticated. Although recently they've stopped planting computer chips and started using engineered viruses. They've moved on to nanobiology. That's what people on abducted.com say, that the aliens are always one step ahead of us.

What are you talking about? asked Tahel.

That abductions website. I'll show you. They see animals. We should ask Kalanit if she remembers seeing animals, the eyes of a deer or a squirrel.

I don't understand what you're talking about.

To make sure they don't remember what the aliens look like, they blur their memories with pictures of animals. That's a well-known fact. Whenever people try to recall what happened, they get a headache.

My mom, she said. She's supposed to come get me soon. She thought of Kalanit in the room. Her hand feeling around on the floor until she detects a bent nail. She uses it to poke at the cuff around her ankle, scratching her skin, bleeding a little. She bites her lip and keeps going. A click is sounded and the cuff falls. She picks up the plate and crawls silently, then stops behind the door and smashes the plate against the floor. The aperture in the door opens. The strange eyes look around for her unsuccess- fully. Curses sound in a thick voice. Her captor opens the door. The nail is hidden between Kalanit's fingers, which are closed in a fist. The captor walks inside with a confident step. Kalanit punches his neck, stabbing him. He falls to the ground and Kala- nit watches with satisfaction as he twitches. She is wild and filthy from her time in captivity . . . Yes, Yalon's question about how she made it over clean and why she didn't share her tale of heroism required an answer. Do you think the police officer is right? she asked.

Hodaya Sasi's sister. You know, they don't look anything like each other. Hodaya is tall and skinny, and that one?

I'm dead thirsty, said Tahel.

He left the room and returned with a bottle of Coke and glasses. Tahel took a seat in front of his computer screen. What are you doing? he asked. Don't look at my computer without permission.

Relax, she said. I just texted my uncle we were going to skype him. She clicked the icon. Elish's image appeared. He was skinny as always, but now his skinniness looked more like gauntness, like an old, plucked rooster she'd seen a kid holding last Yom Kippur. A light bulb glowed through his hair. His chin was cov- ered with a mixture of black-and-white stubble. She said, You need to shave, Elish.

He chortled.

So what do you think? she asked. Yalon breathed behind her. The stream of air on the side of her neck, below her ear, was soft and warm, paced like heartbeats, a calming rhythm. The sweet smell of Coke he emitted was pleasant too.

What did you think? said Yalon.

Good evening to you too, said Elish.

What? said Yalon.

Tahel said, He thinks we're being rude.

Elish nodded.

Why? asked Yalon. What did we do?

Never mind, said Tahel. What do you think happened?

I don't know, said Elish. It's certainly an odd story.

Odd, said Tahel. Just odd. Have you ever heard anything like this?

Elish said nothing.

Yalon said, Sure, people who were abducted by aliens.

At this stage, said Elish, it's as good a theory as any. But I—

What are you saying, Tahel cut him off, that it's a rational explanation?

No, said Elish. Only that without any evidence, any explanation is feasible, even the most unfounded one.

So how do we get evidence? asked Tahel.

Elish said, That's none of our business. Kalanit is back, and that's what matters. Maybe she really does have a neurological condition that causes her to forget.

You don't believe that, said Tahel. You don't believe that at all. What would Benny Zehaviv do?

Elish said, But we're not Benny Zehaviv.

Who's Benny Zehaviv? asked Yalon. The guy you dressed up as for Purim, with the baseball cap and the gut?

Yeah, said Tahel. He's Elish's detective.

But you said Elish was the detective.

Yes, she said, but in the books he writes he writes about Benny Zehaviv.

Young lady, a voice sliced through her, you and I are going to have a long conversation. She and Yalon turned around with a start. Her mother was standing in the doorway. She came nearer, glanced at Elish on the screen. You again, she said.

Good evening, Yaffa, said Elish.

Goodbye, she said. And get a life, *ya Allah*, stop dragging my daughter into this nonsense.

9

Asquare of sunlight was thrown in from the south. I didn't imagine the place would get so chilly in late April. I opened all the windows. Flashes of nylon, flutters of fabric, state flags in the wind. The month of Iyar did not make any impression here in terms of changing birds. The birds screeched all year long. I would have wrung their necks and pulled the song out of their chests. My hand dipped in the bit of heat distractedly, heating to the verge of burning.

I knew Ariel Piron was a questionable type. Manny Lahav warned me against him. He said his name came up often in investigations of cases that had nothing to do with marital law. He informed me that the fraud department was building a case against him. But the research for my first novel was expanding. I couldn't put order into the facts, distill them into a suitable story, a believable one, at least to me. And he was the divorce lawyer of the murder suspect in the case Manny had given me. Ariel avoided me with various excuses. Finally, I hired him to handle my divorce from Ronnit. From the moment I became his client, he let his tongue run loose. He turned out to be a reliable source of rumors. The guesswork industry was absorbed into the walls of his office, or perhaps he had bugged the town. Maybe the rose-ringed parakeets that had taken over Tel Aviv were his agents. Most of the news he gave me turned out to be lies or embellishments. His mouth flowed, he was excitable. I replied coolly to anything he said, which exacerbated his attempts to convince me and loosened his guard. A few supposedly unrelated anecdotes that he told me at different times, losing them in the flood of words, were in fact a series of tracks he didn't realize he was leaving. I told Manny about him, and he passed the information on. Perhaps I shouldn't have told. The temptation to direct the trial and the punishment was too powerful for me to resist. The police raided his office. Betty Stein called to yell at me. So instead of making up a solution to the mystery, I was investigating it, she accused. No wonder I'd been blocked for months. This wasn't what she'd gotten me that advance for. When was I going to send her the final chapters of my manuscript?

I tried to get hold of Ronnit. Her phone was disconnected. So I wrote a letter and mailed it to her parents' house, like in olden days. I wrote I was sorry, that I didn't know what went wrong, and that I had no good news about the matter she'd assigned to me.

Before she left, she said she had no energy to take care of it. A month earlier, we were sitting in Larnaca. Passover was on the horizon, even on that gentile island. She was saying how much she loved the holiday, how she looked forward to the Passover seder. We decided to spend the first holiday at my mother's. She was infatuated with Tahel and looked up to my mother. She said my mother remembered everything her parents had forgotten. I asked what she meant. She said, You know, the tradition, the cooking. My parents, they've forgotten everything, as if they were born in Israel. I said we could save up and take a trip to Morocco. She said yes, she wanted to visit Fes, she wanted to sit on the beach in Mogador, she dreamed of wandering the market in Marrakesh. A bumblebee bounced between the crowns of carrot beds, gleaming in a ray of dazzles. I reached for her hand on the armrest. Our fingers laced. She's left-handed, her right hand is weak, but she squeezed my hand with the force granted by happiness. She even said it herself, I feel like my body is coming back to life.

Then she said, Where are you, where are you? These were

different days. The Israeli spring progressed as usual, Tel Aviv bathing in the pollution of its beauty, its hidden hurt, the knowledge that it had no right to exist, and yet here it was, inflaming in its deafness. The streets were thriving. The streets burned with traffic. Missiles were shot at Sderot from time to time, mortar bombs fell in Kfar Aza, choppers tore through the afternoon sky.

I said, But I am here. I thought our quick civil service would put her mind at ease. I thought Ronnit had returned from it feeling confident. She had that glow I'd seen in her when we first met, when I was still a private investigator and she was a med student. But Ronnit said, Where are you? Every time I need you it's like I'm walking into a dark room, feeling around among things, all of them cold, all of them could be you.

I said I had no idea whom she was talking about. I was here, right next to her. True, I'd had less free time since we got back. I'd spent more time doing research at the journalism archives, gathering clues, I had to finish writing my novel, my deadline was around the corner and I still had no idea how to solve the mystery, I couldn't just make it up, so I was holed up in my office a little bit, so what, Betty Stein was pressuring me, she wasn't happy with the last chapters I sent, she said the story'd become too abstract, I had to learn as I go, I wasn't asking her to understand, just to trust me, the money I made from selling my share of the investigation firm to Eliya was running out, so was the advance Betty'd negotiated from the Israeli publishing house, and Ronnit hadn't found a job, what did she expect?

Ronnit said, Listen to me. I spoke to Yaffa. She had an ultrasound today. She's having a son. Then Ronnit got carried away in an imagined description of the fetus's perfection. His fingers, she said, and his feet, that's what I love about babies, they're so complete, so themselves. She was convinced he would get Bobby's eyes. Tahel, she said, didn't get much of her father, so this kid surely will.

I said I had no idea what she was talking about. I told her about the plot of the book. It was Manny's suggestion that I focus on that unsolved case. The problem was that, allegedly, the man all evidence pointed to had no motive for murdering his wife. Not money, not a dark secret. It couldn't just be a whim. Maybe an unwanted pregnancy. But was that even reasonable cause?

She said I wasn't listening, that I was making noise so that no one could find me. You're all over the room, she said, you're not a bat that needs to generate noise all around. She said she couldn't do this, she had to make up her mind now. She cried in the dark, spent two days resting at her parents', then came back. She said that was it, she'd come for her things. I asked her what she wanted to do about our marriage. She said she had no energy, she was exhausted, and that if I ever loved her, I should at least take care of this, procure an annulment.

10

In one of the Benny Zehaviv books, Tahel read that the moon's filament had annihilated itself from above. She paused to ponder the description. She wasn't sure she liked it. Often, as she considered the moon, she wondered if it suited how the moon looked. Tonight, for instance, when a piece of it hung, yellow and stubborn outside the window, and she sensed its presence even behind the drawn curtains. The description Elish wrote was far from apt. The moon was more like a wound with glowing pus, threatening to burst if the skin was pierced with the right pin.

She sat down in bed and turned on the reading light. At least she'd beaten her mother at one thing. She was spared Oshri's sobs and moans that disguised themselves as snores and mumbling.

On the way home, her mother retained her calculating silence, its burning rage scorching the skin. At home she erupted. How did Tahel dare defy her? Just that afternoon a missile landed not far from their house, and then she went out without letting anyone know, leaving Oshri alone.

Tahel said Oshri wasn't alone. Mom and Grandma Zehava were both home at the time. Besides, she rode fast, taking a route that had a bomb shelter or a safe area every five hundred meters. That was exactly why they moved to Sderot, because everything was safe and they didn't have to be afraid to go outside. And why did she have to be cooped up inside all summer?

Because all your other friends are living it up, her mother

said, partying in the streets all day, isn't that right? Call Elinoar and Racheli and ask them what they've been up to.

Elinoar and Racheli had gone to stay with their aunt and uncle in Ma'alot and in Safed, respectively. Her mother knew that. Elinoar had asked around about Yalon after Tahel met him at the Purim party and spent the whole evening sitting alone with him, talking. Elinoar said she found out from her neighbor, who said she knew Yalon's cousin, that the two boys touched dicks when they were in fifth grade. Then Racheli proposed to Elinoar that the two of them touch nipples, and now they thought they might be a little bit lesbian, and it didn't suit them to hang out with regular girls, who just had periods. Then they started pronouncing her name "Tzahel." So what, Tahel said, just because everyone else is miserable means I have to be miserable too? Yalon's grandmother's house is completely safe.

Beats me how some parents go out of the country and leave their kid alone.

They took his two little brothers with them, said Tahel. She almost repeated the name Yalon called them, the babieses. People constantly corrected him, the *babies*, but he insisted— the babieses. If they can't tell the difference between babies and babieses, he said, that's their problem. Tahel said, But what does that have to do with anything?

You're detained.

What?

Detained.

Like the Palestinians? she asked.

No, like, you're grounded, but with supervision.

You can't keep people oppressed without rights for long.

What? her mother said.

You can't—

I heard you the first time. Elish told you that.

No, I read it online.

If you keep bugging me, I'll take away your hour of internet too, understand? Elish told you that, didn't he? I heard him arguing with your father a few months ago and he used the same words.

He's right.

Those terrorists shoot at civilians indiscriminately. You think they care you're a little girl?

I was talking about what you're doing.

Her mother lost her cool again, repeating the same arguments, the same phrasing of an irrational punishment. What was this meant to be besides punishment that could teach her nothing, the sole purpose of which was to reassure her mother that she wasn't sitting idly by? Tahel didn't give up. She received permission to return to her room.

She glanced outside. The moon was still doing its thing. The distant thunder of bombing dwindled, turning into a faraway rustle. The darkness no longer cut through with flares, with the flashing of lights from jets hovering stealthily. But whispers rose from inside the house. At first she thought her senses were fooling her, but still they sounded, meek yet ongoing. She pressed her knees to her chest, wrapping her arms around her legs, but her neck stretched and bent to the side. She liked to imagine herself as a bird in moments such as these, tilting its head as it listened.

She got up, opened the door to her room, and looked down the hallway that ended at the living room. The whispers were coming from there, as did a dull light, like a stain. She assumed they originated in the kitchen. She crossed the distance with a bated heart. Halfway down the hallway, the whispering stopped and the light went out. Tahel crossed the hallway. Her mother was standing at the windows facing the front yard, her back to her, paralyzed, waiting for something. She was holding a glass with a little water and wearing shorts and a T-shirt, her hair lumpy and mussed.

Tahel didn't know what had sloughed off her mother, but something had, and the nakedness that remained scratched her throat. She whispered, Mom, and her mother shook awake, almost jumping out of her skin. She turned to face Tahel, her eyes wide. *Smallah*, she said.

Is everything all right? Tahel asked.

Her mother downed the glass of water and walked over to the sink. She never drank water straight from the tap. The mineral water cooler was close by. She said, Yes, yes, everything's fine.

Tahel said nothing.

Her mother said, yes, it was just that Dad was spending the night up north and she was a little worried.

Worried about what? It's pretty safe up there, said Tahel.

Yes, said her mother. Worry wasn't a logical thing. She was just worried.

Tahel stood beside her. Her mother's body was stiff with alertness. Why in the dark? she asked. She looked outside too. The shard of the moon was not visible from this side of the house, but it put some brightness into the night. The lake water returned its gleam. The eucalyptus thicket was recumbent like a dark animal, staring back. Her mother's hand reached and squeezed her shoulder. What? said Tahel.

Nothing, said her mother. Go back to sleep, there's nothing there.

Tahel thought that if she had kids one day, she wouldn't lie to them. Kids learned quickly to tell when their parents were lying. How did they forget that as they grew older?

11

The dream master came to me and showed me my father for the second time, standing in a clothing store and picking out shirts. To my question, he answered that the next day he had to return to prison to complete his sentence, he'd decided to join the study program there and finish his degree. I debated whether to tell him he was dead, to be glad he didn't know, or if we should both keep quiet about this fact we were well aware of. The next morning, I considered telling my mother that my father had been visiting me in dreams. I guessed she'd say I was disturbing his eternal rest and should let go. That's what she told Yaffa when, as a young girl, she shared her nightly visions with our mother. Even back then I could tell my mother wanted to keep him all to herself.

Manny called to ask if Betty had gotten ahold of me. I told him I'd made an appointment with her for later that week. He said he'd heard my entire family lived in Sderot now. I asked how he knew. He said, What, Zehava doesn't tell you anything? What do you do all day long? I told him I had errands to run. I forgot to take my car to its annual test and I had to go to the post office too. He said, No, Elish, what do you do all day long? I said, I read, I think, I stroll. Stroll, he said. And what do you do when there's a siren? I said, Same as everyone else, I go out to the stairwell and go down one floor. He said his people were saying the Iron Dome was one big bluff. And believe me, he said, these guys know what they're talking about. I said they were experts in developing war games, not in artillery or ballistics, and anyway the argument had to do with interception percentages, if I understood it correctly. Now every toddler thinks they're a security expert. He said young people today knew everything. I laughed against my will. I asked, In that case, why do they still use your services as a security consultant? He said nothing. He said, But they're making software for advanced weapons. Virtual, I said. He asked if I knew a video game console could also be used as a guidance system for missile launching. I said Hamas was doing a fairly good job with nothing but pipes and explosives. He said nothing again. I could feel the weight of his silence on the other end of the line. I told him I might want to clarify something with him that— He didn't wait for me to finish. He said, Sure, sure, we haven't met for a drink in a long time. He asked if I was writing another Benny Zehaviv novel. He'd remembered a few cases that might— I cut him off. No, I said, this is about something else, but right now I've got to run.

I was in the middle of my car checkup when my phone dinged. Tahel texted, asking if we could FaceTime. I tried to decide what I should text back. The tester said, What's going on with you? Step on the gas pedal all the way down.

I asked Tahel how come she could use the internet unsupervised. She said Yalon let her borrow his iPad, with a cellular connection and a data package. I told her I didn't know if it was all right for me to help her disobey her mother. She said, This is important. She respected her mother's rules, she understood their purpose. I smiled. Her cunning had improved since she was a little girl, but it was still no less transparent. We can talk for ten minutes, I said. She was sitting out in the yard. I could see the new house towering behind her, the flat roof, the glass, the modernity Yaffa wished to sustain her. Listen, said Tahel, you've got to help me and Yalon investigate. She told me Kalanit had been released from the hospital after spending the night in the emergency room. She wasn't hospitalized. No beds were available at the hospital because of wounded soldiers, and they didn't keep any patients around unless it was an emergency.

Tahel said the doctors said she was fine and told her to ask for referrals for all sorts of tests at the clinic.

I said, If she's fine, why should we intervene? Tahel said Yalon reported she was staying with them and was still a little shocked, but recovering. I said she was young and would forget. Tahel said Yalon was convinced aliens abducted her. He was following her around everywhere. I said, It truly is a bizarre case, but the world is full of them. Full of what? she asked. I said, Full of moments when reality trembles. Tahel said nothing for a few seconds. What do you mean? she said. I said, Never mind.

She asked, Like in the books you gave me, where the children cross over to a wonderland? I said, Not exactly. I had no idea she'd read those books. She never gave a sign. Almost a decade ago, in a sort of uncontrollable twitch, I'd bought a ticket to the Dead Can Dance reunion concert. Near me, in the back of the stifling room, close to the sound system, a young couple swayed along with a nine-year-old boy, holding on to the railing separating the two levels of the room. Once in a while his father lifted him up so he could see better, putting him down when the boy's weight became too much. I saw the boy's gaping eyes, saw his parents' gazes aimed at him, alert to his expressions and reactions. I could imagine what they were searching for—the realization that he was witnessing their lives, their younger years, the opening of their souls way back when, the thrill, the promise they'd felt. Of all the exhibits, all the evidence in the unending sentence against them, they chose to entrust him with the complex enchantment of this band as a key to discovering the people they used to be. The electricity went through me too. As did the yearning, the embalmed vibration. I gifted Tahel with books at every opportunity. Adventure books, fantasy books, detective novels, books for young adults. She only responded to *Encyclopedia Brown* and *Harriet the Spy*. Yaffa lost her mind when she found out that eighteen months earlier she'd read the entire Benny Zehaviv series, locking herself in her room for a month and devouring them all. I'd given Yaffa and Bobby a signed copy of each book that was published, and they devoted a special display shelf to them in their old living room.

Like what, then? asked Tahel. Maybe we should discuss this another time, I said. She said she wasn't so little anymore and there was no need to keep anything from her. I didn't expect this kind of treatment from you, Uncle Elish, she said. Still, I told her, being an adult means knowing when knowledge is harmful, when it's better to let go.

12

Evidence, thought Tahel. Elish said we need evidence. Fine, she'd get evidence. But where to start? Encyclopedia Brown and Sherlock Holmes and Benny Zehaviv all already had a trail when they began their investigations, but she had no leads. Kalanit, she thought.

She clicked on the Facebook app and signed in using the account she'd created on Yalon's computer. She searched for Kalanit Shaubi. There were three girls by that name. She found the right one. There had been no activity in the past few days. She scrolled back through her friends' posts. Shalva Matzliach, Kalanit's roommate, had asked for help tracking her down. She wrote, Our Kalanit is missing. If you've seen her, please comment below. Tahel looked through the comments. A few fake expressions of sorrow, a few religious girls typing out prayers for her safe return, a few conjectures that she might have been kidnapped by Arabs, some rants and arguments about the operation in Gaza, and lots of comments from disgusting boys making propositions. She looked at Shalva's profile picture. Her aggressively straightened hair did not soften the impression created by her too-close eyes and bulbous nose. Tahel sighed. She touched her own crooked nose. Once, Oshri had teased her at a Friday-night dinner. What did he call her? Gonzo. She must have been supposed to feel insulted by the name. Look at that dragon nose you got, he said. In response, Elish said, It adds character. Her mother said, Would sir please refrain from intervening in the children's fights?

She went to Hodaya Sasi's Facebook page. She truly did not

look like her sister. She looked skinny and tall in her photos, and big breasted. There were videos her friends had filmed of her participating in long-jump competitions. Her breasts shook when she jumped. Tahel was filled with embarrassment and returned to Shalva's page. She stared at the screen. When Sima called her, the roommate said she knew nothing, but maybe she did. Maybe Kalanit was behaving strangely before she left. Maybe someone followed her to the bus stop, and Shalva didn't remember seeing it. There had to be some kind of clue. The bus, she thought. Someone, the driver. She had to find out who the driver was.

She opened the browser. An image darkened the screen. Oshri was standing beside her, looking. Wow, he said, where'd you get the iPad?

Get in the house, she said.

But you're the one who's grounded, and you're not allowed to go outside.

I'm allowed to sit in the yard.

No, you're not.

He gave her a long look. She returned it. Their eyes locked. She fluttered in the deep, expressionless blue of his eyes. Oshri could have been a beautiful boy. She ordered him in the darkness of her brain, in the effort, to give in. He sat down across from her, lowered his head, and said, Do you know when Dad's getting back?

Tonight.

He said, Mom's worried about him. Then he looked away toward the lake and the trees. When he returned his eyes to her, true terror shone in them, unlike the fearfulness that regularly sabotaged the possibility of his beauty, different from his usual whininess. He rubbed his left arm, scrubbing it with his right hand.

She said, What?

Nothing, he said, shivering.

SHIMON
ADAF

Her phone beeped. Red Color, Oshri sang, jumping to his feet. He took hold of her shirt and pulled, Come on, come on. Grandma Zehava was already at the door to the safe room, making a calming gesture and smiling. Don't panic, *aoladi*, she said. Red Color, Red Color. Their grandmother rubbed Oshri's cheek. Enough, *kapara*. He buried his face in her embrace.

They waited, but the explosion didn't come. A few minutes later, Tahel said, It was a false alarm. Grandma Zehava got up and said, Stay in here, just in case.

The iPad, said Tahel. I left it in the yard. You see, it's all because . . . She fell silent. Oshri was looking at her with that same panic. What's wrong? she asked when their grandma stepped outside.

Nothing. When I'm big, I'll go to the army—

Yeah, yeah, and you'll kill all the Arabs, I already heard.

Mom and Dad say they don't want you to talk to Uncle Elish anymore, that he's putting ideas in your head.

That's what they said? she asked.

I listened. They were on the phone.

So what?

Mom told Dad he had to get back today. She doesn't like staying in this empty neighborhood.

There's another family in the neighborhood. The Dadons.

No, Oshri said victoriously. See, you don't even know. They left this morning after that missile fell here yesterday. They have a little girl.

How do you know?

I told you, I was listening.

Oh, then why did you ask when Dad was coming back?

Because Mom told him a thousand times to make every possible effort. That means he isn't coming, right?

160

13

On the phone, Tahel told Yalon she was grounded and suggested he come over and bring Kalanit with him. She's not that fat, she said. Tell her she can ride the bike I left at your place.

Hang on, I'll ask. On the other side of the line, she heard him say, Can you ride a bike? Then he told Tahel, Yeah, she can.

I didn't hear her answering you.

She nodded. She isn't talking yet, but she responds.

She served them ice tea and cookies. It was a good thing Grandma Zehava was there. Everything was fresh. The laundry smelled good too. Kalanit didn't immediately agree to sit in the yard. When she followed Yalon, who always walked around the house rather than through it, she let out a small, stifled yelp when the lake was revealed to her, the thicket whose reflection was a dark lump in the water. She stood, petrified. Yalon pulled on her arm, pleading with her to keep going, and she moved along with difficulty, unwillingly. They sat her down in a chair, her back to whatever had terrorized her. And Tahel closed her fingers around the teacup and told her to drink. So what, she doesn't say anything? said Tahel. You don't say anything?

Kalanit took small sips. Her alertness slowly loosened, her body melting into the seat. Yalon reported that the hospital said there were no signs of a concussion or any other damage.

Tahel said, So you already questioned her?

Yalon said, Of course not. Sima won't leave her alone. I used the opportunity when she went shopping and we came over.

Is it hard? Tahel asked her.

Kalanit looked at her imploringly.

Having your mother around you all the time?

Kalanit nodded.

Do you remember anything from the bus ride? Tahel asked.

Kalanit flinched.

Do you remember animal eyes, maybe? Yalon asked.

A quizzical expression spread over her face again.

When you try to remember what happened, do you see animal eyes? Do you get a headache?

Enough already, said Tahel, enough with your silly theory.

Kalanit looked them over.

He thinks you've been abducted by aliens.

Kalanit's body disclosed no reaction.

Did something strange happen on the bus, did weird people get on? Tahel asked.

Like what? asked Yalon.

I don't know. Suspicious.

Kalanit nodded, a minuscule gesture.

Do you remember what the driver looked like?

What's that got to do with anything? Yalon asked.

Yes, said Tahel, it might have something to do with it. You said we need to know the details.

Yeah, but do you ever remember the faces of bus drivers?

Yeah, sure, can't you describe Shula?

Shula who?

Shula from the number 1 bus.

Shula, is that that cow's name?

She's not a cow. She's just a little big.

I didn't mean a cow like fat. I meant she behaves like a cow.

How does she behave?

I don't know. My dad said that.

Your dad can't stand anyone.

That's not true.

It is so. He's a snob.

A what?

A snob. Everyone says so. Ever since you got money, your dad.

How do you know what we were like before? Hold on, how do you know her name is Shula? You've only lived in Sderot since—

Because I take an interest in people.

Knowing someone's name isn't taking an interest.

It is so.

No, to—

A giggle cut off their altercation. They turned to look at Kalanit. They'd almost forgotten she was there. Cute, she said. She pointed to her right cheek and her teeth. Yalon opened his mouth. Tahel understood right away. Once, she and Yalon were sitting on the bench at the quad outside the school, waiting for Yalon's father to pick them up. Elinoar and Racheli passed by. Racheli said, Elini, did you ever notice that Yalon and Tzahel have the same braces? And Elinoar said, Rachey, did you notice that Tzahel and Yalon have the same dimple on their right cheek? What a pair, they both said together, and kept on walking, giggling as they went.

Tahel focused and reached out to Kalanit with her brain, commanding her to remember, to dive deep and pull something out. So what do you remember? she asked.

Kalanit looked behind her. Then at the two of them. She picked up a cookie from the plate and took a small bite, pensive. Nothing, she said.

14

At midnight, or some other time of darkness, she once again found her mother standing in the kitchen, looking outside. She followed her motions as much as possible in the dimness thickening the space. Once again a lunar glittering on the water, the eucalyptus fort resting in its own ancient silence. She imagined her mother's body was tensing up at the sight of something outside that she herself couldn't see due to darkness and distance. Her mother's head tilted this way and that, as if trying to locate the source of sounds. Tahel thought about how she needed some night-vision goggles or, better yet, night-vision cameras. She'd ask Yalon if his father happened to have any. She returned to her bed quietly, set the alarm on her phone, and forced herself to sleep. Her thoughts shifted beneath the hard exterior of her decision. How could Kalanit remember nothing? Well, she remembered getting on the bus and riding it. She even remembered that the soldier sitting ahead of her was tearing into a falafel and the smell of *amba* was suffocating. Tahel imagined that the *amba* contained a hypnotizing drug whose smell softened Kalanit, making her compliant, and then at the stop the soldier ordered her to get off with him and dragged Kalanit along behind him. They walk down dirt paths, arrive at a boulder, and the soldier peels the mask off his face. He's actually an old man. It gets dark and Kalanit is tired and sleepy. He taps the boulder and the boulder moves, revealing a staircase. Down in the shadows, more people wait. He leads Kalanit into a cell and closes the door behind her.

Kalanit's questioning was harrowing. Most of it was performed through hand gestures. She spoke a few words, but no full sentences. How come in the Benny Zehaviv stories everyone talked and was ready to talk? A crumb of anger collected somewhere. She fought it off, but it grew hotter. She gritted her teeth. Suddenly, she realized she was stifling a scream into her pillow, that tears were leaking from her eyes against her will.

The alarm sliced through her dream, masquerading as a different ring, a rustle emerging from a veiled woman urging her to get up. Her mother was sitting at the long kitchen island, the wood bright against her tan arms, her eyes bloodred. The lake burned with sunrise through the French windows, through the nets covering them, pathetic in daylight. Why are you up so early? her mother asked. I told Grandma Zehava to let you sleep in. Who knows how often we'll have to stay up because of a siren? Want some chocolate milk?

I'll make myself some coffee.

Since when do you drink coffee?

Tahel spoke matter-of-factly as she boiled water and added sugar and instant coffee to her cup. She said she understood she'd behaved irresponsibly and she wanted to ask for an opportunity to make it right. She poured some milk into the dark liquid and glanced at her mother from the corner of her eye. Her mother turned to her, slightly surprised.

Tahel sat across from her, a steaming cup across from a cooling cup in the weak chill that remained from the nighttime air-conditioning. She said she understood the punishment, but wanted to offer a deal.

Her mother said she had to get ready for work. Maybe they could talk about it when she got home. Tahel said she knew Dad was up north working on his project and that Grandma Zehava didn't have the energy to run around after them, and that Grandma Zehava was a guest and needed to rest, and so Tahel promised to watch Oshri every minute of the day.

Her mother asked how this offer was any different from

Tahel's current obligation. Tahel said, It isn't fair for Oshri to be punished because of me. Her mother nodded. Fine, she said. Then she added, Your father's coming home tonight.

So she put together the delegation. She called Yalon, waking him up, and urged him to come over. She said, There's something we need to discover in the eucalyptus thicket. She proudly informed Oshri that he was invited to join them.

Oshri said no. She looked him over to make sure he wasn't trying to bargain, that he hadn't identified an opportunity to extort her. But his objection was clear and bordered on the terror she recognized in him the previous day.

She asked if he was afraid there would be a Red Color siren while they were outside. He said that wasn't it. What, then? He said nothing. Oshri, she said persuasively, you know Dad's coming home today.

He nodded and shrugged.

Oshri, she said, this is important. I'm not doing it for me.

I won't go in the thicket.

She asked him to explain. He didn't answer. With trepidation, she asked if he had also found their mother in the kitchen. He said yes, the night after the missile fell. She said she was there too but didn't see him. He said he stood in the back of the room, watching.

So what do you think? she asked.

That there's some animal there. Maybe a monster. I can't see it. But. Then he said nothing.

But what? she yelled. What?

Nothing, he said. You wouldn't get it.

Why?

You're always mocking me. You think I'm a wuss.

She said nothing.

He said, Not in the day. At night. I feel like there's something in the thicket.

How? Explain it to me. This time she spoke in a determined order.

Zehava came out. Don't fight, *aoladi*.

We're not fighting, said Tahel.

She pulled Oshri into the house. They stood before the windows. She turned off the lights and looked. But she couldn't see anything. I have to talk to Elish.

Oshri said he didn't like Uncle Elish, that he always followed evil. What do you mean? she asked. He said, Evil follows him.

That's nonsense.

Yeah, yeah.

Don't you want to know what's going on? she asked.

I already know.

She said he was just being stubborn. She said she and Yalon would keep him safe. He took a long look outside, then said, Under one condition. That you go back to sleeping with me in the safe room.

No, she said. I finally—why, actually?

Oshri said he'd be less afraid that way.

You see? she said.

Not for me. I'd be less afraid for you.

Why are you afraid for me?

Promise not to tell anyone. Swear.

I swear.

He said ever since they moved into the house he had an ice worm in his body. Sometimes it started in his left wrist and crawled up his left arm all the way to his heart. It happened a lot when he looked at the thicket. That's what woke him up that night, the worm crawling through his flesh.

15

Tahel's phone rang as they were standing across from the monument. Humidity bound the eucalyptus trees, and the three of them were sweating. The blades of leaves contoured sharply on the backdrop of the broken glimmer of treetops. She sighed, but answered the call. What, Mom? Her mother started yelling. What did she think she was doing? Now she was putting her brother at risk too. Where did they disappear to? Tahel said they were right there in the neighborhood. Her mother said that later that night she and Tahel's father would sit her down for a conversation, and that right now she'd better pick herself up and get home immediately.

When Yalon first arrived, he'd asked what they were looking for. Oshri reached out and pointed at the thicket.

But what? asked Yalon.

Tahel said, When we find it, we'll know.

The thicket was bustling with daytime—wing-flapping, buzzing. From up close they could hear birds descending to dip in the water. So many mites, said Oshri.

What could pass through here at night? Tahel wondered out loud.

Yalon said, Maybe *Bobarisa*.

Oshri laughed.

What? said Tahel. *Bobarisa*? What does that disgusting food have to do with anything?

Disgusting? Yalon protested. You don't understand anything.

What is it? asked Oshri. That milky steak grandma makes?

Yeah, said Tahel. It's a cow's udder.

Really? said Oshri. Gross.

See, said Tahel.

Kuti says you have to be careful when roasting it, said Yalon. Maybe your grandma overcooks it.

So what were you talking about, a *bobarisa* passing through here?

Oh, said Yalon. Oz Barbisa. You don't know him.

No.

He and his buddies climb the hill to watch the bombing in Gaza. They bring beer with them.

Beer.

Yeah. They're in high school. He used to be Hodaya Sasi's boyfriend, even though he's older.

Tahel said nothing. She wanted Yalon to stop talking too. She commanded him to do so with her mind.

Oshri said, They wouldn't come at night.

Right, said Yalon. Not at night.

Oshri said, So it has to be something else.

Anyway, said Yalon. They bring beer, and I heard they bring drugs too.

Why won't he shut up? Tahel thought. Shut up. Shut up.

Hodaya Sasi too.

Shut up, she said.

Yalon looked at her. A thread of insult burned into his eyes.

They roamed the thicket, the heat between them, the disordered music of hidden life, the thicket burst with it. Webs on small bushes, hastes of color, flowers as round as coins. If any shade fell in the thicket, life was indifferent to it.

Tahel considered suggesting they go back. Oshri said, This way. And, indeed, a kind of expansion was evident among the gray tree trunks, the spiciness of summer evaporated: an abandoned path. They reached a small clearing. At its center rose an unchiseled, micalike lump of granite, surrounded by a circle of stones. A brass plaque was engraved with large letters:

THE SARAH MATATOV MEMORIAL HEROISM GROVE

A smaller plaque underneath it read:

SDEROT RESIDENTS, HURT BY MISSILE ATTACKS,
BEAR THEIR WOUNDS WITH PRIDE

Black letters surrounding the granite face were harder to decipher. They read:

WE SHALL NEVER CEASE GROWING
IN NUMBERS AND STRENGTH

Yalon took pictures of the monument with his phone from every possible angle.

Who's Sarah Matatov? asked Oshri.

Tahel said nothing. With effort, she could see the Lakeside neighborhood through the trees.

Why is it so hidden? Yalon asked.

She didn't answer.

Zehava waited for them in the yard. Perhaps she'd seen them leaving or noticed their mussed clothing and the scent of the thicket that had clung to them. She knew where they'd been right away.

Their father got home in the afternoon. Signs of distance were visible in him. Not his tired work clothes, but an inner layer underneath his skin, a different type of seeing bound to his eyeballs, clouding them over. Tahel thought he didn't seem happy to be back. An urgent lightning bolt of discontent like she'd never experienced passed through the house, a thick volley of scolds and rebukes. They confiscated her phone. Her hour of internet, when she normally received possession of the computer's cellular adapter, was taken away. So were her outdoor rights. It took no effort for her to fulfill her promise to Oshri: she was sentenced to return to the safe room anyway, as an unmanned aerial vehicle was intercepted in the Israeli airspace that day. She and Oshri sat on their beds. They were ordered to close the door, but Oshri kept it wide open.

Out in the living room, their mother tried to whisper below the reports blaring on the TV. It was pointless. Her discussion with their father erupted. Their mother said he couldn't go away to another construction site for several nights straight again. He couldn't leave them alone. He said they weren't alone, that Zehava was there, and that he could ask his sister to come too if that would help. Their mother snorted. He said that he finally had some work, and they had a mortgage to pay. The construction had been pricier than they'd planned because they were so eager to finish everything fast and compromise on nothing.

Their mother said, You mean I was so eager to finish everything fast. You mean I didn't compromise.

Their father told her not to put words in his mouth. Their mother said now she was sorry they'd moved to this godforsaken neighborhood and that she wanted him around, that she would ask for overtime at the factory if money was the issue. She said the house gave her the creeps at night. Their father said this was what she'd wanted, this house. He said, What's wrong with you? You're behaving like a little girl.

Tahel's phone rang. Oshri looked at her. He whispered, Yalon. She nodded. Yes, they heard their mother say dryly. Tahel's grounded. Her phone is confiscated until further notice. She said Tahel was becoming a difficult kid, difficult, and that it was his fault. She'd become more difficult recently, and he couldn't go away anymore, Oshri was afraid of the sirens. Their father said she was overreacting, that a few days away would only make the kids appreciate him more. He chortled. Then he promised to put the job off until next week. In the meantime, he'd install the pergola she wanted in the backyard and would go to Seadya's nursery and get some ferns and climbing plants on credit.

16

I was the first one to suggest we break up. Ronnit said I didn't know how to fight, that I saw every small disruption as a sign of the end, maybe because this was the only serious relationship I've ever been in, not including fantasies. I said, In that case, why were you in such a rush to move in with me? We were about to head out to my mother's for Friday-night dinner. I kept glancing at the clock. Ronnit put on and took off dresses. I told her it was only my mother. She said, Still. She lingered in the shower. It was still chilly outside, and the hot water was a real pleasure. I'd told her before that my mother didn't like it when we showed up after the start of Shabbat. It ruined her sense of sacredness. Sense of sacredness, Ronnit said. But your mother isn't exactly religious. I told her I didn't intervene in her little rituals. She's clinging too much to your father's memory, she said. Even after all these years. Maybe that's why you . . .

I what? I asked. She didn't answer. She sank back into her choices. Which outfit is better? she asked, presenting me with two choices. I told her as far as I was concerned she could wear jeans and a T-shirt.

The month of Adar was apparent even in the dullness of the air toward dusk, its rising into it, the hasty departure of sunlight from the surfaces of noon. Beneath the cool breeze that made Ronnit shiver was already a warm outburst of days rushing in, the blossoming contained at all times in the buds of the plant. Ronnit said she'd forgotten her shawl. I calculated the time it would take us to get there. The razor of sunset was waiting on the border of our ride. We didn't have time. Ronnit said she didn't want to catch a cold. She hurried back into the apartment. Time crushed between my teeth until she came back downstairs, her shoulders draped with a delicate, silky shawl.

I drove like a madman. Ronnit said, Slow down, slow down. I said, The road is empty. Before we got on the Ayalon Highway, the Azrieli Towers and their overly delayed destruction to our left, I turned on the radio. The CD slot stared at me as always. Ronnit lowered the volume beneath the capabilities of my hearing. I asked why she turned it down without asking first, and she said sometimes I lost myself in the listening and left her out.

I asked when that ever happened. When had she found me listening to music? She said it didn't matter because I didn't even notice. I asked what she meant when she said I left her out. She said, Out, out, what's there to explain? I'm not like you, Elish.

Like me how? I asked. The line of cars ahead of us slowed down near Ashdod. I noticed it too late and slammed the brakes. Her body was thrown forward, the seat belt holding her in place. What's with your driving? she yelled.

We were late, of course. Ashkelon was already bathed in pale darkness. No cars moved in the Antiquities neighborhood. Ronnit stepped out of the car, swaying. What happened, why are you late? my mother asked as we walked in. I said, There was heavy traffic. Ronnit said, Zehava, do you have any soda? I have motion sickness. Tahel ran in from the living room. I ducked down to hug her. She peeked at Ronnit from between my arms. You're pretty, she said. The words were well formed in Tahel's mouth, but her speech wandered, cutting off. My mother handed Ronnit a glass, the bubbles fluttering on its periphery, in the clear. She said, We prefer not to eat or drink before the kiddush prayer. Ronnit scrunched her nose and drank. Where's your mom? I asked Tahel. She broke into an unidentified, tuneless song, widening her eyes at Ronnit. My mother answered instead of her. Yaffa is tired because of the pregnancy. It's hard on her. Ronnit offered Tahel her hand. Tahel released herself from the cage of my arms and went with her.

Bobby returned from synagogue, singing in his deep voice. My mother sang with him, greeting the angels who entered along with him. Ronnit rolled her eyes from her spot on the couch. They walked to the set table. I leaned down and whispered to Ronnit, Not now. Don't take your anger with me out on my mother.

My mother couldn't calm down from the disruption either. A veil of bitterness took over her motions. When Ronnit offered to help serve the food, she answered curtly that there was no need, she would leave her the dishes to wash at the end. Ronnit barely tasted a thing. Don't you like the food? asked Bobby. My mother pulled away the plate of fish he'd wiped dry with a piece of challah and replaced it with a plate of meat and chicken, roasted and stuffed with rice and inner organs, gizzard and spleen. Nothing beats Zehava's food, Bobby added. Right, Taheli? Tahel was busy soaking a piece of challah with the juice from the tomatoes in her special salad. Ronnit said she couldn't get over her car sickness from my driving. Bobby said, A Shabbat driver. He laughed. Tahel said, Mom's going to bring me a baby soon. No, Bobby said, she's making you a little brother. Do you already know? my mother asked. If it's a boy? said Bobby. No. But it has to be. That's the rule. My mother said, By how tired Yaffa is and the size of her belly, it's definitely a boy. Tahel asked Ronnit, Where are your kids? Through tight lips, Ronnit said, Ask your uncle. He doesn't like children.

Why do you say that? my mother said. *Shebah'allah.* Ronnit said, Ask him, he'll tell you. Tahel broke into her random song again. This isn't the time or the place, I said. Of course not, said Ronnit. Then, to my mother: Zehava, he told me very clearly that he doesn't want children. And that means I don't like children? I asked. Let's not split hairs, said Ronnit. Did you say that, or not? Bobby said, There's no such thing as not wanting kids. It's

twisted. And anyway, the woman decides if she should get pregnant. I said, All right, I think we've exhausted the subject.

The Tel Aviv chain of lights cut in front of us. I broke the silence. I said, This whole mess, it's payback for Laura, isn't it? She
didn't answer. So, yes, I said, I feel a little bad about how things
ended between the two of you, but I could tell right away she was
a thief. Is that what you want, a thieving friend who slowly
makes all your jewelry disappear? She said, No, Elish, you
couldn't tell she was a thief. You went and looked into it and
found out she had a police record for shoplifting. Then you left
the spare change in a prominent spot and installed a hidden
camera, and then you came to me like some big hero with foot-
age of her slipping the change into her pocket. She'd tensed into
silence when I showed her the video one of Manny's experts extracted from the camera I'd asked him to install in the bedroom,
and now she tensed up again in the car. When we got home, she
put some folded sheets for me in the living room. I asked, So
that's it, we're breaking up? She didn't answer. Maybe it's better
this way, I said.

The interrupted sleep became slumber. I saw dawn through
the cracks in the shutters before I was conquered. Ronnit
crossed the living room on her way to the balcony. The sound
made me jump. I got up awkwardly and followed her out. She sat
there, shivering with her cup of tea. I said, What do you want to
do? She said, Go brush your teeth, you have morning breath. I
brushed my teeth, then returned to the balcony. She said it
wasn't that Laura was a thief. That if she wasn't a thief, I would
have found some other fault with her. I said she was mistaken,
that I just wanted to protect her. She said, You can't threaten to
break up with me every time things go wrong. I won't live under
threat. I said, Tell me, what's so difficult about this? She said, I
don't feel safe, Elish. I asked what I could do to make her feel
better, if she wanted to go out to breakfast. She said, Let's get
married.

17

I don't know why, during that conversation with Tahel, before I hung up, her gaze frightened me. It wasn't her usual directness or boldness, but a plea that peeked through without her knowledge, for me to help her linger in childhood a little longer, to delay the departure and dissipation of her component slags, converting into components of a different being, outside her control. There was almost a muffled scream in her eyes. And I felt hollow. I felt that stifled request echoing inside me while I was drawn to it, a tensing that was entirely a sorrow, profound, expansive, of memory. I too, in turn, said no, and my refusal was no help. Her eyes followed me, gluing to my back. Or perhaps something of the trip to Europe had stayed with me. I walked through Tel Aviv, the doorway of hell, like an exterior extension. It seemed the space of the apartment had doubled. I got up and counted the floor tiles, just to make sure a miracle hadn't occurred.

I called my mother. What's up? I asked. She said, With all these missiles falling on central Israel, Sderot seems safer. Maybe it's a good thing. Finally, people in Tel Aviv would know what they've been going through. I asked why she thought people didn't. She said, All these protesters. I said, They're protesting the war. She said, But it strengthens Hamas. I said, Their argument is that as soon as we can't show compassion about a dead child, Hamas has won. She said, But why do they kill their own? I said I wasn't a spokesperson for Hamas. She said the news said they executed Palestinians who opposed them. I said, Looks like the direction we're heading in. I asked about Tahel. She said,

She's grounded. I asked my mother to put her on the phone. My mother said, Her mother won't let her. I asked if Bobby was back. She said, Yes, he's in the backyard. Been welding all morning. I said it was important I speak to Tahel. She said, Okay, but don't let Yaffa find out. She'll give me hell if she hears about it.

Tahel's words were thick with restrained anger. I could feel her effort. I told her Yalon left me a message to let me know her phone had been taken away. She said, Really? A small joy lit up in her voice. I asked her to tell me what happened. She said all that happened was that she went with Yalon and Oshri to tour the thicket on the other side of the lake to look for missile parts. I asked if she was sure that's all that happened. She said yes. She asked when I was coming down to investigate. Investigate what? Kalanit. She explained that, thanks to her and Yalon, the girl was speaking again. I asked why she took Oshri on the tour of the thicket. She said she'd promised her mother she'd watch him. I said I'd assumed she was smarter than that. She said I had to find out what was going on with Kalanit. That I had to come to Sderot. I said her mother wouldn't want to have me. She said their neighbors, the Dadons, just left town, and that Mr. Dadon was friends with Bobby, they went to the same synagogue, the one Yalon's family attended. I said that nevertheless, she hadn't given me a good enough reason yet.

Why don't you believe me? she asked. Believe what? I asked. Why we went to the thicket? I said nothing. She said, No one can fool you. I stayed silent. She said, Mom's afraid at night. Oshri and I think there's something in the thicket. Her words trembled as she spoke. I said, Maybe she doesn't like being alone in that large neighborhood with all the building skeletons and ghostly spaces. No, she said, even yesterday, when Dad was home. Oshri woke me up in the middle of the night and we went out of the safe room. She was in the kitchen, watching, listening.

18

Betty asked that we move the meeting to her office. With the failure of the humanitarian cease-fire and the death of the soldiers that interrupted it, she didn't feel comfortable or safe going out. There was a safe space on her floor. I ignored her advice and walked over. I was still a guest, and therefore exempt from the horrors of war. The coffee shops hadn't been abandoned, nor were they thriving. Their dwellers wore the masks of distraction, ease, joyfulness, exaggerated concentration on trifles, couples' chattering, random encounters. The public laundromats were also working full-time. I paused to watch the revolving drums, the exhibition of single life, made up of flipping through newspapers, leafing through a book, the twitching of city life.

The siren started as I walked into the building on Yedidya Frenkel Street. I was dripping with sweat from my wanderings. The inside of my baseball cap was damp. The air-conditioning bit my skin. Betty steered me into their concrete fortress. Her hair was dyed pink this time. She'd gained weight. I complimented her choice of color. Don't suck up, Elish. I know I've gained weight. It's from all the traveling. It spoils my diet. How was France? Other people were in the safe room. I told her the French were not my audience. Oh, she said, it's just this time we're in. It'll pass. All in all, Tomas is pleased. Someone in the room asked if the attack was over. She'd just made coffee and it would be a shame to let it get cold. According to the Home Front Command, we have to wait at least ten minutes, said one man.

Big deal, those guidelines are for families with children, the coffee maker said. Sons of bitches, he said flatly. Shooting at kids. He seemed to be repeating that line regularly. And the next one too: But when we shoot at their children, the whole world gets upset.

Betty looked him over. She asked why I hadn't attended the most recent protest against the war. Those animals, she said. You wouldn't believe that human garbage. That asswipe singer and his thugs broke into the protester crowd with baseball bats. The police intervened, but you could tell they didn't really want to block them.

Traitor, the man said. You should be ashamed of yourself, protesting while our soldiers are fighting to protect you, demoralizing them like that. His hands balled into fists. She said, I'm fighting to keep them from dying. Who do you think you are, that they should die for your male ego? Betty, we'd better go back, said the coffee maker. I think it's safe now.

Seriously, though, why didn't you come? Betty asked again. The coffee maker walked into her office and asked if I wanted something to drink. I said a cup of tea would be nice. I haven't introduced you to Letty, my new secretary. Letty and Betty, I said. Is that a joke? Kind of, she said. Her name is Letitia. Letty moved a stray lock of hair and began to list their teas. I stopped her at Darjeeling. I told Betty, A gathering of people, regardless of the cause, does not reinforce my faith in humankind, or my affection for it. Why bother? Oh, she said, I forgot about your secondhand individualism. From every corner of her office, characters from her enormous action-figure collection stared back at us. On a bench at the Marseille train station, I'd found a state-of-the-art Batman action figure with moving joints. I took it with me as a kind of talisman. The woman next to me on the train smiled when I pulled it out of my pocket during the ride to look at it.

So what's up? Betty asked when my tea arrived. Letty said, Let it steep for two or three minutes. I asked how she knew that was the ideal period of time. She said, The instructions on the box say so. I asked if she ever tried defying them. She looked at Betty and said, You were right about him. Then she chuckled.

I told Betty nothing had changed. I'd shelved the sixth Benny Zehaviv novel. What do you do with all your free time? she asked. I said, I told you I was bored with writing. She told me she went to the London Book Fair and they asked her there about the new book from the series, and she was already getting emails regarding the Frankfurt Book Fair asking the same questions. I want to make you a financial offer. I told her not to bother. Benny Zehaviv was lost. She said, You know thrillers and detective novels are the bestselling genre in the world. After supernatural YA, I said. Yes, she said. But I don't see anyone buying that genre from Israel. They're thirsty for detective novels. Why don't you write a new series? I said, Manny won't like that. She said, I trust you to find a way to include him in the writing process.

Letty walked in, all aglow. She said, The rocket fell in Kiryat Ono. They're talking about shutting down the airport. Betty raised an eyebrow. Very good, she said. A few days and it'll start hurting the economy. Maybe when they start feeling the repercussions in their pockets, these animals will begin to grasp how bad this war is. Letty walked out. Betty said, Sad, isn't it? After a few quiet months, people will go back to thinking about housing prices. They won't remember this barbaric heat, their murderous rage. This wave of fascism is a result of alienation, she said. And to think a false ideology can create such intense emotional experiences, and for what?

I'm thinking of going down to Sderot for a while, I said. There's a mystery there that's been preoccupying me. It might turn out to be a lead on a book. Betty leaned toward me. Are you sure, Sderot? I said yes. She said, We're organizing an empathy rally against the war down there next Wednesday. It'll be no effort on your part. I said, We'll see. She said, But remember, you have to make things up. Don't get all tangled up again, trying to find out the truth. I said, I won't, I just needed to absorb the atmosphere. I asked if she thought Sderot was in the international consciousness. She said, Now that you've gained some recognition, it shouldn't be an issue.

19

Heat alone remained on the street. Herzl Street was humming with air conditioners and faces drawn behind windowpanes. It was a little over a decade since I'd stood there. In my mind fluttered a solution that had no response in the world, a solution intended to remain out of sight, in the sole possession of the detective and the murderer he'd tracked down. I felt an enormous beast rising to leave Tel Aviv, the buildings bearing witness to the missed disaster. A dimension of the city had died out, an aspect of it had wilted, though I hadn't known yet, hadn't grasped that my days as a detective were over. I could continue to amuse myself with stakeouts, photographs, evidence, without answering the prodding question: What did the investigation mean?

All the detective literature I loved, which had prepared me for something, if literature can still prepare us for life, if it ever could, had tried to point to more—to the fact that in the mere act of investigation we dream up our investigative skills. Edgar Allan Poe begins his first detective story by determining that our powers of analysis remain unanalyzed themselves. There is a level of ourselves at which we put to the test our very urge to ask, its conditions of existence, the action it inspires in us, its secret spell, the deceits it coaxes us to construct just so we can experience momentary relief. So we can let go.

Manny tried hard to pull me out of the bog of helplessness afterward. I don't know why him, of all people. He searched for me, came to EE Investigations, where he found out I was on indefinite leave and that Eliya, my business partner, and her husband were in negotiations with me about buying out my portion of the business. He thought consulting on another case might help me, but I turned him away. He insisted that I take a look at it. I said I wasn't interested.

A few months later, he called me again, asking me to attend a meeting. He came over and made me come downstairs. The rooms of my apartment were in disarray. He asked what was wrong. I said I had to get rid of all my CDs. He pointed to the living room stereo system. I said, There's some music I still need.

Betty Stein waited at the coffee shop on the corner of Bar Giora Street, a hundred meters from my apartment. So this is the candidate, she said, sizing me up. I looked at her with confusion. You didn't prep him, she said. Locks of her black hair were bleached or dyed purple, alternating. Her face seemed to have been chiseled out of a potato, clean of makeup. Her bare arms were sprinkled with tattoos, anime characters intertwined with calligraphy. That's when I noticed the difference in Manny's appearance. His eternal pressed baby-blue shirt had been replaced with a T-shirt with a Doctor Strange print on a backdrop of the moon and temple ruins, a gaping Eye of Agamotto on his necklace, above it the fire-crowned skull of Dormammu. The print bent around Manny's gut.

He said we should get down to business. In recent months he'd been putting out feelers to figure out what kind of opportunities he might be able to find in the private sector. He was considering early retirement. I was surprised. He said yes, there was nothing to do about it, he wouldn't be getting much further in the police force, and he couldn't wait until age fifty-six to find his place in the private sector. Anyway, he said one of his friends suggested he speak with Betty.

Betty introduced herself. She was a literary agent. But she didn't wait for writers to come to her. Instead, she initiated. She followed global trends, and she noticed the detective genre market expanding. I asked, Regional detective literature? Yes, she said. It's the most primitive form of anthropological literature. A specific society, its codes and issues, its dramas, are presented through a mystery. Imagine a sixty-thousand-word news article full of cliff-hangers.

I said that wasn't the kind of detective literature I read. She said, It's the kind people are looking for. It's like this, it has to be realistic and gray on the face of it. I said I'd thought the role of literature was to excite. Yes, she said, completely gray. The trick is to convince readers it's believable, even though they want to give in to reading about bloodcurdling events. It's supposed to create a realistic effect without being realistic. Nobody cares about reality, she said, but people want to believe they're living substantial lives. What do you think is the deal with reality TV shows? I said I didn't watch those. Manny said, Human filth, the kind we only used to see in interrogation rooms, is now all over the screen without a hint of shame. Yes, said Betty Stein. It's easy to say, and easier to point to the well-oiled production, to the idea that what are presented as spontaneous events are actually scripted and directed. But nobody discusses the simple principle that people these days no longer feel tangible. True, reality TV creates a false sense of social mobility. Anyone can be famous. But that's just a secondary effect. The main effect, she said. She gestured with her arms, hitting the edges of the table, making it shake. Manny quickly protected his cup of coffee with his hand. I looked at the liquid in my teacup rising and falling, slitting dark tracks against the glass. The important effect, said Betty, is that these shows make viewers feel like they themselves have psychology, depth, that their personality flaws aren't just meaningless issues, but a foundation for a bleeding experience. That their lives have substance, just like those of their documented counterparts.

Hold on, hold on, hold on, said Manny. Do you think that's good or bad? Betty said, Good and bad are irrelevant terms here. What's irrelevant? asked Manny. What's the point of your insights if you don't use them to improve things? Betty said, Fuck good and bad, I'm not here to fix anyone. What I care about is making a profit off of my insights.

I said I didn't understand where I fit in. Manny said Betty had approached him. She said a senior police officer, with all the cases he knew and his interrogation experience and know-how, was the right foundation. Then she needed to find a ghostwriter. Not that you're a ghostwriter, God forbid. I suggested you because you used to be a private investigator and you write books. I wrote one book, I said. Still. I looked at the book before this meeting, said Betty. Pretty promising. You know how to do research. You know how to weave facts to create a story. And I thought, said Manny, that I'd let you look over a few unsolved cases I came across. Betty nodded. I'll give you the details, he said, and you can take it from there.

20

Tahel didn't have to convince Oshri to go work with their father, which made her plan much easier. They just walked over and offered. Their father was standing in the yard, his head wrapped in fabric, bare chested and sweating, iron rods at his feet. Oshri asked how they could help. Come here, said their father, ruffling his hair. Oshri smiled at Tahel, but there was no mischief in his eyes. They were severe. For the first time, Tahel wondered when Oshri had become aware of her schemes. How long had he been studying them? They carried poles and held them in place. Grandma Zehava brought out a pitcher of her ice tea. The exhausted mint leaves moved up and down as she poured it. Why don't you sit in the shade for a while? she said. Her father said, We made good progress. Yaffa's going to be pleased. The outline of the pergola was revealed, four netted pillars and a convex roof. Now we just need to weld a few supporting beams, said their father, and paint it all white. Then we need to plant and tie the plants. I'll leave that to your mother. Pretty good for two days' work. It's lucky Hamas gave us a break today.

Zehava said, A house in Ashkelon was hit. A direct hit.

Tahel thought at her father, Say yes when I ask you. Say yes.

Near us? Oshri asked.

No, said Zehava. On the other side.

Their father said, We don't live there anymore.

Oshri said, But we might move back.

Tahel thought at Oshri: Shift the conversation to the subject of the internet.

Their father said, Why would we go back?

Oshri said, Because Mom doesn't like living here anymore.

Tahel thought at him, No, no, don't talk about that.

Who told you that, Mom?

No, I just think so.

No, said their father. We're staying.

Tahel turned the power of her thoughts toward Grandma Zehava. Say something, she thought. Mention the internet.

Grandma Zehava said, And there are more than six hundred dead in Gaza.

Very good, their father said. Not as many terrorists.

Zehava said, I can't stop thinking about the dead kids at the beach. Why did they shoot them? Didn't the army see they were kids?

You talked to your leftist son again, didn't you? I'd send all of them to live in Gaza.

Say something about the internet, Tahel thought so hard that new beads of sweat pooled on her forehead.

I saw it on television, Grandma said.

The internet too, said Oshri.

Tahel sighed with relief.

What's wrong? asked their father.

Oh, she said, it's just, the internet reminded me that I'm grounded.

Their father said, Oshri, who said you could go on news websites?

Oshri said, It was the *Snoopy* news flash.

Their father said, This whole country is crazy. Why do they even report that on TV. And on kids' websites too?

Oshri said, It's hard not to have a computer and the internet.

What? said their father.

Oshri sipped his tea. It isn't fair not to let us use the computer when we're home all day.

Their father looked at Tahel. How many days have you been grounded?

She said, Two.

Fine, he said. Let's finish our work. You'll see, your mom will let you off the hook when she sees the pergola tonight.

Tahel followed her mother and felt Oshri's eyes following her, but it didn't matter to her. The evening sun roamed toward the lake, and the thickened, heavy, day-heaped light shone at its observers. Their mother ran her fingers in long motions down the pergola, as if wanting but not daring to touch the iron. It emitted the sour aroma of fresh paint, and the intensity of paint thinner burned the nostrils. When she turned toward the door, her eyes were filled with a glimmer Tahel could not decipher. They burned from within. She handed Tahel the wireless adapter. You and Oshri can have an hour of computer time, sharp. Split the time. She tried to imbue her voice with the usual hardness of her imperative, but the excitement that boiled over into it sabotaged her intentions. The command sounded unmoored in her mouth.

Oshri said he would download the stuff he needed in the background and she could surf the Web throughout the entire hour. She asked if he was all right and he said yes, everything was fine. He watched her running her searches. She didn't find much. Kalanit had taken bus number 353, departing last Thursday at four in the afternoon from Beersheba. She got off that bus last Sunday at ten past five in the afternoon at the Begin/Neve Eshkol stop in Sderot. An attempt to track down the names of drivers according to the ride led to the Metropolitan Bus drivers' union Facebook page and to the Ministry of Transportation website, where the necessary information for submitting a complaint on improper behavior during a ride was listed: route, time of departure, bus license plate number. She searched for information on license plate numbers in vain. Tahel leaned back in her chair and pondered. Then she asked Oshri if he could borrow

Grandma Zehava's phone. It was as if he'd been waiting for her to ask. He ran out and returned with the phone.

A grumpy man's voice answered the Metropolitan Bus Company information line. He softened instantly upon hearing her voice, which was naturally high, and which she'd cutened even more. Yes, kid, how can I help? She said she lived in Sderot and was a young reporter for a local newspaper. Oshri looked at her with wonder. She said she wanted to interview a driver who had a regular Sderot route but she didn't know if they had regular drivers. He said of course they did, but why? Because she thought they were heroes for continuing to drive from Beersheba to Sderot in spite of the rockets and the war. The man snorted, probably a chuckle gone wrong. She asked if the drivers had regular hours. He said usually yes. She asked how she could get ahold of a list of drivers, because she'd already looked online but couldn't find one.

Listen, kid, said the man. Give me the bus number.

She said, Three five three.

He said, Yes, there are a few regular drivers on that line.

She said she needed one.

He said, I'll give you the nicest one.

She said, I know who the nicest one is. My grandma came to visit us last Thursday. She took the bus that left Beersheba at four o'clock. She was carrying heavy grocery bags and the driver helped her, so I think he's the nicest and deserves it the most.

Such wonderful children in this country, said the man. Gold, gold. He said the name of that driver was Levy Todros and he lived in Netivot, but she would have to get ahold of his phone number herself because he wasn't allowed to give it out.

Oshri burst out laughing when she hung up. When he calmed down, he asked how she'd come up with that prank.

She said, From the Benny Zehaviv books. He's always impersonating people and making up stories. Todros, interesting.

She went on the phone company's information website and searched for a number for Levy Todros in Netivot. The website delivered the home number for a Levy and Hannah Todros.

Yalon's gonna die when he hears about this, she told Oshri. The driver is our literature teacher's husband.

21

Manny suggested we meet in Jaffa, of all places, someplace in the flea market. Of all the emptying-outs of the greater Tel Aviv area, the one in the heart of Jaffa appealed to him the most. No tourists, he said, no partygoers. I told him he was exaggerating. The Tel Aviv nightlife didn't really stop. We were both partially right. As soon as we sat down, the server informed us of the location of the safe area and access routes. Some safe area, said Manny, going into the building's stairwell and climbing to the second floor is an instinct by this point. I said that was a theory nobody could be bothered to test. What theory, instinct? he asked. No, I said, that a building's stairwell is a relatively safe space. He sipped his beer and thought about it. I'll ask our people, he said. He was wearing a shirt with a print of *The Dark Knight*, the bat signal emerging from Gotham's burning architecture. I hated the current Batman filmic incarnation. Humidity choked the alley. To the right of us was a café favored by tourists, its bulbs spreading hollow light, blue doors, blurry structures. Half of the pub's tables were folded and leaned against each other, but laughter sounded, distracted attentions floating through space. My body was on the cusp of boiling, the weight of the air resting upon me. Manny looked relaxed. The shirts he bought, he said, were moisture wicking.

I asked what his people said about the forming cease-fire. He said it wasn't going to last. I said they were designing war games. A cease-fire was a strategic move, not a condition to aspire to. He said from the moment they started that media twist about the tunnels, the chances of a cease-fire dropped dramatically. Sounds like one of your theories, he said. He was also surprised when those serious guys told him about it, but they were right. Think about it, the government knew about the tunnels beforehand, and the Gaza invasion was not accompanied by the achievement of some purpose, a real threat whose elimination would justify combat, all our losses. And all of a sudden, a few days later, you start hearing about the tunnels everywhere, like an aggressive marketing campaign for the war.

I made a remark I'd made before—that spending time with the young guys, as he referred to them, was doing him a world of good. It made his thinking more flexible. He said he wished his wife would understand. I thought with the same anguish I had in the past about his wife, the pleasantness of family life, the grandchildren, both born and expected, about the acceptance of the reduction of experience that is aging, about the escape efforts that, from the outside, might be perceived as pointless. I told him I planned to spend some time in Sderot, live there for a while.

Why? he asked. I asked if he remembered the story the giant told me at the hospital. Dmitry, I think, was his name. He said he remembered I thought the case wasn't challenging enough. I told him about Kalanit. He tensed up, just as I had the first time I heard about the same mystery repeating. A sensory organ within him, stronger and larger than his regular ones, more than the sum of their parts, awakened. He said, We have to check. I said I needed help. Yes, he said, of course, where do we start? I asked if he could find an address and number for Dmitry, since he placed a complaint. It was filed last June at the Holon police. Do they have precincts in Holon or is it one central station? I wondered. He said, Ayalon Precinct. He said he still had a few good friends there. Then he added, At least you've found something to fill the days with.

The insinuation of my silence was lost on him. He said, You

know I'm only speaking out of concern. It's been more than a year, since you were hospitalized, that you've been wandering aimlessly in the desert. Tel Aviv really is a desert, I said. He said, You know what I mean, you've stopped writing, you aren't working, you don't have—he fell silent. I said, I don't have a relationship, a family. Yes, he said. I asked how he could honestly tell me that any of the things he just listed gave meaning to his life. He shifted uncomfortably, downed the remainder of the beer in his glass, and waved his hand. A speedy server replaced the glasses with full ones. That's the second beer you get during happy hour, he said. He replaced my glass without being asked.

Not each thing by itself, said Manny, but one thing and another, together they gather to form meaning. Or to evade it, I said. To substitute meaning with a thousand rituals, people, emotional needs, which signify it.

Whatever you say, said Manny. I'm just glad you've found something, a center of gravity. I could feel the change when we walked in, he said. It's starting inside of you, this sunrise. I didn't ask for an explanation. Ronnit once said, Your burning isn't aimed at me. I heard her silent question—If you're capable of burning, why can't you direct it at me?—and I glossed over it with similar silence. Manny had pressured me to take on the project that Betty suggested. He circled me like a predator until I agreed to give it a shot. I debated with him which case we should open. He showed me that simple murder case, in which he was convinced beyond all doubt that the husband was the killer, but could not find one solid piece of evidence. He had his inner certainties and circumstantial evidence. That was enough for him. It wasn't enough for his commanders.

Where will you live, he asked, with your sister? I said no, in a different house in the neighborhood. Bobby had spoken to the Dadons, who were glad to have someone they knew, if remotely, take care of the house while they were gone. Someone willing to move in at a day's notice and pay rent.

22

Tahel hoped the airport would remain closed for a long time and that Yalon's parents would stay out of the country longer. Yalon hadn't been in touch for two days, and she felt waves of dreariness rising from the lake, covering the house, flowing into the rooms. She made the mistake of clicking on the link Elinoar and Racheli sent to their mailing list. They'd created a Facebook page called "From North to South, Blessings of Peace," where they posted selfies. Each one took one of herself separately. They arranged their pictures in pairs and added captions. In one pair, for example, Racheli held chocolate hearts in her selfie and Elinoar presented a carton of milk in hers. Below the collage they wrote, *Chocolates and dairy for the brave boys in the military*. Another pair was made up of videos converted into GIFs. Elinoar blew a kiss and Racheli blinked. The animated selfie collage received the caption *Kisses and blinks for armor without chinks*. In the third pair, Racheli gripped a bouquet of wilted flowers on the right, while on the left Elinoar palmed a bunch of red beads. The caption read, *Flowers and vermilion for bombed civilians*. And so on and so forth. The comments ranged from "You're fun" to "It's heartwarming to see the support from today's youth" and "You're our only way to win" to "Retarded girls, you should make this page friends-only, you have no idea what kind of perverts are out there."

In the late afternoon she went over the main points with Oshri, just to speak them out loud, give them tangibility. Oshri suggested they open some documents on the computer. She said the computer wasn't safe because when their mother got angry, she made it password protected. But the idea in itself was good. She grabbed a notebook. On its cover she wrote, *TYO Investigations*, and below she added, *The Case of the Enchanted Thicket*.

What's TYO? asked Oshri.

Our acronym, Tahel, Yalon, Oshri.

Maybe it should be the TYO Gang, he said.

No, she said, TYO Investigations, just like EE Investigations.

On the first page, she described the Sarah Matatov Heroism Grove. Online, she found out that Sarah Matatov was an immigrant from the Caucasus who was killed in a missile attack in 2007. The attack was especially bad. Besides her death, the bodyguard of the minister of defense at the time, who was living in Sderot, was wounded and had to have his leg removed. She checked on a map the sites where the missiles hit. It happened on the other side of town. So why did they build the memorial in the thicket? More questions came up than answers were found. She wondered if anyone ever solved a mystery using the internet, or if real information was still to be found in the world. She turned the notebook over and wrote on the other side, *TYO Investigations, The Secret of the Disappearing Student.* Then she added the information about Kalanit and Levy Todros.

They both lost themselves in thought. Oshri, their father called out from the front yard, it's cool enough outside now, grab the ball and get out here.

A bitter expression took over Oshri's face for a moment, then he overcame it, sat up, and walked out. A few minutes later, she heard him shouting, Tahel, Tahel, Yalon is here. She hurried out. Their father and Oshri looked like carbon copies of each other, bare chested, tan, already glistening with sweat. The sun touched the tops of the eucalyptuses. The lake shined like a tearing eye. Their father kept the ball in place under his foot and asked Yalon if his father was back. Yalon nodded, fingering the strap of his backpack and moving his weight from one foot to the next. He said his father gave him a ride over.

Then why didn't he come in? their father asked. Yaffa, he called out, see if—

Yalon cut him off. He was gone. But his mother would come pick him up in an hour. He asked if Tahel and Oshri were allowed to go with him.

Their father shook his head. Tahel is grounded, he said.

Mom, said Tahèl, I'm going outside to show Yalon the pergola. Their mother smiled weakly at Yalon. She asked if he wanted anything to drink. That's all right, said Yalon. They walked past Grandma Zehava, who was sitting in the living room and watching an episode of one of the shows Yaffa recorded for her, about people in Netanya or Kiryat Gat, where life was even more boring than in Sderot. Yalon looked at the pergola. He said, You went with white. Tahel pointed at the pillars and the pots leaning on them.

When the paint dries, my mom is going to plant plants, she said.

Yes, said Yalon.

She remembered there was a vine canopy five times bigger alongside the pool in Yalon's house. The pool was abandoned anyway because of the military operation.

I tried to tell my father, Yalon said, about Kalanit, but he's not interested, he's worried about my cousin.

Tahel said nothing.

He's in Gaza, he said.

Elish isn't interested either, said Tahel. I swear I tried. What are we going to do? I thought we'd make some progress before Sima and Kalanit go home.

No, said Yalon, but she's staying, they're staying. I asked my grandma. She said she can't let them leave before Kalanit feels better anyway. Besides, she needs the help.

I thought your parents help her, said Tahel.

My mother is going to Grofit and taking the babieses with her.

What's Grofit? Tahel asked.

A kibbutz in the Arava, he said. It's hard for her with the missiles and the war.

And your dad is staying.

Yeah, he said. And I am too. He has a lot of work.

And he isn't helping your grandma? she asked.

Yalon said, She says he isn't, that she never imagined her beloved son would turn out to be such an egomaniac.

Tahel said, She means your dad.

Yeah, duh, Yalon said awkwardly.

He said nothing. Tahel said nothing.

Oh, she suddenly said, I'm such an idiot. I found out the name of the driver of the bus Kalanit got on last week, Levy Todros.

Yalon opened his mouth. She quickly added, Hannah Todros is his wife. We need to find an excuse for calling her.

But it's summer vacation, he said.

Yeah.

We could email her.

Would she read it during the summer? Tahel asked.

Why not try?

She pondered this option for a few seconds. All right, she said.

Yalon said, Good, I'm glad I came prepared. He pulled out an iPad from his small backpack. I'm almost out of data for the month, he said.

No problem, said Tahel. We'll write the email, then get on the school's online system and send it. Can you access it from your iPad?

Yeah, there's a tablet app for it. Didn't you know?

They wrote to Hannah Todros that the library was closed because of the war. Not "because," said Tahel, write "in light of," it's more official. The library was closed in light of the war, they wrote, and they were left with nothing to do. They asked Hannah to help them by recommending some books, or possibly, if she

didn't mind, letting them borrow some from her. Yalon wondered out loud if the wording was too rude. Tahel said it wasn't.
She said Hannah would be glad.

No, said Yalon, she'll think we're pranking her, wanna bet?

They drank from the glasses her mother had served them.
She told Tahel, Your guests will get dehydrated by the time you
offer them anything.

When she left, Yalon asked if Tahel had seen Elinoar and
Racheli's Facebook page.

Yeah, said Tahel. I don't get how their parents let them.

They don't, said Yalon, they shut it down. But it went viral.

That page?

He showed her a few Facebook pages that replicated the
selfie pairs, turning them into threes and group albums. The
captions became more and more bizarre. Yalon said before they
shut down the page, Elinoar and Racheli created personal greetings. He said he'd downloaded theirs.

Our what? said Tahel.

They made us two, he said.

A picture of Racheli holding a broom appeared on the iPad
screen. In Elinoar's picture, she was holding a phone to her ear.
The caption read, *A broom and a phone for Tzahel and Yalon.* The
second pair was a little more thought-out, using animated selfies. They'd taken shots of their profiles and edited them to face
each other. Each girl was waving her own weapon, Elinoar using
a seashell, Racheli a ruler. They appeared to be sparring beyond
the white line that separated them. Below, the caption read, *A
ruler and a shell for Yalon and Tzahel.*

Tahel looked at the selfie pair for a long time. She missed
them. She said, Most repulsive girls in the universe.

Yalon said, But it is a little funny.

She pursed her lips with effort. He was already smiling.
Yeah, she said, a little funny. They both laughed.

23

Oshri woke Tahel up in the middle of the night and they stood outside the living room and listened to their parents talking in a whisper. Bobby had noticed Yaffa's absence from the bed and found her standing by the window, looking out. Tahel said they were both already quite close to the other end of the living room, the one leading to the safe room and the other rooms. Bobby demanded to know what was going on with Yaffa. She said she was worried, that she couldn't remember the last time she was this worried, not even when the kids were born, not even when Oshri had trouble breastfeeding. Bobby asked what she was so worried about. If she was worried about money, she should know he was swamped with orders ever since he started working at the Asor sites, and they could make the mortgage payments. If she was worried about the kids, they were fine, a little unruly, but it was understandable. Tahel's rebelliousness would go away on its own, and Oshri was a very good boy. If she was worried about him or her mother, they were right there, and they were adults. The war wouldn't last forever, we should be thankful for our luck, not worried. Yaffa said she wasn't the problem, the house was the problem, the lake, they were filled with worry. Then they talked about how I was renting out the Dadons' house. I'd told them I was thinking of writing a new book set in the area.

Tahel said, Yay, yay, yay. I said, This is the second time you've mentioned Oshri waking you up. She said, Yes, he can feel it. Feel what? I said. Things, she said, and promised I'd see for myself. She said that Sima and Kalanit were staying at Kuti's so investigating should be easy.

In the car, for some reason, I remembered Tahel's nose-scrunching, an expression of impossible concentration before she erupted into conversation, and I laughed quietly. It had been years, years of driving, and I still despised the inclines on the way to Jerusalem. I planned ruses, tried to leave when traffic was sparse, but my efforts were in vain, the angel appointed to driving continued to harass me. Once again I found myself in heavy traffic on the inclines. I wouldn't drive through a checkpoint road. I had to overcome the shaking of my hand when I slipped the disc into the car's stereo. A decade of abstaining ended just as suddenly as it had begun, with the same casual violence. The purchasing of the album had been performed in the same manner, as if I'd evacuated my body and allowed it to act according to its own habits and desires. But if the matter didn't pertain to me but to the old, foreign being that had returned to take back its previous dwelling, what did it have to do with one of the forces running the universe, which remain indifferent in the face of the breaking of our vows?

I programmed the machine to play tracks four and five on a loop, Mozart's Violin Sonata in E Minor, in the performance recommended by Claude Rosenbloom. A model began to form in my mind, no more images erupting from the flow of music, but glowing geometrical symbols on a viscous black backdrop that swallowed them the moment they appeared. First the bowed etching of the violin, at its edges the eroded piano teeth.

What are you doing, coming here without notice? said Ronnit. What if David had been home? I told her I was certain he was at Jewish studies. Then why did you come? she asked. I'd called from the edge of town and asked if she could meet me at the mall and bring Akiva with her. I could swing by and pick them up. She said no, they'd get there by themselves. The fringes of the tallit beat against Akiva's thighs as he ran over from the stairs. The

yarmulke flew off his head. He paused and froze in place. I signaled to him to come closer. He called out, But it's more than
three steps without a yarmulke on. Other mall-goers overtook
him, indifferent. I picked up the yarmulke and shook off the hint
of dust that may have clung to it, patting it demonstrably against
my hand. Akiva laughed. He jumped up and wrapped his arms
around my neck. I picked him up. You're heavy, I said. But he was
made of air, brittle bones and air, what was Ronnit feeding him,
weeds and seeds?

What did you get me, Uncle Elish? he asked. I said, We're at
the mall, what do you want? Something special, he said. I said,
Luckily I brought it with me. I pulled out the Batman action figure and handed it to him. He retreated, leaning against the seat
where Ronnit placed him. What's wrong? I asked. He said, It's
idolatry.

I looked at Ronnit. She said, What are you looking at me
for? The kid is right. I said, I thought you said you were creating
your own religious framework, not thoughtlessly adopting a
collection of superstitions. She said, But he's right. What is
consumerism culture if not idolatry? I said, But it's a gift, a
symbol of love.

I ordered Akiva a hot chocolate. I asked if she could leave him
with me and go walk around for an hour. What's wrong? she
asked. I told her I'd decided to move to Sderot for the near future
and wanted to see them before I left. You scared me, she said, big
deal, Sderot, half of David's Jewish class is planning on moving
there. Yeah, I said, Yaffa said the Religious Zionist community is
taking over whole neighborhoods, that they're coming with organized budgets to buy apartments. Are you thinking of moving
too? I asked. She said, God forbid, I've paid my dues to the south,
I'm not going back to Sderot. She asked if it was a smart move on
my part because— I said, I'm not thinking about her anymore.
She said she found that hard to believe.

She'd spoken to Yaffa that morning, she said. I glanced at

Akiva. He was diligently and quickly coloring in the clear areas in the drawing placed before him. He looked up at me. His face was awash with otherness. I was too late. If I'd been part of his life in its first months, perhaps a smidgen of essence would awaken in him by virtue of my own essence, beckoning. About what? I asked. She said, Yaffa wanted to ask if I knew of any methods for removing evil spirits. What does that have to do with you? I asked, or have you expanded your business to magic spells? Elish, Elish, she said, don't be so limited, the world is a network of reciprocal relationships, health and sickness are much more than just symptoms and medications. I said, And people say I'm paranoid. She said, That's because you try to fit everything into your logic. You think in such earthly terms of cause and effect. There are no alternatives, I said. She said, You can give in to things, understand them from the inside. I said, That's nonsense, nothing more than fancy phrasing. What you want to say is, let's fool ourselves into believing as hard as we can that reality works according to our heart's desires. That's not what I said, she said. But your argument was going there. Ronnit said, If you already know what I'm going to say, why do you even bother to talk to me?

I asked what she'd suggested to Yaffa. She said, I told her to burn sage and scatter dry *ezovion* twigs in the rooms. *Ezovion*, of all things, I said. Yes, she said. It has spiritual qualities. Akiva started humming to himself. I asked again if she could leave him with me. She said, Half an hour, I'm timing it. I said to Akiva, You want to take a walk outside with me? He asked, Do you have a camera? I asked how he got so interested in photography. She said David's crazy sister went back to Belarus with her husband two years ago and they had just come for a visit. Her kids photographed anything that moved, and Akiva caught the bug. I said, When consumerism culture suits us it ceases to be idolatry. She said, You can't finish a conversation without taking a stab at me, huh, Elish, huh?

24

Betty didn't like the first chapters I sent her. We had long conversations. She said, You've got to get over that philosophical tendency of yours, get back to earth. The era of great detectives who live outside of society is over. We're now in the era of mundane detectives dealing with pedestrian problems. I told her those weren't the detectives I liked. She said she'd noticed.

The detective's character formed with torturous slowness. I wanted him to be a Moroccan guy from a development town. Betty said, You all. As always, when she started an argument in second person plural, she rid herself of any connection to the Jewish diaspora. Her British accent burst into her very local speech patterns. You all, she said, what is it with you and the ethnic tensions? When will you learn? It's an old injustice the Jewish population in Israel keeps poking at so as not to confront the worse crimes of the occupation. Like, go tell some Palestinian you're an oppressed Mizrachi. Oppressed my ass. It's like a Norwegian person complaining to a refugee from Eritrea that he got a five percent pay cut.

I told her she was falling into the simplistic trap of rating misery. She said it wasn't about ratings, but about distinguishing between blowing off steam and a legitimate complaint, that Mizrachi-Ashkenazi relationships hadn't been an issue for years, just nuance. I reminded her that she'd described the project as regional detective literature, and that locality was all about nuances. She said that even if we forgot for a moment about the scalpers of the so-called Mizrachi agenda, all those swamp

merchants, and extracted the truth, it was still too local. Euro-
peans and Americans want to read the same kind of literature
they themselves could have written by watching the news, she
said. The truth is, so do the Israelis. The rule is fairly simple,
she said. If it requires a footnote, the paragraph is better cut
altogether. She said she preferred a Tel Aviv–based detective
with a twist. I went outside to roam the streets. I went down to
Jaffa and then came back up. I haunted the neighborhoods like a
blackbird. One evening, Ronnit said, That's not what I meant
when I told you to dive into things rather than force them to reflect you. You're barely here. I said, I come back all the time, it's
my apartment. She said, In recent weeks it's been more like a
hotel room where you just spend the night. Her body overlapped
mine in bed. A drought year, a dry winter, but the nights were
freezing, cold lingered in the bones, I couldn't extract myself
from the depths of thoughts. She turned her back on me and
said in a hazy voice, Remember Laura's coming to Friday-night
dinner tomorrow. I lay there, unable to move.

I had no special feelings about Laura. In the past two
months I'd heard her and Ronnit having quiet, heated phone
conversations, interrupted by bursts of laughter, lowering toward complaint, rolling in mutual condolences. I didn't listen to
the contents, just the music of it, the thickening rhythm of tenderness and intimacy. I didn't ask how they'd met. Ever since
Ronnit lost interest in Shoshi and Dror, her only friends from
med school, I hadn't noticed any special relationships she'd
formed. I didn't know whether I should be happy about that.

I was almost late for the appointed time. By some mystery I
ended up in the Tel Kabir neighborhood, my feet wandering
south of Florentin, toward the edges of Herzl Street. I always felt
the city ended at that point, blurring and going out toward the
beginning of Herzl Street, that the street emerged out of architectural fog, a derelict industrial zone beyond which was a

demilitarized zone, somewhere inside of which, lost in uncultivated lands, was the Tel Kabir Institute of Pathology.

But in my distraction, I walked on. I crossed the street, the institute behind me. Under a canopy of holy ficus, the new neighborhood name was announced by a metal plaque: NEVE OFER. I whistled. Ugly projects over ugly projects. I went deeper, down Grinboim Street. It seemed the shopping center alongside the square had never known better days. From its early days it had stood there, half collapsing, deserted, the tracks of the ruin of years grooved through it. I sat beside the older men playing backgammon. They spoke Bukhori, cursing occasionally. I visited the grocery store. Like every capsule of global commerce, it was planned as an enclave that had nothing to do with the outside, its vanity exempt from the atrocities of geography.

I wandered some more. The neighborhood had been divided into housing complexes. I walked into the Zunz and Oholei Ya'akov Streets complex. A ring of projects, some of them skyscrapers by Tel Avivian standards, towering eight stories high. In one of the yards stood a man in a yarmulke. The clean January light was sullied by the sneaking of evening. He was chopping branches from an enormous, wild wormwood bush cleaving from the dry dirt. He asked with suspicion what I was doing there. You've been here for a few hours now, he said. I said I was thinking of moving. All around us, in nearly every building, signs offered apartments for sale. He said, This is an old-time family neighborhood. I asked, So what?

He continued to break down wormwood branches. I asked why he needed so much if the bush was growing right there in his yard. He said he was on the neighborhood board and was handing it out to tenants. A Jewish man, he said, must say a hundred blessings every day, and it's a challenge when most acts that require a blessing are forbidden on Shabbat. I said, That's the point of Shabbat, isn't it? He said, I'm handing it out so that they can say the blessing of fragrant trees every time they smell it.

I said I was surprised by the act of solidarity, so foreign to Tel Aviv. He said, I wish everyone was like that. If I wanted to move there, he said, I should know there was a wave of breaking and enterings and vandalism. I asked what the police did about it. He said, They can't be bothered to come down, even though some of the officers live around here. The place is improving, but years ago there were issues with drugs. A singing of "Shalom Alei-chem Malachei Hashalom" invaded the air, castrated by a lousy amplifying system. He said, We have a good synagogue, you're welcome to attend afternoon or evening prayer, we always have a minyan. I stood there, a little choked, stunned. I said, I think I'll come visit some more, make a decision. He said, You'll find cheap apartments here, everybody's moving to Holon.

I knew the name of my detective as soon as I left. Benny Ze-haviv. A police officer of Bukharan descent living in Tel Kabir. I knew he would need, along with the murder case he was investigating, to deal with the police's powerlessness in handling vandalism in his neighborhood. I knew Manny would be amused by the change made to his name, and I knew his signature would be T-shirts with smart-ass prints, and that he would never walk around bareheaded, but always wear a baseball cap.

The other details continued to preoccupy me over dinner. Laura was somewhat stocky, compact, just as Ronnit had described her, hunch shouldered and with nearly no neck, on top of which sat a beautiful skull, a round, childish face with deep eyes. She asked what I did for a living and asked to hear again, from my point of view, how Ronnit and I met, when I knew she was the one, and what it was like for me to move from being a sworn bachelor to living with a partner, what I would say were the most significant changes I had to make. The questions slid right off me. I answered succinctly. I was thinking about Benny Zeha-viv's history, what I had to find out, what made him a detective beyond a random choice of profession, even if I assumed he was sent to study the trade during service in the military police and then joined the civil police upon his honorable discharge. What was his burning?

I got up and left the table halfway through dinner. Ronnit had left chaos in the kitchen—pots and plates on the small table, uncapped bottles. I piled dishes in the sink and turned on the hot water. The window overlooking a naked Persian lilac exhibited a gut-invading night, so clear the stars hung in their cradles like knives. I noticed my hands in the stream of water were freezing. Ronnit had used up all the hot water without turning on the boiler again. I turned off the faucet. In the quiet that fell I heard a hint of Laura's voice. She was saying, You're right, he really doesn't care about anything except his own thoughts.

25

I told Betty I actually wanted to write a novel about a detective trapped in an endless investigation. He dies during it and is brought back to life to continue it. She clicked her tongue. She said she couldn't force me to write what she wanted, but what I wrote as part of our arrangement had a clear character. A few agents abroad had shown interest in the synopsis and outline we'd sent them. An Israeli publisher wanted to sign a contract. Betty said that Benny Zehaviv's character was a good solution. It had new facets to it, but also echoes of well-known detectives such as Columbo.

Anyway, I said, I think I stole the idea from Borges. Mechanically, she spoke that famous piece of nonsense written by one of those self-important witticists: Good artists copy, great artists steal. I said, In that case we're aiming for greatness.

Betty said, We ought to be careful with the Israeli market. We need to build you up as an authority in the detective-literature field. Those who remember you, remember you from your music-writing days. Maybe you should write some more newspaper reviews. We could pitch a monthly column about detective literature. I said I had no interest in that. I could go back to my favorite detective novels, formulate the thoughts that came to me when I read them, perhaps write a series of essays. She said, Not bad, but don't get carried away, you have to maintain the appearance of accessibility.

I wrote a long essay on Poe. I wrote about the way the poet creates in an attempt to rid himself of a weight of emotion that cannot be borne, some agency allowing him to get to know the emotional burden, be it animal or symbol. I wrote that Poe wished to be the master of his own consciousness, of the conditions under which it existed. A raven knocking on the door of a scholar's room, a doppelgänger sister placed in a coffin, a cat distorted to resemble a dead cat, a murderous monkey invading the home of a mother and daughter, a letter whose content could bring about disaster. I wrote about how each version of this dance birthed a new literary form. When the poet is successful in their signification, a detective story is born. The horror story stems from the sign's refusal to remain under control. When it is delayed or canceled, the poet experiences pleasure, and the melancholic poem takes on form.

I wrote an essay about H. P. Lovecraft's "The Call of Cthulhu and Other Weird Stories." I looked at the investigation models he used and the rationale behind them. Lovecraft declares in the beginning of the story that scientific progress would end up moving humanity backward, exposing the terror and madness implicit in the existence that human wisdom had dressed up with the thinnest layer of order. Our myths are veils intended to hide the truth of the monstrous, indecipherable nature of the gods from us, he states. Thus the plot is accordingly made up of three stories of investigation, each sloughing off the defenses provided by its predecessor, moving from knowledge to revelation. The first story unfurls an academic study following the marks and testimonies left behind by the ritual of Cthulhu, one of those other-dimensional alien beings whose proximity maddens the human brain. Next, a police plot is unfolded, in which a police officer investigates true ritualistic events, leading up to the confession of a sailor, the sole survivor of a research delegation. The ship he'd served on had deviated from its course and ended up on an island where the awakening of Cthulhu and its return to earth has altered the nature of reality. The delegation members lose their minds and drown.

I wrote an essay about Borges's story "Death and the Compass." A police interrogator is summoned to solve the murder of a Jewish Talmud and Kabbalah expert. He chooses to place the bulk of the investigation's weight on a sentence found in the scholar's typewriter, heralding the speaking of the first letter of God's sacred name. His supervisor believes it is a case of a robbery gone wrong. A criminal the interrogator had been chasing for years uses the detective's passion for mystery, revolving around a ritualistic murder, and spins it into a trap. I wrote that it could be interpreted as a parody of Poe's detective stories, as a warning of the danger in preferring a well-planned, well-structured plot over a simple occurrence, plagued with arbitrariness, offered by chance. But the story offers many clues that signify that the detective knows that he and the criminal are destined to quarrel forever, for entire lifetimes, that they are archetypes of a story, and that, given this knowledge, choosing interest over truth requires no justifications.

I do not remember such tranquil hours on the verge of bliss like those long hours I spent perusing these stories and carefully putting my thoughts into writing. I was alone again, my own master. The world, transmitted by taps of light and a tangle of shadows, by the needing of others, by their hidden claims, stood still. Betty rejected the essays. She thought they were too detailed and pedantic. She said she was disappointed, she'd thought I would come up with a catchy theory. I asked her, What about the measure of truth? She said we were living in the era of reproduction. No one had the energy to think, and it was enough for a statement to be made by a celebrity to make it true. I told her we should give up the endeavor and instead allow me to continue writing the book. I had a detective and a mystery, and I more or less understood the tone she was looking for. She said, Finally.

I didn't tell her I'd planned to write a fourth, more personal essay about the parasitic nature of detective literature, the forms it has taken over the years—the social novel, the psychological novel, the science fiction novel. I planned to write that those genres did not require a detective, but that the detective took on new volume and character when relying on them. I planned to write that to me the question wasn't why I liked detective literature so much, but what was it about a specific iteration of it, the one clinging to religious writing, that aligned with the map of my scars. I planned to write that I wanted to heal, but that I didn't know what my disease was or how to conjure the image of a healthy human. I planned to write that I was investigating something, and that the mechanism of investigation was growing more tangible to me than the knowledge it was intended to procure.

HOME

1

In the morning, Manny called to give me the information of the police officer who'd handled Dmitry Shtedler's complaint, as well as the phone number and address that Dmitry had left. The officer had said he was willing to talk to me. I was in the middle of packing, which had been cut short half an hour earlier anyway due to a siren. From my window, I saw three smoke stains blooming like meek flowers against the galvanized tin sheet of July. The thunder that preceded them sounded like banging on the other side of the sheet. My mother called to ask if everything was all right and if I was coming. I said, Yes, of course. She sounded as if she had a cold. I asked if she was sick. She said she wasn't sure, she'd felt a blockage in her nostril since the previous morning. Yaffa had already made her a doctor's appointment for the next day.

I called Yossef Magriso, the police officer. He didn't have much to add. He remembered the case because of Dmitry's dimensions. That's why he felt a duty to help him. The misery and helplessness of the soft giant saddened him. As a child, he saw the fathers of his generation growing weak, the men sitting outside grocery stores on overturned beer crates, getting drunk. Dmitry reminded him of them. Otherwise he wouldn't have even looked into it. But the story was odd, he said. Something about the man's niece wasn't right, he could tell, even though he didn't know her or anything about her. I asked if he could put his finger on what was wrong with her. He said that was it, exactly, he came to interview her when she returned, just to check on her and Dmitry. It wasn't a criminal case, he just wanted to show an interest. And something about the way she answered him, something in her voice, caught his attention. She wasn't lying, he said, but it was as if she questioned the truthfulness of her own answers without knowing why. I asked him if he was trained in questioning suspects. He asked why I wanted to know. I said he seemed to have good instincts. He said his dream was to be an interrogator.

2

We drove aimlessly, with no map. Ronnit said, Yes, north, turn here. Highway six? I asked. Why not, she said, let's try something new, something only ours. I said, I wonder how many other people are saying that exact same line right now. You don't have to spoil it, she said. She looked at the sky, its blue cleanliness, a frozen scream of blue. Ronnit said she liked these droughts, a silent, threatening December. I said we couldn't yet determine it was a drought, it could still rain in January. There's no winter here anyway, I said, in recent years it's been nothing but long storms. Ronnit said she was convinced of it, she could feel the purity of nights, she knew Hanukkah would be dry, and by Tu B'shvat it would be nothing but a frozen tundra. I told her she was describing her mood rather than the weather. She was silent. Then she said I always said the wrong thing.

The road ended in Nachal Iron, where we merged onto the normal asphalt system. That way, said Ronnit, pointing at the signs, Megiddo. I asked how we were supposed to get lost with all this signage. She asked if we were planning to get lost. I said yes, a little. A little was not what she wanted. She said she wanted adventure, wanted to put herself away for a few hours. I said that was the same thing. She said, Maybe for you.

We entered the archaeological site, walking into the delicate sketching of ruins, like contours, an outline, staircases about to rise from the layers of time resting here, thousands of years condensed in dust, walls stabilized, ancient rocks humming within them, rocks absorbing the lives of their dwellers. Can you imagine what this used to be, asked Ronnit, the chambers of the palace Solomon built, the ancient princesses that walked through here, came up here all bathed, the servants anointing their bodies with myrrh and frankincense? She spoke of the city residents who lived safely behind fortifications. A small plaque told the story of the Menashe tribe's failure to uproot the town, the human battalions that swept through it, the Canaanites and the Egyptians, the Assyrians and the Persians, the Bronze and Stone. Imagine, said Ronnit, just imagine the richness of the past. I said I was thinking more of the future of the place. She said, What, a doomsday war, Armaggedon? I said I wasn't thinking about that. She laughed. We took a seat in the shade, a battlefield of dust stretching before us.

Let's drive, she said. Let's drive more, maybe to Acre. I said, Always onwards. She said, Right now, yes. She bought a memento, a coin greened by generations of quiet oxygenation. In the car she held it in her hand, weighing it, balancing it. Near Acre she burst into tears. I didn't pull over. I drove into town, toward the sea, the wall. She cried quietly, without interrupting my driving. She said she couldn't stop thinking about the girl from that morning. It was at least the tenth apartment she'd checked. It sounded promising. She set an hour and arrived on time. The tenant opened the door quizzically. She said the apartment wasn't on the market and slammed the door. I found a parking spot. We got out. A breeze rose from the sea, cutting through the bones. She wiped her eyes with a tissue I offered. She said she was sorry, I said it was all right, this was why we were going away, wasn't it? She'd stayed with me for two weeks, tense, closed off. Every hand I offered was returned empty. She slept on the pull-out couch in my living room, apologizing intermittently. It was just an accumulation of bad luck.

Let's get some coffee, I told her. What good will coffee do? she said. I said at least we'd get out of the wind. In spite of the wall, the tiled quad was exposed. Her lips trembled, on the verge of turning blue. Hold me, she said. I put a clumsy arm around her. Heat glowed from her body, trickling into mine. She said, You're even colder than I am. We walked hunched toward the alleys of the Old City. She wrapped her hands around the teacup. With sudden cheer, she said, Let's keep going. Where, I asked, the border with Lebanon? She said, Let's cross it, let's steal through it, go through Beirut, buy some cherries, go to Syria, stop in Damascus, buy some silk, silk and lace, there's got to be something more. More than what? I asked. More than—she gestured all around her—more than this. I said, What, more than Acre, more than the wild waves of the sea, more than the whisper of water creatures, more than the ball of the sun falling into the water, cooling like a furnace through the night? She smiled. You understand me, she said, we're speaking the same language. I looked away.

When we got back in the car, she said, Let's go home. Home, I said. She said yes. She made herself comfortable, kicking off her shoes. Her toenails were painted pale purple. She rested her feet on the dashboard. The heating in the car made my face hot. Nice shade, I said. She looked at it. She said, Shoshi gave me this nail polish, she thinks it's classy. I shrugged. She said, Don't worry, I haven't talked to her lately. Cities numb in their turbidity passed by us, flocks of birds speeding up in their migration. Ronnit said, Get off at this intersection. Where to? I said. She said, Netanya Forest. We stopped again in an oak thicket. The knowledge reserved for trees, deceit of the ages, moved in its own flow, beaming around us. We were the only ones there. Ronnit pressed her clothes against her body, crossed her arms, detached. A strip of darkness had already begun stretching near the horizon. Ronnit said, Look at their roots, how they bend the dirt, how they reach in stubbornly. I said it made me feel sick to think of how terrifying this life is, how tyrannical, and anyway we were both too cold. She said, We should come back in February or March and see the *ezovion* blossom eruptions. She said

she asked herself what it meant to be alone, completely separate, if she built a shed or a tent and lived here. I told her she
wasn't alone. And I don't want to be, she said, I never want to be
alone. It's the same shade, she said back in the car. What shade?
I said. She said, The shade of the nail polish Shoshi gave me, it's
supposed to be lavender. Sure, I said, why not? I asked her if she
was serious when she referred to my apartment as home. She
said, Yes. She asked if it didn't feel like a home to me. I said, I
don't dare. She said, But it's your apartment, isn't it? I said, Still.
She asked, So where is your home? I said, Maybe I don't need
one. She said it was odd that she felt more at home in my place.

I spent the evening in my study, repeatedly going over the details of the murder case, taking down notes, possible plotlines,
cracks in the case through which involuntary information shards
peeked out, the blades of reality in the apertures of the question.
I blunted at the speed of bluntness, my eyes growing heavier. I
rested my head on the table. Ronnit pulled me from my slumber.
She touched my shoulder. I followed her into the bedroom. She'd
changed my sheets. Tiredness evaporated, replaced by this thin
fear. Later, as I lay there, satisfied, sunk into flesh, I asked again
if she was serious. About what? she asked, her fingers still fanning the flames of the skin. If this was her home, I said, if she
wanted to move in with me.

3

Mom, said Tahel, can I go visit Uncle Elish in his new home?

It isn't his new home, her mother answered, he's just a temporary tenant. That's all I need, for him to move into this neighborhood.

Why are you talking like that? said Grandma Zehava.

I don't like the idea of him hanging around here, especially now.

He can help with the kids.

Mom snorted. Give me a break, she said.

He'll come over for dinner later tonight, said Grandma.

Tahel already knew that. She was eavesdropping on the argument between her mother and grandmother. Her grandmother insisted on making a fancy meal, which forced her mother to leave work early and take her grocery shopping. Even though Grandma said she shouldn't bother because she could take the number 1 bus, she'd spotted a stop right outside the neighborhood. And who's going to help you carry the groceries? asked her mother. The stop is at least a kilometer away. Some planning, building a neighborhood and not bothering to offer residents any public transportation.

Her mother stood beside her grandmother in the kitchen. They were immersed in the quiet of cooking, a silent conversation Tahel had been witnessing since she was a small child. When those two start cooking, she thought, they don't need words. She gave her brain the shape of a net lowering and tightening around her mother's brain, crushing her objections. Say yes, she ordered, don't resist me.

What will you do there? her mother asked while vigorously chopping one vegetable or another.

I want to see where he lives.

It's dangerous to walk all that way right now, there could be a Red Color siren any minute. Beats me why he came here, and that idiot Zalman helped him without even asking me first.

I could call Yalon and ask his father to drive him over and pick me up on the way.

What does Yalon have to do with your uncle? her mother asked.

He's curious too. I told him Elish writes books.

On one condition, that you and Elish come back here for dinner at—

Can Oshri come too? asked Tahel.

What, you think your uncle's a monkey at the zoo? said Grandma Zehava.

Where is Oshri? asked her mother.

He's in his room, playing computer games.

Her mother sighed. She wiped her hand on her apron and pulled Tahel's cell phone from her pocket. She dialed Elish's number. No, it's me, Yaffa, she said. She listened. All right, she said. Tahel wants to come over. *Dir balak* if you keep her too long and don't make it to dinner on time.

She handed Tahel the phone. You're going to give it back to me when you get home, she said.

So annoying, thought Tahel, loosening the thought net's grip. At least, she thought, she was getting better at controlling people remotely. She used to not be able to move her mother an inch.

In her fervor, Tahel didn't say goodbye to Yalon's father. The man scared her anyway, the weight of his body, his scheming eyes, questions the purpose of which she could never figure out, feeling herself failing because she couldn't guess his intentions and offer the answers he wanted to hear or to even make him persist in listening to them. Other matters distracted him constantly, as if he were listening to several voices requiring attention all at once. She imagined his insides. Thick darkness filling his barrel-like body, inside of which screamed the creatures he'd swallowed over the years. She didn't like him and didn't understand what her father saw in him, talking about him with such admiration and recounting pointless exchanges they had at synagogue during the kiddush. Oshri told her that after prayer time a table was set in the synagogue yard, covered with food, *hamin* and candy, which he didn't like, except for the hard-boiled egg, already brown, then made browner by being rolled in some kind of spice. Cumin, Grandma Zehava told her when she asked.

Elish stood at the door, waiting. She rushed over, beating Yalon and Oshri, but when she got there, she paused awkwardly, a clumsiness taking hold of her body, which contained a knowledge that differed from her desires, and was blocked. Elish smiled, noticing nothing. He let her pass. She looked around her, at the Dadons' wedding pictures hung in flashy gold frames, a wrinkled baby held in its mother's arms. She looked at the pictures affixed to the refrigerator door with magnets. Every moment of the child's life, documented.

The living room is tastefully furnished, she thought. The red upholstery of the armchair and the green upholstery of the sofa, what did they have to teach her? Benny Zehaviv could deduce a lot from the living quarters of the people he questioned. All she could say right now was that the Dadons were typical Sderot residents. The mother probably tended toward whimsy, which she allowed herself to express only in the clothes she picked for her daughter and the shades she chose for the furniture. She had to ask Elish how she could improve that skill. She had a lot of work ahead of her. Oof, she muttered.

Yalon asked if she was finished wandering and sniffing around.

What? she said. Then she realized Oshri and Yalon were sitting on barstools at the wooden counter, drinking juice out of glasses, and conducting a quiet discussion with Elish. A third glass waited on the counter, full of whispering Coke, ice cubes floating inside. She said, We've got no time to waste, let's go see Kalanit.

Oshri laughed.

What are you laughing about?

Yalon said, We made a bet about the first thing you'd say.

So? she said.

So Oshri guessed right, said Elish.

And what did you say? she asked Yalon.

That you'd tell Elish about the email we wrote to Hannah Todros.

Oh, she said.

Elish gestured for her to join them. We need to set some rules, he said.

Tahel tightened her lips.

Elish said, I have no idea where this investigation is going to lead. But you do nothing without letting me know first. Get it, Tahel?

She nodded. There was a severity to Elish's face she'd never seen before. His entire skinny form was focused, a flame ignited in him, and he was neither old nor young, but a kind of foreign visitor whose age didn't matter. Who's "you"? she asked.

TYO Investigations Inc., said Oshri.

Tahel looked at him and Yalon. Two traitors, she thought.

4

On the way to Kuti Asor's house, some of the ice gathered in Tahel's limbs melted. I wasn't sorry for putting her in her place. There was an abrasion of a different sorrow. At any rate, her enthusiasm returned. She asked if I thought they'd acted wisely. I said I was impressed with their initiative. Yalon said Hannah Todros answered his email and said she'd love to lend them books. How come you didn't tell me? Tahel yelled. Then she added, I told you, I told you. In the rearview mirror I saw Oshri place his two small hands on his ears and turn to look out the car window with a tight smile. Yalon's body leaned toward Tahel's when he handed her his phone. I'm writing her, said Tahel, that we're coming tomorrow. Can you take us to her place tomorrow? she asked. I said we would need her mother's permission. She said to leave that to her.

Mrs. Asor's commanding appearance matched her voice. Shriveled and vital at once, tall of stature even at her age, careful footsteps. Sima Shaubi wouldn't stop thanking me. Her cheeks jiggled and the brightness of her facial skin intensified as she spoke. She said she was so lucky I was there. Little Asor's friend told her I was a private detective and that I had important friends in the Tel Aviv police. Tahel turned her face away from me.

I said we should get to the interview. I placed my tape recorder on the living room table. Come, children, you too, Sima, we'll go out to the porch, said Kuti. I thanked her with a nod. Tahel said she wanted to stay, that her mother said they had to stay inside the house. Kuti said they could go to Yalon's room if they wanted, or down to the bomb shelter.

Kalanit was less detached than in the video taken a week prior. The traces of shock had sunk into the subcutaneous mask of muscle and nerve, apparent only in sudden twitches, a winking, a flinching. I asked how she was feeling. She said she was better, that she hoped to forget about it all as soon as possible. I asked why. She said what good would it do, something happened that she couldn't explain and she didn't want to lose her mind. I asked what she was studying at Ben-Gurion University. She said social work. I asked what she would advise a patient in her condition. She said it depended on the patient's personality. If she was like her, she would recommend the same thing. She knew this because as a girl she once fell in love with a married man who didn't even notice her and she almost went insane. She said, If you fixate on things you can't control, you can get lost. I said we still didn't know for sure if this was the case here.

Kalanit said she remembered nothing, she was just gaining back the sensations she felt during her conversation with her mother when she got off the bus and checked her phone's calendar. How her body drained out, how she moved away from herself. She said she could feel the breaking of some coil that held her in place, then felt herself being dropped, tossed, without a grip. I told her I'd be lying if I said I knew what she meant, that I could only guess the terror, compare it to the terrors I knew from personal experience. She said she could tell I wasn't the panicking type. I told her she had no idea how wrong she was.

I asked her what she remembered of the bus ride. She said a soldier sat in front of her, and the smell of *amba* from his falafel made her feel sick. I asked about other passengers, and she said they weren't sharp in her mind. Someone in the next aisle kept asking what they should do if a siren sounded. There was also a group of men in Orthodox clothing. I asked about the driver. She said, What about him? I gave him a twenty-shekel bill, he gave me change and a ticket. Then she laughed briefly. I understood what Yossef Magriso was talking about. Her answers weren't concrete in her mouth, as if they were spoken from the air near her lips, as if she were listening to them, same as I was.

I asked if she remembered the times in her childhood when she was nearly kidnapped. She wondered how I knew about that. A muscle twitched near her eye. She blinked hard. I told her Sima told me. She said she didn't remember, she was too young, she only remembered what her mother told her, so she had images in her mind. I asked what the kidnapper looked like when she imagined the scene. She said, He looks . . . And then, as if a bulb lit up inside her, as if she'd grasped something, she fell silent. He looked like what? I asked. She said, I don't know, I can only see a shadow when I think about him. She lowered her eyes and scratched her arm. The mosquitoes here, she said, they're quiet but they've got a hell of a poisonous bite. You can't even hear them, then you get up all swollen from bites.

I told her the particular species common in Sderot was a product of genetic enhancement, a military development, it was how the state implanted chemical geolocation compounds in civilians' minds. They should implant them in the Palestinians, damn them, she said. I said the Palestinians' water's been loaded with the stuff for a long time. She looked at me with wonder. I said Sima also mentioned people who would come to talk to her at school. She must remember that. She said she didn't, but there was a smell. A smell? I asked. Yes, she said, they all had the same smell, she didn't recognize it then, but now she was sure, a smell that filled the mouth, lavender, like in soaps and air fresheners, their clothes emitted the sweet, oily scent of laven– She cut herself off. What's wrong? I asked. Her lips trembled. With an effort, she said, Mom, Mom. Sima, I called out, Sima. The house's inhabitants hurried over from both sides of the house, as if they'd been waiting to pounce. Sima came from the porch, Kuti treading behind. From the other side, Tahel, Oshri, and

Yalon rushed over, almost running. What happened, what happened? Tahel asked first.

Sima held Kalanit. I said, She needs to see a professional. A professional? said Sima. A psychologist, said Kuti. We'll take her to the mental health clinic tomorrow. She left the mother to comfort her daughter alone and followed us out of the room. She said, She's hiding things, the girl. I nodded. The children's eyes wandered from Kuti to me and back. Yesterday, Kuti said, early in the morning, I looked out the window and saw her talking to a strange man in the yard. Later, when I asked her who she was talking to, she said no one, that she was just sitting alone, trying to relax.

5

What did you find out? asked Tahel. Elish said nothing. He steered them to the car. Kalanit's expression and the mysterious clue Kuti had provided translated into a stinging in Tahel's palms. Good, she thought, we're getting somewhere.

She was afraid, Oshri said. What was she afraid of?

Yalon said, I told you, that's what happens when the memories start coming back.

And who was that man she was talking to? asked Tahel.

Government agent, one hundred percent.

Which government, Israel's? asked Tahel.

In the movies they're always collaborating with them.

With who? asked Oshri.

With the aliens.

But this isn't a movie.

Exactly, said Elish, we're not in a movie, so let's keep going slowly, carefully.

But tell me what you found out, said Tahel.

Elish said, Not much, a few details, a lot of guesses and conjectures.

Tell us what, said Tahel.

Elish said, I'll elaborate when there's something to elaborate about. In the meantime, we just need to listen to the possibilities, the details, follow the patterns that form. Jumping to conclusions won't help.

Silence fell over Tahel, a muffling blanket of silence. The stinging in her palms faded, then extinguished. Elish pulled up

near Yalon's house. Even against the evening, the silencing of
the streets, the marble expanses of the entrance, the staircase,
the statues imported from China, the wooden door beaming in
wait, were out of place. This similarity to a fortress, thought Tahel, is all wrong, meant for show. When she compared her house
and Yalon's in her mind, the human dimensions of the house her
mother built grew clearer. She wanted to get there already, to get
out of the car, where the air had run out, to go into her temporary safe room.

Are you all right, Tahel? asked Elish when they got out. She
looked at him. There was a strangeness in him again, shifting
from hardness to softness, flickering alternately, glowing and
darkening. She swallowed. Yes, fine, she said.

We'll go to your teacher's house tomorrow, said Elish. You'll
see, we'll slowly gather the evidence.

She nodded and passed him by. At the entrance, Oshri's hand
ran against hers. She flinched. He looked at her alertly, searching for something. Then his lips stretched into a tight smile. He
shook his head. The expression of kindness he wore—she wanted
to hug him. She said, We have to be patient.

Their mother was already circling the table, setting forks
and knives. Into the shower, both of you, she said. And don't linger. We haven't had a siren in a few hours. From her spot on the
living room sofa, Grandma Zehava said, There are bad battles
going on in Gaza.

Tahel stood in front of the mirror, looking at herself. Did she
look right? She leaned closer to the surface, which covered with
steam again. She found no sign of those metamorphoses. Her
throat was still full. She grabbed a towel and dried her hair.

Mom, she said, can I go visit Hannah Todros tomorrow?

Hannah who? said her mother. She passed the salads along.
Elish's expression gave away nothing. He looked over at Grandma
Zehava, her fatigued posture in the chair, her hands gripping

the edge of the table to support her body as she worked hard to get up.

Sit, Mom, said Elish, I'll help Yaffa.

Sit, sit, her mother said, I can handle everything fine.

I'm not Bobby, Elish said, don't protect my honor.

I said I can handle it, said Yaffa.

Hannah, said Tahel, my literature teacher.

Her mother was halfway to the kitchen counter, where the remaining salad bowls were arranged in a row. She stopped and turned to face them.

Elish said, The two of you are overdoing it with the amounts again.

Zalman will be back tomorrow, said Grandma Zehava, he needs something to eat.

Yes, said Elish, like you're not going to make lunch too.

Who has the time for that? said her mother. Mom has a doctor's appointment.

I'll drive her, said Elish.

Her mother nodded. She said, What are you up to in your literature teacher's house?

Tahel said, Yalon suggested it. We've run out of books to read and the library's closed.

I haven't seen you reading a book in weeks, said her mother.

Elish said, I wish I'd known, I would have brought some books with me.

She widened her eyes reproachfully at him. Her mother sat back down. Oshri was already ripping off pieces of bread and loading them with fried eggplant and egg salad, uninterested in the conversation.

You're so hungry, their mother said. What did you do all day?

Oshri answered with his mouth full, Starve.

Tahel said, I couldn't be bothered to read, but now it looks like this war isn't going to end.

Her mother said, It's an operation. They're talking about a cease-fire.

Elish said, No one really wants a cease-fire. It's a ruse on both sides. Hamas wants to arm itself and organize, and Israel wants to recruit global support, so it's making the gesture.

When will they stop shooting at us? said Oshri. Then he hummed, Red Color, Red Color, before stuffing another piece of *matbukha*-soaked bread into his mouth. Tahel looked at it. Like part of a lacerated body, she thought.

Their mother said, Ask your uncle, he's on their side.

All right, said Elish. Right now we have something more important to discuss. Tahel's reading culture.

I want books too, said Oshri, his voice choked from chewing. Their mother laughed. She took hold of a napkin and cleaned, with a near caress, the stains on both sides of his mouth. She said, You don't have to copy your sister.

I'll drive her, said Elish.

Yalon's coming too.

You've become a car service, said their mother. Since when are you so generous?

Yaffa, enough, said Grandma Zehava, can't you see he's making an effort?

No, said their mother, he always has a secret motive.

She shot Tahel a calculating glare. Tahel felt the eyes searching inside her. She thought back, as hard as she could, Let me, let me, let me.

Oshri said, Mom, can I take the entrée by myself?

Their mother averted her eyes. I'll serve you, she said. When you do it yourself, the counter gets covered in sauce. When she returned her eyes to Tahel, they'd thawed a touch. Did Hannah say you could come? she asked.

Tahel whispered, Let me.

Their mother said, Fine, fine, but under one condition: you

read the books, not turn them into a reason to hang out at his place. She pointed at Elish, her voice hardening still.

Oh, come on, Yaffa, what do you think of your brother? said Grandma Zehava. Elish, *aybeh*, what can I get you? She stood up with an effort, holding on to the back of her chair for support.

6

I lay on the sofa in the Dadon family living room. A dwindling moon stood in the window, and not far away a lake gushed from the ground, a pool of viscous fluid, preparing its quiet life for a purpose I could not imagine. The eucalyptus thicket on its other side may have emitted its spiciness. The leaves may have rustled. If they did, the whisper of the air-conditioning overpowered it. I told myself, I'm in Sderot, lying on a sofa, in a neighborhood on the banks of an artificial lake. But the words echoed in the hollow space of my head, pushed off the walls of the skull toward some interior, hovering space. They had no meanings forcing them to sink, or no being to implement them, to recognize their weight and demand in words. I, who was there, stood on the outside. There was the creature, sprawl-limbed on the sofa, there were the words, there were their meanings. But between one existence and the next, an abyss the thickness of a hair opened up, a narrow desolation, impossible to traverse.

Sometimes I was almost convinced there was some international conspiracy preventing me from being who I was; shards of that lost person emerged in dreams, in involuntary recollections, in moments when the present evaporated. Sometimes I woke up from sleeping and felt as if I'd been displaced to a desert island. I knew this feeling in its greatest intensity when I wrote the sixth book in the Benny Zehaviv series. The sturdiness of structure loosened. I could no longer grasp the hidden force carrying me from one sentence to the next, or how in the shift between them, an illusion of reality, of a world, of standing

on the threshold of life, which I constantly searched for in reading, was born.

I thought Ronnit would understand. Perhaps because she
witnessed the birth of the series, because I shared the chal-
lenges with her and she encouraged me, as was her wont, I asked
that she also witness its dying breaths. She came and brought
Akiva with her. In the first year and a half of his life she only
gave me brief updates, never letting me meet him, sending some
pictures instead. Then all of a sudden she returned of her own
volition, announcing she was coming to visit me along with her
son. There was no distance between him and me from the first.
As if my gaze, lingering over his photos, had passed through to
him and he was looking back at me the whole time. He was already saying a few words. I practiced saying my name along with
him. He said, Eyish, Eyish. Ronnit said he kept singsonging the
name at home later and David had no idea of the meaning of
those syllables his son was obsessed with. So we set some dates,
an order, rules of conduct.

We sat sometime, somewhere, a non-intense season hovered
over the Tel Aviv skies. Akiva, two and a half years of age, yearning to run around. I ran around with him. Once in a while I would
pick him up and he would struggle in my embrace, that same
grip we hope our children never desire to be free of, never rush
out of to the disappearance of years, and against which they always rebel, always acquiescing to the ticking of the clock.

I told Ronnit. She said, But it's you, what are you so surprised about? I asked if she could elaborate. She said, What
good would it do? I've told you a thousand times but you didn't
listen. I said, Maybe this time I'm ready. She said, Everyone I've
ever wanted you to be, you've been, but you haven't really been,
understand? I nodded. She said, You aren't now, either, you're
only pretending to understand. Of course she was wrong. At the
Dadon home, the opulence of which was much tackier than the
restrained splendor that Yaffa had imposed on her home, as if

financial means acted in opposition to a sense of moderation, I put on my earphones. The violin in the Sonata for E Minor curved into the phone's speakers, the piano hammers dimpled their dimples in the darkness that followed. The sensation slowly died down. I fell back into myself, into the papier-mâché mold that is Elish Ben Zaken, whose name I can utter and know, with some certainty, sufficient certainty, that it is my own.

annah's attempts to make the living room look warm and inviting were apparent in the positioning of every throw pillow, in the arrangement of children's pictures along the wall, the two children in identical frames, a boy and a girl, smiling innocently. When she caught me training my eyes on the photos, she said, They're in summer camp right now, in Hungary, the donation of a wealthy Jew. So, she told Tahel and Yalon, sweethearts, would you like something to drink? Maybe a Coke, said Tahel. Why maybe? said Hannah. Either a Coke or not a Coke, what's with your generation and the word "maybe"? I said, Same thing our generation had with the word "like." I've never used that expression of flattery, said Hannah. The word "flattery" stuck with me for some reason. In the morning I'd called Dmitry Shtedler's number for the third time. The number you have dialed is not available right now. I called the cell company, said I was from the dentist's office and needed to remind him of his appointment next week. They said he'd stopped his bank payment orders, and his account was currently suspended.

Yalon said, So, yes, Coke, Coke Zero if you've got it. Tahel said, with the same breath, How can I know what you have if you don't tell me? Their sentences blended into each other like this: So yes / how can I / Zero if / know what / you've / you have you don't tell me. Hannah smiled affectionately. They sipped from their glasses. When will this Coke craze end? said Hannah. Yalon said, In six hundred comma three zero zero four years. Tahel said, It won't, Coke keeps changing. Yalon said, That's what I based my calculation on, how many years before every possible combination is found, so that it's still Coke. Hannah stared at them. She said, Why don't you put this much thought into what we learn in class? Yalon said, We try, but . . . You like to read other things, said Hannah. I'm not surprised about you, all your essays are about science fiction, and I asked your mother at the parent-teacher conference and she told me you're crazy about those books. Yalon nodded hard. He said, I like Roger Zelazny, and smiled, his braces shining against the row of teeth yellowing with Coke. I looked at him with slight shock. But you, Hannah asked Tahel, what do you read? Tahel said, *Prydain, Encyclopedia Brown, Harriet the Spy, The Famous Five, The Three Investigators, Sherlock Holmes, Benny Zehaviv. Benny Zehaviv*, Hannah said quizzically, where do I know that name from? She looked at me, and a flash of recognition ignited in her expression. Of course, of course, you wrote a book report about that series. So this is the famous uncle.

I was going to answer when the door opened. A tall, sweaty man walked in, his shorts held by a belt underneath a small paunch. Good evening, he told the air. Good evening, Tahel and Yalon answered in unison. Levy, said Hannah, these are the children who wrote me. Apparently I've had two curious students in my class this whole time and I never even knew it. Well, said Levy, you've only had them in class for a year. Still, still, said Hannah, I complain so much about today's youth and its lack of interest in the world.

I followed the look of ownership Levy ran over the living room and every part of the house visible from his spot near the doorway, as if making sure everything was where it ought to be, everything to his satisfaction. I got up and walked over, offering my hand for a shake. I tightened my fingers as much as possible around his damp hand. He nodded with appreciation. Who are you? he asked. His voice searched for the low frequencies. I said I was Tahel's uncle. He glanced at the living room table. Coke, he said. You feel like something stronger? I winked at Tahel when nobody noticed. She stuck to the plan. She said, Can we maybe go see the books? Yalon jumped up as well. Of course, said Hannah, such enthusiasm.

The beer he gave me had a hoppy spine and was surrounded by a sweet flesh of barley. Good, isn't it? he said. The owner of the liquor store ordered it especially for him, it turned out. He bought it in cases. I asked about his last name. It's a rare name, I said. He said, Yes, it's Portuguese. The story is we were a family of conversos that returned to Judaism. Marranos, I said, like Spinoza. He asked what I did for a living. I told him I wrote books. And you? I asked. He said, Can one make a living writing books? That depends, I said. He said he was a member of the Metropolitan Bus Company. I tapped my bottle on the table. Which line do you drive? I said with a little excitement. I have two regular lines out of Beersheba, he said, three five three and four hundred and seventy. No, I said, it can't be. What? he said. I just love coincidences, I said. He fidgeted on the sofa. What coincidence? A little over a week ago, a relative of mine took the three five three bus and something happened to her. What? he said. We're very professional. I said, No, God forbid, nothing like that, it's just that she's having trouble talking about it. What time did she go? he asked. I said she took the bus that left Beersheba at four o'clock. *Walla*, he said, that's my bus. But everything's always organized on my bus, I don't allow any funny business, if any passenger starts acting out, I pull over and kick them off. I took out my phone and showed him the portrait of Kalanit that Tahel and Yalon took. With the same excitement, I said, But, like, do you remember her? He said, If my wife heard you using that word, she wouldn't leave you alone. And you're a writer. I said, Which word? You mean "like." Yeah, he said, she'd, like, be annoyed. He chuckled to himself. You're all right, he said. He looked at the portrait and shook his head. Then his finger moved on the screen, swiping through the pictures. Is that your son? he asked. Akiva was sitting on the lip of a round red planter, domesticated pansies whispering around him, his hands gathered between his knees, his smile aimed at the camera, flickering on the verge of embarrassment. At the edge of the frame, the decorations on his yarmulke, which I asked him to remove, caught a wild light. I said no, I didn't have any kids, that he was the son of my ex-girlfriend. He looked at me questioningly. Then he said, The best ones get away. I asked if he was speaking from experience. He said, Experience is the father of wisdom. I said, Question is, which experience makes you wisest? He said, Wise men never stop learning. I said those were the men I liked. He laughed. He said the experienced and the learned might be the same men. I said, Possibly. He told me about a classmate of his that he was in love with all through high school. They both grew up in Kiryat Gat and never left the area. I'm here in Netivot and she's in Sderot. Well, was. She practically ran away. From you? I asked. No, he said, from Israel. She ran away with that architect who planned the lake. You must have heard of the lake.

I told him I was living in that neighborhood, temporarily, I was subletting an apartment, my sister built a house there. He said it was an awesome development, that he didn't believe it would actually be built. He and his wife had debated when the lake enterprise was first announced, but on the other hand, there was rezoning happening in Netivot. He asked for Heftzi's advice because she knew all about what was going on in the city's planning and engineering departments. Heftzi? I asked. Yes, he said, Heftzi Columbus, the girl he used to be in love with until he met Hannah, his beloved wife, during military service. Anyway, Heftzi insinuated that he shouldn't be tempted by the Sderot development. She said, he reported, that it was still just a promise and who knew if it would be fulfilled. Then she and the architect ran away together, and Hannah and I were grateful for our luck. We were very surprised when talk didn't stop, and when they initiated the project and actually executed the plans.

I said maybe Heftzi had other motives. He said that wasn't it. That later a corruption affair in City Hall came out. Money laundering. The former mayor Yoram Bitton, who approved the development, was under investigation. Maybe that's what she was afraid of, that we would lose our money.

He looked at my phone again, swiping through the pictures. He looks like a lovely boy, he said, what's his name? Akiva, I said. It really is an Orthodox name, he said. He showed me the picture his finger was lingering over. The viewfinder froze Akiva mid-jump, the fringes of his tallit flying in all four directions of the wind. There was an expression of elation on his face, like a Breslov Hassid in the fervor of devotion. Levy continued to look through my photos. Is that her? he asked. In the picture Ronnit was stooping, Akiva's head leaning against her shoulder. Yes, I said, Ronnit. Lots of women turn to religion after a difficult breakup, he said. He added he'd read a study about it in the newspaper. The phone beeped. You got a message from Yaffa, he said. The screen read, Is everything all right? Yes, I wrote, why? Yaffa wrote, Because there are sirens here. All is quiet in Netivot, I wrote back. She wrote, Stay there until I text you that it's safe to come back. I wrote, No problem.

I pulled Kalanit's portrait from the phone again and showed it to Levy. I asked if he was certain he didn't remember a thing. He asked what happened. I said, She won't tell. Her mother is worried. He said, With all the rockets and the missiles, who's worried about something that happened on a bus? I said, Well, they are.

Judging by the covers of the books Hannah presented to them, Tahel knew she wouldn't want to read them. Yalon didn't show much interest, either.

I imagined as much, said Hannah. What about these, though I assume you've already read them? She presented the first book in a series recounting the tales and struggles of a young wizard.

Too many holes, said Yalon.

Tahel thought, What's going on in the living room, what's Elish talking to Levy about, what's Levy telling him?

Holes? asked Hannah.

I don't like books that make things up.

Don't all books make things up? asked Hannah.

Their conversation hovered on the edge of Tahel's hearing. She aimed her inner attentiveness farther away. Perhaps one of the men would raise his voice and she would catch the drift of the other conversation.

Yes, said Yalon, but some books make things up every few pages just to create tension and you can tell the writers didn't think it through.

Oh, said Hannah, that's what happens in imaginary books. When books deal with reality, they usually have a strong internal logic. Am I right, Tahel? she asked.

Tahel was snatched back into their conversation. Her attentiveness, that long silver tentacle she'd sent forth to probe, was cut off. She said, That depends. The Benny Zehaviv books are based on research.

I'll have to read those at some point, said Hannah. You two are tough customers.

They both smiled in unison, mechanically. Yalon's dimple and braces answered hers.

Last chance, she said. She pointed at a box shoved under a table and asked Yalon to pull it out. Yalon looked at the titles of the books inside it with cries of excitement. He piled them before him. Tahel glanced at the names: *The Knight of the Swords*, *Witch World*, *Hed's Trilogy*, *Ubik*, *The Man in the High Castle*. Hannah picked up the last one. A new translation was recently published, she said. I didn't know we had the old one.

Far in the distance, the living room was quiet. Tahel could just barely detect the pinging of Elish's phone, an incoming text message. Probably her mother, she thought, that pest. She counted two more messages.

Tahel, said Hannah. Does anything appeal to you?

Tahel said, I'll take *The Man in the High Castle*. Is it good for my age?

They sat in an empty, covered shopping center Elish had taken them to. He said, Your mother asked that we wait a little while until they find out if more missiles are going to fall.

Yalon said, But Netivot is less safe.

What do you want to drink? asked Elish.

Tahel was pulled out of her wandering thoughts again.

Are you hungry? he asked.

No, she said. Nothing. So do we have any new leads?

Not really.

What happened in your conversation? You must have found out something. Can I guess?

As far as Levy's concerned, nothing unusual happened. He doesn't remember Kalanit.

So that's it? she asked.

Like I said, nothing much. But we have to wait and see.

What about the man Kalanit talked to? asked Yalon.

That seems to be our only current lead.

So you didn't find out anything, said Tahel.

Nothing of importance at the moment, said Elish.

You should get a milkshake too, Yalon said, mine is really good.

Still, still, said Tahel.

Elish said nothing. Tahel looked him over. She would have activated her mind control powers had she not been confident it wouldn't work on him. To activate them, she had to grasp a bit of the presence nucleus of those under her control. With a hidden sense she could imagine the presence of her father, her mother, Oshri, Grandma Zehava, Yalon, the other kids in her class, even Elinoar and Racheli, in spite of their distance. But not Elish. Anger rose in her. He's evading it too. It's as if he knows where his nucleus is and he's hiding it, like the wizard that concealed his power in the form of a needle in a bird's egg in that fairy tale she read. She said, How can I learn if you won't show me how you investigate?

Yalon took a long pull on his milkshake. The liquid gurgled, the straw choking.

Enough already, she said, why are you still drinking from a straw at your age?

Elish said, First you have to learn to be patient. You're too short-tempered, you never wait.

Wait for what? If I don't know what I'm waiting for, how am I supposed to wait?

When you look at running water, when you turn your eyes to the sky and see clouds, any phenomenon that seemingly has no order to it, the human brain tries to force a pattern. And then you see trembling images in the water, shapes forming in clouds.

What's that got to do with anything? she said.

Elish said, Pay attention. If you don't learn to suspect this natural tendency, you'll get nowhere.

How do you learn? asked Yalon.

How do you learn? asked Tahel.

Their questions stacked on top of each other, impossible to distinguish source from echo. The single question was charged with electricity.

Elish said, You empty your consciousness and let things come.

But I don't understand, said Tahel.

It means you must never jump to conclusions. Imagine your brain is a clean slate. And once in a while, a fact you hear, something you learn, jots down a line, a dot. You don't rush to complete these marks to form a familiar shape. You examine them up close and from a distance, you try different points of view, sneak looks from the corners of your eyes, check in the dark, check in the light, and all of a sudden it happens, you grasp the correct picture among the deceptions.

How can I be sure I'm not just trying to see something that isn't there?

When it happens to you, said Elish, there will be no room for doubt. You'll know.

9

When we were saying goodbye, Hannah told me that her friend was an avid reader of my literature. I'm not a fan of people referring to novels that are the result of careful, commercial planning as literature. But that was Betty Stein's plan all along. She pulled some strings and got a well-known film critic she occasionally hired as a freelance editor to promote the publication of my first novel with shameless praise. Real literary work, he wrote, using the detective structure. Betty beamed. The review set the tone for the ones that followed. Betty said that if I'd only maintained my connections in academia, I would have won an important prize too. She didn't talk up the novels' literary attributes when she sold them to foreign publishers. Maybe they, who have a tradition of detective literature, are harder to fool. Every market has its own dynamic, said Betty Stein.

I shrugged. Hannah said her friend liked that my detective is himself addicted to a series about another detective. I said that too much of literature tried to create the illusion of a literature-less life. I'd always wondered about that. What audience did this kind of literature imagine, and what did it wish to distill for this audience by depicting characters for whom reading or writing was not a driving force in their world?

Tahel's anger and frustration remained like a stinging sensation in my skin even after I dropped her off at home. Oshri came out to meet us. He said a missile hit the wall of a day care, but the place had been empty. He asked Tahel if she'd brought some books for him too. She said impatiently that she could lend him her old books if it was that important to him.

I walked in after them. The light in the living room was dim. At the edge of every inhalation was a pungent bitterness. Burnt sage, I guessed. Yaffa sent the kids off to shower. She said our mother was resting a bit and asked if she should add a dinner plate for me. I asked about Bobby. She said he'd only be back to-morrow. I said it must be hard to have him away at a time like this. She asked what happened at the doctor's that morning, she couldn't get a straight answer out of our mother, she only said she got a referral to see a dermatologist, but what did a derma-tologist have to do with anything?

I said they wanted to eliminate the possibility that the swell-ing was coming from the area above her nose vein. If some cyst was pressing down on it. She said, Why didn't you ask them to do a CT right there? I said they had to first eliminate the other pos-sibilities. Sure, she said, because a CT is expensive, so they're trying to avoid it. She said sometimes I was unexpectedly help-less and she wasn't sure if I was doing it on purpose. I said I'd call for a referral tomorrow.

She asked again if I was staying for dinner, if she should add a plate for me. I said, No, I'll pass, I'm tired. I asked if she was okay. If she wanted me to stay awhile. She said, What for? She said yes, she was a little exhausted. She was having trou-ble sleeping, maybe she got it from me. I said I hoped it was just a phase, otherwise . . . Otherwise what? she said. I said sleeping was like breathing, sometimes the autonomic system forgot how to perform the activity and the body had to be re-trained. I told her I learned, just barely and with great difficulty, but ultimately I learned to sleep at the speed of sleep. She said, You and your nonsense again. I said, Yaffa, every situation has its speed, sometimes we just naturally grasp how to speed up or slow down to meet it, sometimes we acquire the habit, but

typically we aren't accurate. We move at an approximate, esti-
mated speed.

She smiled, a tiny smile. She said, I hope you aren't burden-
ing the kids with this baloney. I told her not to worry, I had no
intention of interfering with her parenting. She said, You'd better not, unless you want me to kick you all the way out of Sderot.
I looked at her and let out a brief laugh.

What, what, said Tahel, why is that funny?

She was standing at the doorway to the kitchen. Her face had
thawed from that ridiculous scrunching, softened. I couldn't
guess what part of our conversation she'd heard. She was wearing a long nightgown, her hair combed, fresh. Are you hungry?
asked Yaffa. Never mind me, Tahel said, Oshri looks like if you
don't give him something to eat soon, he's going to bite someone's leg off. This time Yaffa laughed. Tahel looked at us, pleased.

onnit left me a message to say that she wouldn't be coming that weekend. She was too tired and needed time to think. I silenced my inner sirens. I told myself, Those belong to the former person, that other guy, the detective. The days spent in my study lengthened. I looked over the case Manny had given me. The details were seemingly dull. The body of a woman in the kitchen of her northern Tel Aviv villa, stabbed by a knife, the handle of which bore her own fingerprints along with another set of prints the police could not identify. On her body were signs of a struggle. The alarm system had been neutralized, the door was open. The husband was in the Sinai Peninsula, looking into a potential investment opportunity in a local hotel. It was the mid-1980s, the Lebanon War was rolling through in a corpse-making machine on the northern border, outputting flesh and hard-heartedness. The aversion and atrophy of a veteran, Ashkenazi bourgeoisie that had discovered the gold mine of false ideology—how to fatten its wallet with the yield of national values, battle heritage, victim ethos, purity-of-arms discourse. The usual. But Manny was right, the murder was overly staged; behind the capricious façade of a robbery gone wrong, careful planning was revealed. When was the last time a tight alibi, an alleged lack of motive, and evidence leading to a dead end all came together like this? But his supervisor didn't see much point in continuing the investigation.

I tried to think of a detective character skilled enough to crack this mystery, what qualities he should possess. I got rid of the detective I'd previously come up with, but once again I pictured a detective of exaggerated dimensions, exceeding reality, like the literary detectives I used to love and knew intuitively Betty wouldn't like. I delved into writing the opening scene. And there entered the detective, scorched with experience, with his cutting statements and broad gestures.

Nevertheless, I called Ronnit constantly, asking after her. She didn't pick up. After two weeks, I told her voice mail that if she wasn't going to come up here I'd come down to Beersheba the following weekend. She called back. Her voice trembled. She said she was coming, she needed to talk.

I waited for her outside the train station. It seemed we were sentenced to forever meet in sterilized, anonymous spaces. In that early December, the evening stood in the afternoon, slowly fanning the flames of its darkness. She walked slowly, the hump of her pack on her back. I removed it from her back and hung it off my shoulder. She said, Let's go get some coffee. I might have to go straight back to Beersheba.

I walked with her in silence. She had new worry lines. Not actual lines I could trace, but when I turned my eyes away from her, I saw them clearly in the etching of her face in my mind. She sat across from me, hesitating over how to start. She said she'd decided to drop out of med school. She was sick of it, the year she spent as a military officer, and her traveling, the college degree in life sciences in America. She started med school too late. In the first two years the density of studies, the information overload, the shortness of breath, all blurred the age difference between her and the other students. But now it seemed their lives were opening toward something, they were going out to parties and experiencing for the first time things she'd already lived through. She had no idea how painful the weight of experience and the knowledge of maturity would be. She felt old.

Old? You're twenty-eight, I said. She said, You have no idea of the chasm that separates age twenty-eight from age twenty-three or -four. I said I heard that nowadays youth was prolonged until at least age thirty. She said, Maybe for you. Where I'm from, by age thirty you're already a whole, molded person. A ghostlike server came over and set an herbal tea in front of Ronnit and a coffee with whipped cream in front of me. Ronnit nodded in gratitude. What does it mean to be a whole, molded person? I asked. How does one know? Is there a government office that runs tests and issues licenses? Ronnit said, Maybe there should be an authority that informs you, you're ready to be on your way. It would save so much agony.

I said I'd thought white-collar professions were the passport her social class wanted. Social class? she asked. Milieu, I said. She said she knew she shouldn't discuss this with me. My cynicism would just spoil it. I said I wasn't being cynical, it was just that this was bourgeois wishful thinking. She asked, What's bourgeois about wanting to know you're living the right life? I said, That desire in itself.

Ronnit said, Elish, stay with me for a minute. I said, I am with you. She said, No, you're focused on me, you're about to burn me with your crazy eyes, but you aren't with me. Be someone, be my hater, be my admirer, but be someone who's with me, not some abstract thought, be a body. I said, I wish I knew how to be anything besides a body. She took a long sip of her tea.

I said, Okay, let's think constructively. You want to keep studying. She nodded. I said, What? She said, Something to alleviate my restlessness, not ignite it. We looked through the darkening glass that was the evening light. She said, Did you know it already rained for the first time this year in Beersheba? What a strange year, the rains starting down south. She recalled how she'd dragged me to look at the squills near Yerucham in late August, how I said the prophecy was too hard on the desert land, that the plants' omen was unnecessary. Her throat emitted a hollow sound. I realized too late it was a laugh. I joined in, clacking with my tongue and lips.

What are you going to do in the meantime, I said, until you

figure out your next move? She said she had to find an apartment, get a job. Her parents had invited her to move back in with
them. They'd moved to Meitar. But she couldn't go back, she
wasn't going to fall through the cracks, she had to know her decision meant moving toward a proper place. I asked if she
planned to stay in Beersheba. She shook her head vigorously.
No. Shoshi and Dror knew about her situation too.

Is it that much of a situation, I asked, quitting school? Oh,
she said, I didn't tell you, my landlord is selling the apartment.
She and her roommate received their month's notice. When did
this happen? I asked. Two weeks ago, she said. The eviction notice was what gave way to her thought avalanche. Why didn't you
call right away? I asked. She said she had, but when she heard
my outgoing voice mail message she freaked out. Suddenly, she
said, she realized I couldn't be a conversation partner. That my
doubts would make her fall apart. I said, Shoshi and Dror. She
said yes, they'd offered to house her for a while.

I said, If you're going to move to Tel Aviv, you can stay with me
for the time being. She leaned over her bag, rummaging through
it. She put her hands on the table, then removed them, called the
server, and asked if any pastries were left from that morning. I
pointed outside. The pale darkness of Tel Aviv, a tongue of a
greater, hidden darkness pressuring the outside. She said, That's
it, those days have arrived, huh. I nodded. Ronnit said, All right,
but only for a short while, until I find an apartment, and only if
you let me stay in the living room, just as a roommate.

shri woke her up. She hadn't thought she'd fall asleep. The humming in her head was too loud. His eyes were clear but distant. They performed their regular ritual, sneaking over to the door of the kitchen and watching their mother stand there and look out-side, leaning closer to listen.

She doesn't look as weak tonight, Oshri said when they got back to the room.

You said she didn't even wake up yesterday and the day before.

Yes, she slept, said Oshri.

Maybe you were sleeping.

No, the ice worm, I didn't feel it.

Why do you think she's less weak?

That's what I think, maybe. He aimed his night-light at the doorframe. Above the compressed lead beam was a wreath of branches, dried leaves, and wilted purple bell-like flowers. What's that? she asked.

The witch told her to hang that, said Oshri.

What witch?

The one she calls for advice.

About what?

I don't know, her fear at night. I just heard her and Dad, and she said she called that woman.

We have to ask Elish if he has a better idea.

He can't help.

He can, she said. You weren't asleep?

Oshri said, No, I wasn't sleeping, I'm reading. I'm nervous.

What are you reading? she asked.

Mr. Twigg's Mistake. Why didn't you give it to me sooner?

Oh, that really is a good book. Elish said he read it three times.

It's kind of funny too. I wish—

She waited for him to complete the sentence, but his voice faded to a ponderous hum. He returned the light to glow over his own bed and lost himself in the book.

She turned her face to the wall. How was she going to get better at what she did? Even if she occasionally managed to influence other people's feelings with her brain, like she did that evening with her mother, she was still a lousy detective. Oshri noticed more than she did. She thought about Kalanit, starving and dirty after stabbing the guard in the cell with that bent nail, running, running. Like a wild animal, her clothes stained with the guard's blood and she's wild, like a wild animal she runs on the dirt path, but in the distance she spots a group of men, the men who were dressed up as yeshiva students on the bus, rushing toward her, and she's running, like a wild animal she's running, without a direction. Something, a mixture of cotton balls and pins gathered out of Tahel's breath, locking her throat. She bit her lips. Her eyes grew hot. But she stifled the sound that tried to come out.

The next morning, she sat out front. Oshri lingered in bed. Twinkles jumped on the lake's surface, seeming to fall from the thicket's trees. Small creatures jumped up to bite at the air before diving back down. Reflections trembled on the water. Don't be tempted by images, relax your thoughts, follow things as they come into being without trying to direct them, that was what Elish said.

Grandma Zehava came out to greet her. Tahel looked at her surreptitiously, checking if the swelling on her nose stood out, but she could see no difference. In spite of the heat, Grandma was wearing her layers upon layers of skirts.

Did you eat something this morning? she asked Tahel.

I'm not hungry.

A girl your age can't not be hungry. Look at your brother's appetite, bless him.

Does your nose sore hurt? she asked.

No, it's just a little hard to breathe, don't worry, *ya binti*, it's nothing.

Do you like staying with us, Grandma?

It's comfortable here, a nice home, knock wood. I wish Yaffa was pleased too.

She's never pleased, that mom.

Grandma Zehava laughed.

Why don't you move in with us? said Tahel.

I want you to live with us always, Oshri said from the front door. They turned to face him. His being was still sleepy. He rubbed his eyes. Did you wash your face, did you brush your teeth? Grandma Zehava asked.

He nodded. He came over, barefoot, in shorts, healthy and round. Grandma Zehava kissed him on both cheeks. You're a doll, she said. Want me to make you some cocoa?

He can make it, said Tahel. He knows how to do it himself.

He leaves a mess in the kitchen. Your mother doesn't like him goofing off in there.

So are you moving in? said Oshri.

Grandma Zehava said no, she had a good home that she bought with their grandfather, may he rest in peace. The missiles would stop soon and she'd go back there.

Do you miss Grandpa? asked Oshri.

I miss him a lot when I'm out. But in our house I don't have to miss him.

What did you love most about him? asked Tahel.

That every time I looked at him I saw how pretty I still was, how young I still was. She ran her hand down Tahel's hair, moving it from her face and tucking it behind her ear. Her fingers rubbed the lobe, lingering. The same nocturnal tangle of cotton balls and pins returned to take hold of her throat. Grandma Zehava leaned in and whispered, We met when I was your age.

Tahel's phone, which was on the table, rang. She snatched it. Yalon, she said.

Come, Grandma told Oshri, let's go inside.

So, said Tahel, my plan worked.

Yes, Yalon said on the other end. Are you okay? he asked.

Fine, fine.

You sound a little hoarse. So I convinced my dad to let me stay at Kuti's, and this morning I woke up and watched Kalanit through the window.

And did he come, the man? Tahel nearly yelled the question.

Calm down. Yes, I don't know where he came from. She walked behind the garden's back wall. By the time I found her, he was standing there and they were talking.

You took pictures, I hope.

Of course I did. It's just that—

Send them to me right now.

Listen, there's something weird about them.

What's weird?

I think I'm right. You'll see. I'm sending you a multimedia text. Download WhatsApp already. You're so old.

Like you don't remember the internet on my phone is locked?

I remember, I remember. It's just annoying to send one picture at a time. What a nightmare.

She focused on the phone in her hand, aiming her thought's full intensity at it.

Oshri trudged over. One hand holding his cocoa, the other holding a plate of cookies, a book tucked under his arm. He swayed clumsily with his effort to maintain balance. Grandma said you should eat, he said.

She shook her head.

He sat in front of her, munching on the cookies. Her concentration broke for a second time. She said, Dip them in the cocoa, I can't stand that sound. Her phone dinged.

Oshri got up and stood behind her, close, chewing. Crumbs sprayed the back of her neck. What's that? he said. In stark opposition to the sharpness of the image, the figure standing in front of Kalanit was fuzzy. It had a human form. One could deduce from it a tall, bony man, even wearing a top hat. But it was as if someone had run a wet wipe over his contours, smudging them. When she enlarged the photo, his limbs seemed to be made of dark stains.

12

A superstition made me bypass Ashkelon and drive through the twisting road between Givati Junction and Hodaya Junction. I remembered my father once told me the road had been especially paved for military transportation, convoys. In wartime, cars driving on a road full of twists and turns would be harder to bomb from the air. I remembered a bit of information that had been making the rounds lately, according to which the city of Nagasaki was bombed because workers at a weaponry factory in Hiroshima who'd heard of the approaching American bomber propellers lit up plastics, creating a smoke screen. They kept quiet for years about their act of bravery that sealed the fate of a nearby city. Near the Hodaya Junction, a man's voice emerged from the white chatter of the car radio to announce a siren. Siren in Ashkelon, siren in Gan Yavne, siren in Ashdod. I pulled over and stayed in the car. Somewhere in the heat-wave sky, a train of blaze burned like an engine, like a star straying out of its night. The explosion made the car windows shake. A banal thought passed through me, that these days the sublime was derived from our attitude toward technology. We recoiled toward nature under its pressure or stood, awed, before the horror it was capable of sowing. I opened the windows and kept driving. Dust, soldier clusters, and the scorching of war all blew inside with the furnace of daytime.

That morning, I called the office in Ashkelon and asked to speak to my mother's primary-care doctor. She vehemently refused to give my mother a referral for a CT scan. She said people had started panicking ever since they learned how to look up symptoms online, and they'd started deciding for themselves what tests they needed. I said, So it isn't a financial decision. She said, It's a systemic decision. At any rate, she said I could ask for a discounted test through the medical insurance expansions. I called to find out about my mother's medical insurance. She had a basic policy. I asked if they would cover the cost of the test if I expanded her coverage and met the monthly payment they required for a woman her age. They said they would, but only after I paid for six months. I called a different insurance company. Same response. I called the hospital and made an appointment. Yaffa scolded me when I told her. She said they couldn't chip in, what with their mortgage payments, and they still weren't sure how much money Bobby would be making as a freelancer; he had a tendency to exaggerate for the better. I said I'd pay. She said, I thought you didn't have a job. I said, I might now. I asked if Tahel was still grounded. She said no, they'd returned all her rights on Sunday. Bobby insisted they do it before he left. I asked why Tahel wasn't answering my calls. She said, She's at home with her friend. She sounded pleased.

I parked on Keren ha-Yesod Street in Holon. I didn't like the high-rises. Most of them were built on pillars, taunting earthquakes and rockets. You couldn't safely stand underneath them, and most of them were locked from the outside. How selfish on the part of tenants. Luckily for me, the building at Dmitry Shtedler's address, which Manny had given me, was open. Reality responded to my thoughts. The flapping of the siren's wings rose from both. I hurried inside. I rummaged in my pocket to see if I had my apartment keys on me. If a rocket hit the car, I could return to Tel Aviv by public transportation. Two little girls held hands tightly, wearing matching dresses and bows. They sat underneath the stairwell on the third floor, a young woman towering over them. One of the girls suggested I not stand so close and pointed at the southern wall of the stairwell. That's where they shoot from. The advice she offered seemed to unburden her. Her expression emptied somewhat of the panic that still choked her sister's eyes. An older man rushed out of the apartment across the hall, zipping his pants with some difficulty, his hands moist, showered. He adjusted the yarmulke on his head and cursed. They said there was going to be a cease-fire, he said, we can't trust those people, sons of perverse, rebellious women.

I smiled. He said, Are you from the building? I said I wasn't, I was looking for Dmitry Shtedler's apartment. He narrowed his eyes and said, There's no one here by that name. The *zhlob*, said the brave girl, he left. The terrified girl bit her lips and nodded her agreement. That's not nice, said the young woman, Dannit, that's not polite. But he told me that's what they used to call him. I said, Yes, he's a giant man, hard to miss. Are you looking for him because he's a giant? asked the man. No, I said. He submitted an insurance claim a year ago and we can't get ahold of him. Look at that, said the man, I've been chasing Social Security for five years to get them to raise my disability and they ignore me, and this guy they chase after. I explained that Dmitry's syndrome was endangering him. What syndrome? asked the young woman. I said, Gigantism, it's a hormonal condition. The heart gives out early, it can't maintain blood flow to such large organs. The man chuckled, then burst out laughing. What? said Dannit. The terrified girl let out a broken, flutelike laugh. Pazit, said the young woman, good morning. Dannit said, Mom, I didn't hear an explosion. It should have happened already. Pazit let out a meek yes. They must have intercepted it above Rishon L'zion, said the man, so we can't hear it from here.

I said, Wait a minute, so did you know him or not? He used to give us presents, said Pazit. Dannit said, Why are you telling? It's okay to tell, said Pazit. The young woman tensed up. What did he give you? she asked. Nothing much, said Dannit, marbles, a doll one time, that was when he was crying. Yeah, said Pazit, he was crying because his aunt got lost.

I have heart problems too, said the man, what are you going to give me? I said each lawsuit was handled separately. He said, Here in Holon we're between a rock and a hard place. They shoot rockets at us and they ignore us too. But down south it's a whole festival. Yes, I said, with overpriced tickets. He said, All of our insurance money goes to the south. The country built them safe rooms and safe spaces, and what did we get? I said, With all due respect. *Yalla*, he said, what, you think I don't know about what goes on in Sderot, for example? He had family there, he said, relatives of his wife's. They're all jewelry makers, but one of them got a job at the engineering department because they supported the former mayor. Yoram Bitton, I said. He said, Yeah, during the previous round of bombing. They booked hotel rooms for Sderot residents, and who do you think got those rooms, only those who were connected with municipality workers. They would write down their uncles' names, as if they lived in Sderot too, and got them hooked up with vacations in Eilat and up north.

Mom, said Pazit, can we go inside? Dannit said, Let's wait a little longer, I want to listen. Pazit said, But, Mommy, I need the bathroom. The young woman said, Hold it in. And to the older man she said, You should be ashamed of yourself, spreading this gossip around. He said, What gossip? I was ... Then he said nothing. I said, Oh, you were one of those uncles. He said, And what good did it do? They fired Elkoby, there was a problem with his appointment, they looked into it. Do you know there's an embezzlement investigation going against Yoram Bitton? I nodded. Good, he said, you guys know everything, no wonder you make people's lives miserable, sending spies to follow around poor sick people.

I'm not following Dmitry, his address isn't up-to-date. Our letters are being sent back. Has he been in touch with anyone from the building? I asked. Pazit said, He kept to himself, would sit on the bench by himself. Dannit said, He was gentle. I asked, Did he have a wife, a husband? God forbid, said the man. Today

13

Tahel pedaled fast. She hadn't fastened her helmet straps and the thing banged against her scalp with every bump and protrusion in the road. She arrived at Kuti's house before Yalon. She leaned her bicycle against the fence, leaned her back against a marble pedestal near the gate, folded one leg, and crossed her arms. And yet, when Yalon paused beside her, her face was still flushed with effort, her forehead glistening with sweat. They left their bicycles in the yard and walked inside. Yalon asked if Oshri wasn't joining them, and she shrugged. She said he didn't want to come. When she invited him, he was busy reading *The First Two Lives of Lukas-Kasha*. She preferred the author's *Chronicles of Prydain*, which she thought was even better, as a whole, than the Narnia series. Not as good as the Earthsea series, but still. She felt a tingle of envy when she thought about how Oshri would read them soon, but the excitement of offering him a part of her world that used to be hers, that used to be herself, her secret self, herself in the dark, grew stronger. They moved the books Elish had given her into their shared safe room. She thought their parents probably wouldn't like that.

The two cuties, Kalanit said when they walked into the backyard, a lawn with some guava trees with crumbled leaves that would soon be renewed, a dusty fig tree, a green pomegranate tree whose hard bell fruits Kalanit was staring at, serrated-lipped cups.

She said, Another month of this and they'll have to embalm

them, the pomegranates, I mean. They're sweet, aren't they? You can tell their peels are going to be bright.

Ask my grandmother, she brings a worker in to pick them before Yom Kippur.

Tahel realized that the distant red flames in the background of some of the pictures Yalon took were the pomegranate flowers hardening into fruits. She said, You sit out here every morning?

Yes, said Kalanit. It's nice out here, shaded and pleasant.

Alone, said Tahel.

Yes, said Kalanit, alone.

And no one comes to talk to you? said Yalon.

Why would anyone come? said Kalanit. Who knows I'm here?

Someone must know Sima is here, said Yalon.

Tahel said, But you have been talking to someone, twice already.

Yalon said, You're a guest in my grandma's house. Why are you letting strangers in here?

Kalanit looked at them. Are you all right? she asked.

Yes, said Tahel, we know you've been talking to someone.

Kalanit stared at them. I don't understand what—

Show her, said Tahel as Yalon swiped the screen of his phone.

Who's this? said Yalon.

Kalanit leaned in to look at the photograph presented to her. Her bottom lip trembled. She said, You did this, right?

Did what? asked Tahel.

On your computer. On a software. You added the drawing of the man.

Tahel furrowed her brow. Drawing, why do you say "drawing"?

It's like a drawing someone added, said Kalanit. Why are you doing this to me?

I took these pictures early this morning when you were sitting out here, said Yalon.

Kalanit started to cry. Are you trying to make me lose my mind? Who have I ever hurt? Who?

Tahel flinched, as did Yalon. The actuality of the crying was bigger than they were, more real than the accusation they'd made. She took the phone from Yalon's hands. The man's figure did indeed look like bad photoshop.

Yalon said, Let's go inside. Sima was already hurrying toward them, her hands clad in long plastic gloves.

So strange, Tahel said when the two of them sat down in Yalon's room, she almost convinced me.

Yalon said, Yeah, for a minute I thought maybe something was wrong with me. I almost believed her that I edited the photos.

And did you? asked Tahel.

Are you serious? he asked.

No, I trust you.

What does Elish say? asked Yalon.

I didn't tell him. He tried calling me this morning, but I didn't feel like answering.

You're mad at him about yesterday.

No, it's just that he won't tell us anything, and we're part of this investigation too.

So maybe we should investigate ourselves.

Yes, she said, we can follow Kalanit, she must go out sometimes.

Noon arrived. They worked in shifts, one of them reading, or eating an apple, or surfing the net, the other looking out the window. Sima called Kalanit inside to eat. Then Sima knocked on Yalon's door. She said, Kuti said not to stay in your room all day. They pretended to be deep in a conversation they'd rehearsed in advance. At the dining table, Kuti watched them carefully. Kalanit ate distractedly, Sima slaving around her. Yalon got up for a few moments and Tahel used the opportunity. She gathered the force of her brain into a narrow beam, aiming it at Sima. Sima was easily influenced. Sima told Kalanit, Why don't we go for a walk, get some air?

Kalanit said, I'll go out for a walk by myself in a few hours.

Back at home Grandma Zehava said, Where did you go? It's not good for girls to be out all day.

Tahel said, When's Dad coming home?

I don't know, *ya binti*. Your mother will be back at five.

Oshri said, He'll be here around seven. And Elish is coming over for dinner.

Tahel calculated. That didn't leave much time for surveillance.

14

When I walked in, Tahel was sitting nervously across from Yaffa. My mother's lips opened in a smile, but her face was still scrunched, closed off in a mask of worry. She touched her nose distractedly. The swelling didn't show. What happened? I asked. It's all your fault, said Yaffa. As soon as you got here, she started acting out.

Tahel didn't deign to turn her face toward me. Her back was stiff against the chair, hovering against it. I was in the Tel Aviv area all morning, I said. Make yourself some coffee, something, my mother said. You had a day. I said to Yaffa, Will you tell me what happened? What happened, said Yaffa, is that I left work early and the girl wasn't home. A siren started, and I called and she didn't answer. That's what happened.

I said Tahel must have a reasonable explanation, that she was mature and responsible, I would trust her instead of just shouting. So what, said Yaffa, you think I just shout? I said that wasn't what I meant, but that we ought to give her a chance to defend herself. Yaffa said, I gave her a million chances, she's just in her own mind. My mother nodded and said, Ever since she was a little girl, she was just like you and your father. Yaffa said, Damn it, Mom, don't bring Dad into everything now. What everything, my mother said, he was stubborn, stubborn.

I'm right here, Tahel said, as if against her will. Pay attention to me. Thank you very much for reminding us, young lady, said Yaffa, now go to your room and stay there until your father gets home.

That's no solution, my mother said, punishing her. You should find out what the girl needs. Mom, said Yaffa, give me a break. Did you ever bother to find out what we needed, what I needed? Our mother said nothing. I remembered Yaffa's hastened maturation. I remembered her persuasions, her struggle to gnaw at the borders of the off-limits area my mother erected after my father's death. No, that's not true, I didn't remember it. I realized it in retrospect, too late to help. I was too busy undermining the constant accusations Yaffa aimed at me, my mother's persistent suspicion, her sudden abstaining from touch.

So what did she say? I asked. Yaffa said, At least this time she didn't drag Oshri along with her. I asked if I could go talk to her. Why, said Yaffa, so you can incite her even more? I said, I won't keep anything from you. Yaffa chuckled. My mother said, Can a leopard change his spots? I stood before the two of them. The electric kettle sounded its click. Steam rose from the spout. I looked at the layer of sugar-sprinkled instant coffee Yaffa had poured into the glass. Even when I still drank coffee, I always detested drinking instant coffee from glasses. The clear essence dilutes the flavor. Yaffa said, What are you staring like a fool for, go talk to her. I said, I thought— She said, What, that later you could say that all I did was shout at her without giving her a chance?

Oshri was immersed in a Lloyd Alexander book. He looked up and smiled. He said, Look, Tahel let me borrow all the books you gave her. I asked if he was enjoying them. He said, It's amazing. Are your books like this too? I said, They aren't as good. He said, I'll read them when I finish this pile. I asked him why he decided to start reading just now. He said, I didn't know it was like this. What? I said. He said, That you close your eyes and the words start moving inside of you, the world going with you. I asked what he meant. He said, It's like you're always in the world, but when I'm in a book, the world is inside me. I asked if that never happened to him before with movies or computer games.

He said, I thought about them later, but they weren't inside of me and I wasn't inside of them, not—

Did you hide the ball already? said Tahel. Oh, said Oshri, jumping to his feet. Good thing you reminded me. He pulled the soccer ball from under his bed, slipped it under his arm, and peeked out from the doorway before sneaking out. The book remained open on his bed. He was close to finishing it.

I told you, said Tahel. Remind me, I said. She was sitting on her bed, her knees gathered into her chest. She said, That he can feel it. Yes, I said, can you tell me what happened? Her lips tightened and she shook her head. I asked why she went outside and didn't pick up her phone. She said nothing. I said, All right, if you want me to guess, I'll guess. You silenced your phone because you didn't want to be interrupted, therefore I deduce you were in the middle of some important activity. There's no other reason why you wouldn't answer your mother. It's also easy to guess the activity. You were tracking a suspect. She forced her face to freeze, but her body tilted forward a little, her green eyes shining. You've been investigating the Kalanit mystery, so it's one of two possibilities. Either you were following Kalanit, or that strange man paid her another visit.

Both, she said, then pursed her lips again.

Why would Kalanit go walking around Sderot in wartime— that's a question, I said. I made her, said Tahel. Did you suggest she go outside? I asked. In a way, she said. I said, Still, she needed her own motive to say yes. Tahel nodded. If the strange man came back, maybe something in her conversation with him created the need. Yalon took a picture of them talking, said Tahel, but it's fuzzy.

I asked her to show me. She shook her head no. She said if I wasn't sharing with her, she wouldn't share with me. Fine, I said, let me tell her a story. I told her the details of Dmitry Shtedler's niece's case, his search for her. She cut me off with questions, exaggerating with her own theories. I said, There's no point in jumping to conclusions. She said, You think that strange man had something to do with it? I said, There's no evidence to point either way. She showed me the pictures. I looked them over, surprised. I said, You could think these pictures were– She cut me off. Fake, she said, I know. But they're totally not. Okay, I said, I'll ask Yalon to send them to me. She said, What's the next step? I said, Remember my condition? Yes, she said, to talk to you before. Exactly, I said. All of her fragility beamed behind the façade of rebellion. I said, If anything happened to you, I . . . She said quickly, But we were careful, we agreed that if Kalanit went into an open field, we wouldn't follow her. We stayed close to concrete barricades, and we went inside of one when there was a siren. And Kalanit? I asked. She said, When we came out, we didn't see her anymore.

Oshri came back, ball in hand. I didn't get a chance, he said quietly, Dad just came in.

enlarged the pictures Yalon sent me on the screen of my laptop. They did indeed look like badly processed files. The man standing across from Kalanit was a hastily filled-out sketch, scattering into an image's most elemental parts before my eyes. The rest—Kalanit, Kuti Asor's garden, even the pomegranate glaring like a budding breast, remained sequential, almost smooth.

Bobby walked in with a steady step, expanding his presence to the size of the living room. Tahel, he called. He said, Don't butt in, Elish, this is none of your business. I said, It is my business. I was supposed to watch her, and I had to go to Tel Aviv, and I didn't let my mother know. What's that got to do with anything? he said. Tahel should know how to be responsible. Right, I said, she should, but you're forgetting she's a girl, because sometimes she's as smart as a grown-up. What kind of experience is she supposed to draw from, whose, yours? None of us really grew up in a war zone. He fell silent. Yaffa said, She has to follow our orders. I said, But the orders don't seem real to her, don't you understand? It's like if someone issued a prohibition against going to the beach because of a jellyfish attack.

I saw the determination of their fury being disrupted, the twitch of an eye, the flaring of a nostril, the jutting of a lip, the pulsing of a braid of muscles. I said, Yaffa, Bobby, I take it upon myself to watch Tahel and Oshri. I'm willing to send you an hourly report on their whereabouts. Yaffa said, No need to exaggerate, I could just implant a camera in their backs and be done with it. Bobby remained speechless. I asked if he didn't trust me.

He said, I trust you to watch them, but I don't trust you not to put ideas in their heads. I told him not to worry.

Tahel and Oshri set the table quietly, occasionally commenting to each other. Bobby returned from the shower full of pep. His time away had electrically charged him. I asked him how it was, working for Asor. He said, Awesome, awesome. Yaffa sized him up, calculating. He said, Those pieces of shit of yours from Tel Aviv won't calm down, huh? Zalman, my mother said, watch your language. He said, Believe me, Zehava, they're garbage. Isn't it enough that they're throwing a support rally for Hamas in Rabin Square, but now they're coming here too? Where? said Yaffa. What, said Bobby, haven't you heard? There's a demonstration in Sderot tomorrow. An empathy rally, I said. So you knew about this? said Yaffa. I said, I know a few people who are going. Why, why? said my mother. I said, They're protesting the killing, not supporting one side or the other, they want to show their empathy for the people who live in this area. In Sderot or in Gaza, said Yaffa. I said, In this area. Bobby said, I would put them on trucks and send them to the gas chambers. I said, Someone tried that once. He said, Those traitors, they're worse than terrorists. I said, Bobby, you know my views, I think we should reach a peace agreement. You don't sign contracts with the devil, said Yaffa. I said, So now people who are pro-peace agreement are traitors. Bobby said, Yes. I said, In that case, you'd send me to the gas chambers too. He said, You, because you're my brother-in-law, I'd just remove one of your legs or—

Enough, Tahel shouted. Oshri signaled something to her, time-out, probably. Her furrowed expression was startled back into her usual beauty. What's wrong? said Yaffa. Oshri said, There's a fly here bothering us. Is that any reason to yell? said Yaffa. My mother said, Stop it, Yaffa, let the girl breathe.

I connected my laptop to the enormous screen in the Dadon living room. I pulled up the photos, enlarged them, looked at them from all directions; perhaps some sneaky detail would present itself. While reading Descartes's *Meditations*, I once paused to marvel at a quandary. Beyond the window, we see a coat and a hat. Who can assure us they aren't being donned by an automaton, just a mechanism of strings and springs? How can we be certain they are worn by a person? The marveling was not at the expression of the thought, it did not stand out as part of Descartes's method of skepticism. It was about the act of thinking it, the appearance of the thought. It was as if the navel of doubt were revealed to me, as if I'd happened to stumble upon its keystone link, embedded in the dark. For years I considered standing before it, its emergence and the required decision. Descartes may have elevated reason, its powers and its ability to imbue its contents with the appearance of clarity and consistency, but I could never believe he himself was convinced, that he himself had released himself from the stance, turning his back on it. To a great extent, one can see his successors and his opponents returning to the moment of decision and examining it over and over without denying it, testing the ramifications of a different decision according to their moods, their anxieties, the experiences they had in their formative years.

Spinoza, who took one glance and announced the superiority of reason's skills of architecture; Pascal, who looked deeper, retreating into the bosom of religious thought; Nietzsche, who demanded to make this primal stance a daily experience, in which the seeming order of existence was undermined because of it and reborn. For years I thought the history of the detective literature I was fascinated with could be read similarly. Poe, who outlined his stance within the moment and left it undecided, died suddenly on his bone- and glimmer-cast throne. Conan Doyle was the boy who chose the chest of reason, on its charms and seductions. Chesterton, who strained under the burden of chaos, locked himself in the confessionals of the vicarage. Borges and Lovecraft shared the constant undermining of the gaze, one taking the amusement it instigated, the other slipping darkness into his pocket like a shard of glass, then pulling it out over and over to look at the cracks of the outside. I don't believe any of them was right and cannot picture an axis on which they appear as fathers and sons. I imagine a space in which they are possibilities existing side by side, siblings, princes sent each in his own direction to find their destinies and inheritances. Each time I choose one of their nomadic paths to follow.

shri woke her up. Her sorrow on parting with deep sleep was replaced with alertness, a dry thread descending into her heart's chambers. She whispered, I want to go talk to Mom. He shook his head and mouthed no. She said, Please, please, in the same mouthing. He pulled a new book from the pile, *Finn Family Moomintroll*, and lay back in bed.

Earlier, in the twilight of sleep, in the slow, foggy descent, she'd reached a decision. She didn't stop at the doorway to the kitchen, but walked in with a heavy, sleepy step. Her mother turned sharply. Tahel, she muttered, and Tahel seemed to be horrified out of her disorientation. She said, Mom, you scared me.

What are you doing here? said her mother.

All that salt made me thirsty.

What salt?

Salt, said Tahel, I dreamt I was at the Dead Sea and everything was white and quiet. She let her voice wander and fade.

Yes, her mother said. Often one's feelings turn into images in dreams.

Tahel walked to the fridge and took out the water pitcher. She asked her mother, Want some?

Her mother gestured for her to pour it, though her glass was already two-thirds full.

Mom, said Tahel, what are you doing, standing here in the dark in the middle of the night?

Her mother said, Nothing, just thoughts that won't let me sleep.

You don't tell me anything, you and Dad.

There are some things kids better not hear.

But I can guess.

Her mother said, What?

You're standing at the kitchen window. I deduce you're looking for something outside. Meaning, you hear or see something
from the direction of the lake and the thicket.

Her mother tightened her lips.

You never check where it comes from during the day. From
that, I deduce you think it only exists at night.

Her mother didn't answer.

In that case, this thing, you think it's unnatural.

Her mother's lowered eyes turned toward the French
windows.

Tahel said, Are you worried?

Her mother nodded. She stood up and signaled for Tahel to
join her at the window. Be quiet, she said. The moon, if there
was one, thinned beyond recognizability, but the sky stretched
from one end to the next like the cloth they used to drain fluids
when they prepared cheese at school for Shavuot, a light filter-
ing through it. Within the muffled racket of weapons and war
machines, the thicket stood still. Its reflection, its dark command over the water, was more real. She waited with her
mother.

Now, her mother said, pointing.

Tahel thought she saw a white, woolly vapor moving quickly
between the trees.

And now, the whisper, said her mother.

Tahel strained her ears. She could detect perhaps a weak
echo that did not belong among the sounds of battle.

Did you understand what it said? her mother asked.

No.

Neither did I, but the more I hear it, the clearer the words become. At first it was as if they sounded in the thicket, then in the lake, and it's moving closer.

Tahel asked, Is there no way to stop it?

Her mother said, I've been consulting with someone. We can delay it.

Tahel shivered. She couldn't say for sure whether she heard or saw anything. She shook it off and walked to the light switch. When she touched it, she felt she was igniting the space with flame. Herself too. Her fear evaporated quickly. It worked, she thought, I managed to question her, just like Elish.

During the day, her mother said, in the light, it seems like a hallucination.

Tahel took a seat at the table. Her mother joined.

Are you hungry, maybe? asked Tahel.

I'm not, said her mother, her voice distracted.

I'm glad Uncle Elish is here.

I wonder why.

I'm learning a lot from him.

The two of you were always connected, said her mother. The distraction lingered in her words.

Oshri too.

A brief silence fell.

Oshri what? her mother asked with that same piercing tone of everyday life, the tone that attacked out of habit.

Tahel said, He's reading. He's reading all day long.

Reading.

Books, the books Elish gave me.

Really, I hadn't noticed.

What, he's finishing a book a day, and if it wasn't for Elish—

Her mother said, Do me a favor, don't praise your uncle.

But he—

No buts. Your uncle doesn't do anything out of the kindness of his heart.

He . . . , Tahel said, then fell silent.

Yes, said her mother. He always has a hidden agenda. He gives you something with one hand and takes something with the other.

Tahel said nothing. The heat that emitted from her flowed to her mother.

The problem with him, her mother said, is that it might be years before you figure out what he took.

17

Tahel recommended the best navigation app for getting around Sderot. I downloaded it. Yalon informed Tahel that Kalanit was planning to take another walk again, this time in the evening. I waited outside Kuti Asor's house. The stifling of the day did not evaporate. If anything, it exacerbated as darkness approached. I waited a long time. My watch showed seven. Kalanit's image appeared against the rectangle of light shining from inside the house. She was wearing jogging shorts and a tank top. She'd lost weight, it seemed to me, or perhaps it was just the impression left by the clothes. She might be too skinny. Her legs were smooth and tan. I followed her from a distance. I recorded the route on the app. She seemed to know where she was headed. She walked energetically, not paying much attention to her surroundings.

She climbed up the street. I climbed after her, staying close to the fences outside houses, behind tangles of oleander and hibiscus. The villa neighborhood was interrupted behind us, replaced with somewhat derelict houses, projects aspiring for grandeur. She turned near a closed store whose top floor was used as an apartment. To her right was a deserted youth center, thorns slicing through the tyranny of floor tiles. We walked down the street lined with buildings whose beginnings were modest and endings were cheap boasting. Left at the synagogue, across which Eritreans sat in their underwear in a yard, drinking beer and sharing jokes in stiff syllables. She slowed down. I clung to the bars surrounding the synagogue. Here and there their paint peeled, their rusted essence emerging.

An abandoned playground, climbing nets made of plastic rings, short wooden tunnels, a merry-go-round, and a slide, on which Kalanit rested her hand. The obvious boiling of the metal did not deter her. The man was there, in front of her. Even in the perforated light of late July, even in the vacillation of dusk, the radiance residues of sunshine insisting on burning, his figure stood out in its vagueness, its refusal to stabilize. What was that? It was as if he were being projected onto the scene from a distance, a sophisticated hologram. My animal instincts, on which I ordered eternal silence, acted on their own accord. I lunged at him. I could not stifle my desire to charge. What urged me to attack? But he was no longer there. Kalanit stood, swaying in place, awakening from a deep persuasion.

Kalanit, I said. She said, What, what? Then a thin film of recognition came over her and she said, You won't leave me alone. First that niece of yours and her friend, and now you. I said her mother was worried and asked for my help. She said, So I'm telling you I don't need help. Then she broke into a sudden run. I stood there for a few moments, unable to make up my mind. Then I hurried after her. I couldn't keep up. No one told me she was a runner. She had stamina. She drew away quickly, flickering. I kept going as long as I could.

I no longer took note of my surroundings. My skill of jotting down identifying marks in my consciousness, which I'd worked so hard to acquire, and which, until a few minutes ago, returned to me like an old habit, fell away at once. My efforts became inertia. I ran, passing this thing or that, a school covered with a mighty, corporeal metal roof, a few trees, a square, a main road, projects, what else, a large building rising in the distance, the flicker that was Kalanit swallowed inside it.

I stopped, panting, sweating. I walked toward the building. Nearby were two buses, police and border-police cars. Inside the lobby, police officers, in uniforms and vests, stood at the ready, hands on belt-hanging clubs. A voice came from the auditorium behind them. How could I have forgotten about the empathy rally? I went through the security check. I walked inside. A small audience stood in a semicircle in front of a stage, listening. The voice speaking from it grew clearer. I caught bits of it. The woman was a member of the Sderot urban kibbutz. She believed both sides were suffering and thought extremists on both sides shared the same interests and were the real collaborators. Jeers sounded in an attempt to cut her off, but she was well versed. The flow of her words through the loudspeakers went on uninterrupted. At the side of the auditorium, behind a column of cops, stood a group holding up signs that read TRAITORS, GO TO GAZA and GOODNIGHT, LEFTIES and FIGHT TERROR WITH TERROR and HAMAS HAS NO INNOCENT CHILDREN and LET THE IDF GET TOUGH. Two of the counterdemonstrators broke free from the group and began negotiating with the officer leading the column. I saw bodily gestures. I saw heads shaking. The officer pulled the radio from his belt. I could only hear the rustling of the sentence starting and ending.

Someone spoke my name. I turned to look. Betty waved at me from the edge of the semicircle, her hair dyed pale green. In the intensity of the floodlights bathing the auditorium, I saw her eyes widening. I turned to look. The column of cops retreated like a system of jail doors, and the group of counterdemonstrators galloped toward the stage. I was too exhausted to run, but I tried. I tried to hurry toward Betty. Then a blow to the back of the scalp, a fist to the side of the ribs like a white-hot rod, and a push to the shoulder, breaking my balance. I stumbled. I felt around me. I touched my cell phone. I hadn't noticed it falling. I shoved it in my pants pocket and looked up. Laughter came from the cop column behind me, indistinct cries. The rally-goers had already passed through the auditorium doors with clumsy panic, the counterdemonstrators following suit, pushing, slapping, administering blows, kicking. One of the last to pass through turned to face me before crossing the threshold. His face and his stature were unmistakable. Bobby.

meant to welcome two strangers into my home and await their approval, I certainly am a wine drinker. She said, What are you talking about, their approval? I said, I thought that was the point of this meal. Ronnit laughed nervously.

Back in the apartment she holed up in the kitchen, forbidding me from entering. I sat in my study instead, jotting down some notes, paragraphs, and thoughts about my detective. He'd started taking form a few weeks ago. I imagined him as a kind of offspring of Gogol, reality filling with mischief wherever he goes, as he scatters a series of jokes and absurdities, then pierces through them with a single look, picking out the solution with astute logic. I had no idea how to connect him with the mundane mystery in the case Manny had given me, but I could picture him before my eyes, his gait, the way he carried his being, his presence, his eyes that veiled with random thoughts, his odd gestures. I couldn't reach full concentration that afternoon. A piece of my awareness remained in the kitchen with Ronnit, watching her slicing, chopping, crushing, stirring, recoiling from boiling water and scalding oil.

Dror came in first, Shoshi seeming to clear a path for him. Finally, I said, Dror and Shoshi. She corrected me in a small voice, Shoshi and Dror. At first look, he seemed large and she small, mousy. But when they stood side by side and Ronnit came out of the kitchen to greet them, I noticed they were both of average height, shorter than Ronnit. She stood before them, head somewhat lowered, smile tense. I said, I've heard a lot about you. Dror said, I hope only the truth, our Ronnit'ale has a tendency to exaggerate. Shoshi let out a brief, sharp cry. I almost asked what was wrong, then realized that was the sound of her laughter.

Ronnit placed the chairs on the four sides of the table, each of us facing the other three. Dror clicked his tongue in approval, he liked that kind of thing, he said, clear equality among everyone present. Ronnit placed the salad bowl at the center of the table and retired to the kitchen. I said, Wait, I'll help you serve. No, no, said Shoshi, let her, Ronnit'ale has to learn not to delegate, it's a recipe for laziness. I asked if they were her age. They looked younger than me. Dror said, I hear you're living a life of leisure. I said, I live a life of contemplation. That's what Dror said, said Shoshi, rubbing his arm.

Shoshi tasted the salad, then placed the fork beside her plate. She said sweetly, Ronnit'ale, what I like about you is how your willpower covers for other things. I said, The salad is great. Dror said, Not everyone is blessed with Shoshi's fine palate. I asked Shoshi, Covers for what? The corners of her lips twisted into a smile. She picked up a piece of rye bread. Ronnit said, Ugh, I forgot the butter. She stepped into the kitchen. Shoshi said, For a lack of natural talent, of course, and cried her little cry.

And you're what, I said, med students? Yes, said Shoshi. Ronnit tells me your degree requires a lot of hard work. Dror said, Whoever said it was easy to make a contribution to society? I said, That depends what you define as a contribution. Ronnit walked in with a steaming bowl of pasta. I cleared the salad plates. In the kitchen, I uncorked the wine bottle and returned to the dining room with it. Dror leaned back in his chair, linked his fingers, and gave Ronnit a reproachful look. I brought four wineglasses. Dror and Shoshi turned over the glasses I placed in front of them. The flat stems gathered the light spilling from the chandelier. Their faces were expressionless. Ronnit, I asked, wine? She sat, paralyzed, gaping at me, gaping at her friends. I poured her some. Dror said, That's rude, she didn't ask for any. Shoshi said, Ronnit'ale, as a future doctor you're surely aware of the damage alcohol causes. I said studies showed that a glass of red wine a day helped lower cholesterol levels. Dror said, The masses seek justifications for living their desires. I told him I read Maimonides and Spinoza too. He said with surprise, Really, he had no idea. In that case he was expressing the opinions of more illustrious men. I told him not to make do with expressing, but to go ahead and read them. A life of study was its own reward. Shoshi asked if I owned my apartment. I said I did. She said she assumed I hadn't paid for it merely through a life of study but rather with marketable skills. I said, I was lucky. I can't force others to live like me. And yet, said Dror, you must serve as a false model for somebody.

Ronnit served the ice cream. For spite, I drank another glass of wine, not enjoying it, only keeping at it for the purpose of practicing the sipping motion, exercising my swallowing muscles. Shoshi said, Ugh, Ronnit'ale, you know me and lactose aren't pals. Ronnit's face flushed. She whispered, I'm sorry. Shoshi said, Come on, Ronnit'ale, don't apologize, you must have had a secret agenda. Again she pierced the air with her scream of laughter. Between scoops of ice cream, Dror said that Ronnit'ale's real problem was that she sought security in ways of life that could not guarantee it. I asked if by security they meant property, capital, status. Shoshi nodded. She said, If you want to phrase it like that. We'd rather talk about a contribution to society's financial and ideological stability. Real equality can only take place among equals.

I said, Productivity as an ideal is nothing more than the bourgeoisie's way of establishing its worldview and turning all of us into clones. You found yourself a nice communist, Shoshi told Ronnit. No, I said, you don't have to be a communist to not be a piece of shit. Dror wiped his face with a napkin. I see, he said amiably, then stood up. He walked to the door without another word. Shoshi embarked on a series of actions that appeared to be a gathering of herself—scarves, handbag. Then she followed him to the door with the same silence. Before leaving she muttered, Ronnit'ale, the three of us have to sit down and have a serious conversation soon. Ronnit waited for the echo of their footfalls to fade away. She said, They're my only friends at the university. I said, They aren't your friends, Ronnit. Why didn't you tell me they were in a cult? She furrowed her brow. I asked n my mirror image, on the right side of my chest, a yellow spot emerged, the shock of flesh rising to the surface of the skin. The muscles in my leg were tight. I conducted my morning rituals before going to pick up Tahel and Oshri. I called my mother to ask if Bobby was home. She said he was, but would be leaving in an hour or two. He got a small job. These missiles were causing a ton of damage. She asked if I'd heard that one woman was hit in the attack the previous night. I said I hadn't, but that I'd heard the missile itself.

My phone had rung as soon as I'd walked into the Dadon home. The ghost fist continued to beat in my rib cage, limiting my movement. I pulled the phone from my pocket, but it was still, a thin black surface, a chipped touch screen, while the ringing continued to come from my other pocket. I pulled the phone out. Two missed calls and Betty's name on the screen.

She asked me why I hadn't prepared her for the fact that all of southern Israel was a military zone. When I'd arrived that Sunday, I was only mildly surprised by the army vehicles, the interception batteries, the camps, the soldiers, the pillars of dust. They were like a set waiting to be uncovered behind routine gestures and the tumult of asphalt. She said, Animals, animals. I heard the blood racing in her veins. I heard her senses sharpening with danger. Her voice was high, urgent. I placed the other phone on the coffee table and sat down. I let out an involuntary sigh. I quickly asked how they'd managed to get a permit for the rally. She said they'd had some trouble with that. The city wouldn't allow an outdoor gathering, but one of the peace

activists found a loophole. Family gatherings were not prohib-
ited. So he suggested they organize their get-together as a rally
held in a safe space. The Home Front Command allowed gatherings of up to three hundred people in the Gaza Envelope. I
touched the screen of the other phone. A lock screen message
appeared, a code requested. Are you all right? asked Betty. You
sound distracted. I said, I've had a long day. She said, I understand why you moved there. I can't wait to see what you've been
writing. You have been writing, haven't you? I said I'd talk to her
tomorrow, that I had to wash off the dust and the sweat.

I called Manny. He laughed when I told him about the progress of my investigation. He said, So, for you it isn't a real investigation until you get beaten up. I told him I needed help finding
more information. Shoot, he said. I said, I need some background
information about Sima Shaubi. She's originally from Beit She'an.
He said he'd make some calls. Then he asked, How's it going in
general? Zehava told him I was getting along great with the kids,
that it was a blessing to have me around. I said I had no real idea.
He said, Well, you're one of those people who live retroactively,
who feel things in retrospect. The loudspeaker system emitted
its metallic inauguration. I said, There's a siren. He said, Take
care of—

His voice was swallowed in the loud, swollen whistle of the
passing rocket. I thought about the man who opened his window
in the town of Kiryat Malakhi to look at a rocket flying by and
was hit. I imagined the iron cutting in the flesh of darkness. I
thought of Oshri and Tahel, who are tuned in to the siren fre-
quency, detecting the crackling of loudspeakers before warning
words are transmitted. They can distinguish the different
sounds of impact, estimate the distance of the strike and its nature. I wondered what they would say about the current thunder,
the compressed core of the boom, its soft edges.

They sat around at my place. The morning grew late. Oshri

sat at the kitchen table, his cheek leaning against a closed palm, reading *Comet in Moominland.* Once in a while he looked up and smiled. He said he liked the little animal Sniff, and Snufkin. It's impossible not to love Snufkin, I told him. Tahel leaned over my laptop, working on unlocking the phone I'd found. She lit up when I asked her if she knew some trick for bypassing the pass code. I stood in the kitchen, preparing tea bags from the infusions I'd brought with me. Why are you filling them? asked Oshri. I hadn't noticed him abandoning the book and coming to stand by my side. I told him I liked to control the amount and flavor of the tea. I explained the distinction between the different kinds and let him smell them. He asked if he could try some. I asked what appealed to him. He pointed at Blue of London. I said it was a fantastic Earl Grey. Tahel wasn't interested. Her whole body hunched over the computer as she typed, her finger roaming over the mouse touch pad. Her name sounded from outside. She said, Good, Yalon's here, he can help. I went out to greet him. He leaned his bicycle against the fence and ran inside. Without any pleasantries, he stood in the middle of the living room and said, The woman who got hit last night is Kalanit.

I looked at their faces. Oshri slurped some of the tea and let it linger against his tongue, the roof of his mouth. His eyes were turned inward, to the action of thinking. Tahel's face shifted from excitement to terror as she considered the implications of this news. She said, What, what, there's nothing about it online.

Yalon's face emptied of the flush of strained cycling and exposed the paleness that had come over it. He stuttered, She . . . She . . . She . . . I told him to take a deep breath. I demonstrated. His stuttering gradually subsided. That word syllable, "she," that blocked him fell away. He said, Was lightly wounded. Sima says she has cuts on her hands, and—she didn't have any identification, it took them a while, she was alone there, alone, bleeding and not talking. Sima says she isn't talking now, either. Tahel asked, What was she doing by the public library? Who goes there at night? Yalon said, And because there was no one around, the rescue team took her to the hospital without informing anyone. He said, Sima says that eventually she reacted. Sima says eventually she pulled out her phone and pointed at her mother's name.

We have to go visit her, said Tahel. I said, I don't think now is the right time. Yalon repeated, She was alone and didn't talk. Oshri was in his own world, rolling the tea against his tongue. Tahel pushed me. I said I had to think, to forget about her for the time being and focus on unlocking the phone. But why is that important now? Tahel said. What's the phone got to do with the mystery? I said, It's got nothing to do with it, but someone lost their phone and I'd like to give it back. She said, Some phone, how come no one called since last night to find out where it is. Yalon looked helpless. I told him the hospital had experience in treating people suffering from shock. He said, And what about the missile injury? I said, She'll recover quickly. Tahel said, So how come? I told Yalon, Maybe an alien abduction would have been better. He stared at me for a few seconds. Tahel said, The phone might be in flight mode. I said, All the more reason.

My phone rang. I stared at Ronnit's name for a moment. Then I pulled out my tape recorder and went to the hallway. I said, Yes, Ronnit, what's up, is everything all right? Ronnit said, No, I need help. I said, I'm in Sderot. She said, David was arrested and I need to get him out. I said, What happened? She said, I don't know, he got mixed up with some gang. Slow down, I said, what gang? She said, A few guys from his kolel, they were preparing for an operation. An operation, I said. She said, They were going to deface some Arab businesses. I said, Ah, Wlodia was going to have his own little *Kristallnacht*. She said, Elish, this is no time for cynicism. I said I wasn't being cynical. She said, Can you help or not? I said, With what? She said, Don't you have that friend, the cop? I said I didn't think he could help. His connections were in central Israel. She said, Who can't help, you or him? I said, Don't you think David deserves to be punished? She said, Just tell me yes or no. I said, I'm leaning toward no. She said, Can you at least come here and watch Akiva?

20

Elish said he would have to make a few calls and find things out and that in the meantime they should go back to their own affairs. Tahel wanted to argue and say they had to rethink their whole approach. But Elish's presence was sucked back into his body, concentrating to the point of ringing with action and intent, and it muted her. She and Yalon focused their efforts on the computer. Yalon's presence was nothing but a bother. That rare correlation that happened sometimes when they smiled, when they discovered they'd been thinking similar thoughts, was gone, and she had to fight against him, order him to focus, scold him. That, she found, made her even sharper. She found the bypassing trick in one of the forums that Yalon reluctantly suggested.

By the time Elish finished making his calls, the phone was unlocked. She handed it over ceremoniously. He smiled at her, but there was a sorrow she couldn't understand in his smile. Tahel wondered, Who's this Ronnit person who changes him like this?

Yalon asked, Do you think it's because of us?

Tahel said, What's because of us?

He inhaled loudly and said to Elish, Can I use the computer? I want to show Tahel some things.

Elish nodded and examined the phone. Yalon turned to face Oshri and invited him to join them, but Oshri shook his head and returned to his book, occasionally sipping his tea and looking foggily into the air, immersed in his own mind. He was starting to annoy her again, that Oshri.

Look, said Yalon, turning the screen toward her. Hodaya Sasi went with Bobarisa to take pictures with some soldiers.

What? Elish said, surprised. She cooked the soldiers *bobarisa*?

No, said Tahel, Bobarisa is this disgusting kid that's feelin' himself.

She looked at the pictures. Hodaya with her arms wrapped around soldiers in clean uniforms near the Sderot train station, Bobarisa making the V sign with his fingers, kneeling beside three other soldiers. Hodaya holding a rifle and wearing a beret, the metal barrel squished against her breasts. Yalon paused on the image.

Who are these kids? asked Elish.

Tahel said, I don't know, boys from Sderot.

Yalon started to speak admiringly about Bobarisa's acts of bravery, and the more he talked, the more normal his voice became, hoarse but confident. He told about the chain of military unit flags that Oz Barbisa hung on a wire between his yard and his house, about his ascent to the observation hill to watch the bombing of Gaza and document it, and about Hodaya Sasi, who, to go by the pictures and status updates she posted, was the soldiers' sweetheart.

In short, disgusting, said Tahel.

Elish's phone rang. He walked over to the kitchen island and said, Two hours, all right, are you sure you can't make it? . . . Fine, hold on, let me write this down. He pulled out a small notepad that Tahel had never seen before, his pen-wielding hand engraving in it quickly. He told them, I have to get ready for a drive, so I'm going to take you back to Grandma Zehava. Be good.

He left the notepad on the wooden counter in the kitchen. Tahel walked over to take a look. She couldn't decipher his handwriting. It looked like the legs of dead flies. Yalon sat in front of the computer, completely absorbed in the photos of Hodaya and Bobarisa and the soldiers. Oshri was lost in his book with his cup of tea. She walked over to the window overlooking the lake. The water looked different from here, the scum burned, the eucalyptus thicket looked shriveled in the heat, pathetic.

Elish emerged from the hallway, showered and meticulously dressed, a hint of arrogance almost apparent in his usually sloppy appearance, even the faint echo of cologne.

Tahel said, Does this drive have to do with the Kalanit investigation?

Elish said it didn't. He put on his watch.

Tahel said, What then?

Elish said, It's personal.

Tahel said, When are we going to make progress with the investigation?

Elish opened the door and signaled for them to come. Yalon got on his bike and rode away.

In the car, Tahel said, You haven't answered me.

The minute-long drive stretched to eternity, as did Elish's silence. He pulled over outside the house, and Grandma Zehava came out to meet them. Oshri walked over, the book gripped in his hand, his mind in higher realms. Elish turned to face Tahel. She tensed with anticipation, but his face was full of the same sorrow she'd detected earlier. No, it was compassion. He said, Tahel, you don't get it. Kalanit may have been injured because of us. Our investigation is over.

21

Manny called to ask how it went. I said it went smoothly. I played my part. In the meantime, he'd found details about Sima Shaubi. Her husband died of cancer. Local rumor had it that Sima was planning to leave him. He was a violent man. She'd filed several complaints against him, as well as a restraining order, which she later rescinded. Once Kalanit enlisted, she rented her own apartment and husband and wife lived separately. Near the end of Kalanit's mandatory service he was diagnosed with pancreatic cancer. He died within a matter of months. Kalanit went traveling. Sima moved to Sderot. I said, Something must have happened, still, within that general, dull story. There are holes of interest, dark spots. Sima says people attempted to kidnap Kalanit on several occasions. Manny said, This case truly interests you. I said, I don't like loose ends. Manny said, The world is full of loose ends. I said, Yes, I've been learning that the hard way.

An officer waited for me at the reception desk at the police station in Jerusalem. He said, All you have to do is sit here and wait for a few hours, those are the orders I received. I nodded at him. Outside the police station, in the Jerusalem furnace that annihilated the brain inside its skull, two groups formed. On one side, Religious Zionist men in shirts and women in hats and headscarves holding up signs that read WARRIORS FOR ISRAELI LIBERTY; on the other side, seven or eight young men and women crying DOWN WITH RACISM in Hebrew, then in Arabic. I assumed they were repeating the same slogan in both languages.

My chest hurt from sitting on the wooden bench. I couldn't

focus on the book I'd brought with me, a new translation of *Ob-lomov*. The recumbence on the sofa, the life that goes by in and of itself, without ceremony or the appearance of a center of grav-ity, but there is gravity—not the kind that fills with life in the course of performing one's daily routines, but the hidden kind that emerges when we aren't paying attention. If we could de-vote ourselves to an intention toward it. But what would remain then? The spirit is no less desolate than one's instinctual re-sponse to the needs of the flesh. I got up and paced. The officer came over and asked me to be patient. I told him not to worry, I wasn't pacing because of impatience, but because of existence itself. He shrugged.

Eventually, they brought Wlodia to me. Previously, I'd only seen him in pictures. He was smaller than I'd imagined, but he had a savage fervor about him. His eyes bugged out like the eyes of a rodent, gray and threatening to pop out of their sockets. His yeshiva-student outfit was rumpled, the shirt wrinkled, the fringes wild over the black slacks. I signed his bail forms and led him outside. The burning dryness of noon did not drive away the two groups. They retreated to the shade, sitting around, gulping down water bottles. Their members jumped back on their feet when we stepped outside. Hands reached out from the Warriors for Israeli Liberty cluster to pat Wlodia's back encouragingly. His head was lowered. He only looked back up when someone from the Down with Racism group called out, Judo-Nazi. The of-ficers standing at the doorway to the station lunged to separate the groups, which had advanced on each other again now that the artificial cease-fire was shattered by the name-calling.

I dragged Wlodia to the parking lot. In the car, he said, So you're Elish. His accent, a skin on the surface of the Hebrew. I nodded. I said, I'm taking you home. He said, So you know. I said, Yes, that took courage. He said, I caught myself at the last minute, how I, a Jew, was becoming like the gentiles in Russia. I said, Yes, it's sad that preventing the violation of human rights is considered an act of bravery. We parked near their building. I saw Ronnit's head peeking out the window. I looked Wlodia over. He relaxed, his fervor abated. I pictured Akiva's face next to his, Akiva's eyes as I saw them then, bathed with otherness. There was no otherness there, only a belonging I hadn't known. An essence responding to another essence, resembling it in nature. Wlodia said, Akiva won't stop talking about you, Uncle Elish, Uncle Elish. He suggested I stay for a late lunch or at least a cup of coffee. Ronnit stepped out of the building, Akiva holding her hand. I told Wlodia I had to get back to Tel Aviv, to my own problems in need of solving. He touched my shoulder in gratitude as he opened the car door. I told him he had to tell Ronnit that he was the one who'd called the police to report the vandalism. He said, I think she already guessed it.

22

Ma'ayan

09:43 Reminder: tonight around ten o'clock, my birthday party, at my place. There's no safe room, there's a stairwell. Bring whatever you want to drink and whoever you want. Please RSVP.

11:48 Happy birthday

Yaron

12:05 Yes! HBD

Gil

12:12 PFF Yaron can't you just write happy birthday? It's just happy birthday why do you need an acronym?

12:13 what's "PFF" short for?

Gil

12:13 Pretty Fucking Funny

Yaron

12:15 Palestine Free-For-all
Gil you coming?

Gil

12:15 yes
Hang on, sending an acronym
Y.E.S.

Yaron

12:16 a real shortcut!

Farkash we expect you to be there

> 12:18 CICJBTD (Course
> I'm Coming Just Building a
> Teleportation Device)

Yaron

12:19 That's a special shortcut! That's what a poet's shortcut
looks like! Not like our simple people's

> 12:20 Next time I'll use
> exclamation points at the
> end of my shortcut too!!!!!

Yaron

12:21 How you doing Farkash?

> 12:22 F.I.N.E. T.R.Y.I.N.G.
> T.O. W.R.I.T.E. B.U.M.M.E.D.
> A.B.O.U.T. W.H.A.T'S.
> H.A.P.P.E.N.I.N.G. I.N.
> I.S.R.A.E.L.

Gil

12:22 Why does this conversation remind me of a cartoon

> 12:23 I think that's your
> world of associations right
> now.

Gil

12:24 It's always been my world except now I have an excuse

> 12:25 Oh. Are you watching
> Adventure Time?

Gil

12:25 Have you seen Doctor Who?

12:25 The trailer? Yes
For season eight

Gil

12:25 No, the first episode

Efrat

12:25 Your kidding! It aired already?

12:26 The first episode
hasn't been aired yet

Gil

12:26 Yes
It aired

12:26 There was a special
where the doctor changed

Gil

12:26 Including a dinosaur

Efrat

12:27 Gil, talk clearly. This is important. The season is supposed to
start in August. Did you watch the first episode?

Gil

12:27 Yes

Efrat

12:27 Where

12:28 That happened on
season 7, didn't it?

Efrat

12:28 I don't remember a dinosaur

Gil
12:28 An entire episode about why the doctor is old

Efrat
12:29 Ugh, Gil

Gil
12:29 I'm serious
There was a dinosaur

Ma'ayan
12:29 Hey guys, this conversation is hard to follow

Gil
12:29 And he's Scottish! And not so moral

Ma'ayan
12:29 Thanks for the birthday wishes ☺

Efrat
12:30 Ma'ayani, I'm having trouble following too

Ma'ayan
12:33 Totally
Nahum I've missed you. When are you getting back?

12:33 Soon

Gil
12:36 In Heidelberg again?

12:37 Uh-huh

Gil
12:38 Well at least you aren't suffering from racism

Ma'ayan
12:38 Germany? Racism?

Gil

12:40 Over here it's almost Nazi Germany with all this new nation-
alism. Pretty soon you'll have to wear a red star to show you aren't
a nationalist there are already lists going

> 12:43 These days left wing
> in Israel is just an inch to
> the left of extremist ultra-
> orthodox like the Kahane
> Lives party

Gil

12:44 The left is dead that's what people are shouting

Ma'ayan

12:44 How did Kahane die? Seriously I don't remember

Yaron

12:45 Left wingers are just people like Gil for example

Gil

12:45 I'm not left wing I love wars

Efrat

12:45 He was murdered I think

Ma'ayan

12:46 Who murdered him?

Yaron

12:46 You're still just people

Ma'ayan

12:48 Gil make me a dessert for tonight

Yaron

12:48 Ma'ayan why don't we go out to the Margosa?

Gil
12:48 Why would we?

Ma'ayan
12:49 I don't feel like going out, I like it better when people come over

Gil
12:49 I'm bringing dessert

Ma'ayan
12:50 Bless your heart :)

Yaron
12:50 Got any soft drugs?

Gil
12:50 No, just cheap booze

12:50 I'll mail you some Wiener schnitzel and sauerkraut

Ma'ayan
12:50 There's a new snack, Bamba and Bissli mixed together

Yaron
12:50 Mmm

Gil
12:50 Why?

12:51 Seriously? Is it a product of genetic engineering?

Ma'ayan
12:53 Totally serious. Efrat told me about it and today I bought some

SHIMON
ADAF

12:53 So they're finally
integrating peanut DNA
with wheat DNA

Gil
12:54 That kind of thing doesn't exist in Heidelberg

Ma'ayan
12:54 Now we just need to name the next snack Iron Dome

Gil
12:55 Is it going to be liver flavored and be shaped like the tip of a dick?

Ma'ayan
12:55 Gross

Gil
12:55 There's iron in liver

Ma'ayan
12:56 Eww

Yaron
12:56 That's 2014 left wingers for you . . .

Ma'ayan
12:58 Nahum, we'll miss you tonight

12:59 Eat drink and be
merry, People of Pompeii

recognized the name of the cell phone owner immediately. Nahum Farkash. Swiping the touch screen naturally summoned the chat app. I wondered, If Farkash was writing from Heidelberg, how could his phone be in Israel? Tahel was right, the phone was in airplane mode. I connected it to the wireless network, and the inbox filled up with texts. In the chat app, I asked that one of his friends let Mr. Farkash know I found his phone and offered my number as well.

I knew that my time in Sderot would resurrect the memory of Dalia Shushan, but I didn't think it would happen so randomly. Farkash was known by his nickname, the Sderot Poet. He insisted on staying in town even when the other artists left. Back in the day, I read a eulogizing poem he'd written following Dalia's death. Many of her lines were imbedded in it, but they did not respond well to the meter into which they'd been cast. I was not a fan of his habit of fashioning his Moroccan identity into a crown to magnify himself. Moroccan identity is a way of experiencing the world, not a skin that can be scrubbed or an object to be exhibited. It isn't the contents of things, but the act of speaking. It shows itself, as a philosopher I once favored used to say. The eulogizing poem Farkash had written for Dalia ultimately addressed, I deduced, a general readership of European descent and ended with the words "Grass shall grow from your cheeks and yet still you shall not understand."

He said he was glad to finally meet me, that he had no idea I was in Sderot, that he thought he'd seen me at the rally the previous night, that he loved what I wrote about Blasé—

I stopped him there. I said, I was a different person back then, I have no desire to reminisce. He said, Okay. I handed him the phone but he hesitated at the door. I invited him to come in and have a seat. He said he'd read one of my books and had a pleasant reading experience. But . . . , I said. He said, But what? I asked if he wanted something to drink. He said, Water, if you don't happen to have alcohol. I said I had a bottle of wine from the grocery store somewhere, nothing fancy. He said, But I wondered what your question was. How does detective literature serve you, to find out what, the question of justice, the agony, the meaning of life, what? I asked if a story wasn't enough, the thrill offered by the mystery, the character of the detective. He said, What's the point of a literature revolving around an investigation if it doesn't itself ask a question? I don't understand literature that doesn't ask a question.

I opened the wine bottle with effort. The pain in my ribs had diminished, becoming a dull signal. The tightness in my leg muscles bothered me more. I was still unable to slow down to meet it, to hurt at the speed of hurt. He asked, Did you get beat up at the rally too? I said, Yes, is it that obvious? He laughed. He said, Actually, isn't it weird for you to be here? This neighborhood is so surreal. I said, Yeah, it feels unfinished, and I don't just mean the construction, but the intention of things to become realized within our existence. He sipped suspiciously from the glass of wine I'd served him. He said, I know, everyone in Sderot is confused that the project was even executed and is actually successful. It belonged in the realm of forgotten dreams, dreams destined for dust. He added that if he ever had the patience for prose, he'd write a fantasy novel set in a Sderot in which all these false passions came true. And most surprising, he said, is that everything that was supposed to prevent this development from becoming a reality actually happened. The architect in charge ran away with the seed money for planning and digging and with one of the municipal employees. The mayor was suspected of embezzlement and money laundering and is still under investigation. And yet, and yet, he gestured toward the view outside the window, the hallucination took on iron flesh-and-glass bones.

I said I'd been there for almost a week and heard more about corruption than about Qassam rockets. He said, People don't get that residents are more concerned about the rot in this town than about the war. He said that a few years ago a journalist called him to ask for ideas for an article about Sderot from a fresh angle. Farkash told him to research residents' sense of distress about the fact that donations to the city all made their way into the pockets of municipal employees and their associates. The journalist was unmoved. Farkash suggested he write the article from a personal point of view, through the story of Sarah Matatov, who was killed by a Qassam. She was an immigrant from the former Soviet Union whose elderly mother died in Israel, leaving her completely alone. One morning she woke up with an ominous feeling. She ran among the buses sent from Eilat hotels to pick up Sderot residents, begging for a seat on one of the buses headed to the resorts, claiming that if she stayed in Sderot, she'd be dead by the end of the day. But she had no connections in City Hall, so she was sent back home. She was killed by a Qassam that afternoon. The journalist didn't care about that either. Farkash told him about the unfounded development the mayor was planning together with a questionable landscape architect and suggested he check that out, that it was a recipe for disaster as far as the mood in Sderot. The journalist wasn't interested.

I said I didn't understand. If the architect fled with the money, how did they build the lake and how was there still an embezzlement investigation going against the mayor? He said this was what he knew: The architect, Georges Arguile was his name, had conspired with Heftzi Columbus, the mayor's office manager, and the two of them took off with a copious amount of money donated by a British Jewish organization for the purpose of sprucing up the town. A year went by, the election was nearing, the eternal mayor announced a rezoning and a continuation of the erection of the Lakeside neighborhood. The embezzlement investigation was unrelated, as far as he knew.

I said there was no way to avoid corruption. He said that Israel had always been a financial story, from the redemption of lands in the late nineteenth century to this day. It was just that it was getting harder to cover up the gnawed foundations with the fissured concrete cloaks of Zionism. So it became hysterical, required to invent new wars every other day. One war per decade used to be enough, but now the lulls were growing shorter, and more distractions were required to keep the lie from falling apart. I asked him if he didn't believe in the necessity of Israel's existence. He said he wanted to live in a Jewish sovereignty, that he wanted to live among Hebrew speakers, that he wanted to take his experience, his parents' experience, his Moroccan heritage, and find out how all of those could blend into a Jewish Hebrew existence and transform it. But to do that he didn't need to fight the Palestinians. He had to fight against the fat men in suits scalping national ideas to inflate their children's bank accounts. The Palestinians would have to wage the same battle too at some point if they were sane and thirsty for life. He said solving the conflict would begin with a financial agreement.

I said, And you plan to do all that from Heidelberg. He chuckled. He said, You couldn't resist the temptation, huh? I said, The phone turned on onto your conversation. He said, How did you unlock it, anyway? I said, My niece. He said, Why do we even bother? Then he added, Heidelberg is an inside joke among my friends. I used to be obsessed with it, then one day I just went there. I asked, Because of Hegel? He said, No, a less spiritual reason. So now every time I go off the grid they ask if I'm in Heidelberg.

ahel was thinking how she never wanted to see Elish again, but she still hoped he'd call, text that he was sorry, and promise to help her solve the Kalanit case. She added the name Dmitry Shtedler to her notebook, on the side of *The Secret of the Disappearing Student.* She planned how she'd behave at Friday-night dinner. She'd ignore him, give him the cold shoulder, turn away disinterestedly. But Grandma Zehava told her mother that Elish wouldn't make it. He said he was too tired and hadn't imagined how difficult moving to Sderot would be.

What's this nonsense? her mother said. He's eight hundred meters away, what is he talking about, too tired? She dialed Elish's number with broken finger taps. Tahel observed her typical, ready-to-go discontent, the oxygen it emitted into the air of the living room.

What's going on with you now?

So what?

The kids are here, they want you to come.

What's that got to do with Zalman?

Won't sit with him at the same table? Are you nuts or what?

Fine, fine, don't do me any favors.

She hung up and sighed. He'll never be a decent human being, she told Grandma Zehava. It finally looked like he was taking responsibility and following through on his commitment. He actually reported on the kids every hour, and they're getting attached to him, I can tell. Then all of a sudden he behaves like this.

Grandma Zehava said, He takes after his father, doesn't like attachments.

Don't start that Dad business again.

Tahel's father walked in, returning from synagogue, Oshri dragging his feet behind him. He broke into his song, "Welcome, Angels," and Grandma Zehava accompanied him. She had a warm voice that reminded Tahel of molten gold. Tahel thought about how she'd like to fill the lake with that singing, which could melt all the evil lurking in the thicket, approaching the—

Come help me serve, her mother said.

She got up and walked into the kitchen. She didn't listen to the dinner-table conversation. It was the usual topics: the situation, government policy, plans to surround Gaza with a moat that would collapse every tunnel the Palestinians dug into Israeli territory, streaming fuel into the tunnels and setting them on fire. She lent an ear in anticipation of a Red Color announcement that would interrupt the flow.

She used her hour of internet time researching forgetfulness and disappearances, blacking out for long periods. Blacking out for short periods was common among people suffering from epilepsy. Kalanit may have experienced a similar fit for three days, but in epileptics the people around them could always notice the paralysis, and Kalanit remembered the bus ride. Tahel checked Yalon's Facebook page. Hodaya Sasi and Oz Barbisa had approved his friend requests. He'd deleted the list of his favorite books and movies from his profile.

Look, Oshri said when she gave him her place at the computer, you've got to see this. On the screen appeared images of strange fish. That's a blobfish, said Oshri. He was named the ugliest animal in the world. The blobfish had a human face drawn into an expression of desperation and anguish, swollen, dead. And this, he said, is a goblin shark. The shark's purple skin was wrinkled, and a long horn jutted out from the center of its forehead. It looked like a hastily made sock puppet. He pulled up a picture of a leafy seadragon, which resembled a twig swept into the depths, then switched to images of glowing sea creatures. Look here, he said. He started up a video that was saved on the hard disk. Illuminated depths in which vermin floated. Look at this, he said. Some movement could be detected in the background. He said, This fish, he knows how to change the angles of his eyes so they reflect the light that enters the water.

So? she said. Big deal.

Don't you get it? he said. The reflection makes the fish disappear in the flow of light.

She looked closer. Again, movement and dissipation.

Pretty, isn't it? he said.

Why are you bothering me with your nonsense?

I thought you'd like it.

Why? she asked.

Because.

You're a smartass now, huh?

What's wrong with you?

Don't you ask what's wrong with me, you midget.

She stepped out of the room. The blood bubbled in her veins, hard this time. She had spent the entire afternoon thinking up ways of getting Elish to make up with her. The same chaos that ran through her insides began to take place outside. They sat in the backyard, in the temporary shade of the pergola they'd helped build. Night trickled in slowly, dripping. Oshri read. In spite of her irritation with him, she marveled at his output. Part of his face was concealed by *The Exploits of Moominpappa*. Their father arrived with heavy footfalls. He asked Oshri, Can't you hear me yelling for you?

Oshri said, No, I didn't hear.

I didn't hear either, Tahel said reluctantly.

You stay out of this, Tahel, said their father. I was calling you to come play.

I'm in the middle of a book, said Oshri.

So, said their father, put the book down and come on.

Oshri said nothing.

Why are you so quiet? asked their father.

Maybe we can wait five minutes, until it gets darker.

Now, said their father.

Oshri said, Ugh, I don't want to.

Tahel glared at him with the same amazement that sealed their father's eyes.

What—did you say? he asked.

That I don't want to.

Ungrateful, said their father. What's going on with you? You got all cheeky. First you don't wake up in time for synagogue. I still owe you a punishment after the Shabbat is over.

Oshri said, All we do is sit around there.

Where? asked their father.

At synagogue. We don't go there to pray.

Their father asked, Then why do we go, smart-ass?

Tahel's mouth turned dry. She gestured to Oshri with her head, but he just gripped the open book on both sides. He said, So you can talk to Yalon's dad.

25

I wondered what reason I still had for lingering in Sderot. Though during Shabbat, a thought that echoed my mother's tone persisted—what did I have back in Tel Aviv? Why couldn't I sell my apartment and move down here? One could get used to war and Qassams.

My mother said Bobby was away at one of the construction sites up north again. Tahel was distant when I arrived, but gradually shed her tenseness the longer I sat before her in silence. She said, We can't just drop the Kalanit investigation in the middle, we've got to keep going. I asked, Who's we? She said, You and I. I asked about Oshri and Yalon. She said Oshri was being punished. Punished? I said. Yeah, said my mother, who walked in from the laundry room. He's getting rude. Tahel said, He told the truth. I said, There are ways of telling the truth. What happened? She told me. I looked at my mother. She said, What can you do, the boy is growing up, he can't stay a cute baby forever. I said, I suppose that isn't Yaffa's version. She said, Sunday is always full of work from Shabbat.

We walked outside. No threat had cut through the face of the morning so far. The greening pond, in its efforts to be a lake, glimmered with the force of day, an uninterrupted ray of serenity in life. Even though a wind blew, the rustle of leaves in the thicket traveled across the water all the way to us. And Yalon? I asked Tahel. She said, He's busy with other things. I said, They're talking about a permanent cease-fire, I heard. She nodded. She said, His mother will be back with the babieses soon.

She said, Elish, please. I asked her what she thought we

could do. She said we had to watch the ward where Kalanit was hospitalized in Beersheba, see if the stranger was visiting her again, then follow him, catch him, and question him. I asked if she'd made sure Kalanit wasn't already released from the hospital. It was only a light injury, and there was no excess of free beds in the hospital right now. She said she texted Yalon but he hadn't answered yet. Her voice lowered when she said this, growing hoarse. I said, Look, we've made quite a bit of progress, we've eliminated a few possibilities. She said, That isn't enough. Then she asked, What possibilities? I said, We can be sure Kalanit didn't make something up because there's a precedent. I said, We know she herself isn't aware of what's happening to her because she spends most of her time feeling anxious and panicked. I said the obvious conclusion was that the Kalanit case was a symptom of the mystery, not its source. Tahel said, But what does that mean? I said, We've only heard of two cases. What if it's a bigger phenomenon, and the sequence of time is interrupted for young women, maybe men too, at different times and places all over the world? Tahel said, So we need to tell someone, the FBI, Interpol, Manny must know people there. I said, You realize we have no resources for investigating this. She said, But we can't just abandon it like this. I said we had to choose the mysteries we could bear. She said, You're always saying things I don't understand, you're doing it on purpose, to confuse me. She said, But there is something you can do, isn't there? She said, You'll leave soon too.

I said nothing. I was astounded. But not astounded. She sat before me, wild, ready to pounce, and simultaneously made of glass, evaporating. A big fish from the depths behind her would soon jump out and carry her who knew where. I opened my mouth to answer and didn't know what I was going to say. The phone rang. I grabbed it mechanically. Ronnit's name flickered across the screen.

She asked how I was doing. She apologized for only calling

to thank me now and asked what had gotten into me on Thursday that made me run off like that. I could have at least stayed for coffee. I said, Perhaps. She said, So what's going on with you, still in Sderot? I mumbled an affirmative response. The entire time, Tahel's eyes were on me. I got up and went inside. I told Ronnit, I'm glad it worked out. She said, It took him all Shabbat long to tell me, I knew he wasn't the type. I heard her voice going up at the ends of sentences, the tongue taking off as it rolled the syllables into her mouthpiece. I picked up one of the dry *ezovion* twigs Yaffa had scattered over the house. I held it to my nose. I said, Good, great, how's Akiva? She said, What's with you? You sound out of it. I said, There are a few matters here that demand my attention. She said, I wanted to tell you something, but you know what, now isn't the time, I'll call you another day. Have a good week, a quiet week. I thought, Hollow words.

I went into the safe room to talk to Oshri. He was lying on the bed, staring. Beside him, open and overturned on the floor of the room, was a copy of *Mio, My Son*. The opaque LED glow was trapped between the ceiling and the cover. I asked if everything was all right. He sat up and said yes. His expression was suddenly full of life. He asked if I thought Mio was actually a lost prince or if he was only dreaming it. I asked if it mattered. He said, But even if he is a prince, I'm not sure I would want to take his place. I told him the next book he should read was *The Phantom Tollbooth*. He asked why. I said he had to experience lots of journeys to learn that it was impossible to say in advance which one was worth embarking on. He said he thought he understood what I meant. He picked up the book. He asked shyly if, once his punishment was over, he could come over and try other kinds of tea. I said yes, of course he could. And books too, I added, Whenever he wanted to read, I would be glad to offer guidance, though at some point he would have to start picking them himself.

Tahel walked in. She'd changed. Her posture was straighter,

her gestures precise, controlled. She said, Last try, let's compare notes. What notes? I asked. She said, Your investigation notes and mine, like the ones Benny Zehaviv makes. I said, But I don't have any notes. She said, You have that notepad. I said, You're perceptive. She smiled.

She pulled a notebook out of the dresser drawer. The cover read *TYO Investigations* and, beneath that, *The Secret of the Disappearing Student.* The first page contained three names: Kalanit Shaubi, Levy Todros, Dmitry Shtedler. There was a page dedicated to each one afterward, containing a summary of information regarding that person. The rest of the notebook was empty. I asked if that was it. She shrugged. She said, Do you have anything to add? Oshri said, There's another side. What? said Tahel. Oshri said, The other side of the notebook. I turned it over. The other side read *The Case of the Enchanted Thicket.* The name Sarah Matatov appeared on the first page. The next one detailed the circumstances of her death and the location of the monument in the heroism grove named after her. I asked, What does Sarah Matatov have to do with anything? Tahel said, We wanted to find out what was scaring Mom in the thicket. And the monument is in the middle of the thicket? I asked quietly. Not really, it's close to the water, said Tahel. I said, How do you get there? Tahel said, Yalon took pictures, I can show you on the computer. I turned the notebook over. *The Secret of the Disappearing Student.* I turned it over again. *The Case of the Enchanted Thicket.* I turned the notebook over and over in my hands like a hot coal. I'm such an idiot, I finally muttered. What, said Tahel, what?

26

Tahel noticed once more how Elish's realness returned to him, how he manifested. Gently, he put down the notebook and said, You're a genius. You're both geniuses. He called Grandma Zehava into the room and told her he had to go out for an hour. Tahel followed his actions with her eyes. He picked up his phone to text her mother. She held her breath. He didn't notice. He slipped it back into his pocket and rushed off.

Earlier, when he'd walked into the room to talk to Oshri, temptation got the best of her, and she slid her finger along the touch screen of his phone, which was on the kitchen table next to one of her mother's dry twigs of purple flowers. The phone shook off its dimness and glowed once more. She looked at his most recent calls. Ronnit. Who's Ronnit? There was no picture or last name attached to her contact listing, just Ronnit. She examined his apps and opened the photo app. Only two albums were in his photo library. One was devoted to Kalanit, a portrait she and Yalon had sent him, pictures of her with the blurry stranger. The other contained pictures of a boy, small, religious, with a yarmulke and *payot* and fringes, in the midst of different activities, jumping, climbing a jungle gym, posing for the camera, retreating from it. They were all taken on the same day and at the same time, a few days before Elish moved to the Lakeside neighborhood. In the final picture in the album, the boy appeared with a woman, also religious, wearing a headscarf, their heads close together, nearly touching, her arms around him. Tahel sent herself the photo, as well as another of the boy sitting alone on a low stone wall, almost bashful, his eyes nevertheless challenging the lens. Then she erased the outgoing messages.

In the bedroom, she wondered out loud what had happened. Oshri ignored her. He already had his nose back in his book. She looked at the pictures on her phone, zooming in on the child's face. Something in his eyes was familiar, threatening in its familiarity. She swiped to the next picture. That's Ronnit, she thought. Who's Ronnit?

Ronnit is the witch, said Oshri, as if talking in his sleep, or as if he were a ventriloquist's dummy.

What? she said.

You asked who's Ronnit, he said, tilting the book to look at her. I told you Mom talked to a witch to—

Yes, she said, not that it helped.

Oshri said nothing. Last night the two of them stood in the doorway to the kitchen and looked inside. Their mother was standing there, covering her ears. Then she turned toward them without warning and they pushed against the wall, squeezing into the shelter of the narrow door beam. She didn't notice them, but they could see tears running down her cheeks.

I wonder if it's the same Ronnit, said Tahel.

I think Grandma knows her, said Oshri.

Yeah, why?

She and Mom were talking about her.

Oh, she said. Thanks.

Oshri didn't answer. The book separated them again.

Grandma Zehava was in the laundry room. Tahel recalled that when Mom talked about the plans for the house, she said she needed a spacious laundry room. She didn't want a machine in the kitchen and she didn't want to see piles of clean laundry in the living room. Grandma sat in the laundry room, a pile of colorful clothing at her feet, mostly Tahel's and Oshri's pants and shirts. She asked Grandma if she needed help.

Grandma Zehava said, No, *yidoroni*, but come sit with me for a bit.

Tahel looked at her face, searching for the clogged vein. There was a baby-blue bump on the side of her nose. The shock of that first evening at home when she saw Grandma pricking her finger with a blood sugar monitor, then injecting herself with insulin, returned to her, accompanied by a slashing sensation. Grandma folded the clothes quickly. Tahel picked up a shirt from the pile and tried to fold it. It crumpled between her hands, balling and spreading out again.

Grandma Zehava smiled. She said, You're a big girl and you still don't know how to fold your own clothes.

She took the shirt from her and showed her the lines along which the folding was to be performed, how to place the sleeves, how to take the collar into account.

Tahel asked, Does Elish have a friend named Ronnit?

Grandma Zehava paused in her folding. She said, Where did you hear that name?

Tahel said, Nowhere, I just heard it.

I told your mother you remember her.

Me, I know her? asked Tahel.

Yes, she was in love with you when you were little. As soon as she came over, you'd go off with her. How you cried when your mother told you she wouldn't be coming anymore.

How old was I?

Not even three.

How am I supposed to remember something like that?

I told your mother not to call her. It's a shame. Let bygones be bygones.

Was she Elish's girlfriend? asked Tahel.

Yes. Go get my bag from the dresser in my room.

Tahel returned, bag in hand. Grandma Zehava fished out a small photo album. She said, Your mother doesn't like me carrying this around. The first page of the album was a faded black-and-white image of a young man in a suit.

That's your grandfather, may he rest in peace.

Tahel didn't like the change in her grandmother's voice. It seemed to come from deep inside a tunnel, full of echoes and echoes of echoes. She grabbed the album and flipped through it quickly. Grandma stopped her.

She said, There you are when you were little. What a doll. I'd walk with you down the street and people would always stop me to say, What a doll, what a doll.

Tahel flipped the page.

And there's you and Elish and Ronnit, said Grandma.

She pulled the photo from its plastic casing. Elish seemed to have been glued into the image, foreign to the background, the setting. The colors were bright, almost burnt against the paper. There was no doubt, Ronnit's head was exposed in this picture, but she was merely a younger version of the woman in Elish's digital photo album.

joints painted blue, like interwoven veins, a thick pipe emerging from the ground, then swallowed in it again. I descended down the other side of the hill, the side facing Gaza. Near the end of the slope a cylinder shot out of the ground, also blue, stretching down the bottom of the hill until it dipped into the rising ground. I touched the iron, then pulled my hand away. Inside this burning were additional burnings, swarming in the deep. I thought back to the trip to Montpellier with Claude Rosenbloom, I thought about Mathieu Clause and the Elgar quote he referenced, about the actor hiding behind the scenes, and I thought about how reality was composed of a series of near replicas and imprecise repetitions, immediately creating a sense of familiarity and a summoning of the encounter with the new. I considered the way the Sonata in E Minor attempts to achieve the exact same impression. I thought about Descartes's unoriginal argument that even in our wildest dreams we create what is foreign to our experience out of parts of our experience, that the disturbed and the unusual are unreasonable arrangements of what we already know. I thought about a pond trapped in the belly of the hill. I ascended the hill again, marking with my eyes the emergence of the pipe from the ground, then went down, following its route. It circled the thicket almost completely, then sank back into a fallow field between the thicket and the edge of the neighborhood, concealed. I'd come this way and hadn't noticed it. There was no logic to the route. If I was guessing right, and sediments accumulated in the belly of this hill, just like in the belly of the mountain in Montpellier, and the pipe was part of a drainage or routing system moving rainwater from the inside of the hill to the concavity of the lake, then what was the reason for this convolution? A pipe emerging from the other side, passing through the thicket, would have been more economical and efficient.

I called Yaffa. She answered quickly, with whispered worry. I told her everything was fine with the kids, our mother was watching them and I'd be back soon. She said, I'm glad you called. I want to talk, but not on the phone. I said, No problem. I asked how she'd heard about the lakeside development. She said she'd read a small news item about it in the paper. It was about a ceremony, the dedication of some monument, but she recognized the opportunity. I asked when this happened. She said, 2010, I think. Bobby was convinced it was a hoax, and he wasn't the only one. Why? I asked. She said the landscape architect who'd designed it had fled the scene. Georges Arguile, I said. She said she didn't know that was his name. He took off with the money, but the mayor insisted on restarting the work and raised more funds. I said, The mayor who's under investigation. She said, Yes, the previous mayor, Yoram Bitton. Bobby thought the development was just an election ruse meant to fill the pockets of contractors who supported Bitton and that's why the land was sold so cheap. People hesitated to buy it. Otherwise we couldn't have afforded it. I told her they were lucky. She said she wasn't so sure anymore. I asked why. She said, Forget it.

I asked if she remembered where she saw the news item. She said it was in the *Southern Wind*, it was distributed in Ashkelon too, and what was with all these questions? I said, Never mind, hang on. I flipped through my notepad and asked if she'd ever heard of Sarah Matatov. She said she hadn't, though that name sounded familiar. I asked if she knew anybody in City Hall. She said, No, only that Bobby's relatives sent him to talk to a guy called Elkoby, who they thought could help. He worked there for a while. I said, Elkoby from the engineering department? Yeah, yeah, she said, a total loser, it was so obvious the title was tailor-made for him. She wasn't surprised when he was fired along with the other freeloaders. I asked if she'd heard of Heftzi Columbus. She said she hadn't, although that name rang a bell too. Then she said, Elish, have you started up with all that questionable business again? I said I hadn't. She told me not to lie, she could hear in my voice that I was changing back.

very August we said this was the first time it had ever been so hot. The day bubbled around the infected lung of the Ninth of Av, and we said, Summer this year is real hell. I remembered. Ronnit said, Inferno, inferno, the humidity doesn't even break in the evening. I said it only seemed to get worse, the sea emitting the hours of heat back at us.

We were becoming more and more shackled in a trap of intimacy, searching. Darkness in the Jaffa air. To Ronnit, Jaffa seemed like a demilitarized zone where stealth was possible. I didn't ask why she needed that sense of surreptitiousness. I came. The owner of the Yafa Bar served us a plate of *maqluba*. Afterward Ronnit said, Let's go down to the port. I said, There's nothing to see there besides crumbling warehouses. Ronnit said, Still.

She told me about medical school. She thought it would get easier with time. She said she was feeling more and more doubtful of her ability to care for others. I said, Ability or need? She said that right now, as far as she was concerned, the two were the same. I asked about changing tracks to medical research. She said she hadn't fully figured out yet what she was interested in. I reminded her that the first time we met, she said she wanted to decode that nebulous knowledge people call the secret of life. She said she hadn't lost interest in that, she was just questioning the way, but that she had no intention of quitting medical school anyway. Shoshi and Dror claimed that a slight push against the bumps in the road would smooth things out. I asked which one of them had said it. She said, When you meet them, you'll understand, I've never met such a harmonious couple.

I pointed at the partially ruined edifices of the port, cast in dimness. I said the city was planning on renovating the port and turning it into a commercial center. She asked how I knew that. I said, Residual information from the days when I cared to know. She asked me to talk a little more about myself. I said I didn't have much to say.

I expected there to be fishermen here, she said. We walked toward Tel Aviv. The wall along the small cliff was orphaned. I asked her what kind of landscape fishermen would have completed, in her imagination. She said, An image of detachment, a life going on without anything to do with us. I said, That's typically our tragedy, isn't it? She said, What is? I said, That life doesn't stop for the sake of death, disease, despair, war, just walks indifferently toward the future. She said, You're so depressing.

I'm dripping, I said. East of the boardwalk was the recreation area, a zone made up of sheets of linen and twinkle lights and the sweet apple aroma of hookah, and lots of tourists, sipping overpriced bad alcohol. I said, There you go, a live performance: the harms of exoticism. She said, They're having fun, what do you care?

I said she was surprising me. She asked how. I said she was the one who always claimed details were not enough. She said, That depends on context. I said, No, details reveal their hidden organizing principle. She said, Fine, so tell me one thing you learned about me from the collection of my details. I said, You've got night blindness. She paused and said, How did you guess? I said, The way you narrow your eyes in dim lighting, the way you lean in, the hesitant steps whenever we move from light to darkness. She nodded. I asked if she wanted to go north to Tel Aviv.

The Irgun Museum stood, perforated, awaiting fighters to rise
from the dead to liberate the city from its new occupiers, the real
estate owners plotting underground.

She said, Yes, is there air-conditioning in your apartment? I
said, You think I'd survive in Tel Aviv without it? We hailed a
taxi. On the way, she asked me to remind her to call Shoshi and
Dror. I nodded.

She wandered through my apartment, looking at the living
room, the balcony, the roof, the bedroom, the study. So this is
where you write? she asked. I said it was and apologized for the
mess. The case Manny had given me was open on the desk. Images of the murdered woman, bleeding on the kitchen floor,
peeked out in black and white. She asked how I could bear those
materials. I went to the desk and started to clean up. I hadn't
noticed she'd already moved on.

I found her in the living room, standing still beside the stereo system, her back to me. She turned around, holding the album *One Mile and Two Days Before Sunset*. She said, Do you
still listen to this? You said you lost interest in music. I said,
There are outliers. She rubbed the head of the boy in the cover
image with her finger, running it over the strip of sky shining
against the dark. She said, I'm sorry, I think I'll spend the night
at Shoshi and Dror's after all. I listened to the sound of her footsteps fading in the stairwell for hours later. She didn't come
back.

29

The door to the jewelry store was locked. I tapped on the glass between the iron bars. The man inside, his image an assemblage of spots against the glass blockade, pointed to the right. Beside the door was a small bell. I rang it. He opened the door. A guy who compensated for the smallness of his skull with an enormous Afro. Thick curls. When he smiled, his teeth looked sharp. I asked if it was necessary for me to ring the bell for the door to open. His smile widened, exposing wrinkles in the corners of his eyes, his age.

I looked at his display table. Necklaces, rings, chains, earrings, semiprecious gems. He asked how he could help. I said I was surprised people locked their stores in Sderot. He said, You aren't from here. I said I wasn't, I was just visiting. He said, Where from? I said, Tel Aviv. Tel Aviv, he said with appreciation, why, don't people lock up there? I said they did. He said, Then why not in Sderot? Just because it's a small place, you expect there not to be pieces of shit here? I said, Well, everybody knows everybody. He said, Don't you know that's the worst situation? Your neighbor stabs you in the back, then smiles at you the next morning as if nothing happened. I said, I'm familiar with that. He said, From Tel Aviv? I said, No, from research I once conducted for one of my books.

Books, he said, you don't look like a writer to me. I said, What do I look like to you? A clerk, at best, he said, and believe me, bro, no one can read people better than me. I said, Okay, what kind of clerk then? He said, VAT inspections. I said, Don't get carried away. Anyway, he could google me. He said, You people, you'll do anything to stay undercover. Social Security agents are like spies, with surveillance equipment and whatnot, why don't you in the VAT office do the same? I said I was Zalman Danino's brother-in-law. He said, Well, why didn't you say so? I know his relatives. What are you doing, buying, selling, or repairing?

I said I was there on a different matter. I was conducting research for a book. He said, About Sderot? I said, Among other things. He said, And you're staying with the Daninos. I said, Close, in the Lakeside neighborhood. He said, Don't remind me of that goddamned cursed name. You're the one who rented Dadon's house. What a coward that guy is. *Inshallah* he moves to Tel Aviv and gets hit by a missile. His sharp teeth emerged between his lips. The bell rang. He opened the door for a middle-aged woman. *Sabah el hir, ya azhizha*, he said, laughing. She didn't answer. She pulled out a velvet satchel and opened it to reveal a pearl bracelet. She said, Look, one pearl already fell off. She presented it on the counter. Elkoby said it was no problem, he could fix it. He reached for the bracelet and she smacked his hand. From her purse, she pulled out a cell phone and took a picture of the bracelet. Then she wrapped it back up and handed it to him. *Ya azhizha*, he said, don't you trust us? She said, I don't even trust God, you want me to trust people?

Why did you say that, I asked once she'd left, that the name Lakeside is cursed? He sized me up with his eyes. What's the book you're writing? I said, It's about special projects in Israel. A special project, he said, big deal. I said Zalman's relatives told me Elkoby was fired because of an inspection. I told you, he said, you guys sniff at every hole. Someone from the state comptroller's office came to look at appointments. What business is it of the state comptroller who the mayor appoints? I said nothing. I said, I want to know a little about the architect who designed the lake. He said, So what do you want from me? I said, I heard you worked in the engineering department during that time. Maybe you can refer me to people who knew him.

He said, That snob, and like, what, is he coming to show off here in Sderot? Georges Arguile, my ass. He's just George Arji. I asked if the man didn't have close friends. He said, He mostly hung out with the mayor and Heftzi. I said, Heftzi Columbus. He tensed up. What have you heard? I said I heard nothing, that her name just came up. He said, I'm telling you, I have no idea what she saw in him. I said, I heard they were a couple. Pff, he said, that fairy. I said, I heard they ran away together. He said, I don't buy it, that running away story. I said, Why? He said, Because, number one, Heftzi wasn't interested in him. And number two, she wasn't the type. I said, How do you know? He said, I know. He blinked and looked away. I stood there, hesitating, on the verge of something. The next required step used to come easily to me, without any remorse. With a voice sealing around the edges, Elkoby said, If you aren't going to buy anything, you'd better leave. I left. Traffic in the shopping center was sparse. I plopped down on a bench in the shade. I never asked for happiness. Asking for happiness seemed like challenging the gods, speaking a name in vain. All I wanted was to linger in the cracks, in pockets of time and space given to a different authority, where reality had run its course or had yet to take place at all. Images from my hospitalization the previous summer rose in my mind again, that same uplifting that was disrupted by a black landslide. Every medical student seemed capable of unimaginable grace. Every specialist a wing-clipped, limb-amputated angel. I looked around. But I'd already removed myself from the line of messengers in this world. In the doorway of a pizzeria a few young men sipped coffee in the orphaned space. Two girls skipped down a staircase, pausing at the sidewalk. The eyes of one of them sparkled, perhaps with tears.

I rang Elkoby's bell again. What do you want? he said. The air-conditioning bathed my face. I said I was discreet and never disclosed my sources. He said, How does discreet help me? He swallowed. He touched the gold ring on his finger. I said, Who

30

Grandma Zehava asked Elish if everything was all right with him. And really, Tahel thought, he'd been looking lost, confused. She wanted to know what he thought, she wanted to talk to him, to see if she could get him to talk, the way he taught her. But her mother said, Tahel, Uncle Elish and I need to have a conversation. Take the cellular adapter and go use the computer in the safe room.

Oshri was sitting in the shaded part of the front yard, looking at the water. When she came out, he said, It's a shame there's no river connecting the lake to the sea. We could have built a boat and sailed away to a life of adventure.

I need a favor, she said.

No, you only get me in trouble.

It's not a complicated one. I need you to go check where Mom and Elish are sitting.

He looked at her and said, You want to listen to their conversation.

She nodded.

He came back after a minute and said, They're in the backyard. And Grandma Zehava is in the living room.

Oh, she said. She asked if he wanted her time with the cellular adapter. He took it.

She bypassed the house along the northern wall, standing flush against it, until she heard her mother saying, Are you sure?

Elish asked, Did he deny it?

Her mother said, He said he was meeting friends.

Yes, for the purpose of beating up protesters.

Her mother said nothing. Then she said, The situation is becoming impossible. People are tense, they're looking for ways to blow off steam.

Being theoretical is no longer legitimate, Elish said. Everything is real. Anyone who thinks civilians shouldn't criticize government actions or even just protest the violation of basic human rights may as well have beat them up himself.

Then why are you still here? her mother asked. You know what people think, and you know why.

I have an unresolved matter, he said.

Her mother said, I'm so pissed off, they postponed Mom's CT scan. I told you we can't trust the public health services.

She didn't tell me.

When did you last ask her how she was doing? For you it's enough that she's around. You know she won't complain.

When did they reschedule it for? asked Elish.

Two weeks. And we already made plans for taking her on Thursday. I don't know—

I'll take her.

Do you plan to stay in Sderot that long? asked her mother.

Tahel held her breath, a small, trembling inhalation, the mouth and lungs lost for a few moments.

No, I'll come from Tel Aviv.

They said nothing. Tahel listened to their sipping and nibbling.

Her mother said, Elish, it's not that I'm not happy that the kids like you. It's not that I'm ungrateful.

Tahel waited for the rest of the sentence that never came. The new trembling, the lingering of the important, restrained word, which flowed to her from nights of standing in the kitchen, now took over her completely.

But . . . , said Elish.

Her mother said, Tahel is a lost cause. She was a rebel from the moment she was born, it's her nature. She walks her own path. But Oshri, at least leave me Oshri.

Tahel could imagine the mystification on Elish's face. No, she thought, he never shows his mystification. Instead he waits, lurking, for the intention of the speaker to be revealed. That suspicion, she had to learn how to activate it, how to reach the gist of things. She thought, Oshri.

Elish said, like an echo, Oshri, his voice toneless. What's the problem with Oshri?

Until a week ago he used to be a quiet child. Now all of a sudden he's rebelling, reading all day long.

He's just refusing to accept arbitrary authority, it's an age thing.

He's not even ten yet, what age, he's a child.

When I was ten . . . , said Elish, then fell silent. Her mother joined his silence. Finally, Elish said, You should be glad. You know how many parents have to fight to get their kids reading?

He was doing fine without reading.

I don't understand. Don't you want your child to live up to his potential? He's sensitive and smart.

Some kinds of smart only confuse people.

Nonsense.

Elish, I'm asking you, let me keep him.

When have I ever taken something from you?

Her mother guffawed.

What's going on, Yaffa? asked Elish.

What do you mean, what's going on?

You look exhausted, you're searching for reasons to worry.

No, I'm not.

You need to rest. Why don't you go someplace, Eilat maybe, the kids too? They need some activity. They're cooped up at home all day long.

And how are we supposed to pay for that? asked her mother.

I thought Bobby was making more money now.

Her mother sighed.

Yaffa, there are natural remedies that can help you. Valerian, essences—

Did you speak to Ronnit? she asked.

Ronnit?

Yes.

Why? Elish asked.

She also offered me valer—

You talked to her?

Briefly. I asked her advice about all sorts of things. Are you up-to-date? asked her mother.

Up-to-date about what?

I don't know, everything that's going on with her. Her kid is almost four. Cute kid. A little *dos*.

Elish said nothing.

Some name she gave him, Akiva.

A rustle sounded. Perhaps Elish shifted in his seat.

Her mother said, I never understood why you were in such a rush to break up, I'm sure—

I suppose I'll call her soon.

Her mother said, So you promise?

I told you, I have a little research to finish up here, an idea for a book. This town of yours, I don't understand why there isn't free access to blueprints.

Sderot, she said. What are you getting into this time?

Manny promised to find out who I should call to ask to see—

Her mother said, It's getting so hot out here. Say you promise.

Tahel's knees were stiff from standing, but she forced them into motion. She hurried inside through the front door. The computer was on but Oshri wasn't in the room. She logged out of his user account and logged into hers. She opened the picture of

Ronnit and Akiva. She wasn't surprised to realize how naturally lying came to him. But what was it about this Ronnit that made Elish want to hide her? She zoomed in on their faces until they filled the screen, her eyes moving from mother to son and back again, searching for something.

31

Manny said his influence and connections only went so far. I didn't doubt that. He said he looked into it, and an investigation against Yoram Bitton had been ongoing at Lahav 433 since 2010. It turned out that his close relatives became surprisingly rich the previous year, but the money transfers left few tracks. Moreover, according to the paper trail, Georges Arguile had stolen the majority of the money before he and his lover fled. And how about the blueprints for the lake development? I asked. He said, Those plans are usually available for residents to view at the engineering department of City Hall. He'd had a brief conversation with the local chief of police. He'd held the role for a long time, and the investigators warned Manny not to share any information, they didn't know who else was involved in the embezzlement. At any rate, the chief of police said that he couldn't grant permission to access documents, and that I could file a complaint with the state comptroller. A dead end, I said. Yes, Manny said, but he did manage to find one nugget of information: the name of the company that had prepared the plans, Aqua/Tech. I asked how he found that out. He said, Tell me what the deal is, what's this got to do with the disappearances of Kalanit Shaubi and Dmitry Shtedler's niece? I said they had nothing to do with each other. The mystery I was trying to solve had forced itself upon me. He said, Do tell. I said, As soon as I know the story, you'll be the first to hear it. What are you suspecting? he asked. I said, That's the thing, I'm still waiting for suspicions to come up.

He said, with a thin film of sorrow over his words, Soon enough you'll be asking to buy back your share of the investigation firm from Eliya. I said no, he shouldn't even joke about that, I was done with—

He cut me off. With what? he said. With the secrecy, with the madness around—

I cut him off. I said, Aqua/Tech, why do I think I know that name?

Elish, come on, you can't just c—

I said, Manny, how did you get that name? He said, You have your tricks and I have mine. I said, Did one of the boys from the office help you? He said if he'd asked for their help, he'd already be in possession of a digital copy of the blueprints. I asked why he didn't, then. Manny said if I wanted to subject the world's resources to my investigation, I'd have to first convince those controlling the resources that my goal was worthy. I said nothing. He said he knew the meaning of his words was not lost on me. I said, Yes, it's just that I remembered where I know the name Aqua/Tech from.

I pulled out my wallet, into the hidden pocket of which, its own pharynx, I shoved every business card I received, until it swelled up so much that in periodic fits of revulsion I emptied it and chucked its contents in the trash. I pulled out all the cards, looking through them. There, Nikolaos Patipeu, the Cypriot sci-fi author. I remembered right, the company he worked for was Aqua/Tech. I wrote him an email asking how he was doing, how his flight back went, if it was as long and harrowing as he'd suspected. I wrote him that I needed some advice and would love to talk on Skype or another app. I read the company's home page. They specialized in the planning of unique water systems. Israel was mentioned among the countries in which they had projects, but the nature of the enterprises was left undetailed. I looked at the photo gallery. One of them showed the observation hill, the pipe that emerged from it, but it was photographed from an angle that did not contain any clear identifying signs—the contour of the city, architectural decisions, the tracks of human involvement.

Nikolaos wrote me back in a matter of minutes. Then an incoming FaceTime call. His portrait on the screen before me. The video streaming was delayed as usual, a trail of marks following the event, moving in its own private, honeyed pace. We exchanged greetings and brief updates. Two days earlier, he'd learned that his most recent book was included on the short list for an international science fiction prize. He was in a jolly mood. He asked how he could help.

I told him about the lake and the route of the pipe leading to it. I said I was searching for the enterprise's plans, and that the city was blocking access. He didn't ask about my reasons. He touched his collar button; the blinking of his eyes crossed the sea like the light of a dying star. His gaze shifted right. He dedicated himself to typing. He said that the database included a referral to two blueprints. Meaning? I said. He said, From my terminal I can only pull up the referrals. The person who was in charge of the project is Tiresias Cosmopolus, from the headquarters in Athens, he said. I'm going to write him and ask him to speak with you as a personal favor.

Tahel and Oshri were with me at the Dadon home. They kept surprisingly quiet. I let Oshri try a fairly mild Darjeeling mix, Margaret's Hope. He said he liked the spiciness of it. I showed him my marking system. Whenever I felt nervous, I filled single-use paper tea bags with different tea infusions. Each flavor was accompanied by a certain color in my mind. Sometimes the connection was simple; for instance, for jasmine green tea, the color in my mind was green. Other times the connection was not as obvious, but understandable, such as purple shades for Earl Grey mixes. Other times it was capricious; for instance, all types of Darjeeling belonged to the red family of colors. Oshri sipped the tea, holding the liquid in his mouth, looking askance. He

said, It's more orange. I nodded. I said I bought spools of different colored threads and tied the bags with the appropriate color
or shade.

As I explained this, I sneaked looks at Tahel. She shifted her
eyes between us and the screen of the phone in her hand, smiling to herself uncontrollably. I asked her if she wanted tea too.
She said no. I asked if everything was all right. She said yes, but
her voice betrayed her, speckled with the dark splotches of uncer-
tainty. She asked what exactly I understood from her notebook
that I wasn't telling. I told her not to worry, I'd update her, that I
was waiting for answers. I said the titles of her notebooks would
make good book titles. Oshri said he was debating what to read
next—*The Brothers Lionheart* or *The Phantom Tollbooth*. Last
night Tahel told him *The Brothers Lionheart* would upset him,
but that was after—

Tahel said, Elish, you got an email. I said, What? She said,
Didn't you hear the email alert?

I went to the computer. A polite email from Tiresias in which
he apologized for the delay in getting back to me. It was true that
he'd been in charge of the blueprints, but the person who'd examined and mapped the area was Agatha Tierman, from the
Warsaw office, who was cc'd on the email.

That book isn't appropriate for his age, right, Elish? said Tahel. I said, I don't know what's appropriate for your age, Oshri.
The Brothers Lionheart is a sorrowful book. Tahel nodded. She
said, Maybe when this whole thing is figured out. I asked what
thing she was referring to. She said, With Mom. She's suffering
at night. Who's writing you so much?

A message slid into the top right corner of my screen, announcing an email from Ms. Tierman before sliding back out.
She would be happy to answer my questions. She'd received the
details from Tiresias and Nikolaos. If I was free to FaceTime,
she'd be available in an hour.

32

Yalon finally came for a visit. Tahel had debated whether to write him and ask what was up and decided against it. That afternoon he wrote that he was on his way, and she wrote that she was at Elish's.

Yalon dropped his bike on the grass out front as usual. He nodded at Elish, who was sitting at his computer in the kitchen and looked up at him when he entered.

To Oshri he said, What's up, my man, what are you reading? He looked at the cover of the book. He said, What an amazing book. High five.

Oshri said, Tahel thinks it's sad.

Yalon said, Girls always think books are sad. Then he paused and said, Or maybe I didn't understand it. I read it two years ago. They're actually dead, the two brothers, aren't they?

Oshri nodded.

Yalon said, That's what I thought. Cool, then.

What happened to him? Tahel thought. Where does everybody go when they step out of themselves? There was a springiness and a coquetry in his steps. The haircut she'd forced on him was freshened, the ends recently cut, sharper around his face. He smiled wide at her, his braces brighter than usual. Enormous headphones wrapped around his neck.

Tahel stepped outside. He followed her out. What's going on with Kalanit? she asked.

Kalanit, he said, who knows? Sima's still at Kuti's, but she says she wants to move to Beersheba.

Didn't she move back in with you? she asked.

She isn't coming back to Sderot, but who cares?

I do.

Why?

Because.

Are you all right? he asked.

No.

Is something wrong?

No.

Listen to this, on Sunday I went with my dad to a work site up north.

Where my dad works? she asked.

No, a different one, near Acre.

Oh.

On the way home we stopped at McDonald's. I got a piece of chicken stuck in my braces and it wouldn't come out. I'm pushing it with a toothpick but I can't get it out. My dad tries too and ends up bending my braces. So instead of going home, we went to the orthodontist. They gave me a replacement last night.

They replaced your dad? she asked.

Funny. The braces. But while we were sitting in the waiting room, Barbisa walks in.

So?

Isn't it weird?

No, she said, was it in Ashkelon?

Yeah.

So what's weird about it? I go to the same orthodontist.

Oh, he said. Anyway, he comes in, Hey, man, what's up? Long story short, he broke his tooth in a fight.

Well, he's an *ars*.

What are you talking about, *ars*, he's the coolest. They went to fight with demonstrators like the–

I don't want to hear it.

But here's the thing, they invited me to a party they're having in the bomb shelter near–

Who's they?

He and Hodaya Sasi. To raise morale for young people in—

Are you going? she asked.

Obviously.

Why is it obvious?

Because what am I supposed to do, stay bored in front of the TV and the computer again?

What's going on with you? she asked.

You want to come or not?

She walked into the Dadon house. Her head was lowered. Her throat bubbling. Yalon called after her, You didn't answer me. She shrugged without turning around. She stood in the doorway, fighting against the rebellion of her throat and her eyes. When she straightened her back, she saw Elish watching her. What's he looking at me like that for? she thought.

She said, Can you take me home?

Of course, but—

Oshri, are you coming? I promised Grandma we'll have lunch with her.

Oshri looked at his teacup, still half-full. He said, Okay, okay, but you owe me.

Tahel sat with Grandma Zehava and watched recorded episodes of the show about the boring lives of people in Kiryat Gat or Netanya. She asked herself if that was what Yalon wanted, to be like that. She thought about Kalanit, the group of men dressed up as yeshiva boys and the impostor soldier bringing her into their lab, hypnotizing her until all she could remember was the bus ride, then returning her to the bus stop in Sderot. Returning her, and she didn't know that someone else was implanted inside her, waiting for the right moment to blow up, like a bomb. She asked her grandmother, When you were little, what did you want to be?

Grandma said, I wanted to be a bride. I was always imagining how I would be as a bride.

I don't think about that at all.

Times have changed, *yidoroni*. Today's women aren't like they used to be. Look at your mother. They can show their power outside too, not just at home.

What do you think I'll be? she asked.

That's up to you. If I had my way, you'd be the prime minister.

Tahel pressed against her, Grandma Zehava's arm wrapping around her. She protected her from all directions, like the ancient creature, bound from the heavens and the beatings of the earth, that she was before her hair turned white. Her grandmother kissed her cheek. She said, Don't you worry too, there's too much worry in this house.

But worry was the last thing on Tahel's mind. At that moment she was already charged for action. She got up and went into her old room. She dialed Ronnit's number, which she'd copied from Elish's contacts.

33

Agatha called on time. I took Tahel and Oshri home. Tahel walked, hunched, down the path leading to the gate. My mother came outside and urged me to stay for lunch. I said, I've got to get back, I'm waiting for a call at the Dadon house. My mother said, Look how much weight you lost, you've stopped eating since you came to Sderot.

Agatha's face appeared on the screen. Dark hair, sapphire, obstinate eyes, heavy accent. She was eager to hear what had come of the project.

I asked if no one had informed her that it had been executed. She said they were not asked to supervise the paving and digging, that a local contractor had performed the work, which was rather unusual, but then again the entire development was bizarre. It had known its ups and downs. She elaborated, I listened.

At the end of 2008 the City of Sderot hired the company to conduct a survey. The work order was signed by an architect whose name she didn't know. The document looked questionable. But the mayor's office manager was so enthusiastic and wonderful and full of faith that she caught her excitement.

I asked if she was talking about Heftzi Columbus.

She said, Yes, terrific girl, I heard she'd left. I said I'd fill her in on everything in a minute.

She took a small starter team with her. The concern that she might be complicit in some elaborate ruse was replaced by a concern that this might be an unfeasible dream, a false vision. Heftzi came with them. She seemed to be very familiar with the territory. She showed them the remaining rainwater in the large eucalyptus thicket, said she and the architect believed there was a hidden reservoir in the area, which left tracks in the form of the enormous puddle. Agatha didn't like Monsieur Arguile. He was too slick. She came from a society where wearing Frenchness as a cultural uniform was revolting, and she recognized the corruption it allowed and camouflaged.

But they were right. The company dug a series of holes between the trees to check the springing of the water and the flow routes. They located the source—in the depths of a hill on the edge of the thicket was a small aquifer. It was polluted, but the precipitation collected in it every year could certainly be used for an ornamental lake.

She returned to Poland and sent Tiresias the findings and data. He prepared and submitted some initial blueprints. From an engineering point of view, it was one of the simplest projects they were ever involved in, including in terms of its forecasted success rate. The real problem was how to insert pipes into the hill so they could maximally drain the precipitation into an aqueduct. The pipe's route didn't even take any thought. She said she'd just sent me a minimized copy. I opened it. I'd guessed right—the pipe was meant to form a straight line between the hill and the designated lake. Payment for the plans was received, said Agatha. And that was it. A year went by, and the City of Sderot contacted them again. Heftzi Columbus and Monsieur Arguile were no longer in the picture. Heftzi was replaced by a determined, stubborn, unfriendly woman. The woman requested new plans that would bypass the part of the thicket that would not be uprooted. She didn't explain, just said that area of the thicket was a sensitive matter. Again, a team was sent for examination and mapping, this time without Agatha, who was preoccupied with another project. If I wanted, she could refer me to the person who was in charge of the second survey. She heard that the mayor had placed the team members under close supervision.

ello? Ronnit said on the other end. The greeting thinned with grumbling, its tone metallic over the speakerphone.

Ronnit? asked Tahel.

Yes.

It's Tahel.

Tahel? asked Ronnit.

Elish's niece.

Tahel, said Ronnit, sweetheart. The mechanical pronunciation faded away and her voice was filled with tones Tahel could not identify, perhaps warmth and richness, perhaps reminiscence, it flowed onto her. Tahelush, Tahel, she said. Then she cascaded upon her, what was going on with her, it had been years, years, she must be a young woman now, and she must be as beautiful as she was as a child, turning heads, but, wait, why was she calling, was everything all right, was she—

Tahel said, Everything is fine, I just need your help.

Hang on, hang on, say, what's new with you? I hear you have a brother now?

Tahel asked, You never met Oshri?

No, Elish and I broke up when your mother was pregnant with him. Didn't they tell you?

No.

I'm sorry, said Ronnit, that I stopped coming just like that. I had to get out, I . . .

She fell silent.

Tahel said, I don't remember.

It doesn't matter if you remember or not, I behaved terribly. And I missed you so much. I wanted to ask your mother to bring you over, but I couldn't, I couldn't.

Tahel bit her lips.

Ronnit said, Do you forgive me?

Tahel said, Sure.

Ronnit said, It's almost the month of Elul, almost the High Holy Days. Your forgiveness means a lot.

Tahel said, I forgive you.

On Ronnit's end of the line she heard the demanding, squealing voice of a child, like Oshri's voice when he was in his disgusting, fearsome stage, a tyrant. Tahel thought about how she hated boys.

What, said Ronnit, Aki, you already had three fruit Popsicles today. The sugar isn't good for you, it makes you crazy. Sorry, she said to Tahel, my son. This summer just won't end.

Tahel said, I called to ask you—

Her mother's shout pierced the background noise.

No, Ronnit said cuttingly, you're not getting any more. And to Tahel she said, As soon as they become used to processed sugar, it's the beginning of the end, they're nothing but slaves to industrialized food.

Tahel asked, Do you know that Uncle Elish is in Sderot?

Ronnit answered with her own question: Am I supposed to know?

I have no idea.

Well, I don't know.

He came to visit, stayed for a little over a week, and he's leaving soon. My mother wants to have a goodbye dinner for him.

I always envied how close your family is.

I want to make a PowerPoint presentation.

Okay.

So I'm looking for some old pictures of Elish.

I don't have any, if that's what you're asking. I don't keep pictures, and Elish never gets his photo taken.

Yes, that's why. I thought maybe you'd have a picture of him with Akiva.

Ronnit's voice stretched out of her mouth, bendy, yearning to tear. She said, Why would I have that?

Because I heard he's his godfather.

Who told you that, she demanded, Elish?

No, I just figured it out.

Listen, Tahel, don't interfere in other people's business.

I'm not interfering, I'm just—

Mom, Mom. Akiva's squealing came nearer.

Akiva, said Ronnit, I'll be done in a second and then I'll be with you. You're a big boy now, these attention-seeking tricks are beneath you. And you, she said to Tahel, what do you want, what do you all want?

Tahel said, I don't understand—

Did Elish tell you to call me?

He doesn't know I'm calling you. I told you, it's a surpr—

Enough, she suddenly shouted. Akiva, go sit at the table. Why, why are you doing this, why can't you all leave other people's small happiness intact, leave it innocent?

Tahel said nothing.

Ronnit's voice cracked. Tell whoever sent you to call to pull out their hooks and leave Akiva alone.

The phone was flush against Tahel's ear. Even in its silence she heard another sound chiming inside, rustling, recorded, repeating some secret, some knowledge that had become a secret not because of any terrifying element within it, but as a result of people's efforts to hide it from the light.

35

There was nothing deceptive about June that year. It entered from the start with all of its summer hubbub, entered with the ruckus of metal armor, entered with its purity of stars, entered with their poison, entered with the blight of the Persian lilac's leaves, entered with the gleaming of acacia flowers, entered with the silky wounding of the poinciana tree, entered in the scorching hours, entered in sizzling hours in the frying pans of noon, entered with moisture nets, entered with the disruption of the skin, entered with an uneasiness of sleep.

I agreed to a partnership with Betty Stein and to follow her orders. Manny consulted me about which case I should write about. I learned the details. I thought I had to do deeper research about the lingo police officers used at the time, the information forensic detectives used at the time. I thought it would be nice to write a novel with historically founded elements and a mystery resurfacing from the past. Betty said she'd leave those decisions to me.

With Manny's mediation, I made an appointment with the person who used to be in charge of forensic science at the time. He lived in Herzliya but said he'd come to Tel Aviv and we could meet at the Azrieli Mall. He asked that I wait for him in the passageway between the train and the mall. He said he would be easy to recognize, he walked with a cane.

He was younger than I'd assumed. Twenty years ago, the brake pipes in his car were cut. The bones in his legs shattered, rehabilitation was difficult, and no one believed he would ever walk again. He listened patiently to all my questions and con-jectures. Eventually he said he didn't understand—I said I was writing a book, but I seemed to be more preoccupied with find-ing the perpetrator. I said that wasn't it, I just needed to get used to the liberty writing afforded, and that in the meantime I was trying to paint an accurate picture. He said, If we couldn't catch the husband, why should you be able to? I said, Oh, in my book the murderer is going to be someone unexpected. He said that was his problem with detective novels, all the wisecracking.

As we said goodbye, he said he'd be happy to provide further consultation. I walked him back to the train station. He limped alongside me. He looked around him and said he didn't under-stand why these places invested so much in a gorgeous and orig-inal exterior when inside all shopping malls looked the same.

That year, from the start, June entered with the flesh-stabbing of the holiday of Shavuot, entered with the refractions of chrome patterns, entered with skies of glass and sandalwood, entered with the thickness of blood, entered with the creaking of cock-roaches' joints, entered with the armies of jellyfish, entered with the vengefulness of drivers, entered in rivers of molten asphalt.

For some reason, I lingered by the entrance for a while. In the stairs rising toward it, I first saw Ronnit's visage, the darkness of her eyes sinking into themselves, her thick braid, then her chest, her stomach, her legs, until she stood before me, whole. Like me, the shock of the encounter ran through her.

I persuaded her to sit, though she was on her way to see Shoshi and Dror, her school friends who'd spent the summer in Dror's parents' apartment in Givatayim, and they didn't like people to be late. When you set a time with them, it meant some-thing. She was just stopping through to buy them a quick gift.

I walked into the bookstore, grabbed a book, and asked the cashier to gift wrap it. She said I didn't know Shoshi and Dror's taste. I said it was a book everybody loved. She said, You say that like it's a bad thing. She kept glancing at her watch. She really was in a rush. She asked how my book was coming along. I told her I'd just started writing it. She said she was convinced I'd be in the middle of working, I was so excited when we spoke at the time, and she thought it was so funny that I recorded the conversation. I didn't remember. I didn't remember which part of my pre-prepared system of lies I'd told her during my investigation of Dalia Shushan's death. I stuttered. I said I'd abandoned that, that I was working on a different book. She asked if it was about music too. I said that's what I'd abandoned, the music, or perhaps it abandoned me, I added. I said I'd been hired to write a detective novel. She smiled. She said, Searching is good for the soul. I asked how she was doing.

That year, from the start, June entered with its weight and proportions, entered with the ebony trembling of the evening, entered with the depths of the honeycomb, entered with the width of the sea.

She was still a medical student, she said. She'd broken up with her boyfriend and was now living with a roommate in Beersheba. She got up to leave, took a few steps, then hesitated and returned. She said she was glad to hear we'd both left Dalia behind, that we could let go. She said her number had changed. She jotted the new number on a piece of paper and handed it to me. She said she came to Tel Aviv once a week.

36

Manny insisted. I told him I had to find these two pieces of information, and that I could find out myself, but it would take too long. He said, So what am I to you, a shortcut? I said, No, you're a friend. He said, If I'm a friend, why don't you fill me in, when are you going to stop being so possessive of your investigation? I said, Manny, this is the last favor, don't make this hard on me. If you can contact Border Control and check what dates Vivian Kahiri left and returned to Israel in November 2010 and pull the date Heftzi Columbus left the country from her file, I promise to tell you the whole story. That's the problem, he said, you never let anyone peek behind the scenes so that you can wow them with your magic show. I thought you'd grown up. I hung up. I thought long and hard. I called him back. I said, Fine, I suspect Vivian Kahiri is connected to the disappearance of Georges Arguile and Heftzi Columbus. I told him about the rerouting of the drainage pipe, about the lake. I said I thought it all had something to do with the embezzlement investigation against the former mayor, Yoram Bitton. Manny asked, The embezzlement investigation against Yoram Bitton? I said, Yes. He said, Are you convinced? I said I wouldn't know for certain until I had the information I requested. He said, In that case, I'll find out.

He got back to me the next day. I said, You have secrets too, you keep things to yourself too. He said, What are you talking about, Elish, what am I hiding from you? I said I never asked about the nature of the contacts he had to keep as part of his security consulting, and how expansive his areas of responsibility actually were. I told him I'd recognized his close relationship with the national fraud department during the Ariel Piron investigation. He said, What difference does it make to you as long as you benefit from it? I said, The benefit is mutual. He said, Do you seriously think that's what our friendship is founded on, the exchange of information? I said, I don't know anymore, the world is full of schemes. He said, Elish, Elish, you've got to leave Sderot.

I called the Egyptian woman. I introduced myself and said I was conducting research for a documentary film about the lake enterprise in Sderot. Her panic reached me through the distance between us. She said, But what do I– Then she fell silent. I told her I heard she was a good friend of Heftzi Columbus's. She gasped. I was, she said, then one day she left and that was it, like. Then dryness demolished her speech. I said, Like the earth swallowed her. Yes, she whispered. I said, The police case is still open. She hung up. I waited.

She called an hour later. She said, Why did you mention the police investigation? I said, I'm in contact with the person in charge of the case. She asked if that person knew I was calling her. I said they didn't, that I hadn't mentioned her. The next thing she said faded into mumbling. I said, Vivian, I'm discreet, meet me for a quick conversation. I promise not to mention your name or give it to anyone else. She said, That doesn't work for me. I said, In return for access to the investigation materials, I promised to give the police detective any relevant lead I find, you see, I'm in charge of sorting through the information. She thought it over for a long time. She said, Off the record. I said, A simple conversation. She said she lived in Holon. We made a plan to meet at the café in the designer store outside the cultural center.

37

In my mind, the map of the country appeared as a series of concentric circles spreading out of Gaza, the infected hub. The trajectories of different missiles determined the diameters of circles. Each circle existed in and of itself, in a fortress of acclimation. The horror involved a drive, moving from one circle to the next. I slipped the Grumiaux and Haskil album into the CD player, and Sonata in E Minor played on a loop. I thought about how I ought to invest in a better sound system. The map of the country faded away, replaced by the full diagram of the first part of the piece, twists and stutters, that whole haunted giddiness of the violin, as if on our way to a house of feasting we found ourselves heading to a house of mourning. I parked in the cultural center's parking lot, a red cube beside a cylindrical belly, striped with yellow.

I patted my chest, my arms, my legs, and told Vivian, As promised, no recording devices. She smiled. Her forty years of age were evident in her smile, the damage to her teeth, the deviation of lipstick from thin lips, the silent rebellion of the skin against the layer of makeup, the coarsening of the nose, the darkness of the line reinforcing the eyebrows, the growing audacity of the henna dye in her hair. She looked me over, black irises, primed like fingernails. I asked her to tell me a little about the lake project. She said she didn't know much, only what she'd heard from Heftzi. She looked around her, above, toward the slope of the building shading us, shifted in the designer armchair, making the round artificial-wood table tremble with her motion. I reached out to steady it. Vivian sipped her coffee. She wiped the foam off her mouth with a napkin. I asked why she left Sderot. That hellhole, she said, do you really have to ask? I said yes. She said she left last year. She went to visit a relative who was in the hospital and met someone in the sitting area outside. They moved in together a few months ago.

I said, It's a well-known fact that hospital yards are used as laboratories for social experiments. They scatter substances in them that disrupt the brain's perception of time. She sipped her coffee again and said nothing. I asked if he looked anything like Georges Arguile. Who? she asked. Your man, I said. She laughed. She said she wouldn't dream of dating Arguile. What's wrong with today's men? she said. They're like girls, going to the gym and watching their weight, skinny like models. She preferred her men big, with some flesh on them.

She asked if I knew it had been Heftzi's idea to begin with, said the film ought to start with that fact. Heftzi's, I asked, not Georges Arguile's? No, she said, all that clown knew how to do was recognize opportunities to make a buck. He had no vision. I said, All right, Heftzi then. She said, She was in love with that thicket, Heftzi. Every year, in Purim, when the anemones bloomed, she got excited like a little girl. The entire area behind it became like carpets of anemones. She would cross the entire thicket. The accumulation of water there amazed her, she wouldn't stop thinking about it. Then she read an article about Georges Arguile and his ecological projects, got ahold of his number, and nagged him until he came to take a look. And the guy just took ownership of the whole thing. But it made no difference to Heftzi. As soon as he said they could build a lake there, she became even more obsessed and she started pushing, the mayor, Arguile. She would give detailed reports of the online research she did until she reached that Greek water-system engineering company, and how she was sure that company would totally fit their project, and how she couldn't wait for the surveying team to arrive. Vivian told her story in one breath, almost reciting or hitting the bullet points in a carefully prepared and memorized list.

So what happened? I asked. Vivian said she didn't know. One day Heftzi just didn't show up to work. The next day Vivian got an email from her saying she was in Crete with Arguile. And that was it, she hadn't heard from her since. I said, You traveled too around that time, to visit your family in France. She tensed up. What's that got to do with anything? she said. That trip was planned weeks in advance. I said, I heard you're a French citizen. She put her cup down. What have you heard? she said. I said, That you have a French passport in addition to your Israeli one. She said, I have to go. I said, Stay. I pulled out my notepad. I said, According to Border Control, you didn't leave Israel at all in November 2010, but you did come back as a foreign resident. She said, That's a registration error. Then it dawned on her. How do you even have this information? she asked. I said, Vivian, do you really believe Heftzi is alive? She said, What, what? I said, Do you think she vanished into thin air, leaving no trace? She said, No, Heftzi's in South America with Georges. For a moment, without my being able to dam it, the image of Piedad Zorita glowed in my mind, standing by the elevator in the lobby of the decrepit Hotel Ibis in Sète, looking at me, intoxicated like me, asking an unbearably large question.

I said, So you do know where she is. She said, I only know what Georges told me. She said, Heftzi was miserable. You have no idea what a shitty family she comes from, what she did to get out. She deserves this, she deserves a better life, so what, so a little money disappeared from City Hall, where's the crime in that, they're all corrupt anyway, why shouldn't Heftzi have a little fun, did anyone even give her any credit for that lake, do you have any idea how much money was wasted on building it and maintaining it? No justice, no justice.

I said, So you helped her disappear. She nodded. In the mois-ture of her eyes, the darkness of the irises transformed into two lead fuses. She said, Georges came to me, the evening of the day she didn't show up to work. He said he and Heftzi wanted to run away, that her brother had been extorting her for money for weeks. I knew what her situation was. The few weeks before that she'd closed off, didn't want to talk. I agreed to help. He said he had a flight ticket for the end of that week and all I needed to do was come with him, leave the country using her passport and ticket. He said he had some connections, that he could get my picture in her passport.

I asked if he'd told her it was a deception intended to stop anyone from tracking Heftzi down. She said he had. He told her a friend of his had agreed to cover his own tracks in the same fashion and that they'd made plans to meet in Germany, each traveling through a different country. I said, So you went to France. Yes, she said, from Paris I used my own passport to fly to Frankfurt, and from there I took a train to Heidelberg.

I said, Heidelberg. Yes, she said, Georges has friends there who promised to help smuggle them to South America. I said, And did you see Heftzi? She said, No, I just gave the passport back to Georges. He said she got delayed, she made part of the journey by boat, and I had to get back to Israel.

How convenient, I said. She said, What? I said, That one Sat-urday Heftzi vanished, and ever since then her existence has relied on indirect reports. Vivian said she got an email from Heftzi that she deleted right away, saying she was happy. I said, I hope so, for her sake. She said, Remember, you promised, it's like a contract, you promised not to get me involved. I nodded. She left.

What does that mean? Manny asked when I reported back to him. I said, What it means is that Heftzi Columbus never left Israel. She may have never left Sderot. So where do you think

38

Oshri didn't like the white tea infusion I brought back from Tel Aviv. He said it tasted like hot water. I told him to let the leaves brew longer, that the tones of scorched toasting would deepen. He persisted in his lack of enthusiasm. I brewed a pot of Grand Yunnan Imperial. He said, That feels good in the mouth. It's part of the oranges, but its yellow is stronger than the other one's. I said, The Margaret's Hope. He said yes. It had an edge of honey, the yellow stands out more. I nodded. I invited Tahel to join us and taste some. She shook her head. She was already isolated in that careful observation of us, as if trying to distinguish our true movements from ones aimed at camouflage, her notebook rolled up in her hand. Oshri said, *The Brothers Lionheart* isn't a sad book at all. Yalon was right. Nangijala is a fun land.

Tahel crushed the notebook, the circumference of the cylinder. She asked if I was packed up already. I said I'd pack after dinner. She asked why I wasn't spending the night in Sderot and going back tomorrow. I said there was no way of knowing how long the cease-fire would last. She said, You drove around even when there were missiles.

I said, What about TYO Investigations Inc.? She said, We shut it down. I said, It's a little early to retire. She said she wanted to give me the notebook as a gift, that I might come up with more ideas, and that I wasn't sharing them with her anyway. I smiled. I said, You're headed in the right direction. She smiled back. She said, But really, maybe you should write a book about the adventures of an investigation agency. I said, I think that's the type of

book you should write. Tahel said, Writing books is boring. I
want to be the one they write books about. Oshri said, But I want
to. I said, What? He said, To write books. I said, Don't tell your
mother about that plan just yet.

The phone rang. I glanced at it. Ronnit. I ignored the call. I
walked outside to the front yard. Tahel followed me out, barefoot.
I imagined the tickle of the grass on the skin of her sole. Occasionally she raised one foot and rubbed it against her calf. The lake
swallowed the flow from the aqueduct on the hill. The surface
was ruptured for a moment by hungry mouths that left behind
circular trembles. I told her about the convoluted route of the
pipe, about Heftzi Columbus's discovery. She laughed. She said,
What, Heftzi Columbus discovered the hill? I said no, just the
possibility of a lake. I told her not to worry, that things would
work out soon. How? she said. I said her mother's problem was
solved. Yaffa didn't know it yet, but the problem was solved. How,
she said, how? I told her to trust me.

Bobby returned unannounced in the late afternoon. Yaffa
didn't insinuate a thing. When I walked inside, she asked me to
come with her to the backyard. I did. Bobby was sitting beneath
the pergola, sipping a beer in short, curt motions. Without another word, Yaffa left us. I sat at the table. Bobby avoided my
eyes. I lingered for long moments. The departure of the sun did
not lessen the burden, the miners' air, the air of those trapped in
a collapsed mine.

Suddenly, Bobby laughed quietly to himself. The bottom of
the bottle hit the plastic table. Listen to this joke, he said, you'll
die. There once were three sisters, Lara, Tara, and Farra. Lara
had a lot of luck, Tara got a nip and tuck, and Farra really liked to–

I said nothing.

He said, Come on, Elish. Listen to this one, listen. A man sees
a little girl playing alone at a playground. He says, Hey, kid, if
you give me a kiss, I'll give you a piece of candy. The girl says,
Forget that, give me the whole bag and I'll suck your dick.

His head was lowered. Still he said, Come on, already, give us a smile.

I said nothing.

He said, Listen to this one. A hunter is trying to catch a bear. The bear tells him, If you shoot me, I'll go with you, but if you miss, I'm going to fuck you in the ass. The first day, the hunter shoots and misses, so the bear bangs him. The second day, the hunter shoots and misses, so the bear bangs him again. The third day, the hunter shoots and misses, and the bear says, What are you, a hunter or a homo? I laughed for like an hour when Amos told me. What's wrong with you, man, I . . . His voice died down. I said, I wish it were that simple, Bobby. But when did it become complicated, he asked, when? I said, When we left childhood.

My mother begged me to stay. I said I couldn't. She said, You come and go, thinking about nobody but yourself. I sat in the car. Yaffa tapped on the window. She said, Zalman got a free vacation in Eilat next Thursday as a bonus from Asor. I said, Excellent, the kids will be glad. She said, But it's the same day as Mom's CT. I told her I would keep my promise of driving our mother there.

I got back to my apartment. Areas that were in the dark came to light, and areas that were bright retreated into hiding. Like a body whose injury we do not notice until pain arrives to announce it and whose mending we do not notice until pain disappears. We cannot claim that the wound was ever evidence of anything besides a malfunction.

39

Manny leaked me details from the investigation. It was classified. The Sarah Matatov monument was ripped from the ground, its foundations pulled out one by one. Beneath a cover of concrete, Heftzi Columbus's corpse lay in wait. On the body, forensics found hair belonging to Yoram Bitton. Manny said the fraud department had been chasing him for the past few years, constructing a case, and that the finding of the body broke him. He confessed to everything.

I asked how the police had a DNA sample for comparison. He said the investigation started when residents complained about a villa Bitton's son had built, which was not up to code. There had already been some suspicions about Bitton regarding possible embezzlement of donation money. The son got into fights with his neighbors, hit children who invaded his property, and got arrested. A sample of his DNA was in the database. Manny suggested they compare it to the DNA in the hair. That was enough to get a court order.

I said, So you had an interest in this after all. He said the head of the team that built the case was a longtime colleague. He consulted with him a few times with regards to the case. He was convinced that part of the embezzlement had to do with the creation of the lake, but that case was allegedly resolved, an extradition order had been issued against Georges Arguile and Heftzi Columbus. He said that when he heard I'd moved to Sderot to sniff around, he told his friend he couldn't think of anyone better for the mission, and that if there was any dirt, he could trust me to scratch it out. I hung up. He was consistent, calling me for daily updates.

The development was indeed Heftzi's dream. From the moment she read the article about Arguile, she couldn't put it out of her mind. She convinced him to come see for himself, invited him to the office, the mayor said. Arguile enticed him, he said. After Operation Cast Lead, Bitton's stock in Sderot had plummeted. He could no longer recruit the support of traditional family clans. They wanted a younger candidate, someone energetic, who would smile gratefully while his strings were pulled. Arguile knew how to reach people. He knew how to identify their needs and present himself as a godsend to handle their troubles. The mayor had a fancy vocabulary, said Manny, acquired over years of public activity in synagogues. He was enchanted by Arguile's silver tongue, his French charm, as well as by Heftzi's adoration for the man. Heftzi, whose wisdom had rescued Bitton from every bind. So the two men conspired to create an imaginary project, a hole that would suck in all donation funds. Some of the money would pad the pockets of the new contracting companies taking hold of the town by tipping the bids in their direction and inflating price quotes. In return, the contractors would provide their support, thus securing his reelection. The rest of the money would be split between him and Arguile. So far it was a perfect plan.

The problems started when they hired a surveying team from a Greek company. Arguile thought it was a brilliant move. There was no better way to cover the tracks of transactions than to conduct business with international companies. Pyrrhic victory, said the mayor. Pyrrhic victory. Heftzi was right. They found an aqueduct that could be used if part of the thicket was uprooted and the land deforested. But Arguile was spooked and started sabotaging the work, trying to fake data, piling difficulties. And Heftzi became suspicious. At first she shared her suspicions with Bitton, but he reassured her. Then, he thought, she

realized he was in on it. She got hold of the planning and engineering company Aqua/Tech's plans and recommendations.

On Friday night, Heftzi went to Arguile's apartment to confront him. He denied the allegations and she forced him to join
her at the site of the survey. I'm not sure what happened, said
Bitton. Arguile said it was an accident, that he slapped her and
she fell, hitting her head on some iron, and died. The coroner, he
was told, determined that the cause of death was not the head
injury. She was strangled to death. Manny said at this point Bitton broke into tears.

The surveying team had dug a series of holes in the thicket
in an attempt to locate the water's drainage routes. Arguile told
Bitton he panicked. He called him and screamed at him to come.
He did. He was foolish, greedy. He helped Arguile dump the body
in one of the holes. They covered her up, filling the hole halfway,
tightening the dirt. The following week, Bitton instructed city
employees to cast concrete over the holes. He said it was time
they erected a monument to celebrate the heroism of Sderot residents living through Qassam attacks. His advisers asked whom
the monument should be dedicated to. He said, Sarah Matatov,
and that the entire thicket would be dedicated to her. A few days
earlier, Heftzi had left a newspaper on his desk. She'd marked
an item in it. The poet Nahum Farkash had performed a song in
Matatov's memory at a concert in Tel Aviv.

He knew Arguile had fled the country. He contacted the fraud
department and reported the disappearance of the money placed
in the hands of the architect. Fraud. The money remained in his
secret bank account. Then Heftzi haunted his thoughts. Not
Heftzi per se, but rather the discovery of the body. He realized he
could no longer shelve the plans. There were too many rumors
among city residents about the lake project. The rezoning permit for a new neighborhood had been sent to the Israel Land
Administration, and if he lost the election, no one could assure
him the plans wouldn't be carried out without him.

He realized he had to see the project through. He channeled part of the money at his disposal to ordering renewed plans for the drainage route from Aqua/Tech and went on a fundraising tour in the United States. He always marveled at the guilt that agonized American Jews and at how easy it was to wring out money when one painted them a picture of the blood sacrifice required to maintain the chosen land.

40

Her mother oversaw the packing. Oshri tried to sneak a few books into his bag, but she said, We're taking a break from everything, get it? Everything, including reading.

He was holding *A Wizard of Earthsea*. He said, Just this one, it's short, I can read it on the way there.

Her mother said, Only on the way there, and I'm checking your bag before we leave.

Elish had been right. Tahel waited for Oshri to come get her for three nights. She returned to her own bedroom, but left the door ajar for him. He didn't come. She asked him if he was sure he hadn't fallen asleep. He said he had, that their mother wasn't in need anymore. On the fourth night she set her alarm for midnight. But she couldn't sleep anyway, just as on the nights before, her thoughts disrupting her rest. She thought about Kalanit, waiting at the Beersheba central bus terminal for the bus to Sderot, dark eyes detecting her, that strange man who had some kind of device that didn't allow cameras to record his image. She thought about him, watching, making a call. A young man in uniform comes out from one of the terminal doors. He buys a falafel, adds *amba*, then pulls a vial of a hypnosis drug from his pocket. A group of religious-looking men hurry out from another door, joining the line in their black clothing, the suits and hats. She tried to think about something else. Elish, for example. He and Ronnit and the little boy, Akiva. What a filthy name. She felt sick. She returned to cling to thoughts of Kalanit, recounting the scheme, one step at a time. The dripping of the hypnosis drug into the *amba*, the whisper of the soldier to follow him. But for what, for what? The alarm clock finally went off. The kitchen was empty, not counting the quiet activity of still life, the economy required for its silence.

Is your bag packed? her mother asked.

She nodded. The power of falling asleep had returned to her in the past few nights. She retired to her bed in the early evening and woke up again in the middle of the night. There had been digging in the thicket that day, and the air was bursting with dirt particles. She called Elish to ask what they were going to find. He told her not to panic, but that they were going to excavate a dead body. She waited with bated breath for the findings to become known. She thought Yalon would definitely call to find out what happened. He didn't. Elinoar and Racheli texted that she had to go take pictures of the excavations and send them to them. She didn't reply. She got out of bed. The circle of brightness in the ceiling glowed. Her mother stood in the kitchen, chopping vegetables. She turned when Tahel walked in.

She said, It's hard to sleep with all this dust, huh? I don't understand how your father and Oshri can do it.

Tahel said, Yeah, I'm thirsty all the time.

Her mother bit into a piece of carrot, crunching it. She handed her a strip of cucumber. Want some? she asked.

Her mother's motions were back to normal—the puncturing into Tahel's and Oshri's business, the dictatorial, matter-of-fact assertions. But Tahel saw the wounded organs. She decided she no longer had any use for the foolish power of influencing people with her mind, that she preferred the power that allowed her to see their cracks.

She asked her mother, We won't leave before Elish gets here, right?

Her mother said, Yes, he's taking Grandma to her checkup.

She walked inside. Grandma Zehava was sitting on the sofa, her purse in her lap, wearing a formal dress and blouse. Tahel said, Grandma, it's just a checkup.

Her grandmother said, People get dressed up for court too.

Tahel leaned in. The vein on the side of her grandmother's nose was more prominent. She said, Maybe you and Elish can come to Eilat after you finish at the doctor's.

Grandma Zehava smiled. She said, Elish is taking me back to Ashkelon, to my home.

Tahel said, So you're leaving too.

Her grandmother said, I'll spend three days there and then we'll see, my things are still here.

You'll be alone on Shabbat.

Her grandmother said, Elish will come.

Oshri hurried in. He said, Elish is waiting outside, he doesn't want to come in.

Elish was leaning against his car, wearing sunglasses. The engine was running, rattling. Elish opened the passenger-side door for Grandma Zehava. A frozen gust of air escaped from inside. Tahel thought that now that he had a tiny shadow that she knew, like a hole, he was more down-to-earth. Her throat filled with a mixture of lint and pins.

He asked how she was doing.

She asked, Did they find the killer?

They know who it is, but he fled the country a few years ago.

But they'll catch him eventually.

Elish said, There are no assurances.

The Interpol will catch him.

Elish smiled.

And Kalanit? she said.

I stopped following that case. But you didn't tell me about you.

She said, What about me?

Are you worried about Yalon?

She said, Pathetic. He joined Bobarisa and Hodaya Sasi's group.

Elish said, Not everybody can be like everybody. Most of those who can't must learn that fact slowly, by trial and error.

And if he is like everyone else? said Tahel.

Would you still be interested in him?

She looked at Elish harshly, tightening her lips. After he and Grandma Zehava left, Oshri came up to her. Look, he said, look at all this tea Elish left for me. He held up a jar filled with lumpy tea bags tied with different-colored strings.

41

During the first minutes of the drive I tried to shake off Tahel's gaze without much success. Why had I refused to recognize the signs in her so far, the signs that she belonged to the category of human beings whose entrance into the kingdom of consciousness was made through the wrong door? A kid who lost a contest and now her eyes were full of burning. She would overcome. But her heart had already stopped at that point, and there would be no correcting the halting. An aperture had been pierced inside her time. For the rest of her life, she would return to it through forked, branched remembrances, to the void of the missing beat.

My mother said something. What? I asked. She said, Such heroes, pointing to a row of APCs. I suddenly realized that until that point the road to Beersheba had seemed to clean itself of military presence. I said I was wondering if the war could really end this way. She said, Too many crying mothers. I wondered how Heftzi Columbus's mother reacted to the news about her daughter. Ultimately, the identity of the body had to be reported. The guesswork never stopped. The noose tightening around Yoram Bitton's neck provided plenty of material for conversations. My mother said that her neighbors in Ashkelon called for juicy details. She told them she didn't know anything they didn't.

Betty was excited. Manny told her about some of the findings. We had a meeting in which she urged me to write about it all. I said I had to think about it. I called Sima Shaubi to ask about Kalanit. She said that, praise the Lord, Kalanit was in an outpatient clinic at the Mental Health Center in Beersheba.

Sima picked her up from there every afternoon. She was improving, talking a lot, eating again. Her therapist said she'd recover from her trauma quickly. I asked if the therapist or the nurses reported any unusual events. She asked why there should be any unusual events, hadn't the kid suffered enough? I said I was glad they were both ready to forget. Forget what, said Sima, the Qassam hitting her daughter? That was something she would never forget.

Is it scary, my mother asked, the CT scan? I said it wasn't, that she would lie down on a padded table, and a metallic circle emitting X-ray radiation would move over her face quickly, like an amusement park ride. She said, I'm too old to enjoy an amusement park. Your father liked that kind of thing, he chased innovations. I would be happy if someone just gave me a cream to put on it. She asked if I talked to Ronnit. I hummed a noncommittal response.

I'd waited a few days before calling her back. Ronnit asked what kept me from calling and said she had important news. I said nothing. Victoriously, she told me she was five weeks pregnant. I said, Congratulations. She said, You weren't expecting that. I asked why she assumed I gave it any thought. She said, I know you, I've seen you looking at Akiva and thinking, Those *dosim* have a million kids, so what's wrong with this picture, where are his brothers and sisters, David must be . . . She fell silent. David must be what? I asked. She said, Elish, I'm not a young woman anymore. At my age, I'm at high risk. I won't have any more children. I said, I wish I could take two years off my life and give them to you. That's the problem, she said, it's easy for you to give what's difficult, but you can never give what's easy. I asked what she wanted. She said, A little peace and quiet. I turned off the tape recorder.

My mother asked if I remembered the time we went to Beersheba. Someone had imported a game I wanted to play and I got Yaffa all excited about it so she'd convinced our father. I said,

Space Invaders. She said, Is that what it was called? She said,
Your father was more excited than the two of you. He wanted to
buy a game like that too. I said I remembered: He spoiled it for
us. She said, Don't talk that way, everything was perfe—

She was cut off by the ringing of my phone. My mother said,
Don't pick up.

When she went into the examination room, I glanced at the
screen. Vivian Kahiri. I looked at my mother lying on the table,
the metallic circle near her head. Every hour I spent idling, wandering, staring, I stole away from her. I could no longer bear the
image. The human and that which was about to be bruised, and
the pangs of blood with every beat. I stepped outside to call Vivian back. She was choked with tears. She'd heard about Heftzi
and was climbing the walls. If it wasn't for her, they would have
already . . . Her crying broke down her sentences, turning her
speech into bursts of growling. Someone took the phone from
her. A man, his voice low and deep. In a Russian accent, he said
Vivian couldn't talk anymore and asked if he should take a message. I said, Who is this, Dmitry? His "yes" was charged with a
question. I said, Dmitry Shtedler, were you hospitalized last
year at—

The phone went silent. He hung up.